C.C. Humphreys is the author of eight previous novels including *The French Executioner*, which was runner-up for the CWA Steel Dagger. His series of Jack Absolute novels have been published in many languages around the world. He lives with his family in Vancouver, Canada.

Vlad

THE LAST CONFESSION

C.C. HUMPHREYS

An Orion paperback

First published in Great Britain in 2009
by Orion
This paperback edition published in 2009
by Orion Books Ltd,
Orion House, 5 Upper St Martin's Lane,
London WC2H 9EA

An Hachette UK Company

1 3 5 7 9 10 8 6 4 2

Copyright © C.C. Humphreys 2009

A CIP catalogue record for this book is available
from the British Library.

ISBN 978-1-4091-0372-1

Typeset at The Spartan Press Ltd,
Lymington, Hants

Printed and bound in Canada by Webcom Inc.

The Orion Publishing Group's policy is to use papers that
are natural, renewable and recyclable products and
made from wood grown in sustainable forests. The logging
and manufacturing processes are expected to conform to
the environmental regulations of the country of origin.

www.orionbooks.co.uk

To Alma Lee, lady of letters, adviser and inspiration.
and
In memory of Kate Jones, the very best of literary agents,
and of friends. Sorely missed.

DRAMATIS PERSONAE

THE DRACULESTI
Vlad Dracul – 'The Dragon'
The Dragon's Sons:
Mircea Dracula
Vlad Dracula
Radu Dracula

THE WITNESSES
Ion Tremblac
Ilona Ferenc
Brother Vasilie, the Hermit

HEARING THE LAST CONFESSION
Petru Iordache, Spatar of Poenari Castle
Janos Horvathy, Count of Pecs
Cardinal Domenico Grimani, Papal Legate

AT THE TURKISH COURT
Hamza agha, later Hamza pasha
Murad Han, Sultan of Rum
His son, Mehmet Celebi, soon to be 'Fatih' or 'The
Conqueror'
Abdulraschid, his favourite
Hibah, mistress of concubines
Tarub, maid
Abdulkarim, or Sweyn the Swede, janissary

THE HOSTAGES AT EDIRNE
The Mardic Brothers, Serbian
Constantin, Bosnian
Zoran, Croatian
Petre, Transylvanian

AT TOKAT
Abdul-Mahir, torturer
Wadi, torturer
Samuil, the Christian martyr

THE WALLACHIAN BOYARS
Albu 'cel Mare'. ('The Great')
Udriste
Codrea, vornic (judge)
Turcul
Gales
Buriu, spatar, commander of cavalry
Dobrita
Cazan, Dracul's logofat, or chancellor
The Metropolitan, head of the Orthodox Church in
Wallachia

DRACULA'S VITESJI
Black Ilie
Laughing Gregor
Stoica the Silent

PRETENDERS TO THE WALLACHIAN THRONE
Vladislav Dan
Basarab Laiota

OTHERS
Matthew Corvinus, 'the Crow', King of Hungary
Brother Vasilie, Vlad's confessor
Thomas Catavolinos, Ambassador
Abdulmunsif, Ambassador
Abdulaziz, Ambassador
Mihailoglu Ali Bey, Radu's army commander
Jan Jiskra, Corvinus's mercenary commander
Elisabeta, Dracula's first wife
Vlad, Dracula's son
Ilona Szilagy, Dracula's second wife
Janos Varency, thief-taker
Roman, Moldavian
Old Kristo, gatekeeper
Hekim Yakub, physician

TO THE READER . . .

In the bitter winter of 1431, in the town of Sighisoara, a second son was born to Vlad Dracul, Voivode (or Warlord) of Transylvania. He was christened Vlad and, like his elder brother, was given the surname Dracul-*a* – Son of Dracul.

In the 'limba Romana' that they spoke 'Dracul' meant 'the Dragon'. Or 'the Devil'. So Vlad Dracula was the Devil's Son.

He acquired other titles in his life. Voivode of Ungro-Wallachia. Lord of Amlas and Fagaras. Brother of the secret 'fraternatis draconem' – the Order of the Dragon. His own people called him Vlad Tepes. His Turkish enemies called him Kaziklu Bey. Both meant – The Impaler.

The land he won and lost and ruled was Wallachia, the central province of present-day Romania. Caught between the expanding Hungarian Kingdom and the all-conquering Turks, between the Crescent and the Cross, Wallachian princes were expected to be the dutiful vassal of one or the other.

Dracula had different ideas. Different ways of executing them.

Finally killed in battle in 1476, his head was chopped off and sent as a gift to his most bitter foe, Mehmet, Sultan of the Turks. It was mounted upon a stake on the walls of Constantinople. There it rotted.

A few mourned him; most did not.

I make no judgement. I leave that to those who heard his last confession – and, of course, to you, the Reader.

'I am a man. Nothing human is alien to me.'
Terence

Confession

'Have you committed a sin? Then enter the Church and repent your sin. For here is the physician, not the judge: here one is not investigated but receives remission of sins.'

— ST JOHN CHRYSOSTOM

– I –

The Summons

Wallachia, March 1481

All was still in the forest. The last snowflakes of the sudden storm had just fallen. Everything paused.

In the crook of a copper beech sat a man. His arms were crossed, gloved hands folded into his lap, the right beneath to support the weight of the goshawk on his left. They had been there for a long time, as long as the blizzard lasted. Man and bird – part of the stillness, part of the silence. Both had their eyes closed. Neither were asleep.

They were waiting for the first sound. Something else to recognise that the storm had passed, be the first to stir before the next one arrived.

There. A twitch of nostrils, their pinkness the only colour in a white world. A sniff – the first sound, followed by the faintest of breezes coming up the valley. The hare could not scent those behind her.

It was hardly a sound – but the man and the hawk both opened their eyes. The bird's were red, fire-red, hell-red, because she was old, nine years old, five past her prime when she could take ten hares, a half-dozen squirrels, a brace of stoats all in a day. Not for their flesh, she didn't need so much. Not for the skins that clothed the man on whose fist she sat. For the pure pleasure of the kill.

Four eyes stared at the snow pack in the glade, seeking the source of the sound they couldn't have heard.

The hare pushed her whole head above the snow-crust. When the blizzard came, she had been caught between stands of beech and aspen, digging for a root. Surprised by the sudden white ferocity, she had frozen. The new snow was as deep as her body but her rear legs rested on the hard pack beneath. Shelter was just twenty leaps away. There, among the deadfalls, she would be safe.

In the tree, the man raised his fist, a wall of soft snow tumbling from his arm, thunder in the silence.

The hare leapt. Young, fast, she was halfway to safety when the man flung out his arm and the bird fell from the tree. Five beats and into its glide. The hare wove, so winter-lean that in the shallower snow near the tree line she skimmed the soft surface. Before it, a fallen branch made an arch, like a cathedral's porch.

The hawk struck, talons thrusting through fur, into flesh. The hare twisted, ripping one triumvirate of claws free, a spray of blood following, a red arrowhead pointing towards darkness and the sanctuary of wood.

Then the jerking stopped and all was still in the forest again.

The man dropped carefully from the tree, groaned, despite the softness he fell into. Snow tumbled from his coat, from its alternating stripes of hare, squirrel and weasel, from the pyramid of wolf-skin on his head. He moved slowly forward, brushing the dirty white beard that curled thickly up to his cheekbones clear of ice.

Stooping, he wrapped his fingers around the bird's back, pulled gently. Hawk and hare slid from the drift. The bird released instantly, her eyes fixed on the leather pouch at the man's waist. With his free hand he reached in and pulled out a piece of fresh flesh. She took it, making a small noise in her throat.

The hare stared up, unblinking in terror. For a moment the man stared back. Then he moved his thumb slightly, pushed down and snapped the neck.

It made such a little sound. Too little for the snap that came a moment after to be an echo. He listened . . . and soon heard men trying not to be heard.

Another snap, this one from down the valley. More men there, and that told him. There was little game on this small mountain at the end of winter; these men were coming for him.

He was surprised they were coming now, through the new snow. But the blizzard had hit fast, winter's late shock, so they must have set out before it began. There were only a few ways off the mountain and, if he knew them all, he assumed the men who hunted him did, too. They would spread like a net through the trees – soldiers and woodcutters and gypsies. They would have dogs . . . *There.* A short bark came from below, another responding from above, neck chains jerked too late to silence them.

He'd known they would come for him eventually.

Dropping the hare's corpse into his pouch, he made his left hand into a fist. The hawk hopped onto it instantly, red eyes watching his.

'It is time,' he whispered.

She put her head slightly to one side, as if in question. But she knew as well as he. The blizzard had been an echo of winter only.

'Go,' he said. 'Find a mate . . .'

He broke off. Every spring he'd let her go, then find her nest in the late summer, take her fledgling, train it, sell it to a dealer in the town for a dozen gold pieces, so prized was a broken-in bird. But this year? She was old, and perhaps would not mate. Besides, the men moving towards them from below, from above? Perhaps he would be the one who didn't return.

'Go,' he said again, and flung out his arm.

Five beats and glide. Yet before she passed between two trees, and perhaps out of his life, she flipped briefly onto her back, as she would to take a pigeon. Her talons stretched, as if in salute. Then she was gone.

He closed his eyes, listened, then moved in the opposite direction to the hawk's flight. Soon the trunks grew closer, branches twining overhead, and the snow was not so deep. He broke into a stumbling run.

Hunter had become the hunted. Now he was the one seeking sanctuary . . .

Mist rose. Despite the tapestries upon the walls, the sheep-skins under her feet, winter still seeped into her cell. So the water in the tub sent its heat up into the chill and, where it met stone, turned to liquid. Drops joined, ran and halted as ice.

She had removed all her clothes, save for her shift. Shivering, one foot on top of the other, she waited. The water was just off the boil, still almost unbearable to the touch. Yet it had to keep its heat, for she needed to lie in it a long time, for the easing of her pains, for her pleasure.

She thrust an arm in. It reddened but she could keep it there. It was almost time.

She uncorked a flask, tipped it carefully, watching the viscous liquid drip out. Two heartbeats, enough, the steam savoured now with camomile, with clary sage, with sandal-wood. She closed her eyes, breathed, sighed. It was fresh, young, but it lacked something in the base. Oil of Bergamot, she thought. She wouldn't be able to get any till the Turkish traders came to the Spring Fair. One month away.

She was shaking with cold now, yet still she waited. She'd been taught – long ago, by those who knew this well – that pleasure delayed was pleasure doubled. Yet she waited for another reason also. When she removed her shift, she would see her body once more. There were no mirrors in the convent. She, who used to stare at herself delightedly in the finest Venetian glass, had not looked in one in the nineteen years since she took Holy Orders. The body that princes once fought for had changed.

She shivered again, not only from the cold. It was the moment. The water, perfect. The mingled scent, perfect. Her body . . . as it was. She crossed her arms, gripped cloth at her broad hips, pulled it up, over. Looked.

A month before, in a village near Targoviste, a statue of the Virgin had blossomed stigmata. The wounds of Christ the Son appearing on Mary the Mother, on each of her palms, at her ankles, weeping blood. Thousands had come to marvel, from all over Wallachia, some even struggling across the passes from Transylvania, despite the hardest winter in anyone's memory.

How many would come to see her wounds?

She lowered herself slowly into the tub, groaning at the exquisite pain. Finally she lay back and traced her fingertip along purple lines that stood proud of the reddening skin, aching with the sudden heat. Aching more with the memory of the man who gave them to her. Aching most when she recalled the other ways he touched her.

Water flooded her, penetrated her, released her, her wounds and her memories. Scent and heat made her mind slide, away from pain, to pleasure; thence to joy. Her orphans growing stronger with each day, just three lost to the winter, brought too late even for her care. The rest, all five, thriving. On her cot lay a plait woven of rosemary sprigs, that the littlest, Florica, had given her only that morning. It was threaded through with a lock of her wheaten hair. The child could spare it, had as much as she herself once had, before she married Christ.

She felt the hammering on the convent's main door at the same time she heard it. Three strikes that travelled through stone, up wood, rippling the surface of the water. But she did not open her eyes. The Matins bell had called the novitiates to prayer some time before. No visitor would be admitted to the convent till dawn, however great their hurt.

Thump. Thump. Thump. Whoever it was did not use the iron knocker upon the wood. And then, recognising the sound, she sat up. She had heard it once before, on the day the scars were made.

7

The door was being struck with the pommel of a sword.

She heard the distant scrape of the door grille, the whining of Old Kristo the gatekeeper, then a low voice, commanding. She could not hear the words. But she knew what they were. She'd always believed she would hear them, one day.

'*By order of the Voivode, I am here to arrest . . .*'

The gate was opening and she was rising. There were sheets to dry herself upon, but she barely used them. It was more important to be clothed, concealed. Then, just as she was about to pull the shift over her head, she stopped. For the man whose metal-shod feet were now striking sparks on the courtyard flagstones probably knew who she was. He was coming to ask her about the last man to see her naked, the first to see her wounds. The man whose corpse she had prepared for the grave five years before.

All things end. Nineteen years of life in the convent were over. Nun, Abbess, these were just titles, already in the past with her others – Slave, Concubine, Royal Mistress. She was only sorry that she wouldn't be there to see her orphans grow stronger; but others would take care of them, sure.

She was not shivering yet. And suddenly she wondered how it would be to see herself again, naked in the mirror of another man's eyes.

Throwing the shift aside, she picked up the plait woven of rosemary and young girl's hair. Rosemary, she'd told Florica only that morning, was the herb of remembrance. So now, holding it before her, she remembered everything and turned smiling to the opening door . . .

In the perfect darkness of the dungeon, the knight was hunting.

He did not move. Not simply because he was near blind, that did not matter much there. But every terrain required a different skill, each type of prey a different technique. Some quarry you pursued, some you drew. In the five years he had lived in constant night, he had learned the way of this, his

8

world, as once he had read valleys and forests, deserts and seas. He had shaped it, from what was available to him. The floor reeds had not been changed since the autumn and so were thick with filth; when the temperature rose above freezing, as it had that day, it made them malleable. So he had fashioned passageways from them that a creature, as hungry as himself, might follow. They twisted and bent round the cell, a labyrinth with him at its centre. He had not made it too easy, all game was wary; but the starving less so, and there was mouldy bread at his feet.

He waited, but not in the dungeon. There was no need for him there. A part of him had to stay to listen but the rest was free to depart, to other hunting grounds, bigger game. He did not just think himself elsewhere, in memory. He went wherever he chose, with whomever he chose.

One was always there. As boy, as youth, as man.

Yes! They are in the Fagaras now, among those peaks, chasing down those valleys. They are boys, barely ten, but still they have left the others far behind, for they have the best horses and the greatest skill in handling them. And they have the desire, not just for the kill. For the beating of the other. Winning is all, for now, for ever.

Their quarry is boar. There is one that they saw and lost in this valley before, a monstrous silverback with tusks like scimitars.

The boar breaks cover. Their spurs redden with blood from their stallions' flanks as they strive to reach it first. There is a grove just ahead, whose interlocked boughs will not admit hunter and steed, only prey. So they kick in their heels, stride matching stride. It is a long throw, a last chance. He takes it, throws and his steel blade slices over the silvered back, its razored edge drawing blood, slowing, not halting. His companion, his brother in all but blood, has thrown also, but thrown true. The boar tumbles, over and over, until the tree that would have saved it, halts it. It is dying, yet it lives. And for the last moments of its life it is at its most dangerous.

'Don't,' he murmurs, in sudden fear, as his companion slides from his saddle, another boar spear already in his hand. 'Wait till it is dead.'

It was strange. Most faces faded from memory, from dreams. Even the most familiar – parents, children, lovers, enemies. His never had.

He pauses now, looks up from beneath that black hair, with those green eyes. The smile comes. 'How many times, Ion,' he says, in that soft voice. 'You have to look into their eyes as they die.'

In memory indistinguishable from dream, his friend advances. The boar rises, bellowing, blood pouring from its mouth, the shaft quivering in its side. It charges and the boy plants himself, his spear couched like a lance in the lists. As the beast swerves, the boy steps to the side, thrusts. The leaf-shaped blade takes the animal in its chest but doesn't halt it. Steel precedes shaft into flesh as the boar pushes the length of the weapon up its body. Only when it reaches the steadying hand, when it has absorbed almost all the wood, does it stop, lay its great head down, lower a tusk onto the hand, gently, like a caress.

'Die well,' says the Dragon's son, smiling.

Far above, a bolt was shot. It was a whisper of a sound but a shriek in that silence. While he'd been hunting elsewhere, he had heard another beast, snuffling its way out of the sluice pipe. The noise had sent it back. He cried out now in frustration, his chance for fresh flesh gone – all because they were bringing in a prisoner, one destined for a cell far above his own.

Then another door opened and he jerked his face up, as if to see through stone. Rarely did a prisoner make it to the second level. Someone of higher rank perhaps, or more heinous crime? He sighed. At the second level, a grille would be cut high into the wall and though his eyesight was poor now, he'd still be able to see the patch of sky change shade. Better, he'd be able to scent . . . a hound's fur wet with snow, applewood burning, mulling wine. Hear . . . the snort of a horse, the cry of a baby, laughter at some jest.

Then, on the level directly above his, a bolt was worked loose. He was excited now, lost prey forgotten. It was not his feeding day; yet someone *was* coming. He lifted his eyelids open with his fingers and thumbs to make sure he didn't blink. The rare flicker of light beyond the opened grille was all that stopped him going totally blind.

He knelt, pressing his lips to the ceiling, moistening them on wet moss. The cell door above creaked open. But then he heard just a single footfall . . . and cowered down, crying out. For guards always came in pairs. Only a priest or a killer would come alone.

His eyes were wide now without need of fingers, terror in the sound of that one man approaching the round stone in the floor. For if he was a killer and not a priest . . .

He groped before him for the sharpened bone, clutched it, pressed the sharpened tip into the pulse in his neck. He had seen prisoners tortured to death. He had tortured some himself. He had always vowed that he would not die that way.

Yet he did not thrust. He could have killed himself before, ended this misery. But to do so before he had made his last confession? Then the torments he'd suffered for these five years would last for all eternity. Worse! Unless he was absolved of his sins, the suicide's fate would be as nothing to his – for the ninth, last and deepest circle of hell, just like the *oubliette* in the castle of Bucharest, was reserved only for traitors.

He heard the clink of metal. It was not the bolt on the grille being pulled back. It was a bar slipped under a hook. And then the stone, that had not been lifted in five years, was.

The torch flaring above him was like a desert sun at noon. A dark shape held it high. Priest or killer?

He pressed bone tip into flesh. Yet still he could not drive it in, could only croak his one, his ultimate hope. 'Father, I have sinned against heaven and before you.'

For a moment of silence, nothing moved. Then an arm reached slowly down . . .

– II –
The Chamber

He reached for her as he always did, just before he woke, as he had every morning for twenty years. For a time, there had been nameless others beside him and, touching their softness, he'd sometimes mistaken it for another's, woken with joy, one moment of it. But the bitterness of the next moment, when realisation turned to despair, meant that he had long chosen to sleep alone. Companions were dispatched after they had fulfilled their function, assuaged some need. For ten years, he had not even bothered with that.

Janos Horvathy, Count of Pecs, reached, realised . . . yet kept his single eye closed. He was trying to see Katarina's face. Sometimes he could, for that brief instant of reaching, of realising – the only time he could. He had her portrait, but that showed merely her beauty; nothing of what he truly loved – the feel of her skin, her calmness, her laugh.

No. This morning she wouldn't come, even so briefly, her features dissolving into a memory of inadequate paint. A breeze flapped the beeswax-dipped cloth in the arrow slit, admitting a little light, making the room even colder. At first he wondered why his servants had not repaired it; and then he remembered that he was not in his own castle in Hungary. He was in another man's castle, in another country.

And then he remembered why. Remembered that today might be the beginning of the lifting of the curse that had killed his wife twenty years before; that had sent their three children to the family vault, one lost to childbirth, one to battle, one to plague.

A knock at the door. 'Yes?' he called.

A man entered. It was Petru, the young Spatar who held this fortress for his prince, the Voivode of Wallachia. He stood in the doorway, shifting from foot to foot, as nervous as he had been when the Count had first arrived the day before. Horvathy understood why. It wasn't often that one of the highest noblemen of Hungary came to such a remote place with such a purpose. And before he'd arrived, Petru had had to make many arrangements, in the greatest secrecy.

'Is all ready?' Horvathy asked.

The man licked his lips. 'I . . . I believe so, my lord. If you would . . .' He gestured to the stairs behind him.

'I will. Wait for me.'

The knight bowed, closed the door behind him. Horvathy slid from beneath the furs, sat for a moment on the bed's edge, rubbing the thick grey stubble of his hair. The bed-chamber, despite the breeze, was no colder than his own back in Pecs. Besides, he'd discovered long since that the castle for which he'd traded his soul could never be warmed when no one he loved could survive within it.

He dressed swiftly then went in search of warmth. Not for his body, he'd never really required that. For his soul.

'My lord,' the young Spatar said, pushing the door inwards, stepping back.

Horvathy entered. The hall, lit by four reed torches and dawn's light beyond the arrow slits, was as modest as the rest of the castle – a rectangular stone chamber twenty paces long, a dozen wide, its walls lined with cheap tapestries, its floor strewn with skins, both trying to retain the warmth of the large fire at its top, eastern end and largely failing to do so. It was a functional room at the centre of a simple fortress. Ordinary.

Yet what had been placed in the room made it . . . not ordinary.

14

He looked around, then at the young man before him. 'Tell me what you have done.'

'I have obeyed the orders of my prince, the Voivode of Wallachia.' Petru held up a sheaf of parchment. 'To the letter, I trust.'

'And how did these orders come to you?'

'They were left in the night outside the gate, three weeks ago, in a satchel. They bear the Voivode's seal but . . .' He licked his lips. '. . . But another paper warned that the Voivode was not to be contacted further, or acknowledged in any way.'

Horvathy nodded. The Voivode knew as well as any the danger in the game they were playing. 'And was anything else left?'

'Yes, my lord.' The younger man swallowed. 'The satchel was weighted down with the several parts of a hand-and-a-half sword. A blade, quillons, the pommel. There was an order to re-forge it. I had to send to Curtea de Arges for a blacksmith. He arrived this morning, has begun. Our forge is poor here but he says he has all he needs.'

'Not quite all,' replied Horvathy, reaching inside his doublet. 'He will need these.' He pulled out two circles of steel, the size of finger and thumb joined. Their edges were rough, for they had been gouged from the pommel of a sword. 'Here,' he said. 'These were sent to me, with the summons that brought me here.' His one eye was fixed on the younger man's two, awaiting the reaction.

It came, in a gasp. 'The Dragon!'

'You recognise it?'

'Certainly, my lord.' Petru turned the pieces over in his fingers, wincing as the serrated edges drew blood. 'It is the symbol both of the man who built this castle and the sacred Order he led. The man, the Order, both dishonoured, disgraced . . .'

The suddenness of Horvathy's lunge startled Petru. The Count was a head taller than the knight, bent now over him.

'I'd be careful about terms like dishonour and disgrace, Spatar,' he shouted, his scarred face a hand's width away. 'Because I am a Dragon, too.'

He held the stare, his one grey eye gleaming, all the brighter by its contrast with the other puckered socket.

Petru stuttered, 'I . . . I . . . I meant no offence, Count Horvathy. I merely . . . repeat what I have heard . . .'

The stare held a moment longer. Then the older man turned away, spoke more quietly. 'You repeat gossip, gleaned from tales of one Dragon – Vlad Dracula, your former Prince. Yet part of what you say is true – it is his dark deeds that have tainted the Order to which he swore his oath. Tales that have all but destroyed it.'

'All but?' Petru said, carefully. 'It is destroyed, surely, is it not?'

The Hungarian breathed deeply. 'Until it is slain by St Mihail's magic lance, a Dragon cannot die. It sleeps only. Sleeps perhaps one day to waken . . .' Horvathy's voice faded, behind the hand lifted to his face.

'My lord, I . . .' Petru took a step towards the Count, his tone cautious. 'I was raised to honour the Dragon. I dreamt of becoming a brother. If it could awaken, with honour, I would ride beneath its banner gladly. And I would not ride alone.'

Horvathy turned. Saw the yearning in the younger man's gaze. He had once had such hunger, such ambition. When he had two eyes. Before he was a Dragon. Before he was cursed.

He breathed deeply. He had also startled himself with his sudden anger. And he knew it should not be directed at the youth before him, but at himself. He reached up, running his finger over the scar where an eye had been. Perhaps this was the day of redemption of all sins, the beginning of hope. Others must have thought so too. Or else, why all these elaborate, secret arrangements?

He turned back to them now. In a calmer voice he said, 'Tell me what else you have done.'

The younger man nodded, relief clear on his face. He gestured to the dais, raised before the fireplace, to the three chairs upon it. 'We shall sit there, my lord, closest to the warmth. The chairs are the most comfortable I possess. My wife was sorry to give hers up, heavy as she is with our first child . . .' He cut himself off, flushing, and to cover his embarrassment led the way past the dais to a table beside it. 'And here is the best that a humble fortress at winter's end can provide for sustenance.'

Horvathy looked down at the table which was well-stocked with wine, rough bread, cinder-coated goat's cheese, herb-encrusted sausage. Then he saw what lay beside the food. 'And what are these?' he said, though he knew.

'They came in the satchel, my lord. The Voivode ordered them to be displayed.' Petru lifted the top one. On its front page a crude woodcut depicted a nobleman eating his dinner among ranks of bodies twitching on stakes. Before him a servant hacked limbs, severed noses and ears. ' "The Story of a Bloodthirsty Madman",' Petru read aloud, then offered the pamphlet. 'Do you wish to read, my lord?'

'No,' Horvathy replied, curtly. He had seen them before, many times. 'And now,' he said, turning back.

He had avoided looking at them, after the first glance into the hall, though they were the biggest things there. For they spoke, too clearly to his innermost thoughts. To sin. To redemption. To absolution, sought and never found.

The three confessionals stood in a line in the very centre of the room, facing the dais. Each was divided into two cubicles, one for supplicant, one for priest. Their curtains were open, and Horvathy could see that they had been adapted for long periods of sitting. There were cushions, wolfskins. 'Why these?' he said softly, moving forward, laying his hand upon the dark-stained wood.

'The Voivode ordered them, my lord,' Petru said, joining him. 'And this was the hardest command to fulfil. As you know, we of the Orthodox faith do not have them, but are

17

happy to kneel before our priests in plain sight at the altar screen door. So I was forced to go to those damned Catholic Saxons across the border here in Transylvania, who cheated me as is their way . . .' He broke off, flushed. 'I . . . mean no disrespect, Count Horvathy. I know you are of the Roman faith.'

Horvathy waved him down. 'Do not concern yourself, Spatar.' He stepped into the priest's side of the cubicle. 'What's this?' he said, folding down a hinged table.

'I had them installed. The orders spoke of scribes who would sit there. The . . . confessions are to be written down, are they not?'

'They are. I have brought the scribes. You thought well.' Horvathy rose swiftly. 'And the last?' He squinted to the shadows at the far end of the hall, opposite the fireplace. 'What is there?'

'Ah. This is perhaps the only time I have exceeded my orders.' He gestured and Horvathy followed him, to another table. 'There is plainer food for the scribes, for the . . . witnesses.' He swallowed. 'But my Latin is weak and I was unsure exactly what the Voivode meant by . . . *quaestio*. If some sort of interrogation is planned, I thought . . .'

He pointed to objects on the table. Horvathy reached down, touched the metal head cage, pressed a fingertip into one of the spurs within it. He glanced over the other implements – the bone-crushing boot, the thumb screws, the flesh tongs. Hardly a complete set; just what the Spatar travelled with to enforce the Voivode's will at the local villages, no doubt.

Sucking at his finger – the spur had drawn blood – he nodded. He did not believe they would be necessary. But he did not want to condemn the Spatar's zeal. Then he noticed, beyond the table, something embedded in the wall. 'What's that?' he murmured.

The younger man smiled. 'A curiosity. It is said that the former Voivode punished his traitorous nobles by forcing them and their families to work as slaves here and build this castle. Like so many tales told of him I did not believe it. Until I found . . . this.' He pulled a candle from his pocket, went and lit it at one of the reed torches burning in a sconce, returned. Lowering the light, still smiling, he said, 'See, my lord. And feel.'

Without thinking, Horvathy did both. Knew instantly what jutted from the mortar between two bricks.

It was the jawbone of a child.

He snatched his hand back, leaving a speck of his blood on the begrimed baby tooth. He had heard the story of the castle building, too. Like so many told of Dracula, it had always seemed unlikely. Like so many, it was undoubtedly, at least partly, true.

Janos Horvathy, Count of Pecs, glanced back down the hall at the three confessionals. The tales that were to come from them were going to be similar. And worse. Far worse. Suddenly, all the hope he'd had when he first received the facings from the Dragon's sword, the hope that had sustained him across the snow-clogged valleys of Transylvania to this remote fortress in Wallachia, slipped away. What tales could emerge here that would exonerate such evil? What confession could be told that would free the Dragon order of its disgrace – and him of his curse?

He raised his finger to his missing eye, placed a spot of blood there, too, rubbed it away. 'Send the rest of the sword to the blacksmith. And call them. Call them all.'

With a bow, Petru turned to obey.

– III –

Confessions

The first to come were the scribes, tonsured monks, each carrying their stand of inks, their parchment and quills, their little knives. They went to the priest's side of the confessionals, placed their equipment upon the shelf, pulled down the hinged writing table that Petru had had fitted, then, settled, drew the curtain.

A moment later, Bogdan, second-in-command at Poenari, appeared. He had been sent to rendezvous with the Count's party a day's ride away and guide them to the castle. During the journey, Horvathy had asked him about the prisoners he had collected, by order of the Voivode – the first of whom Bogdan was now half-carrying into the hall. This man – a former knight, Horvathy had been told – crouched for a moment in the doorway, unable to stand upright after five years in an *oubliette*, a cell that was half his height tall. It accounted for his walk, like a crab upon a beach, and his near-blindness, for he had almost never seen the light. It also accounted for his scent, which even a thorough scrubbing in the horse trough in the castle yard had barely begun to diminish.

Aided by Bogdan, the prisoner pulled himself onto the seat of the first confessional, squatting there, his knees drawn up under the shift he wore. A light came into his eyes, as he inhaled the aroma of incense and polish. He reached up and touched the grille, then gave a gurgle of joy. Bogdan drew the curtain.

The second prisoner, the woman, was also clothed in a

shift. Bogdan had told how he'd gone to the convent to seize the abbess, and had found no reverend old lady but a naked lunatic, thrusting a woven plait at him. He had not taken it – all knew that was the first way a witch ensnared her victim. He had not paused to study her nakedness. He had simply wrapped her in blankets and thrown her into a cart.

Her head was uncovered now, and beneath the stubble her skin shone in the firelight. Her eyes were bright, too, as she took in what was before her. Bogdan did not touch or guide her. Petru, standing before the dais, pointed to the middle confessional, stepping well back as she passed. When she had settled, he drew the second curtain across.

And finally came the hermit, a reeking pile of hair flopping forward over his downcast eyes, his thick beard moving around his mouth, words formed on hidden lips, sound-lessly. Since Petru had captured him himself – in a cave within the very forest surrounding Poenari Castle – the man had not spoken.

Petru looked up at the Count. 'Now, my lord?' Horvathy nodded and Petru turned back to his lieutenant. 'Go tell His Eminence that all is ready.'

A bow, and the soldier was gone. Now it was about to begin, Horvathy felt nothing, save a curious lethargy. His one eye glazed as he stared near his feet. Around him, the hall was filled with little sounds. Flame-crackle, of fire and torch, the sharpening of feather quills, a low moaning. Then, through the arrow slits, he heard first the sharp bark of a raven and then the '*kree-ak, kree-ak*' of a hunting hawk. He lifted his head to it, wished he were hunting, too.

The door opened. A man walked in.

He looked as out of place in that sparse room as a peacock in a hen coop. In contrast to the grey-clad men who waited for him, he was dressed in bright scarlet robes, and compared to their wolf-like leanness, he was fat, a heifer, not even a bull. When he mounted the platform, he breathed heavily, as if he were climbing a tower. When he pulled back his hood, the face revealed was sunk into a neck of jowls, black eyes studded into flesh like raisins into a pastry. His hair was short, blond, thick and held under a red cap. He fell into his chair.

The Hungarian gestured the Spatar to his seat. But he did not sit himself. Instead, he looked before him and spoke directly at the three confessionals. As he did, from each came the scratching of quill on parchment.

'Let it be known that I am Janos Horvathy,' he said, speaking clearly, slowly, 'Count of Pecs. I have been sent here by command of my liege Lord, my King, Matthias Corvinus of Hungary, to . . . to interrogate you.' He stumbled a little on the lie then gestured around the hall. 'And though I find this method, all this . . . somewhat strange, I do not question the commands of the Voivode of Wallachia, in whose realm, and by whose grace, this interrogation takes place.' He nodded to the younger man. 'Let it also be noted that Petru Iordache, Spatar of Poenari, has fulfilled his sovereign's commands to the last detail.' He sat, then looked at the Cardinal.

'Must I?' the bovine churchman sighed.

Horvathy pointed to the confessionals. 'All will be noted down. You have those you report to, as have I. We must have an exact record.'

'Oh, a record?' Wincing as he leaned forward and took some weight upon his swollen feet, the man spat, 'Well then, for the record, I am Domenico Grimani, Cardinal of Urbino and, as Papal Legate to the court of King Matthias, I represent Sixtus IV. And for the record, I think the Holy Father would be amazed to see me here, in these barbarous mountains, taking part in a . . . pageant!'

'A pageant!'

The Cardinal did not flinch at Horvathy's roar. 'You asked me to accompany you on this journey, Count. You said I was needed to judge something. But the cold, the hideous inns, the appalling roads – well, they have driven the reason for my being here quite out of my head.' He raised a fat hand to his forehead, assumed a mockery of thinking. 'Was it to listen to the tale of a monster? Was it to see if we can *rehabilitate* Dracula?' The Cardinal laughed, pointed before him. 'And all this? Was it so that the secret fraternity he led, and buried with his horrors, can rise again?' He was shaking with laughter now. 'For the record . . . who cares?'

'I do!' roared the man beside him. 'Perhaps you forget – though somehow, I doubt it – that the fraternity you mock is "fraternatis draconem" – the sacred Order of the Dragon. Of which I and my father were – are! – proud brothers. Founded for the sole purpose of fighting the infidel and the heretic. Hungary's enemies, Christ's enemies, the Pope's enemies, Cardinal Grimani.' Horvathy's voice lowered again, in volume if not in passion. 'And the man you speak of was not its leader, but its most famous member for a time. He was the one who last rode under the Dragon banner against the Turks. And under it, nearly beat them. Would have beaten them, perhaps, if the Pope, my King and, yes . . .' he faltered, '. . . his fellow Dragons had not forsaken him.'

As the Cardinal had shaken with laughter, so the Count now did with rage. But, breathing deeply, he sat back and went on more calmly. 'And I will remind you why you are here, Cardinal. Why you agreed to accompany me to this "barbarous" land.' He leaned forward, speaking as much for the scribes as for the Roman. 'It is because a restored Order of the Dragon could once again become Christ's cutting edge, uniting leaders in every state in the Balkans, and in lands beyond, under our banner. And thereby – need I remind you of this? – helping to lift the scimitar that presses on Rome's throat.'

'My lord Horvathy,' the Cardinal replied, oil replacing ice in his voice, 'I apologise. I meant no slur on your Order, which undoubtedly was once a great weapon for Christendom's cause. But I am confused – is it not an impossible task, to whiten the name of someone so black? Surely, the whole world knows of Dracula's infamy, his cruelty, his depravity.'

'What the world knows' – the Count's tone calmed also – 'is the story his conquerors told. And since they controlled so many printing presses, it was their stories that were widely spread.' He gestured to the table, the pile of pamphlets there. 'But if the Holy Father were to forgive . . . why then, are there not presses also in Rome, in Buda, ready to print other stories? A different version of the truth?'

'Ah, truth.' The Cardinal smiled, outwardly this time. 'The truth of history. I've often wondered what that is. Is the truth what we seek here? Or just a version of it that will suit all our ambitions?' He sighed. 'But you are right, Count Horvathy. The presses are weapons as strong as your broadsword and axe. Stronger in some ways. I've often thought: if the Devil had a Bible in print, would he be as unpopular as he is now?' A smile came at Petru's gasp. Then he leaned forward. 'So what truth is it you would have them tell?'

'That we will hear,' replied the Count. 'What we seek may not be possible. It may be that the monster is all that will emerge from the telling. But since the Turks now have a foothold in Italy, at Otranto, and the Sultan's standard has been raised before the walls of lost Constantinople – and who knows where he will lead his army? – is it not a tale in desperate need of hearing?'

Grimani sat back, a conciliatory smile now on his face. When he replied, he spoke slowly, clearly. For the record. 'Very well, my lord. I acknowledge that the times are perilous. You have asked me here to be a judge. So let me begin with this.' He looked at the line of confessionals. 'Who waits here behind these curtains? And why have they been chosen to tell us this tale?'

'Let them answer.' The Count motioned Petru forward.

The Spatar rapped hard upon the first confessional. 'Who are you?' he demanded.

The knight had been listening to the voices. He heard so

many in a day, it had been hard to tell if these were any more real. But he'd suddenly recognised the voice of one of the judges; more, he'd realised that he had met the man before, in the days of sight and sin. That, and the fact that he now understood just why he'd been freed from the darkness, brought his mind, which had spun in circles of insanity for long years, slowly to a stop.

'My name is Ion Tremblac,' he said. And saying it, he remembered that it was true.

Gasps came, one from the Count as the recognition was returned, one female and from the central confessional.

Petru went on. 'And how did you know Dracula, the former Voivode of Wallachia, whose tale we seek to hear this day?'

'How? From boyhood, I took every stride beside him. Rode stirrup to stirrup with him to the hunt, to war. Suffered torture, shared triumph. I was his closest companion.' The man began to weep. 'And I betrayed him. Betrayed him!'

A near silence, violated only by the sound of other tears in the second confessional. Horvathy turned to it now, and Petru tapped it once, then crossed himself. 'And you, lady,' he asked. 'Who are you?'

She too had sat there, listening, realising. She had always known that one day she would have to give an account and not just in her prayers. She'd been ready, calm, willing . . . until she'd heard a voice she'd thought never to hear again, of the only man she'd ever called a friend, a man she'd thought long dead. She breathed now to calm herself, wiped her face and when she was ready, spoke. 'I have been known for many years only as the Abbess of the Sisters of Mercy at Clejani. But beneath the veil, I have always been Ilona Ferenc. And from the moment I first saw him, when I was slave to the Sultan, till the hour I prepared his body for the grave, I loved him. For I was his mistress.'

It was the weeping knight's turn to gasp, uncertain again that anything was real, that he was not still in his cell, among his ghosts. For the woman who had just spoken was dead. He'd seen her murdered – viciously murdered. Keening, he began to tap his head against the wood.

From the last confessional came no sound, no movement. When Petru thumped it, the hermit did not stir.

'And you? Speak!' he commanded.

Silence.

'My lord,' said Petru, turning back, 'I do not think he *can* speak. He has lived in a cave on this mountain for many years and no one has ever heard him do so.'

Horvathy bent, spoke loudly. 'Well, man? You were ordered to be brought here as well. Can you tell us who you are? What you were to the person we are here to judge?'

The quills stopped their scratching. The silence extended. Then, just as Petru was about to reach in and drag the hermit to the far end of the hall, and its tools of coercion, a voice came. It was gruff with disuse, barely there. Yet, because of the perfect acoustics of the hall, it carried.

'I knew him. In some ways, better than anyone. I heard of every deed he did. I heard why he did them.' The voice grew stronger. 'For my name is Brother Vasilie. And I was his confessor.'

The quills began moving again, one by one, as the scribes scratched those last few words.

'Interesting,' the Cardinal said. 'And leaving aside, for the moment, that you will be betraying the secrets of the shriving . . .' He settled back into his chair. 'Well, who would speak first then? Who would begin the tale of Dracula?'

In the first confessional, Ion Tremblac thrust forward, his face pushing out the curtain. All could see his features in the cloth, his moving mouth. 'I will,' he said swiftly. He had waited so long. Five years of darkness. Now, here, at last, he could see some light. There was a priest in the room; he was in a confessional. It did not matter that he had been raised in the Orthodox faith that did not use them. God, in any coat, had forsaken him long ago. But however great his sins, this was his one chance to repent, to draw Him back. To be forgiven.

'I will,' Ion said again, before anyone else could. 'Because, you see, I knew him from the beginning . . .'

— PART ONE —

The Fledgling

'It is far easier for one to defend himself against the Turks who is familiar with them than for one who does not know their customs.'

— KONSTANTIN MIHAILOVIC, Serbian janissary

ONE

The Hostage

Edirne, capital of the Turkish Empire, September 1447

'Well? Is there not one of you dullards who can speak this for me?'

Ion Tremblac stared at the curls and swoops of the Arabic letters on the tablet before him, and sighed. Quietly, for it would not do to be heard in despair. If he could not present an answer, the least required was diligent, silent striving. But the letters he'd copied down were becoming less clear, not more so. His mind was just too full! The boys had entered the classroom at dawn, and the sun was now close to its zenith. First there'd been Greek, then mathematics, then some fiendish Persian poetry. When that was done, the scholars had begun to rise, assuming by the sun's position in the sky that the day was done and they were free. But then Hamza, their *agha*, their tutor, had given a teasing smile and said, 'Let us end the day with the words of Allah, the Merciful, the All-Encompassing. Just a short verse from the Qur'an.' The Serbian, Mardic, had actually groaned and been struck for it. Hence Ion's inward sigh. He wanted the wooden *bastinado* that rested beside the tutor's floor pillow to remain there.

'Come, my fledglings, my young hawks. Your dullness would test the patience of the Iman of Tabriz, whose seren-ity was undisturbed when barbarians burned his house around him and who only asked: will someone not open the window?'

Hamza laughed quietly and leaned over his crossed legs, gazing down from his raised dais upon the seven bent heads below. He was obviously expecting some reaction to his words. None came.

'No one?' Now it was Hamza who sighed. 'Go then, you stones. See if some of the Merciful's clean air can clear your heads!' Over the scuffle of boys rising, the little groans as limbs too long crossed were released, he added, 'But we will return to this in the morning. And there will be no tales from Herodotus until we finish it.'

No one was faster to their feet than Ion. He would have been first through the door, too, leading his *orta* into the central passageway of the *enderun kolej*, joining the throng there of other *ortas* released from their studies. Now that he was standing, he could see them over the low partition walls that divided class from class in the big hall, and he ached to join them. All were silent, as was commanded, but he could see the restraint on the faces, the whoop that would erupt as soon as they cleared the doors. But he could not leave. Not when the one who sat next to him was still studying the words. Ion clicked his fingers in front of his friend's face, the gesture obvious.

His impatience had no effect. Hamza, who had stood and was stretching his own cramped limbs, looked down at Ion and his prone companion. He studied the bent head, the midnight-black hair falling like a veil over the face, and smiled. 'Do you have it, my young man?'

The youth's lips moved once more in silent recitation before he looked up. 'I believe so, Hamza *agha*,' he said.

'Then why didn't you speak it before your classmates?'

Turd, thought Ion. Wasn't it obvious? His friend could have answered most questions if he chose. But the rest of the *orta*, made up of other hostages like themselves, were jealous enough already. It was often easiest, and less bruising, to keep silent.

Hamza stepped down from the dais, into a shaft of sunlight. Beneath his black turban, his blue eyes shone in his dark face, a slight smile splitting his blond beard. Seeing him more clearly, Ion saw again that their *agha* was older than them, of course, but perhaps only by seven years. Until his promotion three years previously, he'd been cupbearer to the Sultan. 'Well then,' Hamza said, gesturing down. 'Recite it for me, Vlad Dracula. Let me hear from your mouth the wisdom of the Holy Qur'an.'

Vlad cleared his throat, then spoke. ' "They will ask thee about intoxicants and games of chance. Say: In both there is great sin as well as some benefit for man; but the evil that they cause is greater than the benefit that they bring." '

'Good.' Hamza nodded. 'You mispronounced perhaps three of the words. But the fact that you can pronounce Arabic at all astonishes me.' He came closer, squatted down. 'How many languages is it that you speak?'

Vlad shrugged. Ion spoke for his friend, excitedly. 'Greek, Latin, Frankish . . .'

Vlad gave him a look, bidding silence. Ion knew the look and obeyed.

'And you are fluent in Osmanlica, of course. But Arabic?' Hamza whistled. 'Do you strive to be a *hafiz*?'

'One who can recite all of the Qur'an?' Vlad shook his head. 'No.'

'And yet you can recite much more than almost . . . anyone else I know.' As he spoke, Hamza suddenly punched Ion on the shoulder. When he stepped out of range with a yelp of outrage, the other two laughed.

'I . . . admire it,' replied Vlad. 'And I recite it because the words and the thoughts they hold are beautiful and are meant to be spoken aloud, as the Angel Gabriel spoke them to the Prophet, may peace be upon him. On a page they are just words. Out here . . .' – he waved the air before him – '. . . they are energy, released.'

'I think you are intoxicated with words, my young man.' Hamza rested his hand on Vlad's shoulder, leaned in. 'We are alike in that. And perhaps their truth will lead you to other truths. Even to Allah?'

'Ah, no. That is not the reason I learn and recite. I admire the words, yes, but . . .'

Hamza's smile did not fade. Doubt was good, a stumble away from a fall. 'But?'

Vlad looked up, listened to the last of the *ortas* leaving, the shouts, laughter and challenges, as caged youth exploded into freedom. 'I learn to know you,' he said. 'Truly know you. For the Turk is the power shaking the tree of the world, and your faith is what drives you to do it. Unless I know about that, know everything about you, well . . .' He looked back, directly into the older man's eyes. '. . . How am I ever going to stop you?'

Two gasps came, from both listeners. Hamza recovered first, withdrawing his hand. 'Do you not fear that I will punish you for such talk?' He gestured to the *bastinado*, which he had left by his floor pillow.

'For what, *effendi*?'

'For your rebellious thoughts.'

Vlad frowned. 'Why would you be surprised by them? All hostages are children of rebels. That's why we are hostages – so that our fathers, who rule their lands by Turkish grace – continue to acknowledge their true master. Dracul, my father, gave me and my brother Radu to your . . . care, five years ago. Not so we'd receive the best education it is possible to have but so that, if he rebels again, you can kill us.'

Ion reached, took an elbow. 'Stop . . .'

Vlad shrugged him off. 'Why, Ion? Hamza *agha* knows our story. He has seen hostages come and go, live and die. He helps to give us the best of everything – food, language, philosophy, the arts of war and poetry.' He pointed to his tablet. 'They expose us to their faith, one of tolerance and charity, yet they do not force us to convert, for that is against the word of the Holy Qur'an. If all goes well, they send us back to our lands to deal with all their problems there for them, to pay them tribute in gold and boys, and thank them for the privilege. If all goes badly, well . . .' He smiled. 'Then

34

they spill our well-educated brains upon the ground.' He turned back. 'Do I speak anything but the truth, *effendi*? If so, beat me soundly for a liar, please.'

Hamza regarded him for a long moment, nothing in his expression. Finally, he said, 'How old are you?'

'I will be seventeen in March,' came the reply.

'It is too young to have such cynical thoughts.'

'No, Hamza *agha*,' replied Vlad softly, 'it is only too young to be able to do anything about them.'

They stared at each other for a long moment. Then both smiled again, with Ion looking between them, excluded, suddenly jealous. He would never have the intellect of his friend; and he could plainly see that Hamza and Vlad shared something he would never be a part of.

The silence held, until the Turk rose and turned away. 'Go, my hawk,' he said over his shoulder. 'Your companion is desperate to fly.'

Vlad rose, too, but did not go. '*Effendi*, do you not leave us soon?'

The tutor was stooping to collect books. He straightened. 'How have you heard what has only just been decided?' When Vlad merely shrugged, he shook his head, continued. 'It is true. I travel at the end of the week. On the orders of the Sultan, may Allah always send him health. You know I am not one of your ordinary *agha*s.'

'I know. You are also one of the finest of the Exalted One's falconers. Is that what you are about now?'

Ion shifted. It was not usual to ask questions of an *agha*, only to answer them. To question was seen as impertinence – and was punishable.

Yet the Turk did not reach for the *bastinado* at his feet. 'I go to hunt,' he said softly, 'but not birds.'

Again Ion shifted, aching even more to be gone, away from the warning in the tone. All knew Hamza was a rising power in the state. His falconer's title was real, for all men had a trade, against the day of disaster – even the Sultan himself, for Murad worked metal into horseshoes, bow-rings, arrow-heads. Yet all knew also that if Hamza was about the Sultan's business it was work of intrigue and danger. For Vlad to be even thinking about it . . .

Yet his countryman did not blink. 'Though perhaps you may get the chance to fly? And if you do . . .' He reached inside his lawn shirt, down to the line where it met the baggy red *shalvari* that swathed his legs, and pulled out a bundle wrapped in blue cloth. He held it out.

Hamza reached forward, took the bundle. The cerise silk ribbon gave with a slight tug and he unrolled the cloth. For a moment he studied what he held . . . then he slipped on the gauntlet.

'I could only guess at the measurements,' Vlad said. 'I hope it . . .'

Hamza raised his hand, flexed his fingers. 'You have a good eye, my young man. It fits . . . like a glove!' He smiled, made a fist and lifted it into a sunbeam so he could study the polished leather of its top, the skin that must resist the grip of talon, thick and double-stitched. But beneath, on the softer leather that ran up the inside of the wrist . . . 'What's this?' he asked, peering.

Ion saw golden thread woven in patterns. His Persian was better than his Arabic and he recognised it as such; then knew the words when Hamza recited them aloud. ' "I am trapped. Held in this cage of flesh. And yet I claim to be a hawk flying free." ' The teacher looked up. 'Jalaluddin. Rumi. My favourite among the poets.'

'And mine.'

The Turk read the inscription to himself again silently. 'You have made free with the last line. Does not the poet say, merely, "bird"?'

Vlad's only reply was a slight shrug.

'Well.' Hamza raised the glove, turning it in the light. 'Exquisite work anyway. Now I know what trade you follow, Vlad Dracula, against the day of disaster.' He took the gauntlet off carefully, then looked up and smiled. 'I thank you for it. From now on, when I hunt I will wear it. And when I do, I will remember you.'

'It is all I could desire, *effendi*.'

Bowing slightly, Vlad turned and made for the partition door, a relieved Ion following. They were nearly through it when Hamza's soft voice halted them. 'And do you consider yourself caged, my young man? Because your body is hostage to the Sultan?'

Vlad did not turn. 'You know what else is written, *effendi*,' he said softly. ' "I do not keep hawks. They live with me." ' He smiled, although only Ion saw it. 'And I live with you,' he added, stepping through the door, 'for now.'

Then he was striding down the corridor.

Ion followed, his shoulders hunched against the order to return, perhaps to the *bastinado*'s touch. It did not come.

— TWO —
Rivals

Vlad stood for a moment in the doorway, blinking against the light, accustoming his eyes. Thinking of Hamza. He would miss the man. For the wisdom of his teaching, nearly always delivered with words not blows. For their shared love of many things – Sufi poetry, Greek philosophy, falconry. They had flown together only once, when Hamza had taken his *orta* out of the *kolej* and into the hills. The sakers they'd borrowed from the Sultan's mews tolerated the strangers on whose fists they sat, and three made kills of bustard, including Vlad's. But Hamza had a shungar, a falcon as white as the snows from which it came. He flew it at fowl, at rabbit, and it killed again and again, yet always returned to the fist to nuzzle the hand for flesh. It was then Vlad had noticed his *agha*'s worn glove. That night, he'd begun his task while the others slept.

Mockery interrupted his memories. ' "And I live with you . . . for now!" ' mimicked Ion in a whisper, as they marched toward the sunlight. 'Do you seek to be a mystery to them?'

'I seek to keep my enemy guessing about me, yes.'

'Is Hamza your enemy?'

'Of course. He's a Turk. But I like him anyway.'

Vlad stepped from the hall into the inner court. The noonday sun cast his shadow behind him, onto his other shadow. He could sense all the questions roiling inside Ion and he smiled, wondering which one would burst to the surface first. He glanced back, then up. Had his friend gotten taller overnight? They had both grown in their five years as hostage to the Turk but Ion's growth had nearly all been upwards and only recently out. He still walked with the stumbling gait of a colt unused to his long limbs. Whereas he . . . he would never look down upon many men. Most men would have to step to the side to look past him but . . . he'd have liked some more height!

He stopped suddenly. Ion, trying to sort his questions, stumbled into him. 'Heh,' he said, surprised, instantly wary, stepping back, looking at Vlad's hands.

'Where are you, Ion?'

'Where?' Ion glanced around then realised what was meant. 'The glove? When did you . . . why did you . . . ?'

Vlad recommended walking, both shadows following. 'When did I make the glove? When you were in the tavern, drooling over Brown-Browed Aisha. Why?' He slowed. 'I wonder that myself.'

'Tell me, Vlad,' Ion chuckled, 'for you do nothing without a reason.'

'Do I not?' Vlad sighed. 'Maybe you are right. Maybe I do think too much. Well then . . .' He blew out his lips. 'I made it because I can, and because I delighted in the making. I gave it to Hamza because I like him.' He glanced up. 'Is that reason enough?'

'No, Vlad. Because you like me. And you've never made me a glove, or anything else.'

'True.'

'So tell me.'

'Well then.' Vlad took a breath. 'If you must know there are two reasons apart from the liking. One obvious to any but a simpleton. One less so.'

Ion ignored the jibe. 'The obvious?'

'Hamza is a power in this land. He was Murad's cupbearer, has kept rising through the court. Not bad for a cobbler's son from Laz. This is a man to know. To respect and to earn his respect. We may have to deal with him one day.'

'We?'

'The Draculesti. My father, my brothers and me. The Princes of Wallachia.'

'Hmm! And the other reason?'

'Does he not remind you of the Dragon?'

Ion stopped, open-mouthed. 'Your father? Hah!' He grinned. 'Vlad Dracul is squat, like you . . .'

'Squat? Have a care!'

'Devil-dark, green-eyed, brown-skinned, excessively hairy, like you . . .'

'Are these men you describe or monkeys?'

'While Hamza' – Ion circled a wrist before his face – 'is tall, slim, fair and nearly as handsome as me.' He ran his hand through his long, golden hair, shook it. 'He and I are from a race of angels, while the Draculesti . . .'

He shouldn't have looked away while insulting his friend. Vlad took an arm, put hip to hip, and had him on his back in the dust in a moment. His face was a hand's breadth from Ion's. 'What you say of my father is true. But it's the interior I refer to. They each love life, every facet of it. And yet each would give up all of it – every pleasure, every vice – for what they believe to be right.'

A stone dug into Ion's back. Where Vlad pinned his arm, it hurt. Provoked, he spat, 'I thought you hated your father?'

Vlad's face changed. Mockery died. He stood, pulling Ion to his feet. 'Hate? Why do you say that?'

Ion brushed the dust from his *shalvari*. 'Because he gave you, and your brother, to the Turks as hostages. Sent you away from all you loved – home, mother, sisters . . .'

Vlad wiped the dust from his hands. 'I hated that he did it. The way he did it.'

'He had no choice.'

'No,' Vlad said softly. 'When you are lashed to a cart wheel, kissing the Sultan's arse, you don't have much control over what you do.'

Ion instantly regretted raising that memory of five years

40

before. The Sultan's invitation to confer at Gallipoli. The Dragon taking his two youngest sons on the embassy. But it wasn't an embassy. It was the bringing to heel of a vassal who had played too many games on the side of the Turk's greatest enemy: Hunyadi, the Hungarian 'White Knight'. Dracul, fettered and powerless, did what was required. Swore to pay his annual tribute in gold and in promising boys for the *enderun kolej*. Swore to support only the Sultan in war. Eventually he was unchained, returned to his country. But he had to leave his sons behind as hostages to his word.

Vlad had begun walking again. Ion caught up. 'I am sorry . . .'

'No. It is nothing,' Vlad replied. 'If I hated what he did, that is past now. I understand why he did it. He did what he had to do so he could remain free and do what was right. As we all must.' He looked back. 'Hamza *agha* has taught me that. A glove, my labour upon it, is a small price to pay for such knowledge.'

They had reached the limits of the gardens of the inner court. Stepping through the doorway into the outer court, the sudden increase in sound halted them. Hundreds of youths from all the *orta*s mingled there, raising voices and dust. Standing close to the entrance were the other students of their own *orta*. As one, Vlad and Ion tried to move the other way. Too late.

'Vladia! Oh, Vladia!' More kissing sounds came. 'Your nose, how brown it is! How far up the *agha*'s shitter did you shove it this time?'

Vlad stopped, so Ion had to. After years in the same *orta*, all the hostages knew the others' sensitivities. Vlad's nose was one. His relationship with Hamza was another. The Serbian, Gheorghes Mardic, had hit with both. With a sigh, Ion followed Vlad to the group, each member bearing the same mocking smile on their faces, the same excitement in their eyes. This confrontation had been building for a week, since the day at the wrestling turf when Vlad had thrown both

Mardics and then everyone else, one after the other. Separately, they could not defeat him. Together . . .

Vlad halted a few paces away, hands at his side. 'You have something to say to me, Mardic Maximus?'

The larger of the Serbian brothers – and they were both hefty – nodded. 'You heard me, Vlad . . . Nares!' Laughter came at the title. 'But I am happy to repeat myself. That huge thing you call your nose is covered in shit. Turkish shit.' He peered exaggeratedly. 'And now you are closer I can see . . . brown eyebrows! Brown in your hair!' He nodded. 'Did you get your whole head up the *agha*'s arse?'

Ion took a step to the side, so he could watch Vlad more clearly. When he smiled, Ion readied himself. It was a signal, of sorts.

The others must have thought so too for they suddenly bunched together, like a spear blade – the Serbians at the front, Petre the Transylvanian to their right, the Croatian Zoran to their left, the smaller Bosnian Constantin just behind.

'Five to two,' breathed Vlad, still smiling. 'Wallachian odds.'

'Five to three, brother.'

The shrill voice came from the midst of another *orta*.

'Radu,' Vlad said without looking, 'stay back. Leave this to us.'

'And miss the fun?' A boy stepped up beside his brother, providing an immediate contrast. For Radu was fairer than Vlad, his hair as long but dark brown not midnight black, and shot through with reds; his eyes were blue as well as the Dragon's green; while his nose was small and in proportion to a face whose skin was unblemished and rose-hued. 'Besides,' he said, settling, imitating his brother's stance, arms to the side, one leg slightly forward, weight spread, 'I learned a new move yesterday – "How to Break a Bosnian's Back".' He looked at Constantin. 'I cannot wait to try it.'

Vlad shifted slightly. They had fought as a three before and it always came at a cost. Radu was just eleven, his body still more child than youth. And his beauty made others both desirous and envious. In a fight they would try to mar it. Vlad and Ion, defending him, often left themselves vulnerable. Yet he was also proud to have his brother there, the Draculesti united.

'Then, brother, let us see what you have learned.'

Vlad waited. The Mardic brothers shuffled their feet. It was clear they had no plan, hadn't thought they'd need one.

The eight youths looked at each other. Then each became aware of the noise that had been building for a while, the vibration under their feet. Closer it came, closer. The two groups simultaneously moved two paces back, beyond the range of sudden attack. Then they all turned to look.

Before them were the equestrian grounds and sweeping across them was a cloud of dust, shapes moving within it, cries emerging from it. All wanted to move from its path, this whirling cone that only thickened as the horses that caused it were brought up onto their hind legs in a sudden halting. Dust filled with debris smashed into them, blinding, stinging, bringing tears and choking. Then it began to settle, and those who rode the whirlwind became clear.

Horsemen, of course. One, in particular, kept his superb white Arab's front hooves flailing long after the others had dropped.

'Mehmet,' Vlad breathed, choking on the name, on the dust.

— THREE —
The Challenge

Vlad stared at the Turkish prince, who finally let his grip slacken and allowed his mount's hooves to fall. He had not seen him for over a year, but he hadn't changed much – at least in his looks. His beard was a little redder, thicker, better trimmed. His nose was still a parrot's beak, thrust out over full lips. There was a definite change in his bearing, though. He had never been a modest youth. But two years before, his father, Murad, had inexplicably abdicated, making his son sultan in his place. Mehmet had been bred to power from the crib, but he was still just a fourteen-year-old ruling one of the most powerful empires in the world. He had ignored his advisers, alienated his most loyal troops, the janissaries, encouraged wild mystics from the mountains, waged foolish wars. The Divan, the Sultan's council, had begged Murad to return, and Murad had agreed. Mehmet was a mere prince again, heir to the throne he'd occupied for two years. Humiliated by being forced to bend again to tutors, to obey rather than command. And Vlad could see how that sat in the boy-man's face: not well.

'Dracula,' he exclaimed, returning the stare. 'Two Dracula. Two sons of the Devil . . . and their little gang of imps.' He glanced around at the others, dismissing them, his gaze returning to Vlad. 'I am glad your father still behaves like a sheep, so his lambs can live.'

'And your father rules again, Mehmet,' replied Vlad evenly, 'to universal rejoicing.'

The prince's redness deepened. He brought his horse

a step closer, forcing the group to give ground. 'I will be sultan again,' he hissed, 'while you will still be a hostage. My hostage! And I will make you suck the dirt from my feet.'

'You'll find it hard to walk then, missing a toe.'

Ion tensed, waiting for the explosion. But after a moment, Mehmet just smiled. 'Little Dragon,' he said. 'Always so bold. Easy to be when you hide behind your status as a hostage. You know I cannot touch you . . . for now.'

'I know you never will, *Little* Prince.'

'No?' Mehmet's smile widened. 'Not even with this?' Reaching over his shoulders, he pulled something from a sheath on his back. All knew it, the javelin about the length of the youth's arm. 'But you could never touch me with a *jereed*, could you?' He looked around. 'None of you Balkan scum have the horse or weapon skill required to get even . . . one hit in eight?'

Ion could hear the guile in the question. Vlad must have, too. Yet still he spoke. 'One in eight, eh? Those are good odds.'

'No, Vlad . . .'

A raised hand halted Ion's words. 'We eight against you and yours?' Vlad said softly. 'I believe we could do that.'

The hiss from the hostages was drowned by the roar from the mounted Turks. Topping it, Mehmet cried, 'But what is *jereed* without a wager?'

'What do you offer?'

'Well.' Mehmet gazed up into the sky. 'They tell me you are friends with Hamza *agha*. That you share his love of the hawk. If you managed to score one hit, I will give you my beauty, my beloved Sayehzade.'

All gasped, mounted and standing. You could buy a house in Edirne for the price of such a bird. Even Vlad was stunned. 'I . . . I have little to offer to compare . . .'

'Exactly!' crowed Mehmet. 'You have a little . . . brother. Radu the Pretty. Wager him against my Sayehzade.'

Radu spat. 'I am not a wager. And I would never . . .'

Vlad's arm went around Radu's shoulder. 'My brother is not mine to give,' he said. 'What else of my little would you take?'

'Well . . .' Mehmet's gaze moved rather obviously from Radu's groin to his brother's. 'You have a little piece of skin there that is yours. Such a little thing that stands between you and Allah, the Most Merciful. It is said that you read the Qur'an as well as I. So why not take the extra step? My father will arrange a great circumcision ceremony for you when you come to the true faith – once our *jereed* have found their eight targets.' He leaned down, smiling. 'What do you say?'

Don't, thought Ion, watching his friend, dreading the answer. Which came.

'My foreskin *is* mine to offer, Prince. And I do.'

Gasps again from the hostages, whoops again from the Turks.

'A deal,' yelled Mehmet, circling his horse in excitement. 'If no *jereed* strikes us before you all are struck, I will order the leather table cloths to be made. I will sharpen the knife myself!' He wheeled back. 'Fetch your mounts and join us upon the field.'

With that, whirling around, he led his men back the way they'd come, their features swiftly swallowed in dust.

'What have you done, Wallachian?' It was the elder Serbian, Gheorghes, who coughed out the words. 'We cannot score one in twenty against them, let alone one in eight. He tricked you with poor odds! They have practised since childhood while we—'

'We ride as well as them,' Vlad replied, his voice strong. 'Throw as true. What we do not do is unite as them. Here, upon the *jereed* field. There, upon our plains, in our mountains.' Vlad gestured north, began to move that way, towards the horse lines, talking as he went. 'We fight as Serb, Croat, Transylvanian, Wallachian – and Hungarian, Franks,

Venetians. All the Christian lands. Separately they chop us up. But once in a while we come together. And when we do, we take Jerusalem. We just never remain together long enough to hold it.'

'Shall we start with your foreskin, Vlad, and conquer the Holy Land tomorrow?'

All laughed at Ion's weary words. Even Vlad.

'So we fight for the Holy Foreskin, not the Holy Cross, is that it?' chortled the Croat.

'No,' said Vlad, serious again. 'We fight because, however much we may hate each other, we have to hate them more. They are the enemy. Of our faith in Christ, however we see it, Orthodox or Catholic. And for our lands. Free, not under the yoke of Islam and the Turk.'

They had reached the horse lines. Grooms, who had seen them approach, were readying their mounts.

'But how will we beat them, united or not?' asked the Transylvanian, Petre.

'I have some ideas about that,' said Vlad. 'Remember we need one score. Only one.'

Around him, his fellow hostages were mounting, each controlling their horses in their own way. All had strapped on spurs, jabbing in, pulling hard on the bits, mastering the beast. Vlad knew a horse could be bidden that way, with pain and cruelty. They would follow their rider's commands. But they would not truly strive for what they did not love.

Unlike Kalafat. Every time he saw his horse there remained a trace of the wonder he'd felt at their first meeting. He'd been allowed to choose from Murad's own stables – and been mocked for his choice, for she was a mare, not even quite grown, and of the Turcoman breed; thus far smaller and slighter than the male destriers, the huge warhorses, that other hostages chose. But it was not for her beauty that he picked her, though her coat was a dappled grey and her mane a thick white shock that gave her her name – Kalafat, the gaudiest of headdresses. He'd picked her because he recognised in her what he had sought in a horse from the moment he began riding – about a week after he started to walk – spirit. He did not seek a dominance, but a partnership. When he climbed onto her, it was as if he merged with her, becoming Centaur, not man and horse. His hands were a whisper on her reins, his thighs a caress along her flanks. And he wore no spurs.

The others passed the racks of javelins, each leaning down to snatch one up, moving out onto the field. Vlad was about to follow, when Ion grabbed his sleeve, pulled him back. 'Why are you doing this?'

Vlad stared into the distance, to where a cloud of dust showed the circling, prancing Turks. '*Kismet.*'

'What?'

'We spoke of it last week.'

'I remember you and Hamza talking of it. The conversation swiftly put the rest of the *orta* to sleep.' Ion grunted. 'It's destiny, is it not?'

'A form of it. Each of us is born with our *kismet* foretold. We cannot alter it. But we can prepare for it.' He pointed into the dust cloud. 'Fighting Turks is the fate I was born to. And Mehmet, who is the same age as me, will lead them.'

'What has that to do with *jereed*?'

'I have to learn to beat him. It will always require great risk. More, some day, than a small piece of skin. I may as well begin now.'

Ion shook his head. 'You are mad.'

Vlad smiled. 'When did you first guess?'

He moved forward, bent low over Kalafat's neck, snatched up a javelin. He threw it high into the air, watched its unwavering descent, raised his hand to catch . . . and dropped it.

Ion lifted his eyebrows. 'Vlad!'

His prince smiled at him. 'Just because I'm mad doesn't mean I am not afraid.' He called out to his horse, a series of clicks in his throat. Immediately, Kalafat bent to the ground, picked the javelin up between her teeth, lifted her head. Leaning down, Vlad took it from her.

'To the field,' he said, to his horse and his friend.

— FOUR —

Jereed

They rode onto the equestrian grounds, a dusty, rough rectangle running from the walls of the *kolej*'s outer court to the first of Edirne's houses. It was about a hundred and twenty paces long, half that wide. Heading back towards the *kolej*'s walls, they passed the red post that marked the small neutral zone, where no competitor could be struck.

The other hostages formed a semi-circle within it. Vlad rode into the middle of them. 'Listen well,' he said urgently, gesturing to the far end of the field where Mehmet and his seven were gathered behind their own red post, in safety, 'for I have a simple way to beat them.'

He dropped to the ground, thrust the butt end of the *jereed* into the dry dirt, drew the rough rectangle of the playing field, the small neutral zones slashed across their ends. 'We all know the Turkish method. In *jereed*, as in war, they ride from their lands . . .' He jabbed the stick into the Turkish safety zone. '. . . And challenge us one at a time. And which Christian knight could refuse a challenge to single combat? So one accepts, chases the challenger, throws, usually misses . . . and another Turk rides out and spears him! But there is nothing in the rules to say we have to fight separately. What if we ride out as eight, call eight of them to the chase? Fight together for once? What if you, Mardics Maximus and Minor, lead us for the honour of Serbia and we others . . .'

'Hide behind us,' interrupted Gheorghes, 'and let us take their *jereed* for you. Then we sit and watch you slide out to take a sneak throw and save your manhood!'

'No! Listen! Listen! This will work. A screen, yes, but armed and—'

'And you behind it,' jeered the Transylvanian. 'Just as your father was when my uncle, Hunyadi, the White Knight of Christendom, needed him at Varna. Kept the Dragon standard folded, let others take all the risk, skulked—'

'Skulked?' yelled the younger Dracula, pushing his horse forward. 'My father? I'll pay you for that—'

'Listen!' shouted Vlad, to no avail. And it was too late anyway. His voice could not quell the tumult. But the sound of a hunting horn did.

They all looked. Two riders sat forty paces away. The one lowering the bugle from his lips was Abdullah-i-Raschid. He was Mehmet's current favourite, a Greek-born slave. Ringlets dropped in well-ordered ranks down either side of his olive-coloured face. 'Petty princes! Low hostages! Scum!' He bowed mockingly, his voice as oiled as his hair. 'Are there two *men* among you? Would any dare to challenge Mehmet's warriors?'

'Wait,' warned Vlad. 'Let us choose—'

'Choose for yourself!' The elder Mardic jabbed in his spurs, jerked his reins, his mount letting out a shrill neigh as it came up onto its rear hooves. As they dropped he cried, 'For Serbia and St Sava!' and kicked hard. His brother did the same. Both spurred onto the field.

The Turks were not surprised. They were ready. With a flick of reins they had turned, within three strides they were at a gallop. The Serbians' charge had brought them close enough for a throw and the younger Mardic leaned back, jerked forward, his *jereed* flying hopelessly wide. He tugged his mount's head around but one Turk turned far quicker, paralleling the desperate Serb's sweep as he tried to get back past the red post. Not swift enough, his frantic bobbing was no distraction. The javelin took him in the side, three paces before safety.

A cry came from the far end, and from the many spectators

51

who crowded the raised walkway above the horse lines. A cry that doubled in triumph as the elder Mardic, pursuing the weaving Abdullah, threw just as the Greek crossed into safety, missed anyway, and was immediately hit by another Turk riding out. Head drooping, he joined his brother and trotted over to the stables, trying to ignore the jeers of those who watched.

'Now,' cried Vlad, 'will you listen? There are still six of us, we—'

'Too late,' said Ion, pointing.

All looked. Two other Turks had joined the one who'd thrown, galloping beside him as he leaned out of his saddle and down his horse's side, snatching up his *jereed*, shaking it aloft in triumph, to more acclamation. He passed twenty paces before the hostages' safe zone and blew his lips out in the unmistakeable sound of derision.

'I'll finish him!' cried the Croatian, Zoran.

'Mine!' yelled the Bosnian.

'No. Mine!' shouted the Transylvanian.

'Wait,' shouted Vlad.

Too late. As all three charged forward, their opponents split, two left, one right, but not at full gallop, slow enough to give hope and a target. Three *jereed* flew; three missed. The Christians tried to divert their horses away from the Turkish safety line, gallop back toward their own. But Mehmet, Abdullah and another rode out, not so fast, steady, the short range not requiring the extra velocity a charging horse would give them.

At least one javelin missed . . . by a hair. For a moment it seemed that Little Zoran would escape. But the Turk's horses were swifter and better handled. One cut ahead of him, making his mount shy away; he had thrown the one *jereed* allowed, could not strike. Neither could the other, slipping to Zoran's other side, enclosing him. But they drove him towards a man who could – Mehmet, who'd snatched up the *jereed* he'd missed with and held his horse unmoving in the centre of the field.

There was nothing Vlad and the others could do. They could only watch as the two straddling horsemen delivered the Croatian to their prince, like hounds driving quarry to the hunter's bow. Mehmet let him come closer, closer, then suddenly he leaned back and hurled his weapon forward. It smashed into the boy's face. From his shriek of agony, just before he tumbled from his mount, all knew that he was badly hurt. When he reached the ground he did not move. Mehmet's arm raised in triumph as he rode back to his line.

Slaves ran out. The game always paused for injury, so Vlad and the others urged their horses forward, reaching the fallen before the running men. In a moment Vlad had dismounted, in another he had the boy turned and his head in his lap.

'Christ save me,' he murmured, crossing himself. The face was wrecked, the nose smashed sideways across the cheek, one eye already blackening, swollen shut. The boy was choking and Vlad sat him up, struck him square in his back. Blood and bone shot onto the dust.

'Jesu,' said Ion, dismounting, kneeling.

On his horse, Radu turned away. 'How . . . ?'

As men ran up, as several reached to lift the unconscious boy, Vlad walked a few paces, then bent down. 'This is how,' he said, picking up Mehmet's *jereed*. The leather, padded cap that would have prevented the worst of the damage was dangling to the side, exposing the turned poplar tip. 'He's gouged out the rivets,' he said. 'He'll deny it, of course, but—'

'The dog!' said Ion, rising, fury shaking him. 'I'll—'

'Wait!' said Vlad, remounting. 'We'll do this. But we'll do it right.' He looked at each of them in turn. 'Will Wallachians heed me at least?'

Both youths nodded. As Zoran was carried away, they rode for their own line. Glancing back, Vlad could see Mehmet, dismounted, surrounded by his seven companions. They were passing a skin bottle amongst them, already celebrating their certain victory with fermented asses' milk. For a moment, Vlad felt a distinct tightening in his groin. Then, mastering himself, he turned to the others. 'Listen carefully. We will have to do with three what I had planned for eight.'

'But brother,' Radu muttered, his voice still tearful, looking nervously to the other end of the field, 'none of them has been hit. They can ride all eight against us. We won't stand a chance.'

'Know your enemy, Radu. Mehmet will not miss a chance to show off to his people . . .' – he gestured to the spectators – 'those he was ruling two months ago, and will no doubt, rule again. He'll want to prove he is invincible. And he'll want to beat me, man against man. If he could wield the knife himself, and remove what separates me from Allah, he would do so.' Vlad winced. 'His weakness is his pride. If three of us ride out to challenge them, only three will take the challenge. He will be one. So this is what we must do.'

He spoke quickly, need driving him. And it was a simple enough plan. His father had once told him that, on the battlefield with all its infinite complications, simplicity was usually best. He could only hope the same applied on the field of *jereed*.

'They are mounting,' Ion said.

'And we already are,' replied Vlad. 'Let's seize the ground.' And, with a touch of heels on Kalafat's flanks, Vlad led his countrymen forward.

Mehmet rose in his stirrups. 'Do you feel, Dragon's son?' he called, clutching himself at the groin. 'Trust me, everything is so much better without the excess flap.'

'I know you are skilled at cutting things off, Mehmet. I have seen the proof of that.' Vlad threw the Turkish prince's *jereed* up in the air and the leather cap flipped back. 'But I don't think I will give you that chance.'

The *jereed* dropped into his hand. In one motion he leaned

back and threw. Mehmet ducked, letting out a squeal of rage. 'You are not allowed to hit us behind the post,' he yelled.

'And I didn't,' said Vlad, wheeling Kalafat away. Outrage held Mehmet still, allowing the three Wallachians to get halfway down the field before the Turks burst forward.

'Here,' said Ion, handing him another javelin, looking back. 'Now?'

'Wait . . . now!'

Radu cried, 'Yah', kicked his heels, swung his horse in an arc to the left. A Turk followed, hurled, missed, turned towards his line. Radu surged in pursuit.

Everyone was riding flat out. Mehmet and Abdullah were thirty paces away, a long throw but one a good *jereed* player could make. But Vlad was counting on Mehmet's fury, his need for the certain kill. So he crouched low over Kalafat's neck and rode stirrup to stirrup with Ion, his friend's tall body a barrier between the enemy and himself.

They were being forced west, towards the horse lines. They could ride out of bounds there, to their shame. Or . . .

'Now,' Vlad shouted, and Ion swung his mount's head hard left, back into the pursuit, Vlad paralleling him, still sheltered. Then, at twenty paces and closing, Vlad swung slightly clear and stood tall.

The sudden closed gap, the sudden target; both Turks leaned back. The slave threw first, leaning out to the side, his javelin flying low and hard and taking Ion in the side. Vlad heard the thump, his friend's harsh cry. But his eyes were on Mehmet, all the way back in his saddle, hurtling forward.

Everything slowed, sound receded, as if the spectators were now whispering their cheers, the horses holding their grunts, the men their cries of pain or triumph. All Vlad could hear clearly was the coming of Mehmet's *jereed*, the wind whistling in the leather pad that flipped back and forth on the tip. Vlad let his own javelin slip from his fingers . . .

Then all was moving fast again. The weapon arriving at his

head, his sudden stoop, his arm shooting up to pluck the *jereed* from the empty space above him. It was a move many strived for and few achieved, drawing cheers, even from Mehmet's team. Not from the prince himself, as he was so engaged in swinging his horse's head away from Vlad, turning it back to his own end of the field and the safety of his line.

But he was turning. Vlad was still moving straight forward, closer, closer, till he was three horse lengths away; not so close that it would be thought unbecoming. Close enough not to miss.

A twitch on the reins moved Kalafat's head to the right. Then, using the full momentum of the charging horse and his own body bent back, he snapped suddenly forward and, just before the Turk crossed to safety, hurled his *jereed* straight into the centre of Mehmet's spine.

Vlad was pleased to hear wood snap, so he must have hurled it hard enough. Mehmet must have thought so, too, because he gave a great cry and appeared to fly out of the saddle, to roll over and over in the dirt. Looking back, Vlad was relieved to see the body moving – he did not think it was either of their destinies for Mehmet to die, by a hostage's hand, this day. But he was even more relieved, as he rode towards the horse lines, to reach down and squeeze himself at the groin.

'Still there,' he murmured. And smiled.

— FIVE —

The Concubine

Most of the crowd were rushing forward to stare at that rarest of sights – a fallen prince. Only a few delayed them, hands reaching to clasp their hands, slap their backs. Christian slaves mostly, temporarily freed by this rare triumph. But Ion pushed through, knowing they must not linger. Soon they were passing those who had been too far back to see, who did not know them.

They mounted stairs to the raised walkway above the equestrian grounds, part battlement to defend the inner city, part passageway above the crowded streets. There were stalls up there, and they settled into the shadows of a juice-seller's awning, half-hidden by a latticed *palanquin* that had been abandoned there, its bearers no doubt among the crowd that chattered its wonder and speculation as it looked down upon the field. Sipping pomegranate juice, they looked, too, watched Mehmet being rolled onto his back, then lifted slowly to his feet. He stayed bent over, hands on knees, talking continuously. His men were looking around – Vlad knew who for – shrugging, stooping to report. They saw him strike at one, then draw his hand back slowly in obvious pain.

'It is his slaves I feel sorry for,' said Ion. 'There will be some beating at his *saray* tonight.'

'And fucking,' said Radu excitedly. 'The men he'll beat, the women he'll fuck. Though it could be the other way around.' He flushed suddenly, remembering how he was nearly the principal in a wager.

'All that fucking!' groaned Ion. 'They say he already has

five concubines. And he's only sixteen, like us!' He gave out a moan. 'While I can't even get Brown-Browed Aisha of the tavern to roll over for me once.'

Vlad smiled. 'At least you are discriminating, Ion. Mehmet doesn't need men or women. He'd fuck a wooden post if it had stood long enough in the sun.'

The laugh – deep, rich, from the belly – startled them. Not because it came from the *palanquin* they'd assumed was empty. Not because it came from a woman. They were startled because they'd been speaking in their native tongue, the 'limba Romana' of Wallachia, their language of secrets, and they'd never met anyone in Edirne who spoke it. Until now.

The *palanquin* was a latticed closet on poles, a seat within, its sides depicting scenes from life – hunting, hawking, feasting. Peering closer now, Vlad could see what he'd missed before – a person within. He looked beyond, to the pole-bearers, one trying to urge the others back to their duties. But they resisted, still drawn to the scene below.

'Who are you?' he whispered, leaning close.

Silence, for an age. Finally, a low, unexpected reply in their tongue. 'I am a concubine.'

'Whose?' said Vlad.

Again, the reply was long in coming. 'The man who the crowd tells me now rolls disgraced in the dirt.'

'Mehmet?'

'Yes. I am his new *godze*. Or will be tomorrow night. You know this word?'

'Chosen girl.'

'Yes.'

Ion had been growing more alarmed as the whispered conversation progressed. 'Come away,' he said, gripping an arm. 'Do you know the whipping you'll get if you are caught talking to a concubine. Especially Mehmet's. Come away now before—'

Vlad pulled his arm free, leaned closer to the lattice-work. 'You speak our tongue. Where are you from?'

'A village near Curtea de Arges. It is—'

'I know where it is,' said Vlad. 'My family has lands nearby.'

'And you are?'

'Dracula,' Vlad whispered. 'Vlad—'

Her gasp interrupted him. 'The Dragon's son!'

'Yes.'

A huge shout came from the horse grounds. More people pressed to the edge of the walkway, blocking the view. 'Radu, go and see what is happening.'

Reluctantly, he rose. 'Yes, brother.'

Vlad turned back to the *palanquin*. 'What is your name?'

'My slave name is Lama.'

' "Darkness of Lips",' whispered Ion.

'Yes. But I was christened Ilona.'

'Ilona,' repeated Vlad. 'It is Hungarian. It means "Star".'

'You speak the tongue?'

'Enough.'

'My father was Hungarian. My mother, Wallachian.'

'And you were taken?'

'In a Turkish raid. I was ten. Sold to a merchant to clean his house. Then the merchant's wife thought I was pretty . . . too pretty . . . and I was sold to a former concubine of the old Sultan. She raised me, taught me . . . to dance, to sing, to please with poetry and the lute.' Her voice came more softly, a husk to it. 'And a hundred other ways to delight a man.'

Despite his unease, Ion shifted, drew a little closer.

'Have you . . . have you known many men?' Vlad asked.

There was a trace of sadness in the question. It brought a second laugh. 'None, lord – though you'd be surprised at the toys to be found on the Street of Potters!' The laughter faded. 'And you do not give away what men will pay extra for. My owner will tell you that. So I am yet a virgin. Till tomorrow night at Mehmet's *sarayi*.'

59

Sadness had not replaced the laughter. Nothing had. And that made Vlad sad. 'Do you want this?'

'Want?' came the echo. '*I* do not . . . want. I exist for other people's wants. That is my *kismet*. I must accept it.'

'*Kismet*?' said Vlad. He looked around at the shifting, excited crowd, bent still nearer, until his lips were almost touching the lattice. 'What if you had a different one? What if you were given a choice?'

An irritated sniff. 'I've never had a choice. How could one come now?'

'Because I could offer you one.'

Beside him, Ion threw himself back. For a few moments, he'd been lost in the girl's voice, in his imagining of the lips she was named for. But then he realised that Vlad was moving beyond even the danger of conversation. Far beyond! He grabbed an arm again. 'No!' This time Vlad did not shrug him off. He just turned and looked at him. Wordless, Ion dropped his hand away.

Her voice came faintly, as Vlad looked back. 'What is this choice you offer me?'

He smiled. 'It is that one between everyone's decision for you and your own.'

Silence again in the *palanquin*, while around them, the crowd's murmur began to build. 'Mehmet! Mehmet!' came the cry, closer and closer. Men were backing up the stairs. The prince and his retinue had to be climbing towards them. Radu, returning, confirmed it with a raised thumb.

'I have a friend here,' Vlad continued, low-voiced, 'a merchant from our land. His barge stands at the docks. He hates the Turks and loves silver. Silver my father will give him if he gets you home.'

'Home?' she asked, as if the word were unknown to her. Then she continued in a stronger voice, touched with anger, 'But if we speak of choice, this is still yours, isn't it? You will choose to do it or not?'

Both pairs of lips were pressed to the lattice now. Only

thin wood separated them. 'I have already chosen,' Vlad whispered. 'It's your turn.'

'What's he doing now?' Radu asked, nervously.

Ion just shook his head.

The surging crowd burst onto the parapet. Many threw themselves onto the ground as Mehmet crested it. His face was distorted by pain. Abdullah supported him on his right side. With his left hand he used a *bastinado* on those who pressed closest. 'Dogs!' he cried. 'Jackals.'

The crowd passed along the walkway; blows, curses and prayers receded. The *palanquin*'s bare-chested pole-bearers were approaching. Vlad had stepped into the awning's shadows as Mehmet passed. Now he came forward again. 'Choose,' he said.

The servants bent to their poles. Their leader shoved his stick into Vlad's chest. He just leaned into it as the *palanquin* was lifted, straining for words. Then, just as the men lifted, he heard them.

'Come for me.'

And she was gone. They watched the litter's slow progress through the still-thick crowd. When Vlad took a step after it, Ion caught his sleeve. 'You cannot . . .' he said.

Vlad looked at his friend, his green eyes expressionless. 'Why?'

'To beat Mehmet at *jereed* is one thing. All saw it was fair. To kidnap his concubine . . .' The eyes did not change. 'Vlad, this is the man who so loves his garden that when one of his prize cucumbers disappeared, he personally slit open the stomachs of seven gardeners to find it.'

'And did find it, I am told. So?'

'So? So he is not a man to have as an enemy!'

'He is already that. Nothing I can do will make him more or less so. And do you know?' He turned to stare, where men were still following, crying the name of Mehmet. 'I truly believe that one day, one of us will be the death of the other.' He reached back, lifted the beaker of pomegranate juice, drained it. The red liquid glimmered, staining his teeth in the smile that came. 'But forget all that, my friend, because . . . didn't you hear her laugh?'

Before Ion could reply, Vlad had laid the cup down. 'Come on,' he said, 'we must follow. We have to know where she lives if we are going to steal her.'

Vlad set off. For a moment, Ion and Radu did not move, just looked at each other. 'We?' they each said, faintly.

— SIX —

The Chosen Girl

It was not all unpleasant, the preparation for her deflowering.

True, they had woken her early, just as the *muezzin* was calling the most faithful to first prayers. Ilona would have slept through that, easily, as she always did. But not this day.

The air was chill when they fetched her from the bed she shared with Afaf, who just grunted and fell back asleep. A cloak covered her but she was not allowed to dress for they needed to consider every part of her. She was led to the stone slab at the entrance to the house's small *hamam*, mounted it. The cloak was pulled away and she stood there and tried not to shiver, her eyes downcast, her expression bland, her hands open-palmed to the side, her weight on her right foot which was turned out so all of her was exposed. The servants moved around, pinching here, prodding there. They were trying to be calm – a girl was often sent out, to be the concubine of some victorious general or provincial governor. Sometimes, rarely, a wife to a state official. But today was different and Ilona could sense the excitement. Within minutes, even the most reticent of servants was chattering.

Today, a girl was being sent to the Sultan.

Or was he the Sultan? Ilona frowned, then relaxed at a snapped command. He had been two months before. And now it was said he wasn't but would be again, with Allah's grace. It confused her but it didn't truly matter. All that did was that he had picked her for some reason, some facet of herself she did not understand. Twenty girls had been paraded before the screen in Mehmet's *saray*. She had not seen him, of course, but he had seen her. Now she was *godze*, the chosen girl.

Hence the excitement as the servants walked round her, and the attention to her every detail. She had been told what this could mean – there may have been five concubines already in Mehmet's *saray* but none had yet borne him a son. If she pleased him enough, and thus drew him often enough to her divan so that he got her with child – with male child . . . well! Concubines who bore sons often became wives. Wives were given freedom and power.

Freedom. She kept the sigh within. *What was that?*

She looked through her lowered lashes as the *kahya kadin*, Hibah herself, came in. Mistress of the house on the Street of Nectar, she rarely bothered with the little details. But now the woman stopped, folded her arms over her enormous stomachs, tipped her head. Then she clapped two fat hands together, her gold bracelets jangling. 'Begin!' she called. 'Bathe her. Bring her.'

It was not all unpleasant, the life of a slave. In the first ten years of her life, when they called her free, she had never had a bath. In the house on Rahiq Street, she had one daily and loved it: the delicious heat of one plunge, the exhilarating shock of another; the steam that enveloped her and opened every pore; the chilled water they rinsed her with before they wrapped her in softest, warmed sheets. Today they took even more time and care. Rubbed longer with the kese mitts, the scented soaps; scraped every part of her, opened and explored every crevice. Her thick, hazel hair was washed in lavender water and coiled down her back. Then she lay on a divan while small women with strong hands rubbed and stroked and pressed to the point of pain, and back, slowly, to delicacy. Finally, the oils were applied. It had been some concern, the scent whose trace must linger into the night. And then a janissary of Hibah's acquaintance had told her that he'd wrestled with Mehmet the week before and the youth had smelled of ginger and şandalwood, a combination that was straightforward, masculine. Hibah had gambled that what pleased in one form of wrestling would please in another and ordered a jar from the Sultan's own perfumers.

Eventually, Ilona sat in another chair, still naked but not cold, for the room was heated by braziers and the press of women, both those who tended and those who urged the tenders on. These lounged on divans, eating sweetmeats and drinking apple tea, though Ilona was only allowed a sparrow's share of each. Her hair was rubbed dry, then managed into ringlets. Apparently, Mehmet's current favourite, Abdulraschid, wore his hair just so. And there was much debate as to which couplet from which poet would be inked onto the skin in a swirl that ran from the nape of her neck, over the swell of breast and belly, and down to climax on the pubis, the redness there from the caustic creams that had removed all hair two days before having finally faded. The woman calligrapher stood awaiting the decision patiently. When they settled on Jalaluddin – something about flight, Ilona did not understand Persian – she tried not to laugh as the brush danced across her skin.

It took the whole day, the preparation for her deflowering. A day of laughter and music, for the *ney* was played throughout, the reed pipe's notes rising now in joy, now with a wistful air. At one point she was commanded to dance. Just enough to remind that she was one of the best that they had ever had. Not enough to raise a sweat.

One by one, the servants completed their tasks and left, till there remained just the three of them: Hibah, who would sell her; Tarub the merry, who would accompany her as far as the prince's divan, and Ilona.

She stood again in neutral stance, eyes downcast, as Hibah walked around and around her, commanding a touch more paint to lips that truly needed none, exchanging one silver toe-ring for another, making sure each bell on her belt gave out a complimentary chime. All except one, which was silent.

Hibah fingered it. 'You can find this? In the dark?'

'Yes, mistress.'

'Close your eyes and show me.'

The belt was laid on the floor. Eyes closed, Ilona bent, searched with her fingers, found the tell-tale ridge, placed a painted nail under it. 'Shall I open it, mistress?'

'And risk staining your veils? Foolish girl! No. As long as you remember to do it before you sleep. By dawn's light men like to see that they've had a virgin. So if you have no blood of your own, which you may not, then use the pigeon's blood within. Rub it on yourself, but especially on him. Daubing the scimitar in gore, eh?' She cackled, then turned to Tarub. 'Have we missed anything?'

Tarub smiled. 'My Lama sheds the pure light of the morning star, as ever.'

'Hmm!' Hibah grunted. 'Purity may be fine in daylight. But men want something different at night.' She turned to Ilona. 'You will remember all we have taught you?'

Ilona's mouth had gone dry. She swallowed, nodded. 'I . . . I think so, mistress.'

'Think?' Hibah replied sharply. 'You must know. Be prepared for anything. All men are different in their desires – and Mehmet is said to be more different than most . . . and as changeable as the Levant wind! He may wish to write poetry to you and worship you as an eastern star, bending before you to pray . . . here!' She slid a finger down Ilona's belly to rest on her pubis. 'He may wish to take you like a boy . . . here!' The finger moved on, pressed, and Ilona felt her guts twist. 'He may want your tears, your laughter or one after the other. Are you prepared to give him anything he desires?'

Fear came again now, the fear that the day's slow preparations had distracted her from. Fear . . . and something else. 'Do I have a choice?' she snapped.

Tarub gasped at the outburst. Hibah raised a hand then lowered it, unwilling to mark the merchandise. 'Stupid girl!

Where do you think you are? Your only choice is in the reading of *his* desires!' She turned to Tarub. 'Veil her!'

Tarub went to the stand, bending to lift the headdress off it, such was the weight of the silver and bronze coins that dangled from its brow. It was an unusual request from Mehmet's emissary, for coins were usually either dowry – or worn by prostitutes to show their wealth and thus their skill. Hibah had snickered that it was perhaps an indication of the role Ilona would be required to play – wife or whore. Perhaps both. The leather cap within had been fitted to Ilona's head before and sat snugly now. The length of coins hung down, obscuring what was before her. Hibah was a shape, stepping back, appraising.

'Good,' came her voice at last. 'Go, Lama of the Dark Lips. Make us proud. May Allah bless you in your enterprise and reward you for your skill.'

As she entered the main corridor of the house, sighs and whispers greeted her. She could only see glimpses through the swinging veil but she could hear and recognise the voices of the girls she'd lived with for these last four years. She'd never see them again. Tears started and she wrenched them back, reaching for the anger she'd felt a moment before. Her eyes were painted . . . and she must not spoil the merchandise, either. This was her fate, this day, the night to come. Written. Unalterable. She had no choice.

And then she gave a little gasp. For she remembered what the day of activity had made her forget. Someone else talking of choice. Offering her what she had never been given before.

As the door swung shut on whispered farewells, as she waited for the one that gave onto the Street of Nectar to open, she felt her surprising anger return. What right had this Dracula to raise any hope in her? What could he do? A hostage! Little better than a prisoner himself, one up from a slave. A slave was defined by having *lost* the right to choose. She would be borne in a *palanquin* to Mehmet's *saray*. He would take her any way he wanted. She would break a vial of

67

pigeon's blood over him if she did not bleed enough. She would choose nothing for herself.

The front door of the house of the concubines swung open. The chair was a squat shape before it, glimpsed through her swinging veil. Six men from the palace guard stood there, armed with halberds. Four others, bare-chested, huge, stood at the poles, coming in and out of her vision. She felt dizzy, swayed. Tarub's hand clutched her elbow, steadying her, guiding her as she would every step of the way. Till the last.

She took one now, descended the stairs. Then, halfway down them, something made her pause. She looked up, over the roof of the litter, across the narrow street, into the doorway opposite, half a dozen steps away. In it stood a man. Veiled, too, a scarf wound around his head, covering his face. Only his eyes showed. And though she had only seen him the once, through latticed wood and thus not clearly, she knew him.

She turned her head sharply to try to see him better. The coins swung again, hid him. When they swung back, the doorway was empty. So she could remember him only in that one glance. Remember eyes as green as a spring hillside in Wallachia. Remember the look in them, the heat in them; the smile.

She smiled herself, at herself. At her anger, snatched away like a pigeon snatched suddenly by a hawk.

SEVEN

The Snatch

He'd seen her. He didn't know if she'd seen him.

As he preceded the *palanquin* down the street, Vlad smiled. He hadn't really seen her, of course. Never had. She'd been encased in lattice-work when they'd talked. She was wearing a metal veil now. He wondered what she looked like beneath it. What if she was hideous? What if that rich voice emerged from the face of an aspiring crone?

He shook his head. It seemed unlikely. Mehmet's tastes were known to be peculiar but Vlad had never heard that they ran to the ugly. Besides, how she looked should make no difference to him. She was a lady from his land, in peril. And though he had listened to many wonderful tales in his time with the Turk, it was the legends from his childhood, sung before his father's fire, that he still loved best. And in the courts of the Christian world it was tales of Arthur and his knights that inspired. He saw himself as Lancelot now, pledged to a Guinevere.

But would the tale have been different if Guinevere had been a hag? Would Troy have fallen if Helen's nose had a wart on the tip? It shouldn't matter. Didn't. Only his promise mattered, and how he fulfilled it. Nothing else.

There were two routes to Mehmet's *saray*. One obvious, one less so. Vlad needed the *palanquin* to take the latter.

The long, twisting Street of Nectar ended in a fork at a fountain. A wider avenue led to the left, though it was somewhat narrowed by stalls on each side and people bunched around them, buying provisions for their suppers.

The other way, narrower still, led slightly uphill past a *mescid*, a small mosque, and, perversely, a row of taverns right next to it. Glancing up that lane, hoping all was in readiness there, Vlad slipped into the throng before the stalls. He had no precise plan, other than chaos. But how to cause it?

The first stall belonged to a seller of watermelons, whole or by the piece. Tied to it by a rope was a donkey, who stood in the way of such creatures, one rear hoof on its tip, eyes glazed in its lowered head, chewing on nothing. Dull beast, Vlad thought, hearing above the haggling and clink of coin the steady approach of booted men, the cry of, 'Make way there!'

He glanced back, saw the silver headdress and heron plume of the *bolukbasi*, the guards' officer, twenty paces away. Biting his lip, he looked before him again, and thought of something. Drawing his *bastinado* from his belt, he lifted the donkey's tail and shoved the forearm's length of stick up the animal's arse.

He had his desire. Instant chaos. A flying hoof missed his head by a wing-beat. He leapt back, into the shelter of a doorway, beyond the reach of flailing hooves. He was still hit by the things that started flying – bits of its master's stall that the donkey destroyed; melon – yet since the beast was tied to the stall, it was also dragging it into the centre of the roadway.

From beneath flung debris, Vlad looked at the guards, halted just ten paces away at the junction. Over the din of braying beast, screaming owner and panicked purchasers, the *bolukbasi*'s voice still carried: 'Clear the road there, dolt!'

The watermelon vendor – an old man with a humped back – took a pace towards them, bent over, hands clasped before him in supplication. 'I will try, *effendi*, but this animal, cursed of Allah . . .'

It was all he could say before the donkey kicked him, catapulting him into the stall opposite, bringing half of it down. His own was dragged further into the street by the raging animal, who finally broke free and went galloping away, the snapped-off strut scything into bystanders.

Surveying the wreckage, the *bolukbasi* shook his head and bellowed an order: 'This way!' Then he led his men up the other road.

Vlad let them get twenty paces ahead, then followed.

'Are you ready?' he whispered.

'Nothing?'

Radu shook his head. He'd been down to the junction for the fourth time. Dropping onto the stool beside Ion he muttered, 'Maybe they've already passed the other way.'

'No. Vlad would have come to get us. He knows we have little time.' Ion looked again at the *mescid* beside the tavern. The *muezzin* had ceased his call to prayer only a few minutes before. Because it was a Friday, hostages were allowed to remain in town till prayers were over. Stay beyond that, and they would feel more than a touch of an *agha*'s *bastinado*.

It was not only the hardness of the stool that made Ion shift. He turned and looked through the bobbing heads of the tavern's occupants to see Aisha, the-yet-to-be-attained, with a wisp of brown hair damp upon her forehead. He watched as she wiped it with a red kerchief, saw a man grab the cloth from her and ostentatiously suck it, to hers and others' laughter.

Ion groaned, and Radu mistook it. 'I know! If he does not come will these not answer the *muezzin*'s call and go to their devotions?'

'These?' Ion forced his gaze away from his beloved. 'These are Bektashi. They have other devotions.'

'I thought they were janissaries?'

'They are.'

'And all janissaries are Moslem, are they not?'

'Yes. Wherever they are from, to join the *orta*s they have to come to Islam.'

Radu frowned, staring. 'And doesn't the Qur'an forbid the drinking of spirits and wine?'

'It does. Your brother could quote you the verse. But that does not stop many drinking. They say that even the Sultan, Murad, is given to bouts of over-indulgence. And many janissaries belong to the Dervish cult of Bektashi. Moslem but different. These of the . . .' He squinted at a bare calf muscle, the elephant tattooed there. '. . . Of the 79th *orta* have adopted Bektashi ways. Unveiled women.' He glanced sourly at the laughing Aisha. 'Unbound hair. Drinking.'

'But . . . ?'

Ion raised a hand. Allow the flood of Radu's questions to begin and it would never stop. 'Go to the crossroads again.'

'But I just came back.'

'Go!'

'Who is the prince's son here?' Radu grumbled, but rose.

Ion glanced into the tavern again but couldn't see Aisha. Gone to fetch more *raki* probably. He had bought several jugs – 'tinder for the flames', Vlad had said. He had a plan for everything, from winning at dice to stealing fledgling hawks from a nest. But Mehmet's concubine was not a baby bird up a tree, to be taken just after its first moult. Ion could only hope that what had been planned would happen soon, before prayers he could hear being sung in the *mescid* next door ended, and the first stroke of the *bastinado* fell on their up-raised Christian backsides.

Then he saw Radu running up the street. Behind him a silver heron's plume bobbed above the crowd. Rising, he did as Vlad had told him.

'Look,' he shouted, 'here come some of Mehmet's arse-lickers!'

Vlad, ten paces behind the *palanquin*, heard the shout, saw the first of the tavern's clientele spill out from under its awning – and smiled. The rivalry between the janissaries and the palace bodyguards was intense. Both were elite troops, the Sultan's chosen. But the *peyk* – halberdiers of the guard – were nearly all Turks and freemen; the janissaries were all Christian converts and still slaves, despite their status. This worsened the enmity between the groups and would, he hoped, help his cause.

He moved till he was within one donkey-length of the covered litter; till, through the folds of his headscarf, he could see the *bolukbasi* of the *peyk* in profile. The man was straining to ignore the comments on his manhood, his parentage and his predilection for bestiality. Vlad knew he had his orders, could not allow himself to be drawn into the tavern brawl Vlad needed. He also knew that if one did not start on its own, he would have to start it.

The guard marched forward in step, lowering their halberds at a snapped command. For a moment, Vlad thought they might escape with nothing but insults, until a huge man stepped into the roadway . . . and lifted up his shirt.

'See how smooth my skin is!' he called. 'See the luxuriance of my hair.' He ran his fingers up a thick blond mat, from groin to chest. 'Show us yours, *effendi*. Let us compare beauties!'

Vlad knew the man. His slave name was Abdulkarim, 'Servant to the Powerful'. But he was known to all by his name and the land of his birth: Sweyn the Swede. No one knew by what byways he had come to be the Sultan's soldier and slave. But all knew what this baring of skin meant. For Mehmet, in his two years as sultan, had adopted Greek customs as well as their dress. To surround himself with men who were happy, he had their spleens cut out; thus removing, from those who survived the operation – and many did, the Persian surgeons were so good – the very seat of moroseness.

It hadn't seemed to work for the *bolukbasi*. 'Out of the way, intemperate dog!' he bellowed, grasping the hilt of his sheathed sword. 'Before I remove your spleen and half your guts with it.'

'Oh, terror!' cried the Swede, fanning himself with his raised shirt. 'But tell me! Could you not also remove a few haemorrhoids?' With that, he turned about and bared his arse.

More jeering. More laughter. For a moment, Vlad thought that the *bolukbasi* was going to draw his sword and thrust it up the tempting target. But then the Swede straightened, robed and, to great cheers, began to move out of the roadway. The officer turned, and gestured his men forward.

Vlad looked around, desperately seeking he knew not what. He saw that some of the younger janissaries were still clutching three-legged stools, willing the fight. Even as he watched, though, these were being reluctantly lowered.

So Vlad bent and snatched one up. He too had seen the tattoos of the *orta* that held the tavern. 'Elephants!' he cried, and hurled the stool straight at the *bolukbasi*'s head. He saw it come, ducked enough so it thumped into his helmet not his face. But the sound of wood on metal rang like another battle-cry. A wave of stools, mugs, jugs came crashing over the guards. Many struck the *palanquin*, which had been hastily dropped by men protecting themselves. Screams came from within it.

'To me!' yelled the *bolukbasi*, blood running from the blow to his head. His men rallied to him, halberds swatting aside thrown wood, points lowering towards the janissaries.

Vlad had moved to the shelter of the far side of the litter. Ion and Radu joined him there.

'What now?' Ion shouted.

They were on the opposite side to the door. Vlad peered through the lattice. He could see two shapes within. 'This,' he said, drawing his dagger, plunging it in just below the roof.

Screams came from one woman inside, but were suddenly cut off as if smothered. Ion joined in the cutting on the other side, sawing down through the thin wood. By the time he reached the bottom, Vlad was already cutting along the edge of the roof. When he reached Ion's cut, the three jabbed their fingers into the gap, and pulled.

The wall of the litter gave with a loud rip. And there, on its floor, crouched a masked and painted *houri*, her hand clamped across the mouth of a servant. Through the veil of coins, eyes glittered.

'Come,' said Vlad, speaking Osmanlica, 'swiftly now. And you . . .' he added, looking at the prone maid, touching the hilt of his dagger back in its sheath, '. . . silence or death!'

Clasping Ilona's hand, he drew her from the wrecked *palanquin*.

Beyond it, the *peyk* had begun to march into the tavern. Wood had been surpassed by steel, bruises by blood. All were focused on the fight, on surviving it, so none saw the four shrouded figures slipping away.

Nestled beside the new stone bridge that Murad had built over the River Ergene was a sprawl of jetties, flat-bottomed barges bumping against them. With night falling, and workers drawn to mosque or tavern, few observed their passage to a certain pier.

'You're late!' called Alexandru, the captain. 'I was just about to cast off.' He looked at the veiled woman. 'This her?'

'Yes.'

'Then get her aboard, so we can be gone. It's dangerous enough what you have been about, Vlad Dracula. And my ship has orders to sail from the port of Enez in two days, with or without me.'

'Here is what I promised you.'

The captain weighed the bag in one hand. 'Seems light.'

'It is. Half what I promised you.'

'Half? Now, wait—'

'My father will give you the other half when you deliver her . . . and this letter.' He handed over a sealed roll. 'Besides, you say you do not do this only for silver?'

The captain looked up at the rooftops of Edirne. 'Five

years I spent chained to one of their galley benches. So if I can pay the goat-fuckers back . . .' He looked back at Vlad. 'You say this will hurt them?'

'Yes,' said Vlad. 'I think it will hurt them very much.'

'Good. Then get her aboard. And I will collect the other half of my fee from the Dragon's hoard – or from you when I return.' With that, he stepped back onto his deck, ordering his crew to their tasks.

Vlad, who had not let go of Ilona's hand, now pulled it, guiding her towards the ramp.

For the first time, she resisted. 'You do not come?' she said.

Vlad paused, held by her, by that voice and the first words she had spoken since the snatch. 'I cannot. I am a hostage and have given my word. To the Turk. To my father. Also' – he swallowed – 'the Sultan is not someone to cross. A few years ago other hostages – sons of the Serbian despot, Gheorghes Brankovic – tried to pass information to their father about the Turk's war preparations. In the terrible castle of Tokat, Murad had red-hot iron shoved into their eyes. So . . . please.'

He pulled her again. Again she resisted. 'Will you not be so punished? For what you have done today?'

'I do not think we were seen. Even your woman saw us as we are, in Turkish dress, our faces hidden. Only you and the captain know us. And he is good Wallachian, if surly. He will see a country-woman home.'

'And then?'

Vlad took another roll of parchment from his pouch. 'Here is a letter written to my father. You will be taken care of.'

'I did not mean that,' Ilona said. 'I meant . . . will I see you again?'

'If Allah wills it,' he replied. 'God, I mean,' he added with a smile. 'I truly have been among these people too long. But yes, I believe it is my *kismet* to return to my land one day.'

'*Kismet*,' she echoed, finally yielding to the pressure of his hand and climbing the ramp. 'Mine changed when I first saw you.'

'Kismet doesn't change,' he replied. 'All this was already written.' Handing her onto the deck, he turned immediately, descending, and as soon as he was clear of the ramp, they hauled it in. Lines were cast off, oars slipped into the water. The barge began to drift slowly from the dock.

They were still only an arm's length apart when the thought came to her. He *hasn't* seen me! Living always beneath a veil, she was used to observing men through one, never being observed herself. But if he did not see her now, how would he ever find her again?

'Vlad,' she called. And as she did, she reached up, lifted. The length of jangling coins stroked her face as they rose. Then she dropped the headdress onto the deck.

She was still close enough to see the change in his green eyes. 'Oh,' he said softly. 'Yes. Yes, I see.'

Beside him, Ion stepped up and gasped. All thoughts of tavern girls swept, with one look at her face, from his mind.

But it was Vlad she looked at, only Vlad's eyes she saw as the barge drifted onto the current. Saw them when his face had become a blur. Saw them still as the ship drifted under a stone arch.

And he still saw hers, and everything else about her.

EIGHT

Warp and Weft
Poenari Castle, 1481

'What is this? A tale of courtly love? If we'd wanted one of those, couldn't we have hired a troubadour?'

The Cardinal's harsh words brought them all back to the hall of Poenari Castle, where no one had fully been for a while. They had been in the story, all of them making it, both tellers and listeners.

Ion had been there again, beside Vlad, serving Vlad, knowing Vlad. Ilona, too, telling of what passed between them. They had both been lost in him. Who he had been. Though five years dead, alive in both of them.

The listeners had been fashioning their own Vlad, according to their needs. For Petru it was simple. He wanted the man who built the castle he commanded to be a hero; more, a *Wallachian* hero. He had heard of a time of justice, order, strength in his land. Of the smiting of Christ's foes. He wanted that time again.

For the Count of Pecs, it was not simple . . . and he shot forward in his chair at the Cardinal's outburst, nervously watched the Italian lever himself from his, watched him waddle across to the table. He needed the man to judge well – and favourably. His wish was for a risen Dragon. Not one washed clean of blood. Who could use such a crippled beast? But if it could rise with fury not depravity, power not barbarism . . . And if Dracula could be forgiven – partly, at least, enough for the purposes of God and Man – then perhaps he could be forgiven, too. Perhaps, the curse that had taken both his eye and his family's lives would be lifted.

The Cardinal stood at the table, pulling nettle leaves off a round of goat's cheese, squashing the pungent whiteness onto coarse bread. The Count joined him, poured wine. 'Your Eminence?' he said. At a nod, Horvathy filled another goblet and both men drank. Petru, meanwhile, gestured to Bogdan, who took water and bread into the confessionals for both prisoners and scribes. It was not kindness. Petru would have done the same for cattle, keeping them alive for their purpose. Then he joined the others.

The Cardinal lowered his voice. Not everything had to be scratched onto parchment. 'Really, Count. This is all quite entertaining. I like a tale on a winter's day as well as any. But this is not the one we came to hear, surely?' He reached down, picked up the top pamphlet from the pile, read aloud. ' "The Story of a Bloodthirsty Madman Called Dracula of Wallachia".' He studied the woodcut under the text, bodies twitching on stakes. 'You say we are here to disprove this?'

'Not . . . disprove exactly. Not all of it, anyway.' The Count bit down on a sausage. 'To hear a different version. To mitigate the worst, perhaps. To single out the best.'

'To re-write history?'

'Eminence, as you said earlier, that is what we all do with history. Use it for our own purposes.' He lifted another pamphlet. 'The men who wrote these certainly did. For profit. For vengeance. History is a tool; more, a weapon. For us. For the Church.'

'For crusade?' The Italian shook his head. 'But the banner of crusade, as you know, is the hardest of all to weave – far more complex than these crudities.' He gestured to the tapestries that lined Poenari's hall. 'If the warp of that banner is the pure white of God, the Cross is the red weft – and it is made up of dozens of different threads and shades. My master, the Pope. Yours, Hungary's king. The princes, nobles . . . and yes, financiers of Europe, all have to be gathered, carefully aligned in the loom, do they not?'

Horvathy nodded. 'They do. But remember, Your

Eminence, it is always the Balkans that is the crucible of Holy War, its leaders the front line in the fight against the Infidel.'

'Vital threads, indeed.' Grimani swallowed, frowned at the wine's harshness, then looked up again into the Count's one eye. 'And you believe you can deliver these leaders, united under the Dragon?'

'I pray so. But prayer is rarely enough, as you know.' He nodded back to the confessionals. 'It is the tale we are hearing that matters. And what we can take from it to tell both our masters.'

Grimani glanced, too. 'And amusing enough though this tale has been, it has given me little so far to recommend, to judge.' He waved a hand at the tapestries on the wall, the woven hunt in progress there. 'So shall we move to the chase? These beaters have driven the game out. Is it not time for the first kill?'

Horvathy drained his goblet, put it down. 'Agreed.' He returned to the dais, mounted, waited till the other two had joined him and sat before he spoke. 'Enough of a young man's dreams. Of tournaments and quests and love. Tell us now of cruelty. Tell us of death.'

Silence, for a while. The scribes' fingers paused over their ink pots. Each narrator had been given a different colour. The cripple's was black. The concubine's, green. The judges' questions, when they came, had been noted down in blue. But it was to a fourth pot, the least used so far, that they reached when the silence ended. For it was Dracula's confessor who spoke now. His voice was still croaky from disuse. Yet it carried into the hall.

'Strange you ask,' he whispered, 'for we were just coming to that.'

Red words flowed across the parchment.

— NINE —

The Blacksmith

They came for him before the dawn. It was a week since the snatch and Vlad had just begun to sleep with both eyes closed again.

They arrived in the dark, down the central passage of the *enderun kolej*, slippered feet silent on the polished wooden floor. They passed most of the partitioned classrooms, where each *orta* studied and slept, and not one page woke to their tread. Only when they gathered at a gap in the partition walls, where the hostage *orta* slept, was a single word whispered.

'Now.'

Vlad heard it and awoke, too late to do anything about it. Not that there was much to be done, with two men at every mattress. One to throw back the woollen coverlet. One to press a curved dagger to the throat.

The yelps of terror woke everyone in the *kolej*. The two eunuchs, who lay on raised beds in the middle of the hall, woke screeching to protect their brood. So also the two senior *aghas*, bursting from their latticed chamber at the hall's end. Yet, when they saw who had come, by the light of lanterns whose gates had now been opened, they cried out only once more, to quiet the boys' terrified whispers.

Vlad recognised, as all did, the red jackets, bright blue *shalvari* and yellow boots of the Sultan's bodyguard. For the moment of panicked waking, he thought it might be the *bolukbasi* of the Peyks who stood in the doorway. But then he remembered that unfortunate had been disembowelled in

Edirne's central square, along with his entire company, as atonement for his failure.

The man in the doorway was not going to fail. 'Which of these uncircumcised dogs is Dracula?' he bellowed at the eunuch beside him.

The man pointed. Immediately, Vlad was pulled by his hair off his mattress, and dragged across the floor to the entrance. 'And the brother?'

'He . . . he . . . . he is with the younger boys, *effendi*,' the eunuch gibbered. 'I . . . I will fetch him.'

'You will show him to my men,' the captain said. 'And you' – he reached down, grabbed Vlad's arm, lifted him by it, twisting it behind his back – 'will come with me!'

With his arm stretched and held high behind him, and the captain's other hand on his neck, Vlad was marched down the passageway, lined by gaping students, to the main door. There he was joined by a white-faced Radu, held in similar style. Without a pause they were pushed out into the inner court, across it. There was a bunching there, as a frightened gatekeeper fumbled for keys. Finding his head beside his brother's Vlad whispered, in their own tongue, 'Remember what we said! Admit nothing.'

'Silence!' shouted the captain, twisting harder. Vlad could not contain his cry. Then they were through the gate, onto the equestrian grounds, moving fast across them. The gatekeeper had dropped the keys in his panic. Bending to pick them up, he did not notice Ion slip through.

The party made their way to the horse lines. Beyond them, the gates of the stables were flung wide. Within, under the glare of reed torches, men and horses moved. The prisoners were marched straight in, taken to the right, past stalls, through a place Vlad had spent some time – the falcons' mews. Bent over, glancing up, Vlad saw sakers, their hooded heads bending to the noise of men, seeking through their blindness. Strangely, he wondered which was Sayehzade, the stake in the *jereed* wager that Mehmet had sullenly failed to deliver. One bird began screaming, wings spread wide, tipping off its perch, held upside-down there by its jesses. He saw legs come forward; someone reached, gathered.

Then they were through the mews; the screams receded but did not cease; another sound came. This was rhythmical, the striking of metal on metal. Only then did Vlad realise where he was being taken; and terror came. He had never thought that the punishment for what he'd done would be death. His only value to the Turk lay in his life – but they were masters of punishments. He had told Ilona of one upon the docks. The hostage sons of the Serbian despot Brankovic had been caught trying to send messages to their father. They had not been killed. Red-hot metal had simply been jabbed into their eyeballs.

The heat of the forge struck him like an open-handed slap. As he was forced onto his knees, Radu beside him, he glimpsed two things, two people: Mehmet, in his brocade jacket and Greek robe, smiling; and beside him, the blacksmith, hooded like a hawk, drawing something glowing from the fire.

Vlad felt his bowels loosen. His *jereed* rival was the one person he did not wish to see there, amidst heating metals. Yet, hating the fear, he reached for his defiance. 'You owe me a hawk,' he shouted.

He was slapped, thrown down onto the hard-packed earth before the anvil. He lay there, squinting up, mesmerised by molten red, and wondered, in a flush that brought sweat to every part of his body, if this was the last thing he would ever see. Beside him, Radu wept.

And then Vlad realised that they were not the only ones on the ground; that everyone there was descending, from feet to knees to bellies. Even, finally, Mehmet, allowing his glittering jacket to lie in the dust. Until there was only one man in the forge still standing.

The blacksmith.

He was dressed as any of his trade. A leather apron

protected him from neck to knee, his hands were encased in thick gauntlets, and his face in the hood, a slit filled with meshed metal before his eyes. They glowed, reflecting the heated iron he held in tongs, which he studied for a moment, then lowered upon the anvil. A hammer fell, in those rhythmic strokes. Then the metal was lifted, plunged into a water trough. Steam engulfed him, as he laid down the hammer, raising the tongs to the eye slit, turning it.

All Vlad had seen was iron. He had made it into the shape he feared – a poker with a molten tip. Now, in the coolness, he saw its true shape, and what it was: a horseshoe.

With a sigh, the blacksmith laid it down upon a pile of others, immediately lifted another bar of metal, laying it back into the coals. Then he raised the hood from his head, speaking as he did.

'Allah be praised for the worthiness of this work. For his is the skill, mine merely the service.'

The hood was set aside. The man turned. And Vlad saw why everyone was lying before him.

'Murad!' he breathed, not so loudly that any could hear, as the Magnificence of the World, the Beacon of Creation, the Sultan of the Turks stepped down from beside the anvil.

— TEN —

Punishments

In the darkness just inside the forge's open doors, an eye pressed to a crack, Ion hesitated. He'd slipped behind them as the others were dragged in. If he slid forward now, lay in the dirt, perhaps they would assume he'd been there all along? He wrapped his fingers around the frame . . . and then he spied the slightest of movements in the shadows behind the forge. Two shapes were there, one each side of Murad. Two of the Sultan's archers, his special bodyguard, arrows fitted to the notch. Ion knew that one drew with his left hand, one with his right, so they could straddle their lord. He also knew they never missed.

He hesitated still . . . and the moment passed. Murad was walking forward and Ion could only stare at the Rock of the World. He had only seen him twice before and from a distance. Here, this close, all that Ion had heard was confirmed. He looked so . . . ordinary, like any labourer on the streets of Edirne. Of middling height but large in chest and shoulders and with a blacksmith's muscled arms, he had an unkempt, grey beard, grey as the eyes in the round, unremarkable face, each feature smeared now with soot. It was said that he could walk among his people on a crowded street and never be noticed. That he often did. And that, unlike his peacock son, the clothes beneath the blacksmith's apron would be drab at best.

Ordinary! And yet not at all. For this was the man who had summoned to Gallipoli the strongest warrior Ion had ever known – Vlad Dracul, Voivode of Wallachia – and chained him to a cart wheel for a week. This the man who, two years before at Varna, took on the strongest army the Christians had put into the field for more than a century and wiped them out. Who then, bizarrely and almost immediately, abdicated in favour of his fourteen-year-old son so he could retire to his island of Manisa and linger with his poets, his contemplation and his wine. Who'd been forced to return after two years because of Mehmet's misrule.

This the man who now stepped forward and lowered his foot onto Vlad's neck. For a while he did not speak. When he did, his voice was low, almost a whisper. 'Dracul-a,' he said, pronouncing it as two words and in the 'limba Romana' – their language; not Osmanlica, the language of his land. 'Dragon's son.' There was something in the tone that Ion, expecting savage retribution for their crime, had not expected to hear: a certain sadness.

'The *aghas* of the *enderun kolej* tell me that you are one of their finest students. That you recite the words of the Holy Qur'an beautifully – as well as the poetry of Persia, and the philosophies of Athens and Rome. That you are as skilled with threads as I am at forges, against the day of disaster. And that you excel at manly pursuits – upon the wrestling turf, on a horse with bow, with *jereed*.' He glanced down at the red brocade jacket of his son, and a slight smile came, then vanished. 'But shall I tell you what does not please me?'

Murad paused, pressed down with his foot. And here it comes, Ion thought, swallowing. He knew Turkish punishments. Had experienced a few. Nothing, he was sure, like the retribution that would be given out for the stealing of a chosen girl.

And then Murad spoke on. 'It does not please me that you are the *Dragon's son*.' The last two words were shouted. As was the subsequent, 'Up!'

He was instantly obeyed, though all rose only to their knees, settled back onto haunches, waited, heads bowed;

Vlad, head now free, arms still pinned, amongst them. Only the Sultan, his watchers in the shadows and Ion behind the forge doors, stood.

Murad went on, his voice soft again. 'Did Dracul think that because he kept his Dragon banner furled I would not notice his eldest son, your brother, Mircea, leading Wallachians against me at Varna? Does he not know that I have spies everywhere reporting each twist he makes?' He glared down. 'And they tell me that though Dracul claims to hate my bitterest enemy, Hunyadi, the accursed White Knight, even as I do, that even now he has made a pact with him. To supply him with troops, marching again under a furled banner. To speed his passage through gates that should be barred against him.'

Murad stepped back to his forge and began to don the gloves he had removed. 'He seems to have forgotten what the word "hostage" means . . . in any language. He must learn the consequences of that.' As he spoke, he lifted the heated tongs from the coals.

'Father!' Mehmet called excitedly. 'May I—'

'Your skill is with plants not metals, my son,' Murad said sharply, 'and when I can teach you how to turn a seed into a cucumber, you may come and work my forge.' Pulling the tongs close, he studied the glowing metal at their end. 'And while I do not desire to punish, do not the commandments of Moses, honoured among prophets, speak of the sins of fathers and their consequences for sons?' He stepped back towards Vlad, metal glowing before him. 'Dracul must be sent a message. A clear one.'

Behind the door, Ion quivered. He had a dagger at his belt. Should he not leap forward now, stab Murad, save his friend's eyes? He would surely die, but die a hero if Murad did, too. Yet his hand never reached to his belt. Nothing moved, apart from a tear down his cheek, as the Sultan bent, bringing his own face close enough to Vlad's for the molten glow to light them both.

'So I say this to you, Dragon's sons. Both of you. Your lessons here are ended. Others begin. You will be taken to the fortress of Tokat. You will have different *agha*s there, learn different subjects. Less refined. Equally edifying. And your father will learn through your suffering the consequences of betrayal.' He lifted the tongs away, stood straight. 'Take them,' he said.

The men who held Vlad jerked him to his feet. Manacles were produced, clamped to his wrists. The men who held the still weeping Radu turned him towards the door.

But then Mehmet stepped before them, raising a hand to halt the guard. 'A boon, father,' he cried.

Murad turned back. 'Ask it.'

'Are there not different ways to send the same message?' He looked across at Vlad, smiled. 'I can think of nothing more beneficial than the lessons that await him at Tokat. But this one . . .' He reached out, laid a finger on Radu's chestnut curls, moved it down, tracing the nose, leaving it lie upon the lips. 'Is there not more than one way to bend a Dragon to one's desires?'

Until that moment, Vlad had felt as if some *djinn* had him in a binding spell. It was not the men that held him but his own will, frozen. This was his fate, to be blinded by a Sultan. There was nothing he could do to save himself. Then his fate changed, and again, he could do nothing but accept it. But when someone else was threatened – his brother, his blood – the spell was shattered.

With a roar, he bent and wrenched his manacled hands from the grip of the man on his left, straightening suddenly to drive the top of his head into the jaw of the other, who fell back. The first man reached for him again, but Vlad brought the metal manacles sweeping up and across, smashing them into his face. He collapsed and Vlad was free, moving towards Mehmet, aware of every little sound now as he had been aware of none before – his brother's weeping, every man's cry, the creak of bowstring pulled hard back by men in the shadows.

'Wait!' Murad cried, arm lifted in command.

The arrows were not needed. Vlad was stocky, shaped like a bull. But even he could not charge through the half-dozen men who leapt forward, punching, kicking and finally hurling him to the ground, an arm's length from his target.

But Mehmet had stepped back, readying himself. And though he still had a hand on Radu, he was no longer holding him tight. Certainly not tightly enough to stop the younger Dracula from grabbing the jewelled handle of the knife in Mehmet's belt.

'Leave me be,' Radu shrieked, drawing it, slashing the blade across the reaching hand.

Mehmet screamed. More guards rushed in. Radu was disarmed, grappled to the floor.

'Are you badly hurt, my son?' said Murad, coming forward again.

'Badly enough,' Mehmet whined, showing the slash across his palm.

Murad reached, closing his son's hand, holding it. 'You will live. And we have learned: even the youngest Dragons have teeth.' He smiled. 'Do you still want him?'

Mehmet nodded, a gleam in his eyes. 'More than ever.'

'Then you shall have him.' Murad raised his voice. 'Take him to my son's *saray*. The other to the wagons. He will leave immediately. The rest of you will go. Only Mehmet will stay.'

'Vlad!' Radu cried.

On the floor, his brother's cry came to him through the fog where blows had sent him. He tried to surge up through it, to fight again. But the Sultan was instantly obeyed, as ever. Men lifted both boys and rushed them from the room.

In a moment, all were gone. All save the Sultan and his son; the two shadows releasing, just, the tension in their bowstrings. And Ion, still frozen behind the door.

For a moment, silence. Ion was sure they would hear his breathing, the fall of his tears. Then footsteps came, soft on the dirt floor. A man entered with a goshawk on one fist.

'Well, Hamza *agha*,' said Murad, 'is my bold Zeki ready to fly?'

'He is ready. To fly for you. To kill for you, *enishte*.'

He calls him *enishte*, 'uncle', Ion thought. Then he remembered how Hamza was only recently appointed a falconer. Before that, the handsome tanner's son from Laz had been Murad's cupbearer. And more, it was said.

The Sultan pulled a piece of raw meat from the pouch at Hamza's waist, luring the bird from his falconer's glove to his own, the jesses effortlessly transferred. With the bird settled, Murad looked up. 'And this other hawk, the Wallachian. Can you make him as biddable? Will he, one day, kill for me, too?'

'I . . . think so, *enishte*. I have some ideas.'

Murad chuckled. 'Oh, I am sure you do. You were always the cleverest of my boys, nephew.' He glanced to the side, and affection left his face. 'I have often urged my son to study you.' While Mehmet coloured, his father looked back. 'These ideas? Would you like to share them?'

'It is as you say, lord. Dracula is a hawk. There are many ways to train one. Some with harshness. Some with love. Some with one after the other. As in this case.' He sighed. 'I believe we can leave the *agha*s of Tokat to deal with the first.'

'I wish I could see that,' murmured Mehmet.

Murad frowned slightly, though not, it seemed, at the interruption. 'It disturbs you, Hamza? You regret the lessons that the hostage is to learn?'

Hamza shrugged. 'Sometimes, with a proud bird, the only way to break it is to soak it with water, then sit out the entire, freezing night with it. I regret that, too, though I sometimes recognise the need.'

Murad leaned forward, lifting Hamza's gloved hand to the fire glow. ' "I am trapped," ' he read aloud. ' "Held in this cage of flesh. And yet I claim to be a hawk flying free." ' He looked up. 'This is what he sewed for you?'

'Yes.'

Murad read again, silently. 'Jalaluddin. He has taken some liberties with the verse.'

'I told him so, *enishte*.'

Murad let the hand drop. 'He has a schoolboy's love for you, does he not?'

Hamza shrugged. 'Perhaps.'

'And you for him?'

Hamza said nothing.

Murad smiled. 'Well, you spoke of how some birds need love *after* harshness.'

The two men had turned towards the forge so that the Sultan could read. Mehmet, striving not to be excluded, had come closer. Ion saw that the three were almost a screen to the archers in the shadows. So he edged around the door.

Eyes followed him. Not human. The goshawk was no doubt a gift from some vassal-prince to the north, for it flew in the same beech forests from which Ion came. He moved, praying silently for a countryman's silence.

It was not kept. '*Kree-ak, kree-ak,*' came the hunting call.

He leapt. And his knees, weakened by shaking, gave . . . and saved his life, for an arrow flew a finger's width above his head and shuddered into the door.

'Hold!' Murad's shout was to the second archer, who had cleared the screen of bodies and was about to shoot. 'Guards!' he called, and five men rushed in, to seize the fallen Wallachian.

'You,' said Murad, turning to the first archer, 'are banished from my service for your miss. And you . . .' he continued, turning back to Ion, 'come here.'

As the disgraced archer left, Ion was dragged forward, pressed to the floor. Murad bent, lifted him by the hair. 'A youth,' he said, 'and dressed like a student. Do you know him, nephew?'

'Yes, *enishte*. His name is Ion Tremblac. A *boyar*'s son from Wallachia, sent to be Vlad's companion.'

'Indeed.' Murad studied him for a moment. 'And now he is turned spy.'

Ion looked up into the Sultan's grey eyes. He knew his death was in them. Strangely, it made him less frightened, now that it was certain. 'No spy, Murad Han. Only a loyal servant to my lord, my friend, Vlad Dracula.'

The words were defiantly spoken, perhaps harsher than he intended. All tensed, waiting for retribution. But Murad's voice was soft when it came. 'The boy has courage, Hamza. Is he as gifted as the one he serves?'

'No. Not close. But then, few are.'

Mehmet stepped forward. 'He was one of those who conspired to hurt me upon the *jereed* field, father. And a spy must be silenced. Give him to me . . .'

A raised hand halted the words. As if he hadn't heard them, Murad continued, 'It would seem a pity to extinguish such a spark. And he may be useful to us.'

'How so, *enishte*?'

'Does he know what they do at Tokat?'

Hamza nodded. 'All know. At night, at the *enderun kolej*, they frighten each other to sleep with tales from those dungeons.'

'Good.' Murad smiled. 'Our message to the Dragon will be better delivered by one of his own people. This boy can tell him what is happening to his sons. He will guess what Mehmet intends for Radu. He will know what lessons the elder will learn at Tokat. He will tell of our restraint in punishing them . . . for now.'

The Sultan reached again into the pouch at Hamza's waist. Pulling out more meat, he fed it to the bird still resting calmly on his fist. 'Mehmet, see that everything is provided to our messenger for his journey. It is time Hamza and I tested the mettle of this bird. To the hunt!'

He moved to the doorway. Guards enfolded him on each side, the one archer joining from the shadows, arrow ever notched on bowstring. At the entrance, Murad paused, looked back at his son who had taken a step towards the prone Ion. 'Remember, Mehmet. The messenger I send must be alive to speak.'

With that, he was gone, Hamza and most of the guards with him. Leaving just the two who held Ion. And Mehmet.

Ion stared up into Mehmet's brown eyes. The shape was the same as his father's. But in Mehmet's there was not a trace of humour or compassion. He raised a hand now as if to strike, then slowly lowered it, finally grasping Ion's hair, moving it gently away from his face.

'Your life is spared, dog. So you can bark your message to your master.' He smiled. 'But that does not mean the message must only be in words.' He looked everywhere around the forge. Finally, his gaze settled on the burning coals. 'Hold him tight. By the head,' he snapped.

He was obeyed. As the men pulled a struggling Ion forward, Mehmet went and searched among a rack of iron rods. Then, with a cry of joy, he pulled one out, shoved it into the fire. Donning a pair of gloves, he spoke. 'You know, dog, that each Sultan has his *tugra* – a unique symbol to affix to documents, like the seals of your princes. Well, sometimes we need to burn our mark on our property – our sheep, our camels, our horses. I thought that when my father took back the throne from me, he got rid of my brand.' He turned the iron in the glowing coals, then lifted it, blew on its end, which glowed a deeper red. 'It appears that he did not.'

There was nothing Ion could do. The hands' grip was unbreakable. He could only close his eyes, pray that the fate of Brankovic's blinded sons was not now to be his own. Murad had said that he must be able to speak. But to see?

It was the relief of a moment when the heat came to his

face, when he heard and smelled the crisping hair. Only that one moment though before the agony came as Mehmet scorched his *tugra* into Ion's flesh.

ELEVEN

Tokat

In a world for ever dark, Vlad had no way to mark the passing of time. The enclosed wagon that had brought him to Tokat had admitted some light. He'd seen seven dawns through its slats. But they had blindfolded him when they'd taken him out, carried him along stone corridors, down endless flights of stairs. And there was not the slightest chink in the walls of his cell. He knew it only by touch, an exploration that had taken mere moments. It was a sloping cylinder of rock, twice his height deep. Halfway up it, a shelf of sorts jutted out on which he could perch, just able to lie upon it to sleep if he curled his knees up to his chin. But if he did sleep, sooner or later he'd fall off, wake to the scraping of his flesh on rough stone, feet or hands plunging into the filthy straw that lined the stone floor and held all his excrement.

There was no way to count the days by his feeding. It could have arrived at the same time every morning or only twice a week. It did not vary. The thinnest of cold barley soup, strings of what could have been meat floating in it; a piece of stone-flattened bread on which he could smell the mould. He ate it all anyway, drank the mug of rank water that came with it. It was too little but he had to keep as strong as possible for whatever lay ahead. He knew the stories of Tokat, of the torture cells. Starving would not help him survive.

He never saw who brought the food or even heard footsteps, just the circular trapdoor opening fast, the food banging against the walls as it was lowered in a net, the door slamming shut. He'd shout, plead, threaten. There was never a response. He'd sink upon his shelf and shiver. He still wore only what he'd slept in at the *enderun kolej*, and the cold was the dark's constant companion.

The only thing he'd sometimes hear, in the brief moments the trapdoor was open, were distant screams.

Once, in his fury, he scooped a handful of his own shit from the floor, waited, more patiently than he'd ever waited for the most elusive of quarry. When the door opened, he hurled it with a great shout. The cry it provoked was as gratifying as the cry Mehmet had given when Vlad's *jereed* took him in the back. But the net was snapped up, the door replaced. And he was able to mark the time in one way at least – by the ravenous hunger that grew and grew.

In the perfect darkness, light only came in dreams indistinguishable from wakefulness. Then, one day or night, voices began to emerge from the harsh brightness, speaking a language he didn't understand, like the twittering of starlings. He squinted against the glare, tried to make out faces through his tears. He never could.

Until, one day or night, into his dream came the shuffle of a chain, the scrape of wood on stone. Light, dull real light, not vision light, the shape of a head before it. A word spoken, one he understood.

'Come.'

Hands reached, hauling him up. He crouched, the two men on either side supporting him because he'd been unable to stand straight in the time he'd been below the ground. He squinted up at them, eyes half-closed against the glare of reed torches. He was dragged, toes scraping the uneven flagstones, trying to push off against them, to get some feeling into his feet. He did not know what awaited him down these dank corridors. But he wanted to stand and face it.

Yet the first thing he faced was water. His guards – thin-faced, turbaned, with fingers of bent steel – flung him into a cell. At its centre was a stone trough. The silent men stood back, arms folded, waiting.

Vlad stumbled forward, dipped a hand. The water was barely warm, but it felt to him like the hottest of *hamam*s after the frigid world he'd inhabited. There were kese mitts, too, of rough woven cloth and not of the first use or cleanliness, but when pressed against his skin . . . ah! Peeling off the rags his *shalvari* and shirt had become, Vlad began to wash. The water turned brown from his shit, pink from the blood that came from the scores of scabbed-over flea bites. But the blood reassured him. It meant he was alive, which he'd often doubted in his cell. And being clean meant he was a man again. Sometimes he'd doubted that, too.

When he was done, a thick wool *gomlek* was thrown at him, the knee-length tunic joyously warm after his summer rags. Sandals, too, which he slipped onto his tattered feet. Then, like the teeth of a millwheel turning, he jerked his body up piece by piece until he stood straight for the first time in an age of darkness. As soon as he did, the silent men were on him, gripping his arms, pulling him down the corridor to another low doorway. Bending, they flung him into the room. His weakened legs made him stumble, fall to his knees. It was darker there too, airless, almost like his cell. But there was light and his gaze went to it. To the red glow of a brazier.

When his eyes had adjusted, he looked around, saw that he was in a windowless vault, large enough so that the ceiling was lost to shadow . . . though not what dangled from it: pulleys, chains, nooses. More things were piled against walls – metal rods, tongs, a rack of knives. There was what looked like the frame of a divan, tipped up on its legs. Beside it stood the skeleton of a suit of armour.

His gaze went back to the brazier. Two shapes had appeared behind it, one large, one smaller; or perhaps they'd been there all the time. As he looked, the larger shape moved, thrusting a metal bar into the coals. It caused an eruption of sparks, a sudden increase in light, and Vlad saw that the two shapes were men.

One stepped forward. 'Welcome, princeling. Welcome to Tokat.'

It was a surprisingly deep voice, considering how small the speaker was. As Vlad's eyes adjusted, he could see that the man wasn't a dwarf, had none of a dwarf's swollen features, but wasn't far above one in height. He was like any other man, but in miniature, with a hooked nose, and eyes that sat under heavy lids as if he craved sleep. He wore a thick wool jacket, buttoned high to the neck. It was covered in coloured threads, sewn in elaborately stitched patterns that looked, at a glance, like a stag hunt.

The second man had bent into the red glow. He was as big as the other was small, his naked stomach a dome under a vast and muscled chest. Both were elaborately tattooed with creatures from myth and life. A Basilisk chased a Manticore into his armpit. A tiger emerged from the cave of the belly hole. There was writing across his huge head, which was bald. Indeed, there was no hair anywhere; though, strange amidst the strangeness, two red lines were painted where eyebrows should be.

'His name is Mahir,' came that deep voice, 'and it means "skilled one". And he is very skilled, as he will show you. He will not tell you, though, for he cannot speak. Show him why, Mahir.'

The man leaned forward over the brazier. He opened his vast mouth. The teeth in them were white, almost excessively so. Perhaps that was because they were set against such a dark, empty cavern. The man had no tongue.

'It was not the first thing Mahir lost,' the other man said, chuckling. 'For he was a eunuch at the harem in Edirne for many years. Then he saw something he shouldn't have, began to speak of it and . . . phish!' He flickered his tongue out, snakelike. 'They made him chew it off himself. Can you imagine that? Perhaps you'd like to try? No?' The dry laugh came again. 'Anyway, Mahir was wasted, chattering his life away at the harem. He lost his tongue and found other skills. As you shall soon learn.'

The warmth Vlad had felt fled. He knew now what he had chosen not to see before. Every item in the chamber was an implement for the infliction of torment. And he was about to learn what each was for. Punishment for his father's sins against the Sultan. He tried to speak, to protest, perhaps to beg. But his voice wouldn't work.

The tiny man spoke again. 'And I am called Wadi. It means "the calm one" . . .' He broke off. 'But why do I keep translating for you? You speak our language well, do you not?'

Vlad managed words. 'Well enough.'

At them Mahir, who had kept his mouth wide open, snapped it shut, and moved to the brazier. He began to place metal instruments upon a rack suspended above the coals.

'You are modest,' continued Wadi, 'for it is reported that you were one of the most proficient of students at the *enderun kolej*. Well,' he said with a smile, 'you are at a different *kolej* now. Your studies will be different, too. More . . .' He gestured at the heating metal. '. . . Practical in nature. And we are not like those *agha*s who taught you before, Mahir and I.'

With that, he suddenly clapped his hands. Just once, and it startled Vlad like an explosion of gunpowder. It begins, he thought. He wanted to run, to flee the chamber. Maybe to grab a metal rod and fight. But he found he could not move his legs. Even when the door opened and half a dozen youths of about his own age came in. Yet they did not rush him, pin him, throw him to the floor. They formed in a semi-circle, dropped to their knees, lowered their foreheads to the stone.

Wadi inclined his head. 'Your fellow students,' he declared. 'Not the quality of *orta* you are used to. Peasant boys these, unable to read, write, quote the Holy Qur'an, debate

99

the poets. But they are strong and quick to learn. And in their own field they will become as gifted as any other graduate, though their talents will not lie in engineering, administration or languages. They will travel as widely perhaps, be as necessary to the success of our Sultan in the Abode of War as any soldier. For as you know – or, if you don't you soon will – every society needs its torturers.'

He returned once more to the brazier. 'So, students,' he continued, 'let us welcome a new addition to our *orta*. He has some catching up to do but I am sure that you will all help him in his studies. And we are honoured, for he is the son of a prince of Wallachia. Never heard of it? Never mind, few have. It is a minor land, owing everything to the indulgence of Murad Han, Asylum of the World, may Allah keep his kingdom. It is the Most Blessed who wills that we teach the princeling our ways. So we obey.'

With that, the small man clapped again. Immediately, the thin men appeared in the doorway, clutching another man between them. This man was weeping. Wadi smiled.

'So welcome, Vlad Dracula. Welcome to your new school.'

TWELVE

The Choice

He was dressed as most Anatolian shepherds in wool *shalvari* and a sheepskin vest over a red-dyed shirt. All were swiftly stripped from him, reducing him to quivering flesh. He clasped his hands around his groin, making the students snicker. He blinked continuously, terror in his large brown eyes. He was chubby, a contrast to the men who still stood beside him and who, at a nod from Wadi, immediately forced the peasant to his knees.

'Any fool can inflict pain, prince,' the *agha* said, 'but it takes a skilful man to sustain it.' He stopped beside the prone man who blinked up at him. 'In that, it is like any art. A lute's string is sounded in such a way that its harmonies vibrate in the air. We do not pluck and dampen it, cutting off its beauties. We seek to extend them.'

Wadi reached suddenly, pinching a fold of flesh on the man's upper arm. He cried out, something in the local dialect. Wadi ignored him. 'But so much depends on the instrument on which we practise. The finest lute will sustain the longest.' He released the man's skin, turned to the students. 'So study your instruments well. Note their health, their flesh, their stamina. And then begin to play.'

And Vlad heard himself speak before he thought to, his voice a croak. 'What crime has he committed?'

The small man's brow creased. 'Crime? What does it matter? We are not judges. It is enough that he has been judged by others. They could have hung him from a tree.

Instead, they sent him here, for they know that we are as much a part of justice as they are.'

He gestured to the two men. Immediately they pulled the peasant to his feet. One snapped manacles to his wrists, the other went to the wall and dragged a rope across, one end of which ran through a pulley, squeaking along a rail above. The other end was swiftly looped through the manacles and secured. Both men then went to the rope's end and pulled, hoisting the naked man's arms above him till he was standing on the tips of his toes. He dangled there, eyes now shut, lips moving in plea or prayer.

Wadi had picked up a stick. He stood before the hanging man. 'I have heard that in Christian lands, torment is used to extract a confession. More, that they use it especially on those of different faiths. Barbarism!' he exclaimed. 'Leaving aside the wisdom as exists in our Sultanate of Rum, that all men may keep the faith they choose without persecution – though the wisest come to Allah, praise him . . .'

'Praise him!'

'. . . what use is a confession extracted by torments? Men will say anything to escape pain. Women, too. Why, if I had the Christian saints Peter and Paul in this room for one hour I could make them deny their God, their Saviour and own their love of Satan.' He looked around at all the attentive faces, his gaze finally resting on Vlad. 'Tell me, princeling – in the *enderun kolej*, did you not divide your time between the practical and the philosophical? From geometry to the dialogues of Socrates? Well, it is the same in our classroom. We too have our philosophy. The philosophy of torment, which has been my lifelong study.' He nodded. 'We torment for two reasons. The first is for information. In war, to discover where the ambushes are laid, or the weak point in a fortification. In peace, where stolen goods or a child may be hidden. The torment used must be fast, intense, unbearable – for what is sought is only fact. But the second reason for torment, that which, like the lute, we sustain for as long as . . .' He smiled. '. . . *Humanly* possible, is this.'

He raised his stick, gesturing for his class to speak. They did, as one.

'We torture others so they cannot torture us.'

The shout echoed around the stone room. It roused the dangling man, who looked up as if called.

Wadi nodded. ' "We torture others so they cannot torture us." Like all great answers, it is so simple. Why do we seek the most ingenious ways of prolonging pain? Not for pain itself. No, that would be mere cruelty. But for an example, as striking and clear as possible. For the warning: This is what happens when you oppose me. This shall be your fate.' He beamed at them. 'Well,' he said, 'enough philosophy. Now for the practical.'

He turned and nodded at Mahir, who had been standing quite still, making a clicking sound in his throat, then tapped his stick upon the table. 'Come, my scholars,' Wadi said. 'Take one each.'

All came forward eagerly, lifting something from a tray. Only Vlad remained still. 'No, prince?' Wadi smiled. 'Well, you will join us soon enough, trust me. When you see the fun to be had. When you realise that this . . .' He struck the naked body beside him hard, and the man cried out. '. . . Is no longer human. Not even animal. It is a concept. And, of course, an example. For your enemies. Perhaps, most particularly, for your friends.'

They'd formed a semi-circle around the peasant. Wadi opened the gate on a lantern, held it up. Mahir came forward and Vlad now saw what he held, what they all held. It was a *bastinado* – but this was not the wooden stick of chastisement from the *enderun kolej*. This was a thin rod of steel, the length of a forearm, no wider than a thumb. Mahir struck the belly with it once and the man gave a yelp, his eyes shooting wide. Then the teacher stepped back.

'Did you take note, students, of Mahir's stroke? Not too

hard, yet not too soft. A balance. You must never break the skin. Do you see the mark it left?' Wadi used his *bastinado* to point it out. 'Hardly anything, is it? A tiny bruise, caused by blood vessels rupturing beneath the surface. But when joined to the next one, and the next one, when there is no clear skin left . . .' He struck, next to Mahir's mark, drawing another cry, adding another welt. 'Well, you will see what happens when a man is transformed to a living bruise.' He waved the students forward. 'Find an area. Work on it. But remember – no blood!'

The blows came. Wadi commented, urging force or restraint. After a while the man's cries turned to coughs. Vlad did not move, did not turn away. He wanted to, more than he'd wanted most things. But he would not show them that weakness.

A *bastinado* had been thrust at him. He had taken it without thinking. With every blow he gripped it tighter, his fingers cramping on steel.

In the torment, there was release.

In the darkness, there was light.

In solitude, there were companions.

They came in his dreams and stayed in his wakefulness. Each came according to his needs, which changed with the hour of the day or night.

'But how can you tell the hour, my son?'

Vlad Dracul, his father, was there, sharing his shelf of rock. He was massive of shoulder, of chest, and yet there was room for the two of them to squat, in the Turkish style, thigh to calf.

'By the type of torment,' Vlad said, ever eager to please his father. He knew the Dragon would be interested. 'Winter mornings are cold. So it is when they practise the warmer styles. Those that require flame.'

'Good boy. Observant boy. Observe them closely, Vlad. Only by knowing them will you be able to defeat them.' He ran a hand, heavy with jewelled rings, through his curly black hair. 'What else do you know of them?'

'I know they are obsessed by food. Are not the colonels of the janissaries known as "soup cooks"? They treat human flesh like they treat mutton. Boil it. Baste it. Grill it and roast it.'

'And do they eat it, too?'

'I have not seen that.'

Strangely, his father began to cry. Vlad had seen him laugh, often. Never cry. It disturbed him. 'Please . . . don't . . .'

'I failed you, boy,' Vlad Dracul wept. 'I am the reason you have to see all that. The reason you are here. I couldn't keep the balance. If I hadn't helped Hunyadi, the Hungarians would have eaten me, spat out my bones. But the Turk found out. Punished me through you. And all for nothing. My time is done. It is too late.' He plunged his face into his hands, shouted, 'Too late! I have prayed nightly – to God, to Saint Gheorghe – to protect my precious boys. Yet here you are. And Radu! Radu!'

Vlad shuddered. 'My brother? What of him?'

The voice came from between fingers. 'You left him. Left him to me.'

The language was different. So was the face that lifted now. Mehmet smiled, ran his tongue over his swollen lips. 'And now he is mine – and far sweeter than any whore you could steal.'

'No!' Vlad screamed, leapt, hands stretched before him to grapple and rend. But he gripped nothing, slipped, his head striking stone. He felt the sticky wetness on his brow, reached up . . . and another hand forestalled him, touching there, caressing there. He knew it instantly for it was the only one that had touched him in that way since his mother had died.

'Ilona,' he whispered, reaching up to the hand that was not there. 'Star.'

'My lord,' she murmured, leaning her face into the light.

He had long since unpinned her hair, uncurled the tight ringlets that Mehmet had ordered. It fell now in hazel waves, framing the near perfect oval of a face that bore no hint of paint and needed none.

'Are you safe, my star?'

'Safe, my lord. Safe in our land. I wait for you there.'

'Wait? No! Do not wait. You are pure, unsullied. Innocent. Do not wait for a monster.'

'You? You are my hero. My saviour. My prince.'

'Monster!' he screamed, reaching forward, trying to shove her away. But his hands met air alone, and he drew them back, covered his face. 'Monster,' he repeated, more quietly. 'For I have become one of them.'

'How?'

He didn't know whose voice it was who asked. It didn't matter now. He'd tell them all – Ilona, Father, Mehmet. The others.

Wadi stood before the glowing furnace, Mahir in darkness behind him, the rest of the *orta* spread in a semi-circle around. The small man had a livid bruise on his cheekbone. 'So, princeling,' he spat, as soon as the jailers brought Vlad into the chamber, 'for months now you have taken no part in your lessons. You have merely . . . *observed.*' He sneered the word. 'But that is not why you are here. To observe. It is not what is required of you. Nor of me.' He reached up, and fingered the bruise upon his cheekbone. 'Others are becoming impatient. I am becoming impatient. So it is time for our lessons to become more . . . direct.'

He nodded to the jailers. They left but returned swiftly, holding another man between them and Vlad saw immediately how different he was to the poor labourers they usually practised upon. In his middle years, he had a trimmed beard and moustache on pale skin and was dressed in clothes from the West – a green velvet doublet, hose, buckled shoes.

'A treat, scholars,' Wadi cried. 'A merchant and a captain, from Rome, no less. An educated man yet stupid enough to try and smuggle spices and slaves and not pay the tariff. So he will pay now.' He smiled. 'His cries and prayers will make such a change from our usual peasant gruntings, eh? It will be a pleasure to hear them. Or . . . not.' He turned to Vlad, his hand reaching up to the welt upon his face. 'For you are educated, too. Perhaps your cries would be even more entertaining?'

Vlad swallowed. 'You would not dare.'

'Would not?' Wadi's laugh was harsh. 'This is my realm, princeling, not yours. And in it, I can do anything I desire.' He turned to the *orta*. 'Strip them both.'

The students lunged, stripped. In moments, Vlad and the merchant stood facing each other, naked save for a loin cloth, their arms pinned.

Wadi reached for something behind him, then stepped forward. He only came to Vlad's chest and he peered up into his eyes. 'What is the motto of our *kolej*? Say it, princeling. Say it.'

Vlad looked away, silent.

'No? Forgotten it?' Wadi looked at the students who held Vlad. 'Tell him.'

Both boys shouted it. 'You torture others so they cannot torture you.'

'You torture others so they cannot torture you,' Wadi repeated softly. Then he brought his hand up and laid a coldness against Vlad's skin. Squinting down, he could see that it was a knife with a blade no longer than the small man's palm; it curved, widened, ended in a square tip. He recognised it . . . for he had used one himself and recently, to cut strips of leather for Hamza *agha*'s glove.

It rested against him but a moment. Then, suddenly, Wadi thrust one corner of the tip into Vlad's chest. Slit, slid, sliced

107

a strip the width of the blade, the length of a finger, before Vlad's scream was seconds old.

Wadi stepped away, turned to the others, holding the strip high. He raised his voice above the moaning. 'Did you all note how easily the skin peels away? How I slipped the flat of the blade in shallowly? Used its keenness, not my strength? This technique is called flaying. And it is said that in the farthest East they can keep a man alive through a thousand cuts. Do we believe it? Can we exceed it? Shall we try?'

'Yes!' came the cry.

He threw the skin onto the brazier. It sizzled there, crisping swiftly to black, burning with a sweet, foul scent. 'Let them go,' he said, to those who held both prisoners.

They were released, Vlad clutching a hand to the blood that flowed between his fingers. He kept upright despite the pain, watched as Wadi came forward, stooped and laid the knife onto the stone floor between the two unclothed men.

'One of you will flay the other,' Wadi said, stepping back. 'And because you are the honoured guest, princeling, and he the criminal, you get to choose.'

Vlad let his hand fall away, stood straight. He couldn't see the torturer clearly through his tears but his voice was strong. 'No,' he said.

Wadi smiled. 'Interesting choice,' he said, turning to the merchant, whose face was distorted by terror, his lips forming words no one could hear. 'Take up the knife. If you can take ten strips from him without killing him, you are free to go.'

Vlad watched the merchant's eyes. Watched the terror in them turn to desperation and then to a kind of hope. Watched him step forward and bend to the flaying knife. The pain at his chest was unbearable. Something shifted inside him. 'No,' he said again. Differently. Bent swiftly as he spoke.

Picked up the knife.

*

Her hand was still in his. He was squeezing it so tightly he thought he would break her fingers. 'I had used one before, Ilona,' he whispered, 'to make a falconer's glove. But flesh was . . . different from leather. And there was blood,' he sobbed, 'so much blood . . .'

'My love! Don't! Don't . . .'

'And do you know?' he whispered. 'He was just the first. Now Wadi has seen what I am like with a blade, he keeps pushing one into my hand.'

The grip on him changed. The skin was rougher and Vlad could feel the scars upon the palm before it pulled away. 'Jesus,' Vlad said, in wonder. In joy. He looked up . . . but form had dissolved into light. Golden, wondrous light.

The Saviour had never visited him before, though Vlad had begged him to come. He had neglected his prayers since his mother died. But not now, not in his cell. 'I am here with you, my son,' came the voice. 'I understand your suffering. For did not my father also send me to torment?'

Vlad knelt, knees grinding into rough stone. 'Forgive me, Lord,' he said, 'my sins.'

'You are forgiven, my son,' came the reply. 'Because you ask, because you repent, because you will atone, your sins are removed. And yet . . .' The voice became harder. '. . . How little there is to forgive. For was it not a Roman you tortured? Did not the Romans nail me to a cross? Is it not written in the Book of Matthew that I shall seek throughout the world all things that offend and commit evil; and shall throw them into the furnace of fire?'

'Lord?' Vlad squinted into the light. 'Do you say . . .'

'Remember my sacrifice. Remember what set you free. I was tortured and murdered so Man might live.'

He heard the feet approaching on the flagstones above. 'Lord,' Vlad cried out, 'what are you telling me?'

The wooden trapdoor was pulled up. There was light, dull light, not heavenly light. That slipped away. But as it faded, voices came: his father, Ilona, Mehmet, Jesus. Speaking as one.

'You torture others so they cannot torture you.'

Hands reaching for him. Real ones now, jerking him from his cell.

THIRTEEN

First Time

For the duration of his imprisonment – how long that was Vlad could not know – his path had always led down, each flight of stairs taking him deep into the bowels of Tokat. This time he was pulled up. It frightened him, this change of routine. He did not know what it could mean. He did not think it would be good.

And then he was thrust through an archway into daylight. It dazzled him, after his life of darkness and flame. It was wonderful, too, the air clean of all foulness, a harsh wind blowing over him that made him shiver with cold and delight. He sniffed it like a hound, opened his senses to everything: to the wind driving ice crystals into his face; to the roiling grey clouds; to a scent in the air that spoke of another land, another season . . .

It is near spring, he thought. I have been held here for close to six months.

He looked around then. He was standing in an arched entranceway to the fortress's main yard. Walls enclosed the space in a star shape, with the usual huddle of straw-roofed huts leaning against them. Horses moved in some, soldiers in others. Within one, a fire glowed, a blacksmith wielding his hammer before it. In yet another, slaves turned a wheel, grinding barley.

To Vlad's life-starved eyes, all was delightful. Until he looked at the figures in the very centre of the courtyard. The students of his *orta* were there, huddled close for warmth,

Wadi in their midst. He saw Vlad immediately, beckoned him.

'Ah, good! Here, princeling, here,' he called. 'I have something special for us today.'

The group parted to admit him – and sitting there, previously screened, was Mahir, bare-chested as ever despite the chill rain. A long wooden stake lay across his thighs. It was about the length of a tall man and half as much again, its circumference matching the meaty forearm that held it. Its end had been chiselled to a roughly rounded point, and Mahir was applying a metalled glove to that, scouring it smooth, eliminating all edge, rendering it into half a globe.

'You will witness something extraordinary here today, princeling. An experiment, almost. For Mahir has never practised this form of his craft. It has not been much used in the Abode of Peace, though often in the cruder realms across the Danube, so we hear. Still, we do like to take the best from our northern vassals.'

Mahir dropped his scouring glove, ran his finger over the end of the stake, squealed in the high-pitched way that was his speech, to show that he was ready.

'Excellent,' said Wadi. 'But before we begin, remember we are not just artisans. We are historians and philosophers. And what we undertake today has an ancient lineage. For did not mighty Sennacherib, King of the Assyrians, practise this technique upon the Israelites? Did they not profit from the lesson and use it in their turn? Their Torah talks of sinful men, fixed upon timber.' He clapped his hands, signal and delight both. 'Yes, my scholars, you are once again heirs to ancient tradition. Regard!'

His clap brought men who had been waiting for it. The first of them came from one hut bearing ropes, another led a donkey from the stables, while from the archway a group appeared, facing inwards, looking at someone in their midst. Then they parted, and Vlad saw a youth, not much older than Vlad himself, with long, fair hair, no turban. He did not resist as he was led towards the apprentice torturers; indeed, he did not seem to have much awareness of what was going on around him. He was staring at the clouds.

'His name is Samuil,' said Wadi, beginning his usual summation of their subject, 'and he comes, perhaps like the technique itself, from somewhere across the Danube. Taken by our Sultan, Balm of the World, on one of his many successful campaigns.'

Vlad stepped closer. Wallachia was across the Danube.

'And he is, of course, a follower of Christ,' Wadi continued. 'No harm in that. Many are who dwell in the Abode of Peace. All we do ask is that they keep their misguided views to themselves.' He pointed to the youth. 'But this one refuses to keep his silence and his Prophet to himself. He has been chastised, flogged, starved. Still he must speak.'

Vlad stared at the young man's raised face. His eyes were closed now, his lips moving.

'So he has been given to us for punishment. And it was Mahir who thought he should receive this one!'

The donkey had arrived, led into the centre of the rough circle, head lowered, as oblivious as the youth. Seeing it, Vlad remembered another donkey, in a street market in Edirne, and what he had done to it. He shivered.

Mahir reached up, withdrew two items from its saddlebags – a razor and a jar. The first he stuck in his belt, then pulled the stopper from the jar and poured its green contents onto the stake's smoothed end. All could smell the sweetness of olive oil.

'Are we ready?'

Mahir gave a squeal of assent. Laying aside the stake he rose, went to the youth and ripped his thin *gomlek* from him. He didn't try to cover his nakedness. Didn't react at all when Mahir picked him up and laid him on the ground, face down, his head between the donkey's rear hooves.

There was a rack fixed to the donkey's back in place of a saddle. Mahir tied the ropes securely to it, triple-knotting them. Then he tied the other ends halfway down the stake before laying it between the youth's bare, spread legs. He looked up, gave a squeal.

Wadi smiled. 'Indeed, Mahir. Let us begin.'

The torturer signalled other men forward, one to hold each limb, one to sit on his back. Then he pulled the razor from his belt . . . and the young man's eyes finally flickered open, searched the faces that regarded him. Finally, his gaze settled on Vlad. And he said one word.

Vlad took a step forward, raised a hand, let it fall. He knew he was the only one there who had understood the word, spoken in the tongue of Wallachia.

Salvation.

And then the word was lost in screaming, as the razor slit his anus to allow easier entrance for the blunted, oiled stake. Mahir guided it in, squealing to Wadi, who began to lead the donkey slowly away. The beast didn't react to the shrieks, the shuddering, the vibrations travelling through rope. It just plodded forward, pulling the stake, despite the slight resistance, which became easier.

Vlad saw the youth pass into unconsciousness when the stake was halfway up his body. He knew he was not dead, by the pulse still throbbing at his temple. It was then that Mahir untied the ropes, beckoned the other students forward. Together, on his command, they hoisted the stake and its load into the air, guiding its end into a hole dug for the purpose. Upright, the body began to slide down of its own weight. But Mahir, though a novice at impalement, understood his trade. For when the youth's feet reached halfway down the stake, he grabbed them, crossing them onto a step that had been fixed into the wood. Then, with three swift strikes of his hammer, he drove a long nail through both feet, making them fast to the wood beneath.

'Salvation!'

Vlad called it, because the youth could not, not with the stake's blunted end now protruding from his mouth. Called it for them both and for Jesus, who had been in his cell and now was here, taking another martyr's hand, as he had taken the other Samuil, the first Christian martyr. This was glory! This was sacrifice! Jesus for Man; Man for Jesus. All suffering dedicated to God.

'Salvation,' he cried again. 'Praise him! Praise God!'

Wadi couldn't know what he was saying. But all could see the ecstasy on his face, hear it in his voice. 'Yes, princeling,' he cried, 'now you see. Now you understand.'

Vlad understood. But not in the way his *agha* meant it. And it was his meaning, not Wadi's, that he took with him when finally they threw him onto the ground and five men struggled to carry him back to his cell. When he wouldn't stop shouting. When he wouldn't stop praising.

— FOURTEEN —
The Passage Hawk

They did not come for him again for several days, although he could not know in a world of perpetual night. They brought him his broth and murky water and he drank it, or poured it out, as he chose. His excrement he smeared on the walls, on himself. The martyr had been covered in it, so he was too. It did not concern him but it concerned the guards, who tried several times to drag him from his hole. Cursing, at last they succeeded.

He crouched on the corridor flagstones, naked and filthy, muttering. He kept looking back, waiting for the others. But no one joined him in the light. They preferred to remain in the darkness.

At last he became aware of someone standing before him, calling him. He looked up, saw a man whose name he had known but could not remember.

'Vlad,' the man called gently.

He looked down again, returned to his muttered prayers.

The man's voice came again. 'Maybe we have gone too far,' he murmured. Then, louder. 'Take him to the *hamam*. Clean him. Shave him. Not like that! Gently now. Use him gently. Give him fresh clothes and put him to bed in my quarters.'

Vlad watched the young, tall, handsome man walk away down the corridor. Compared to the sallow, thin-faced men who stood beside him, the newcomer looked like an ancient God.

'Hamza,' he croaked.

*

'Where are you taking me?'

Hamza started, turned in his saddle to stare at the youth beside him. These were the first words Vlad had spoken in the week since he'd been taken from his cell. The good treatment that followed – the best of food and drink – once he was able to keep the richness down after his months of gruel – the daily bathing, the softest of silks to sleep beneath, under the warmest coverlets – all were received with the same downcast eyes, the same silence. He talked, but only to himself; at least, Hamza saw his lips move. But no sound emerged. Till now.

'I do not take you, my young man. You accompany me.'

Vlad lifted his gaze – another beginning. 'Then I am free to ride the other way?'

'Well . . .' Hamza tipped his head, smiled. 'But why would you choose to do that when I promise you such fine sport.'

He gestured back, beyond the six mounted servants who followed them, to the three wagons. From the first jutted and swung all the paraphernalia of the camp: cook pots, tent poles, canvases and carpets. The second clinked with every sway, filled with the jars and barrels that would make the camp pleasurable. But it was to the third wagon that Hamza was referring. Its thick coverings were stretched high over frames then pegged down, sealing the interior from light. They could not contain the sounds though, the screams that had begun as soon as they left Tokat and, half a day later, had not abated on this road to the mountains.

Vlad glanced. 'What are they?'

'Can you not tell from the screeching? Ugh!' Hamza blocked an ear with a finger. 'Sakers. Eyases, taken from the nest last summer and kept badly by the fool I bought them from. They may be beyond redemption but so may we all.' He looked across. 'Shall we give them a chance? Will you help me redeem them, Prince?'

Vlad kept silent for so long Hamza feared he had slipped

117

back again. At last though, he spoke. 'All this . . . to train falcons?'

'That would indeed be foolish. No. I bring them to amuse while we wait. For there are other hawks at our destination, I hope. They are the reason for our journey.'

It was not quite true. The youth beside him was the reason, hawks the excuse.

'And what is our destination?'

Hamza pointed. 'There.'

Vlad looked up. The mountain road had been climbing for a while. Ahead, it rose in switchbacks.

'Ak Daghari. Highest point in this part of Anatolia. We will be there by tomorrow's nightfall.'

'And there we will meet your hawks?'

'If Allah wills it, yes. Men live up there. Strange, barbarous-tongued men from the far north, a place called the Nether Lands – which I think means it is an arsehole of a place.' He laughed. Vlad didn't, so he went on. 'Yet they have a rare skill in the trapping of passage hawks. And they come so far from their own land because Murad, Light of the Land, rewards them better than any Christian monarch would. It is said that if they take three birds in a summer they have earned their fortune.' Hamza sighed. 'But they only went up at the first snow melt and may not yet have been blessed. Still, we will find ways to amuse ourselves, will we not?'

He gestured to the moving mews but Vlad did not reply, simply lowered his eyes again. Hamza regarded him, wondering if he suspected anything. Then he shrugged. It did not matter. All that did with a falcon was that it learned to fly and come back to the fist. And, of course, that it killed before it returned.

There were no birds awaiting them on Ak Daghari's summit. Just three squat, bearded men who stank of the goats they kept and responded to Hamza's gestures – neither could speak the other's languages – with grunts and gestures of their own.

'It's hard to be certain.' Hamza shook his head. 'But I believe they are telling me that hawks have been sighted but not lured.'

'How are they lured?'

Hamza turned, delighted at one of Vlad's rare questions. 'We will go and watch with them . . . though it is a dull trade. Three in a summer, remember? Yet I believe the theory is that they tie a decoy bird to a pole. On a long tether, so it flies and flaps. A hawk sees it, attacks. They are watching from a blind, they drop the pole, spring a hidden net . . .' As he talked, Hamza led Vlad back to the encampment, set up in a defile hidden below the summit. 'But let us pleasure ourselves with what we have, not what we don't, eh?'

He put an arm around Vlad's shoulder. The younger man tensed, until he recognised the first touch in an age that was not a blow.

Two of the wagons had been emptied, their contents transformed into a small pavilion, entirely carpeted, luxuriously appointed with silk hangings on the walls and deep furs and skins across the two divans, one for each of them. Another, larger, rougher tent had been erected for the servants. Hamza led Vlad past both to the enclosed wagon, as yet untouched. There he began carefully to untie the covering's straps. Yet despite his delicacy, the screaming, which had ceased since the wagon was first unhitched, began again.

Hamza sighed, undoing the straps carelessly now, noisily. 'It is the problem with eyases taken from their nests too soon. They scream for their mothers. The passage hawks are so much better. They rarely scream; and, of course, they already know how to kill.'

Lifting the covering, he beckoned Vlad inside, then followed him, dropped it again. All was dark until the gate of a lantern was opened and a light spilled out; faint, but enough to reveal the source of the screaming – two falcons sitting on perches, their hooded heads bobbing as they tried to locate the source of the disturbance. One began to flap, slipping to the limit of its jesses, hanging upside-down, wings wide and flapping.

'Chk. Chk. My pearl. My jewel. Easy! Rest!' Hamza clucked soothingly, and he pulled on his glove.

It was the sight of it, of the poem carefully stitched in gold upon the finely-tooled leather, that brought Vlad's circling mind, which had sped up and slowed, sped up and slowed ever since he'd watched a countryman impaled, to a complete and final halt. It did not show on his face, though his body gave a little shudder. Yet when he spoke it felt, for the first time in an age, that it was him speaking and not someone else.

'You wear it?'

Hamza turned, hearing the difference in the tone. Saw, even in the poor light, that the younger man was actually looking at him now, not through him. He smiled. 'Always. If my house were to burn down, I think this is what I would seize before I ran.'

He began unwinding the jesses from the still-flapping bird, clucking all the while. 'This one is called Erol – "Strong" or "Courageous". A name given but not yet proven, eh, my beauty?' As he spoke he slipped the bird free of its perch, managed to get it onto his fist where it gradually settled when Hamza produced a piece of raw meat. He nodded towards another glove and Vlad slipped it on. 'That one is for you. A female, so bigger. I think she will never be Sayehzade, the beauty Mehmet lost to you at *jereed* and never sent. But she may serve the Sultan well.' He smiled. 'Her name is Ahktar. It means . . .' His bird began to flap again. 'Be still! Find your courage!'

'Star,' said Vlad, finishing the naming. But as he unwound the jesses, just before he drew the saker onto his fist, he whispered the word again, in a different tongue. One of the very few words he'd spoken aloud in months.

Ilona.

The falcons had had little training, just enough to sit on a fist and take mutton from the finger. So, for a couple of days, the two men spent their time inside the wagon, feeding the birds, talking to them. On the third day, the birds were taken outside and walked about, although they remained hooded. Two days later, at dusk, hoods were taken off for a time, which was expanded on subsequent evenings. Soon they began walking about the camp, out along the banks of a snow-melt stream, Vlad imitating Hamza: taking the hoods off; re-hooding; turning the birds as they walked; forcing them to re-sight. And each night, after they returned the falcons to their mews, they returned to their pavilion, to good, simple food, a glowing brazier and Hamza's talk on the training of birds and other philosophies of life. Vlad listened, but spoke little.

By the tenth dawn no birds had been taken on the mountaintop. But it was time to fly the ones they had.

'It is the hour of risk,' Hamza said, as they went out in the gentlest light of morning. 'We hope the bird will know us enough, trust us enough to return. But there is only one way to be certain.'

They climbed to another, almost bare peak, with just a few trees for cover. Hamza had selected it carefully and they stopped a few hundred paces short of the summit.

'Shall the Courageous One fly first and prove his name?' Hamza said, and immediately began loosening the jesses. Then, gripping them only lightly in his fingers, he removed Erol's hood. The bird blinked repeatedly, eyes swivelling to take in the sudden expanse. Hamza fed it a small piece of meat. Then, he lifted his arm and flung the bird. 'Fly, Baz Shah,' he cried, naming it for the Persian King of Falcons. 'Fly!'

The bird flew. Low to the ground and fast, making for the

summit and its few trees. They lost its dark shape there, and neither of them breathed for what seemed an age. Then Hamza stepped forward, circling the rabbit skin lure at the end of a long rope, whirling it, calling loudly, 'Come, Baz Shah. Come, Courageous One! Return to me!'

For the longest moment, nothing stirred. Then, a black dot detached itself from a branch, transformed from speck to bird by pure speed. And when it struck the lure, it pulled Hamza to his knees.

Erol began to feed. 'Praise be to Allah,' Hamza cried, delighted. They watched the bird rend and tear for a little while. Then Hamza stooped, took its jesses, lured it onto his fist with easier meat. Standing, he beamed at Vlad. 'Your turn.'

Vlad stepped forward, loosening the straps that bound his bird to him, and he to her. Slowly, he took off the hood. The saker, like the other, blinked, gazed around.

Vlad kept his voice low, so only the bird could hear him. 'Go, my beauty. Go, my . . . star!' And, on the word, he flung out his arm.

They watched the shape change from bird, to dot, to nothing as it slipped over the crest of the mountain. They watched it go and Vlad, sensing it, didn't bend to lift the lure.

They waited for a while until finally Hamza said, simply, 'Oh.' He turned to Vlad. 'It happens. To the best of us. To the best of birds. The first time is the riskiest. It . . .'

Vlad began to walk quickly down the hill. Hamza ran to catch up with him, and was surprised at the expression on his face. Not the tears he expected. Something that all his jokes, talk and enthusiasm had not brought. 'You smile?'

'Yes.'

Hamza shook his head, his voice touched with anger. 'Is it because it is the Sultan's falcon? Do you punish him? Or is it that you do not care?'

Vlad stopped, looked up, still smiling. 'But I do care,' he said. 'Ilona is free.'

Hamza frowned. 'Ahktar,' he corrected.

'Oh yes,' Vlad nodded, moving off again. 'Her, too.'

FIFTEEN

Initiation

Two men awaited them at the encampment. The first was one of the incomprehensible trappers. He brought with him his first success.

'A goshawk,' Hamza cried, delightedly, taking the trussed and hooded bird, examining her carefully, a grey-blue stillness in his hands. 'Female, and I would say two years old by her weight.' He looked up. 'The Cook's Bird, they call the goshawk, Vlad. For what it brings to the pot – it will kill again and again and stop killing only when it is exhausted. Her eyes will already be showing a tinge of pink. By the time she is nine they will be entirely red. Filled with the blood of her victims, it is said.' He smiled. 'The Sultan will not grieve for his missing saker when he sees this beauty.'

Then the smile went as he saw the second visitor, a man who seemed made of road dust, so entirely did it cover him from turban to toe. 'A messenger from Murad,' Hamza murmured. Handing the goshawk back, he gestured the trapper towards the mews and beckoned the messenger into his pavilion.

Vlad, holding Erol now, accompanied the bird-catcher. He struggled to contain the saker. Hooded, too, it could not see the goshawk but it could sense her and, shrieking, it dropped from Vlad's fist, pulling to the limits of its jesses, wings flapping.

The goshawk went into a separate compartment. Vlad was helping to secure the mews flaps when he heard soft footsteps behind him. He turned – in time to note the worry on

Hamza's face, swiftly displaced by neutrality. 'News. I have been summoned back to Edirne and . . .'

Vlad, feeling his heart skip, guessed at Hamza's concern and interrupted. 'And you return me to Tokat,' he said, his voice harsh.

Hamza shook his head. 'No. I am to bring you with me.'

Vlad, concealing his relief, studied the face before him, the trouble veiled in it. He would not ask about it, for the moment. 'Do we leave now?'

'At dawn,' came the reply. 'It is sooner than I hoped, for your sake. I think you are still . . . tired.' A smile chased the frown from the face, 'At least we do not return with an empty fist, eh? But with news of the fine passage hawk that will follow us, Allah's gift for Murad.' He rested a hand on the younger man's shoulder. 'So tonight, to celebrate, we will feast.'

The servants built a fire on the banks of the stream that flowed down the mountain. Water was heated in the large cooking kettles and poured into a wide, shallow hole that had been dug into one bank and then lined with tanned camel skins. At the point where the stream looped, a natural pool had formed.

'First, the cold plunge. Come,' said Hamza, beginning to strip off his robes.

'Must I?' said Vlad, reluctantly pulling off his sheepskin coat, eyeing the green-tinged ice-melt. Though spring's warmth lingered in the day, dusk brought a reminder of winter.

'It is not my *hamam* in Edirne, to be sure – to which I invite you on our return – but it will do. Besides,' he said, reaching forward to pull off the *gomlek* that was halfway over Vlad's head, 'just because we are camping with goatherds doesn't mean we have to smell like goats.'

And with that he planted a hand in Vlad's chest and sailed him backwards into the pool.

He had been cold in the dungeon hole. This was a different kind of chill, sudden and intense. He tried to climb out but Hamza had leapt in, blocking his escape. 'Camel-fucker, it's cold!' yelped the Turk. But when Vlad tried to surge past him he pushed him back. 'Wait! The more you suffer here on earth, the greater the delights in paradise.'

They lasted a minute, turning blue, teeth rattling. Finally, Hamza stood, looking down. 'Come,' he said, 'before our manhoods disappear entirely and we are fit only for work at the *harem*.'

A short stagger to the hole the servants had dug for them, a different kind of pain. The heat was almost unbearable and despite their shaking they could only lower themselves into the water slowly. Eventually, they were up to their chins, steam rising about their faces.

'Ah!' sighed Hamza, inhaling the heated air, fragrant with added oils, bergamot, sandalwood. He reached down. 'That's better. My wives will not have to seek another to satisfy them.'

'How many wives do you have, Hamza?'

'Only two, praise be to Allah. I am allowed two more by His will, and I could take concubines in addition if I desired it. I do not. Women!' he shouted suddenly, tipping his head back. 'Blessed are they and a joy to our nights, surely. But the days . . . Mercy, how they will talk! On and on, for hours. About nothing at all!' He looked across. 'Do you not find it so?'

'I . . .' Vlad flushed. 'I have never . . .'

'What? Never?' Hamza sat up, stretching his arms out along the edge of the pool. 'No tavern girl? No cast-off concubine luring you behind her shutters?' Vlad shook his head. 'And there's Mehmet, with his six women . . . no, five actually, since one went mysteriously missing.' He looked across but Vlad could not read anything in the look and kept his own face still. 'Mehmet's already a father and . . . you and he are of an age, are you not?'

126

'I need take Mehmet's example in nothing,' Vlad said forcefully.

'You do not like him.'

'I hate him. He is a bully and a brute and he . . .' Vlad hesitated. There was something he hadn't yet been able to ask. 'My brother, Radu. How does he fare?'

Hamza closed his eyes, slipping his whole body in once more. 'Well enough, I believe. Mehmet has been . . . gentle with him.' He opened his eyes again. 'But you should not dismiss Mehmet with easy words. Bully? Perhaps. Brute? Sometimes. But he has a mind as educated as yours, dreams as large. And always remember – he will have the power, one day, to do something about them.'

'You remind me that I have none. That I am a mere hostage,' Vlad replied bitterly.

'Another easy word, mere. There is not such a thing. You are a hostage to something important. A prince. A power.'

'But not power like Mehmet's.'

'Ah no.' Hamza shook his head. 'And mark this, my young man: with that power, Mehmet means to conquer the world.'

On these words he clapped his hands. A lurking servant appeared, carrying kese mitts. But instead of entering the pool to scrub his master's back, the servant handed the scouring cloths to Hamza and retired.

'Here,' said the Turk, passing a cloth over. 'Sometimes it is necessary to get our own hands dirty to get our backs clean.'

He crossed the pool, slid in behind Vlad who tensed. But the strokes that came were not lascivious but rough, direct, as brutal as any *tellak* in the baths of Edirne. His muscles eased under the pressure. When Hamza offered his back, he returned the favour with a vigour that brought groans.

After a while, Hamza reached up, took Vlad by the wrist, halting him. 'Come, my young man,' he said softly, 'to other pleasures.'

*

Their pavilion had been transformed. The plain sheepskins they slept on had been rolled back, serving as bolsters to beautifully woven Izmiri kilims Vlad had not seen before, dazzling in their shades and patterns. Between the two couches a low table had been set up. Lanterns glowed in the corners, while braziers burned scented oils. The tent was deliciously warm after the chilling walk back from the pool, and thick, silk-lined robes awaited them, along with lamb's wool slippers.

Hamza clapped his hands and servants brought food. This was different from the plain fare they'd eaten so far: goat meat again but herbed kebabs rather than stew; a rich pilaf studded with pistachios, raisins, dried apricots; breads filled with poppy seed jam, encrusted with rosemary and glazed with honey. And instead of the clear river water they usually drank, they sipped sherbets of orange and pomegranate.

To Vlad's mind there was only one thing missing and it was his lingering look into an empty cup that provoked Hamza's question. 'You crave wine, do you not?'

'Crave? No. Desire? Well . . .' He shrugged.

'What was the Koranic verse you quoted so beautifully at the *enderun kolej*?'

Vlad cleared his throat. The Arabic came easily. ' "They will ask thee about intoxicants and games of chance. Say: In both there is great sin as well as some benefit for man; but the evil that they cause is greater than the benefit that they bring." '

'Do you believe that?'

'No. But I am not a Moslem. Besides . . .' He paused.

Hamza leaned forward. 'Besides, many Moslems do not abide by the law. Is that what you were going to say?'

'Perhaps.'

'Including, Murad, Asylum of the World, our Sultan, who loves the wine, some whisper, even to excess.'

'But you, Hamza, do not?'

'I do not. But it is not so much about the Prophet's words,

128

though I honour them.' He smiled. 'I simply do not like the effect it has upon men. Some become sloppy, sentimental, loose of tongue. Others seek to fight for no good reason.' He leaned back. 'No, if I am going to break the commandments of the Holy Qur'an, I believe there are better ways of doing so.'

Vlad frowned. 'What ways?'

Instead of replying, Hamza clapped his hands. Servants came instantly and cleared the remnants of the meal. One brought forward a small brazier, another a metal pot, a third a flask. They bowed, then left.

Hamza had delved into a pouch. He pulled out a brownish lump, held it up, displaying it between finger and thumb.

'What is it?' asked Vlad.

'Other pleasures,' murmured Hamza, reaching forward to crumble it into the heating pot. 'Hashish, from Lebanon. Do you know it?'

'Yes. No,' replied Vlad. 'Some boys in the *kolej* went to certain houses in Edirne, but I . . .' He shook his head. 'What is it like?'

'A dream.' Hamza tipped in liquid from the flask. 'This is a distillation of the fig,' he said. As the pot heated, he added other things. Vlad could scent nutmeg, clove. Hamza stirred silently and, after a little while, took the pot off the brazier. Then he dipped a bronze ladle in, poured the liquid into two small cups. He lifted both, reached one across.

Vlad sat back, thrust out his palm. 'I think not.'

Hamza did not lower the cup. 'I offer you only a temporary oblivion. A dream, Vlad. An escape from now. Nothing more.' When Vlad shook his head again, Hamza continued, softly, 'I can only guess at the horrors you have undergone at Tokat. I begged Murad Han to allow me to journey and end them. This cup will help the healing.' He nodded. 'Trust me.'

He offered the cup again. After a moment, Vlad took it. Hamza lifted his own. 'To dreams.'

Vlad followed Hamza, sipping slowly till the cup was

drained, enjoying the tastes, those he knew, even the slight bitterness that he did not. 'May I have more?' he asked, holding out the cup.

Hamza took it, put it down. Lifting the brazier, he carried it to the corner of the tent. 'Wait,' he said. 'Lie back.'

Vlad did. For a while, his limbs, which had not even eased in the heat of the water, still held him rigid. Then, quite suddenly, they gave, sinking him into the soft cushions. His mind was clear, though. Very clear. Other than that, and his sudden ease, he noticed no difference in himself, nor any of the excesses students from his *orta* had whispered about.

He began to feel cheated. 'Is there not something else?'

'Wait. And . . . look!'

Hamza gestured up. Flames from the brazier's intricate grille made moving shapes on the canvas ceiling. Vlad stared, focused, lost focus. He felt he was both observing the shapes and beginning to float amongst them.

A voice came. Seemingly from far away. Yet it was clear, pure, like a silver bell striking in a church. 'Do you see them?'

'Yes,' Vlad said, his own voice loud to him. 'Stars.'

'Stars?' came the reply. 'I was talking about the camels.'

'What camels?' But suddenly he *could* see camels. Two of them, heads close, humps merging and multiplying. And then he was laughing, at the grotesqueness of it, the beasts' plain stupidity. And the laughter was like a limb that had been long unused, coming into life. Once begun, he couldn't stop, didn't want to. He looked across at Hamza. His face! Every part of it had expanded – the beard, the nose, the eye sockets, the extraordinary blue of the eyes. Yet it did not stay the same, did not remain as Hamza. There were other faces . . .

His father's. His Saviour's.

'No,' Vlad said, trying to sit up. He shook his head, and then another wave of laughter took him. Just Hamza was there, though his teeth were as big and yellow as a camel's in his mouth. 'You promised me oblivion,' Vlad cried. 'I want oblivion! It is my right as a prince!'

'Right?' Hamza cried. 'I have your right right here.'

And with that, laughing wildly, he threw himself on top of Vlad.

A collision of limbs. Arms wrapping, fingers gripping, slipping, finding, losing. Hamza was tall, long-limbed, those limbs like steel coils. Vlad was shorter, compact, his strength centred. They strove for dominance, weakened by laughter, then suddenly beyond it, serious, excited by each throw, each tumble that scattered the cushions, blood pounding in their ears like *kos* drums.

Hamza had him, one long leg thrust through Vlad's, hands gripping his wrists, pushing down, nose almost touching nose. Then Vlad felt the surge within him, caught it, focused it, used it, twisting up, pushing back. He reached a pivot point, thrust over it, and it was Hamza who was below now, his arms on the carpet, his face a finger's width away, so close Vlad could see, even in the half-light of the tent, the fine green spirals in the Turk's cobalt eyes.

They ceased struggling, striving. Held the position, the look. And then Hamza managed to push up, just a little. Just enough to lay his lips upon Vlad's.

'No.' Vlad released the limbs he held, sat up quickly. But he couldn't find the strength to move away, nor to stop Hamza slipping in behind him, hands sliding around his chest, holding him there. 'You are so alone, Vlad,' Hamza whispered. 'Always. You have been through so much. Here. At Tokat.'

Suddenly, Vlad was sobbing. 'I saw . . . terrible things. I did . . .'

Words, memories, tears choked him. 'I know,' came the voice, Hamza's voice, yet not. His hand, not his hand, reaching down.

'No,' said Vlad again, trying to halt the sliding hand. But he didn't have the strength, the will, to do more than say it.

'An end to aloneness, Prince,' said Hamza, and bent Vlad over the cushions.

It was not quite the oblivion he'd been promised. It was dark, the place he slipped into, but he could still feel, a little hurt; later, a little pleasure. And hear too, the voice that said he loved, that asked for love in return. Hear the voice that replied – his own, not his own – saying, 'Yes. Yes, I do. Now. For ever. I do.'

SIXTEEN

Abode of War

They rode at first light – Hamza, Vlad and three of the guards. The camp would be struck behind them, follow at its own pace. The Sultan's summons were urgent. If they rode fast, slept little, and horses were ready at caravanserai along the way, they would be in Edirne in five days.

They rode fast, pushing their mounts to the limit, never beyond it. The speed of their passing prevented conversation and, during their roadside respites, Vlad prevented it again.

'My young man,' said Hamza, stretching out a hand as they lay upon their blankets at the first sunset.

Vlad, wordless, wrapped himself tight and rolled away, offering nothing but his back.

They rode through a land on the cusp of spring and preparing for war. Like the streams that flowed down from snow-headed mountains to join the rivers, their small party was a trickle that soon merged into a flood of men and beasts. The Sultan's '*tug*', his standard of six horsetails, had been raised before his war tent at Edirne and many nations' warriors were surging towards it. Beneath the tails, silver bells chimed. It was said their soft music could be heard from the furthest islands in the Aegean to the pyramids of Egypt. From the mountains of Tartary to the oases of the Sinai desert. It was a summons to the *dar ul harb* – the Abode of War – and it echoed through the passes of Transylvania, down the stone corridors of Carpathian castles, through the courts of kings and the palaces of bishops. The Grand Turk is coming, the tiny bells warned. Know it and despair.

Hamza may not have been able to get Vlad to raise his eyes. But he lifted them at his own bidding, to take in the wonders and begin the tally of his enemies, to know them as his father the Dragon had bid him. Everywhere he looked there were horses – tall, lean mounts from the plains of Anatolia; small, shaggy beasts from the mountains. The former were ridden by *sipahis*, Turkish knights, men of higher rank who would ride into battle in mailcoats and iron helms but here wore the robes and turbans of their homes. They would ignore anyone beneath a Sultan who passed them on the road. The latter were ridden by tribal men, often Tartars, wild with slanted eyes who would consider being overtaken a challenge and would gallop past their party again and again, claiming triumph in shrill ululations, clashing swords on shields, or signalling with a flight of arrows that would pass uncomfortably close.

Stream became river became flood, and progress ever harder. When, at noon on the third day, they were halted at the bridge of Ilgaz, the only way over the River Gokirmak, blocked by a thousand milling, cursing horsemen, Hamza called a halt until nightfall. When the moon rose they resumed, riding all night and well past dawn, repeating the plan at the equally swollen crossing of the Sakarya.

At each halt, Hamza tried to talk. Not of what had happened between them. It was obvious Vlad would not discuss it. But words on hawks, on war, on weaponry all elicited the same response – silence. Only when they were standing on the banks of the Bosporus, on a cliff above the little port of Uskudar, did Vlad speak. One word.

'Constantinople,' he murmured.

Hamza followed his eye-line downstream. The city was a hazy vision of towers and walls in the dusk light. 'Do you dream of visiting it one day, my young man?'

He expected his question to be ignored as ever. He was surprised. Twice.

'I dream of praying . . . there' – he pointed – 'before the altar of Santa Sophia.'

'Indeed?' Though he himself prayed the required five times a day, he had never once seen his companion bend his knee. 'And what will you pray for there, Vlad?'

The younger man turned. For the first time in three days, those green eyes fixed upon his elder's. 'Salvation,' he replied.

Disconcerted, Hamza looked away, back to the dome of the great church, glowing in evening light. 'You know it is the dream of Sultans to turn Santa Sophia into a mosque,' he said. 'And with the Greeks getting weaker by the year, losing their territories, abandoned by allies, betrayed by their own . . .'

But Vlad was already moving away, leading his horse down the steep path to the dock and the waiting ferryboat. Hamza glanced back once at shimmering Constantinople, sighed, and followed.

Two mornings later, they crested the last hill before Edirne, expecting to see the city . . . and saw another city before it. The river of Islam's warriors, rallying to the horsetail standard, flowed here into the turbulent sea of the war camp. It looked like chaos. The outer areas were a jumble of small tents and horse-lines where the *gazis* camped, as wild-eyed and shaggy as their mounts, fired with faith, fermented asses' milk and the paradise that awaited them either in life or death. The neighing of war steeds was not the only animal cry, for vast lines of camels coughed, spat and trumpeted, donkeys brayed their complaints, and mange-ridden dogs howled and fought.

At first, there was order only on the roadway they descended, one of four that separated the sections of the camp and had to be kept clear for the Sultan's messengers riding in from every corner of his and his enemies' realms. But after a long ride through the multitudes, they came at last to a barrier. It was made of red silk and at it their written summons were examined by a heavily armed officer. They were waved through.

The silk palisade separated chaos from order. Beyond it, the tent city was laid out in precise, concentric circles. At first the tents were smaller, plainer towards the outside but as they rode deeper in, these became larger, more opulent pavilions, spread with rich and colourful hangings that could sleep a hundred men but, Vlad knew, mostly only slept one – the *belerbey*, the provincial governor, around whose tent his *sipahis* gathered in their more modest ones. Each pavilion had the governor's standard before it, the number of horse-tails upon it rising as they swept down the avenue. When they saw one with five upon it, they were halted again, this time by a huge officer in a tall, conical hat surmounted by the heron-plume headdress, the *kalafat* after which Vlad's *jereed* horse was named. From the back of the hat dangled the red sleeve that denoted the man a member of the Bektashi order of Dervish. He and six soldiers searched Hamza and Vlad thoroughly, hands roughly probing under their garments, removing their boots and confiscating their daggers. Finally, they were allowed to pass.

'Janissaries,' commented Hamza. Unnecessarily, for Vlad knew the Sultan's elite soldiers well, had trained with them as hard in matters of blade and blow, bow and horse as ever he had studied Latin and the Holy Qur'an in the *enderun kolej*.

The janissary tents were lower, two-man cones of hide, spreading around their own commander's pavilions. These were big enough . . . but nothing to what Hamza and Vlad approached now at the very end of the road; of all roads, for the four spokes of the wheel ended here – at Murad's *otak*. It was a vast and gorgeous palace, held up by three huge poles, enormous silken sheets concealing every scrap of canvas, each depicting an array of trees and flowers like the most luxuriant of gardens.

And there, before its entrance, stood Murad's *tug*, his war standard. Beneath its six horsetails dangled banks of silver bells, giving out the sweet chimes that had rallied the hordes of Islam to their chieftain and made their enemies quake.

Murad was going to war. And lying on the ground beside Hamza, reverencing the *tug*, Vlad wondered two things.

Who this power was to be directed against?

And how any force on earth could stop it?

SEVENTEEN

The Offer

They sat, cross-legged on the ground, and watched the shadow of the *tug* move across the ground. It shortened across the west, vanished at noon, reappeared soon after, slipped towards the east, while *beys*, soldiers and slaves strode, marched or scuttled in and out of Murad's *otak*. They were not forgotten; water was brought at noon, a skewer of meat and bread. But they were not summoned until the shadow had almost touched the eastern-most tent ropes.

A servant appeared, beckoned. Groaning at the stiffness of his limbs, Hamza rose, brushing dirt from his clothing. Vlad squatted for a moment longer, breathed deep, then rose, too.

It was hard to tell the Sultan at first, such was the throng. *Sipahi* horsemen in boots and riding robes, janissary captains in breastplate and mail, the *atecibari*, chief cook of the army, with his symbols of office, spoons and bowls, swinging from his girdle, indicating to all that their father, the Sultan, would feed the whole army on the campaign. The chief cook's presence was as vital here as any illustrious warrior's.

And then Vlad saw Murad, conspicuous because he was, as ever, so inconspicuous in a simple, dark blue tunic that fell to his knees. He stood at a table of charts and lists, at the centre of a throng of officers. To his left, a goldfinch to his father's sparrow, stood Mehmet.

The man who was Sultan, and the man who had been and would, Allah willing, be again both looked up as Vlad and Hamza entered. Mehmet immediately looked down again but Murad held Vlad's gaze until he knelt and pressed his forehead into the carpeted floor.

'Enough for now.' Murad's voice came softly to the prone men. 'All may leave.'

'Father—'

'All, my son. But you may return . . . with this man's brother.'

'He does not wish—'

'I care not for his wishes. I want him here. Now.'

The voice had not lifted in volume. But all could hear the strength in it and reacted. Gaudy slippers came into Vlad's lowered sight, pausing. He caught the faintest whiff of ginger and sandalwood, then Mehmet was gone.

Another pair of slippers. Plain leather. 'Nephew.'

'Eye of the Storm,' replied the falconer, reaching forward to kiss the slipper.

'Prince Dracula.'

He had been readying himself to kiss in his turn. But Murad's use of a title he had never used before made him hesitate. Then he leaned forward, kissed, more fervently than he had planned.

The slippers moved away. 'Rise. You'll both take some wine?' Murad returned to the table, waving away a servant who came forward, lifting the pitcher himself. Behind him two archers, with an audible creak, eased the grip on their bowstrings. 'Ah, not you, Hamza. Your obedience to the word of the Most Merciful is a rebuke to us sinners. Alas!' He turned to Vlad. 'But you will not shame me further by making me drink alone?'

'I will not.'

'Good.' While a servant brought Hamza a mug of sherbet, Murad poured two goblets then brought both forward. 'Drink deep, Prince,' he said, handing one across.

Vlad sipped. The wine was as good as he expected it would be; a nectar after six months of denial.

139

Murad drank, watching him. 'Drink deeper. I think you will need to, to hear the news I must tell you.'

The goblet was halfway to Vlad's mouth. He halted it. 'What news, Sultanim?'

Murad looked at Hamza. 'You have not told him?'

'As you wished, *enishte*. And even if I had chosen to disobey . . .' He glanced across at Vlad. '. . . No time seemed appropriate.'

'Indeed.' Murad raised an eyebrow, catching something in the falconer's tone. He looked again at Vlad. 'Well then. It is my misfortune to be the bearer of sad tidings. I hope you will forgive the messenger.' On Vlad's silence he sighed, and continued. 'There are two things I must tell you, Prince. The first is that your father is dead.'

Vlad only moved a leg, shifting it forward to brace himself. 'How did he die?' he asked softly.

'He was beheaded.'

Vlad, braced, raised the goblet, drank deep, then spoke. 'How?'

All knew he was not enquiring after mechanics. 'Hunyadi ordered it.' He waited for a reaction. None came. 'Hunyadi,' he repeated, 'the Hungarian White Knight they call him, which, considering the blackness of his heart, his cruelty, his treachery . . .' He broke off. 'But you were raised to consider him a crusader hero, were you not? The Scourging Flame of Christendom?'

Still Vlad did not react. Murad glanced at Hamza again then went on. 'But it matters not what you thought of him before. Nor do you need to accept my opinion of my enemy. You need only learn why you should hate him yourself. And learn it from one of your own.'

He gestured. There was movement at the entrance. Vlad did not turn, just kept staring at a point above Murad's head, at a poppy curling in silk there. Only when a man came into the edge of his vision, a man he had not seen for many years, did he turn.

The newcomer was dressed, in contrast to the robes of the Turks, in a heavy, quilted doublet. Sweat shone on the high dome of his forehead, running into the white hair that circled the temples like a ruffled fringe.

'Do you remember . . . I am sorry, titles in your tongue confuse me. You call your noblemen *boyars*, yes? But he is a . . . *jupan*? Is that correct? Yes? Good. Cazan *jupan*. You may not know that he has lately been your father's chancellor.'

The man bowed. 'Prince Vlad.'

The fact that this man also addressed him as prince added to Vlad's confusion. There was something else here, beyond a father's murder. But before he could think what, Cazan was kneeling before him, unrolling the large misshapen bolt of red cloth he held, speaking again. 'Vlad, Dracul's son, from your unhappy land I bring you the prayers of its citizens and this hope for all our futures.'

Satin gave way to steel. Lying in the cloth was a State seal and a sword. Both bore the same symbol, cut into the metal. The Dragon, its tongue thrust out, its scaly tail curled up and around its neck, the cross of Christ resting on its back. And it was seeing the mark of his family that made Vlad realise what was amiss.

'You have brought these to the wrong Dracula, Cazan,' Vlad said, keeping his voice low and even. 'You should present them to my elder brother, Mircea.'

The *jupan* swallowed, hesitated, looked up at Murad. 'And that is the second thing I must tell you,' the Sultan said. 'Your brother – Mircea – is also dead.'

'Beheaded?' Vlad tried to keep his voice even but it cracked slightly.

'Alas, no.' Murad nodded to the other man. 'Tell him, *jupan*. Drink this wine and tell him.'

The goblet was brought over by a servant. Cazan gulped, spilling liquid down his doublet. Wiping his mouth, he turned back to Vlad. 'It was . . . before your father was caught, Prince,' he said. 'Mircea was alone in the palace at Targoviste. All knew that Hunyadi was coming with the man he wanted upon the Wallachian throne – your cousin Vladislav, of the Danesti clan. So the *boyars . . .*' He swallowed. '. . . Some *boyars* killed the few guards left, dragged Mircea from his bed and . . .'

He looked up at Murad who nodded. 'Yes. He needs to hear it all.'

'They blinded him first,' Cazan went on in a rush. 'Red-hot pokers in the eyes. And then they . . .' He broke off, coughing.

'And then they buried him. Apparently, he was still alive when they did.' Murad shook his head. 'Barbarians.'

Cazan wiped his eyes, then bent to the objects before him. 'And so I bring you your father's seal and his sword. Offer them to you, last hope of the Draculesti.'

In a movement as sudden as all his others had been slow, Vlad bent and seized the sword. It was heavy, long, a hand-and-a-half, and when he put his second hand upon it and lifted it high it felt as though a missing limb had been suddenly restored. He remembered now that his father had called it the Dragon's Talon.

'Wait!'

Murad's command halted the arrows that would have killed the man who raised a weapon near the Sultan. In the silence that followed the shout all that could be heard in the tent was the creak of tent rope and bow-string.

Then Murad spoke, softly. 'This is your father's sword, Prince. Yours now. I knew him, a little. We made war upon each other. We made war side by side. For a while we made peace, to both our benefits and our peoples' rejoicing. He was, as much as any in these dog days, a man of his word. He was trying to keep that word when Hunyadi, the black-hearted White Knight, cut off his head and buried your brother alive.' He began to move slowly forward. 'The sword you raise now Dracul would not have raised against me but

142

against his real foes – the men who have usurped his throne. Your throne now, if you will take it.'

He reached Vlad, his hand still raised to hold off the arrows. 'I cannot crown you Prince of Wallachia. That can only be done in your own land, by your own people. But I can give you an army to command. And while I go into Serbia to confront that hated White Knight, you can go to your homeland and use your father's sword to claim what is yours. The throne. The heads of murderers and traitors.'

Vlad had held the sword pointing straight up into the roof, unmoving. Yet now, from weight, from suppressed grief, it began to shake. And Murad, beside him, reached up and gently took it, his hands replacing Vlad's, which slowly fell to his side.

'What a weapon,' Murad said, tipping it to the torchlight. 'I think the sword masters of Toledo exceed even the Damascene in the art.' He looked at Vlad beside the shining blade. 'When a *bey* is made a commander in my army, he is given a *tug*, so that his men will follow his horsetail to victory. But you do things differently in your lands, do you not?' He turned. 'Hamza? When a knight is made in the land of the Franks, does he not kneel and receive the blade upon his body?'

'Yes, Sultanim. Have we not read of this in the great legends of Kral Artus, whom the prince calls Arthur?'

'We have.' Murad lowered the sword, till its tip stood on the carpet, resting his hands on the great curved quillons. 'Shall I give you your command in the same way, Dragon's son?'

All looked at Vlad. His green eyes were downcast, as unmoving as his body. He did not acknowledge that he had heard. Suddenly all became aware again, of tent rope and bow-string.

And then Vlad moved. Dropped to his knees, head bent, neck exposed, arms wide to the side. His voice, when it came, was steady, strong.

'Give me your commands, O Pillar of the World. Lend me your strength, so I may be avenged upon my enemies.'

Murad smiled and raised the sword. As Hamza said, he knew the stories of knighthood, the three strokes of the sword that honoured the Christian Trinity. So he laid the blade flat on Vlad's left shoulder and said, 'Take my strength, Vlad Dracula, Prince of Wallachia.' He raised the blade, lowered it upon the other. 'And I name you *Kilic Bey*, for your mighty sword, and all shall know you as such in our army.' He raised the blade again, brought it down to rest on the dark, thick hair. But before he could speak the final words of blessing, a voice interrupted.

'Vlad! Vlad!'

Vlad turned, the weight of steel still on his head. In the entranceway of the tent stood Mehmet. Before him, with the Turk's hands upon his shoulders, stood Radu Dracula.

The boy had changed in the half-year since Vlad had seen him. He had grown, had nearly reached his brother's height. His brown hair, which had always fallen loose upon his shoulders, was now curled and oiled in the Greek manner. He was dressed much like the man who held him, in a red brocade waistcoat extravagant with gold thread, *shalvari* swathing his legs in deep, cerulean blue.

There was something else about him, in the way he stood, the way he bore the hands that rested on him, as easily as his elder brother bore the steel upon his head. In the long moment of that first stare, Vlad saw what it was. How both surviving sons of the Dragon had succumbed to the Turk. And in the moment of swearing an oath to Murad, he swore another to himself. How he and his would never be powerless again.

Murad lifted the sword. 'Rise, *Kilic Bey*.'

Vlad rose. Radu was released. When he'd first called, it seemed as if he would fly into his brother's arms. Now he moved slowly across, arm extended. 'Brother, are you well?' he said, his voice moving between high and low.

Vlad took the extended arm at the elbow and each clasped the other. 'Well enough, brother.' Still holding him, he turned to Murad. 'Most Mighty, may I ask for my first recruit? His blood, as mine, cries out for revenge.'

He could feel Radu start to shake. He would have known for a while now, about his kin, while Vlad was learning the lessons of Tokat. He would be readier than Vlad himself to act.

But he had mistaken Radu's upset. His brother's arm began to withdraw and he grasped it tighter, tried to keep him. Then he saw it, in eyes like his own, and heard it too in Turkish voices, of father and son.

'He stays with me.'

'Alas, prince, we must keep one of you.'

He let Radu's arm slip, watched him cross back to the comfort of Mehmet, who was making no effort to hide his triumph. One Dracula would ride at the head of a Turkish army. One would remain, a hostage still . . . and something more. And as Vlad looked between the Sultan and his heir, as he gazed for a last time at his brother, he repeated his oath to himself but spoke different words aloud.

'When do I leave?'

EIGHTEEN

First Reign

Targoviste, December 1448, nine months later

Ion Tremblac stood twenty paces before the gates of the Princely Court in Targoviste, staring into the rain. It fell in sheets, had long since transformed his cloak into a sodden lump of wool. He had stood there as the storm approached in clouds that obliterated the stars, in wind that came first as caress and finally as blows that made him stagger. When the storm broke, the few other observers fled. He could not until all hope was gone. If he kept his vigil, withstood all that God threw at him, perhaps the Almighty would relent and send the messenger.

But the Western Road was empty. No man with any sense would be upon it tonight. Only someone with a pressing need and a message to deliver. Bringing either hope or despair.

Ion reached up, pushed aside the sodden hank of hair that hung into his eyes, pulled it back, a gesture as natural to him as breathing and the reason he kept his hair so long. It was not the brand of a criminal he bore upon his forehead; but it *was* a brand and he hated it.

There! A rent torn in the clouds by the swirling wind, a glimpse of moonlight, snatched away. But in its momentary glare, he saw a horse rear up, heard a whinny of terror. The beast skittered in a circle, then plunged on towards the gates. Ion, in the thrill of answered prayer, had only a moment to leap aside. Just before the gatehouse the rider struggled to command the maddened beast. Finally, the horse settled and its rider slumped down across its neck.

'What news, friend?' Ion came forward, took the dangling reins, a hand raised to stroke, to calm.

'Only that it is a cruel night, Ion. And that we should all be in our beds.'

He'd expected a man and a stranger. He was twice wrong. 'Ilona,' he cried, reaching up, helping her down. He held her with one arm as she slumped wearily against him, called for a groom again and again until finally one appeared, a boy of no more than ten. Handing over the reins, he said, 'See to this horse.'

The boy, his shoulders hunched against the storm, his eyes wide, seized the reins, ran off. Putting his arm around her, Ion half-walked, half-carried Ilona into the lee of the gatehouse.

'You are soaked, Ilona.'

'Strange,' she murmured, 'I don't know why.'

Then she laughed. That laugh, first heard through latticed walls in Edirne a year before, had never been forgotten by the man who looked at her wet face now, so different from the one he'd first glimpsed and instantly loved as a barge carried it away from him. No paint now, nothing plucked, framed by hazel hair that fell, soaked and unbound, shadowing hazel eyes. As with the laugh, it was not a face to forget. Ion hadn't. And he suspected that the man upstairs, for all his cares, hadn't, either.

'Come,' he said, taking her arm, 'we must find you dry clothes.'

She resisted the pull. 'Is he here?'

'Ilona—'

'Is he?'

'Yes. But he won't see you. He won't see anyone but messengers.'

'He'll see me,' she said, moving towards the great wooden doors. 'If you tell him who it is.'

Ion did not follow. 'He's different, Ilona. So much has happened to him. Things he won't talk about. And now he waits to hear if his army marches for him or against him. If he will still sit on the throne at midnight, having sat upon it for less than two months.' He stepped closer, reached for her hand. 'Wait for a better day.'

'I have waited for those two months to be summoned,' she replied. 'Two months with nuns, praying and stitching, stitching and praying. God's life,' she laughed, 'I understood why I should not ride through a land at war, that my prince had other concerns. But now, one way or another, that war may be ending. No better day will come.'

He tried again. 'Your clothes . . .'

'If he will not see me, I will change them. If he will see me . . .' She shrugged. '. . . Well.'

Whore, he thought, pushing past her suddenly, throwing open the doors that smashed into the walls beyond. What could he expect? They'd rescued a concubine, hadn't they? What was that if not a whore?

Then he slowed, let her catch up, though he did not look at her, not even when she tucked a hand under his arm. For he remembered how the whole of Dracul's court had tried to corrupt her in the year since the captain had delivered her. The Dragon was one; had her appointed Maid of the Chamber to his own wife to keep her accessible. But Ilona had gently, firmly denied all, from the Voivode down . . . down to Ion. In desperation, he had even asked for her hand, a great honour to a tanner's daughter from a *boyar*'s son. He had been gently, firmly refused. She had been waiting for one man. For one night. This one.

As they passed through the palace, Ion was aware of two things. The emptiness of corridors that should be thronged with soldiers; and a certainty growing within him that the man who waited above would reject what all others had desired. He had not lied when he told her Vlad had changed. When it was proven, when she was rejected, Ion would be waiting. Suddenly filled with hope, he began to walk more swiftly.

At least there were guards still outside his chamber, two nervous youths who lowered their halberds as soon as they rounded the corner. 'It is I,' said Ion.

The halberds were raised. 'Pass, my lord.'

There was a chair to the side of the door. Ion took Ilona's hand, lowered her into it. 'Wait here,' he said. 'Keep her here,' he added to the guards. Then he knocked on the door. After a while, he heard a grunt within. He pushed it open, stepped through, was about to shut it again. Then didn't, left it ajar.

Vlad stood at the table where he'd stood most of the night, his weight resting on fists placed either side of a map. He had long since lost feeling in the knuckles. But he did not move them, offering this little hardship, this small suffering, alongside his prayers. Perhaps the combination would conjure an army from the inked contours of his realm, his Wallachia, spread before him. An army that would rally to the Dragon banner. But the only one he kept seeing, marching from the west, was the army of his enemy, his cousin, Vladislav of the Danesti clan – joined now with his own, the one he'd sent to intercept him.

What had he done? How had he failed? Two months before he'd swept into Targoviste under that same banner. He hadn't even had to unsheathe the Dragon's Talon. The people lined the streets and cheered. The *boyars* knelt before him in the Bisierica Domnesca and swore allegiance. He hadn't been crowned. The Pretender, Vladislav, still had the crown, the circlet of gold that the Prince of Ungro-Wallachia must wear. But his nobles told him he would have it soon enough. One of them, the most powerful, Albu cel Mare, 'the Great', had sworn he would bring it, with Vladislav's head still wearing it, within a month. Vlad had dismissed his Turkish allies, for the Voivode of Wallachia had to stand alone. He had stayed in Targoviste to consolidate his rule, dispatching Albu and three-quarters of his army to the western passes.

That was his great mistake. For though Vladislav and his protector Hunyadi had fought and lost to Murad at Kossovo Polje, the Field of the Blackbirds in Serbia, two months before, Vlad had received no reports of their deaths. He had dispatched Albu cel Mare before he found out they were still alive. And there, on the western reaches of his realm, Hunyadi had his fortress of Hunedoara. There he would have gone, there cel Mare would have met him – and Vladislav Dan. Pretender no more. King again . . . if the man whose boots Vlad heard now was not bringing the granting of his prayers.

'My prince.'

Vlad looked up, tried to read an army in Ion's face as he had tried to find one on the map before him. Failed again. 'What is the word?'

'Nothing new.'

'But I heard a horse. Who came? Or . . .' His voice dropped to a whisper. '. . . Who else left?'

'Someone did come. She . . .'

'She? Who?'

'Ilona.'

Vlad rubbed at his eyes. 'Who?' he repeated.

'The concubine?'

Vlad looked down. For a moment, he just stared. Then he said, simply, 'Oh.'

'She asks to see you.' No reply. Ion felt hope grow. 'She has ridden from the Sisters of Mercy at Rucar, where she has been sheltering with your stepmother.' Still nothing. 'Do you wish to see her?'

Vlad suddenly sat down. Ion could see the swollen redness in the hands that now covered the face. 'No,' came his muffled voice, 'I will see no one but a messenger from the . . . I will see no one.'

'My prince!'

Her cry came from the open doorway, where the two guards were struggling to hold her. 'I told you to keep her out there,' Ion said, stepping forward, arms wide. 'The Voivode will see no one.'

One soldier passed his halberd to the other, bent and wrapped both arms around Ilona's waist. She shrieked, kicked out; the man yelped, squeezed harder.

'Leave her,' said Vlad rising.

'I will deal with her,' Ion said desperately, moving forward. 'Come, Ilona—'

'I said, leave her,' Dracula suddenly roared, 'and leave us.'

'But, my prince—'

Ion couldn't finish his sentence. Vlad's grip on his throat prevented it. He had the taller man up on his toes, fingers like steel bars driving into the skin. 'While I am yet Voivode I will not be questioned, only obeyed. Do that, or desert me like all the others, I care not which. And return only if either a messenger comes from the west or my enemy does.'

With that, he bent at the knees and threw Ion backwards into the guards. The one released Ilona, who sank to the floor. Then all three men stumbled out, closing the door behind them.

Vlad went back to the table, sat, and gazed again at the map before him. Ilona, still on the floor, watched him and, for a time, did not, could not, speak; all she'd planned on saying was lost upon seeing him. Ion had been right. Though she'd only studied him once before, in that moment in Edirne before the boat had drifted beyond sight, she could see that he had changed. The way he held himself. The focus of his stillness. The boy was gone; or rather, she realised in an instant, the boy had been taken away.

'Prince,' she whispered finally.

He started, raising one hand as if to ward her off. 'I'd forgotten you were there,' he said.

'It is different for me, then,' she said, rising. 'Since you offered me a choice in Edirne, there has not been a single moment of any day that I have forgotten you.'

She moved to him and he watched her come, no expression in his huge green eyes. When she stood beside him, she glanced past his face to the map. 'Is all lost?' she asked.

He traced his fingers over the contours of his realm. 'Yes,' he replied softly, then looked up at her. 'You are the first person I have admitted that to. Before I have even admitted it to myself. Why is that?'

"Perhaps because telling anyone else would be handing them a weapon to use against you. But I have no power, so a weapon is useless to me.'

'Perhaps.' He stared down again. 'Do you know Albu cel Mare?'

She nodded, shuddered, remembering the huge and lecherous man kneading bruises into her thigh under the Dragon's table, his wife upon his other side.

'I am almost certain he was one of those who murdered my father,' Vlad continued, 'and buried my elder brother alive in a place I have been unable to find.'

'And yet you gave him your army?'

'I had little choice. The *boyars* side with whom they can gain the most from. I thought I'd offered him enough. So I accepted his kiss of peace, though it burned my face as Judas's kiss must have burned our Saviour's.' He reached up, touched his cheek. 'And he told me what I needed to hear – that he would bring my cousin's head upon a stake.' He shivered. 'While my father's head is lost in some midden, providing scraps for dogs. Dogs like him.'

He lowered his face into his hands. After a moment, she reached for them, moving his fingers aside, laying the tips of hers upon his forehead, moving them through the thick, black hair. Feeling them, he remembered Tokat, her touch in the cell, the brief release of an imagined kindness. The reality of it was different. Not . . . kind. He took her hand, pulled slightly, she bent . . . and water ran from her head onto his.

'Lady,' he cried, standing, 'you are soaked.'

'It comes with riding through a storm.'

'We must get you dry clothes. Come . . .'

He turned towards the door, as she dropped her fingers onto his mouth. 'I do not need other clothes, my prince. I only need to get out of these ones.'

He looked at her and the feeling of the moment before returned, doubled. He pressed his mouth back against her fingers, breathing out, and she ran them over his lips, pushing the lower one down. He bent, lifted her, arms under her knees; hers went around his neck. 'There is a fire here,' he said. 'It will warm you.'

'It will,' she laughed, 'but I suspect you will warm me more.'

'How old are you?' he said, smiling as he carried her towards the flames.

'You asked me that once before, in Edirne. I am a year older than I was then, so seventeen. The same age as you.'

'Well,' he replied, his eyes darkening, 'if experience makes us old, then I am aged beyond my tally.'

'Then we make a pair, my prince,' she said, reaching for the belt around his tunic, 'for I am experienced, too.'

His eyes widened. 'How experienced?'

She laughed. 'Only in some ways of the world. But not in . . . love, except in a schoolroom sense. You prevented that when you stole me, remember?' She removed the belt, dropped it to the floor. 'And you?'

That darkness came again, then disappeared when he smiled. She could see that it was a rare thing, and worth waiting for. 'We make a pair indeed then, lady,' he said, pulling the sodden cloak from her shoulders.

Then he was kissing her, kissing her hard, a young man's kiss. And she, who had been taught a thousand ways to please a sultan, promptly forgot nearly all of them. Nearly all. For, in the house on Rahiq Street, she had been warned about the urgency of a young man's desires, the rush to fulfilment. She'd been told that many men were sad afterwards and she had already seen enough sadness in her prince's eyes to know that when it returned it would return him to its cause – to a family unavenged, a throne won and lost. But for the time she kept him there, before the fire . . .

'Slowly, Vlad,' she whispered, her lips upon his ear. She felt him tense, wondered if her speaking was a mistake. And then, feeling his body ease, she pulled her face back to see his.

He was smiling again. 'As my Star commands,' he said.

Obeying, he stripped her as slowly as she did him, laughing with her when her soaked blouse bunched around her face, trapping her. By the time she'd wrenched it off, though, his laughter had faded. And she saw something else in the fire-glow, something she'd never seen before in a man's eyes. Not lust, she'd witnessed that often enough. Desire – but of the desiring.

'Oh, Ilona,' he said, reaching out. Yet it was she who moved fast now, sliding into him, pressing into his hardness, his every muscle trained and conditioned for the fight; while she was not the waif she'd been when she'd been a Sultan's choice. She was a woman now, and they matched where they joined, soft to hard, silk to steel.

Wet to dry. He moved his mouth over her, his tongue circling, on breasts, belly, down to her inner thigh. And there he paused, breathing deeply, eyes wide. Raising them, look-ing up, murmuring one word: 'Sanctuary.'

'Yours,' she whispered.

He raised his mouth to hers then. Joined there, he lifted her and she wrapped her legs around his hips. He took the two paces to the wall beside the fireplace, pressed her into the tapestry there. He shifted, hovering there like a falcon, the moment before it fell. Until she reached down, clutched him, guided him. And when he sank into her, slower than any falling bird of prey, she gasped, with the little pain, with the delight, the pressing down, the sinking in. On he went, slowly, and when he stopped, when she had him, all of him, she tightened her legs and pulled him in still deeper.

They stood for a while, not moving, eyes wide. Then they began to move, couldn't stop, as all became blur, became frenzy, all she'd learned, forgotten. Suddenly he was lifting her away from the wall and she had to grip him hard at his neck, holding tight as he walked them backwards, laid her down on the table beneath him. She held his head as he rose up to lick her breasts again, circling her hips on him.

He had only dreamed of this before, never experienced it. A part of him, a small part, was separate, marvelling, above the surrender of his flesh. Then he was brought sharply back because suddenly she twisted, spinning her hips around, causing him to cry out in shock and some pain. He was forced from her, watching as she slid before him and lowered her breasts onto the maps.

She looked back over her shoulder, smiling. 'Come,' she invited.

And he was not there. Another memory, another touch – another person, bending thus. Flames moved, casting their conjoined shadows against cloth. Canvas not tapestry . . .

She was expecting delight in the green eyes. She saw something else – that darkness back again, doubled. So in the moment before it swallowed him, she flipped onto her back, pulled him down hard, reaching to slide him inside her again. 'Now, Vlad,' she whispered, biting his ear. 'Now.'

The darkness disappeared. There had been moments when she knew he'd been obeying, taking care. She wanted none of that now.

Neither did he.

NINETEEN

The Fugitive

She'd been right about the sadness.

Afterwards, lying in the warmth of bodies, upon rugs from the Olt valley that were so marvellously woven with flowers they could have been lying on the river's banks and not before a hearth, she felt the body she held so tightly change, revert to what she knew had to be his normal way, a rigid tension. She could feel him gathering himself to rise and held him all the tighter.

'Vlad,' she whispered. 'Prince. What will you do now?'

'Put on my armour. Gather those few who still follow me. Die with my father's sword in my hand.' He spoke coldly now, tried to rise once more.

Again she prevented him. 'Is that the only choice?'

'I cannot see another. I will not flee to the Turk again, to see Mehmet, fresh from his share of the spoils of Kossovo, his hands upon my brother . . .' He broke off, broke free, wrapped a cloak around himself, dropped into his chair.

Ilona picked up his tunic, pulled it over her head, enjoying his scent upon it. She came to him, lifted his long hair aside, placed her hands upon his neck. 'And can you not make peace with Vladislav? You are related, are you not?'

'Cousins. But the Danesti clan hate the Draculesti and always have. As we hate them.' He gripped the arms of his chair. 'And only one of us can have the throne.'

Anger came, as well as sadness. 'Your life is not worth the throne.'

'It is my father's. Mine now. He must take it. But he must kill me to do so, unless I can kill him first.'

'Prince . . .' She moved around, knelt, so she could look up into his eyes, which avoided hers. 'He will not give you the chance. The White Knight, Hunyadi, supports him with all his power. Vladislav has his own army, and probably yours as well, Albu cel Mare at its head. All the other *boyars* will join him.'

'They will. Jackals seeking carrion.'

'So it is not victory you seek. Only martyrdom.'

He glared at her then. 'You question me?'

'Forgive me, lord,' she said, lowering her gaze. 'But when they tell your story after you are dead, do you want it to be the tale of an ass or a lion?' She didn't dare look up, just listened to the sudden harsh breath above her. Then she went on, while she could. 'A lion would bide his time, gather his strength, wait for the hour when the jackals fall out over another carcass – and then pounce.'

She'd gone too far. Knew it in the sounds emerging from the constricted throat above her, the fury about to burst over her. And then she recognised the sound and looked up to see Vlad laughing, his face breaking into unused lines.

'Well, Star of my night,' he said, 'I think perhaps it is Mehmet I rescued and not you, if this is the way you speak to princes. An ass, eh?' He stood swiftly, jabbed his finger down onto the map. 'There, to the north-east. Moldavia, where Bogdan, my uncle, rules. There I can take shelter . . .' – he turned to her – '. . . until the jackals turn on each other again.'

Then they both heard it, the clatter of hooves on cobbles. Vlad went to the fireplace, picked up the weapon leaning there. 'If that is my enemy, then I shall die with this, the Dragon's Talon, in my hand.' He lay the sword down in easy reach. 'If a messenger, confirming what I already suspect to be true, then I will ride for my uncle's court . . . and another chance.'

As he spoke, he was already dressing and beckoned her to do the same. She reached to pull off his tunic, but he stopped her. 'It would be safer for you to dress like a man, for only the storm and St Christoph protected you on the road tonight.' He went to a chest, threw up its lid. 'Here are some more of my clothes.'

They both dressed, as swiftly as they'd disrobed. They were lacing on boots when they heard running footsteps in the corridor, followed by hammering upon the door.

'Stand behind me,' Vlad said, then unsheathed the great sword. 'Come,' he bellowed.

Ion rushed in, stopped when he saw them.

'Are my enemies come?' Vlad asked.

'No, Prince. But a loyal messenger has. He says that Albu cel Mare has joined the Danesti and they march on Targoviste. They will be here before dawn.'

'So.'

Ion looked at Vlad. Then at the woman they both loved. Saw that they were different, both of them. The way they held themselves. Not touching. Not apart. He nodded, took a breath. 'Do we fight?'

'You and me against an army, Ion?'

'A hero's death.'

'No,' Vlad replied, glancing at Ilona, 'an ass's.' He led her forward. 'The victors today will tell the story, and they will not make mine the death of a hero.' He looked at Ion. 'Will you guide Ilona back to the convent, to my stepmother? And then will you follow me?'

'Where?'

'To my uncle in Moldavia.'

Ion shrugged. 'You ask, Prince. You have but to command.'

Vlad shook his head. 'By dawn, I will be a prince no more, but a fugitive on the road.' He reached up to the other man's throat, touched him there on the bruise his previous grip had left. 'A road that is likely to end in some alley, under an assassin's knife. And since I will no longer be a prince, so I cannot command you to such a life, Ion.' He smiled. 'But as a friend, I can but ask.'

Ion reached up and took the hand. 'I am yours, Vlad, as ever.'

'Good.' Vlad shook Ion's hand briefly, then placed Ilona's in it. 'Now go.'

'Wait!' It was Ilona who held back, resisting. 'Is it because I am a woman, and weak, that I cannot also share this road?'

'No,' replied Vlad, 'it is because I love you and if my enemies learn of that they would use you to get to me. I would die, in some room above a tavern, in some alley, trying to protect you. For now, I can only protect myself.'

'Well then,' she said lightly, stepping away, 'I will wait at the convent and pray each day for your swift return.'

He caught her hand as she turned. 'Do not wait, Ilona. If I survive, I will return only when I am strong enough to take my throne back – and keep it.' He squeezed her hand. 'That may take years.'

'Then I will wait the years.' She smiled. 'It is the advantage of serving a mistress who lives in a convent.' She glanced between the two men. 'No temptations.' Raising his hand, she kissed it and, without another word, walked out of the door.

'See her safe, Ion,' Vlad said. 'And catch up with me at my uncle's court, if not upon the road.'

'My prince.'

As Ion's footsteps faded, Vlad gathered a few spare clothes, wrapping them in one of the rugs they'd laid upon. He donned his cloak, picked up his sword, walked down the deserted corridors, noting that his last two guards had fled. Waiting in the shadows of a portico, he watched Ion and Ilona ride out. Then he went to the stables.

Kalafat was there, groomed and fed. Her head jerked up and down in delight at seeing him. Aside from his soldiers, she was the only boon he had asked of Murad. He stroked her golden mane, then saddled her himself. He thought the grooms had all gone but then one, a boy of no more than ten, appeared, tears in his eyes, something rolled up in his arms.

'The other man said to give you this, sir,' he said, before flinging it at Vlad and running out.

Vlad lifted a corner of the dark cloth and glimpsed silver, curved into a Dragon's claw. It was his father's banner, now his, and it had flown for just two months over their palace.

Vlad knelt. And there, in the straw, he made a vow.

'For Almighty God, whom I worship. For my father, whom I loved in life and revere in death. For Wallachia, my land, which deserves better than to be ruled by jackals that fight for the scraps thrown to them by Turks and Hungarians. For all this, and for the blood of the Draculesti, I swear: I will return.'

Then he mounted Kalafat. On a whisper, the Turcoman mare rode into the rain-thick night, taking rider and herself to their unknowable fate.

PART TWO

The Impaler

'I conclude that since some men love as they please but fear when the prince pleases . . . that a wise prince should rely on what he can control, not on what he cannot control.'

— NICCOLO MACHIAVELLI, The Prince

TWENTY

Wilderness Years

Poenari Castle, 1481

In the hall of the castle, it was the woman who had lately been speaking most. There was still a catch in her voice, and what had once lured princes added to the entrancement of the tale. The scribes' pens recorded the words, gave the plain account; but the story expanded in the minds of both teller and listeners. Within them, each of them made for themselves a slightly different version, according to their needs and desires.

All had been startled when the hermit finally spoke. He had commented little before. But it seemed that Vlad had told no one of his time at Tokat; and though the two closest to him had read, in the shadows of his eyes, that horrors had been inflicted there, neither had known what they were – until now. And tears fell as they listened.

However, just as each re-made the story in their own way, so each of them had their own reasons for listening. And as Dracula's first, brief reign ended, each unkinked their limbs and remembered what they were.

Ion had just pronounced Vlad's vow to return. Taking it as a signal, Horvathy rose and made for the table. With a grunt of pain, as he came onto his swollen feet, the Cardinal followed.

Petru signalled his officer to take more water and food into the confessionals. Then he joined the others at the table. 'Is all that true?' he blurted.

The Count turned to him. 'What, especially, Spatar?' he said, through bread and goat's cheese.

Petru gestured irritably at the three confessionals. 'That Dracula came to power on the whim of the Infidels? That he reigned . . . but did not slaughter?'

Horvathy grunted. 'He reigned for just two months, that first time. It takes time to organise a massacre.'

'But the Turk?'

'We all make accommodations with the Turk, young man.' The Cardinal took a deep swig of wine. He was enjoying it more now. It was not the velvet produced near his home in Urbino, of course. But its roughness somehow suited the setting and the tale – which had started to intrigue. 'What did those of the Greek Church say in Constantinople before its fall? "Rather a turban in the Hagia Sophia than a mitre?"' He licked his lips. 'Well, they got their wish. For what some called the greatest cathedral in the world is now a mosque, the Aya Sofya Camii.' He sighed. 'The problem for the Christian powers is that we usually hate each other at least as much as we hate the Mohammedan. What we heard Vlad say upon the javelin field is true – we can come together and take Jerusalem; but we can never stay together long enough to hold it.' He paused, drank again, continued. 'We have always needed something special to unify us.'

The Count studied the clergyman, seeking hope in his words – for the cause of the Dragons; for his own soul's redemption. It was why they were there, to persuade this man, who would then persuade the Pope. 'The Dragon perhaps, Your Eminence?' he breathed, leaning in. Grimani looked up.

'But how did Dracula go from this puppet,' Petru interrupted harshly, through chewed sausage, 'this Turkish catamite,' he spat out the word, 'to the Impaler of legend?'

'If you'll just be quiet, Spatar,' the Count replied, furious, 'I believe that is what we are about to hear.' But when Grimani did not speak, just kept cramming cheese into his mouth, Horvathy sighed and continued impatiently, 'But let me at least fill in some detail, for the record, so we do not live each day of every year of Dracula's life in the wilderness.'

Draining his goblet of wine, he set it down, returned to his chair. The Cardinal followed, scratching his head. 'The wilderness? I thought he fled to his uncle?'

Horvathy faced the confessionals, raised his voice. 'For the record,' he announced, and scribes began to write, 'Dracula's uncle, Prince Bogdan of Moldavia, was murdered by a brother three years after Dracula got to his court, in 1451. Vlad fled again, this time with his cousin, Bogdan's son, Stephen.'

The Spatar smiled. At last, someone of whom there could be no doubt. 'Stephen cel Mare.' He turned to the Cardinal. 'It means "the Great", Your Eminence. And he is. Hammer of the Turks. Greatest of Christian heroes.'

'Indeed?' The Count frowned. 'Or just another pragmatist? For he too has treated with the Turks when he wanted to steal land from fellow Christians. I have fought beside him, against him . . . well!' He shrugged. 'But in 1451 he was just one more pretender with a purse of gold waiting for the man who could bring his head back to Moldavia. As was Vlad – accompanied, I presume, by the man who sits before us.' He looked briefly at Ion's confessional, then raised his voice again for the scribes. 'The fugitives wandered, desperate, near penniless, warding each other's backs from the assassin's knife. Learned to sleep with one eye open.'

Petru shifted in his chair. 'But he returned. Took back his throne as he had vowed.'

'Yes. And by this time he had learned how to keep it, too.'

'How?'

Horvathy looked at the younger man. 'Do you happen to recall what happened in 1453?' he said, his voice thick with sarcasm.

The Spatar noticed the tone. 'Of course,' he snapped. 'Constantinople's fall.'

'Well done! Yes, Murad had died – of apoplexy, after a

drinking bout, it is said – and Mehmet was sultan again. Free to pursue his dream of being the next Alexander, the new Caesar. He prepared long and well, mustered a massive army, brought the best gunner in the world, who built the largest cannon yet seen—'

'Hungarian, wasn't he, Count Horvathy?' the Cardinal interrupted, softly.

'Yes,' came the reply. 'And the cannon was forged by Germans across the border here in Sibiu, while the Serbs sent miners to dig under Constantinople's walls, which Wallachians scaled to the beat of the *kos* drum . . . and the Pope sent not one ship, not one company of soldiers to defend them. So what exactly is your point?'

'Oh, nothing.' The Cardinal smiled, sat back. 'Please continue with your admirable summation.'

The Count grunted, went on. 'There is not much more to tell of the fabled city. Mehmet besieged it, eventually brought down its walls with his cannon, stormed it, ravaged it. The Rome of the East fell. And Christian leaders, who had wrung their hands when they were not sitting on them, realised that an Alexander does not stop with one city, however fabulous. He needs to conquer the world. And that if they did not put aside their quarrels and join together, he would take them one by one.' He licked dry lips. 'It was time for all haters of the Turk to unite.'

Petru leaned forward, excited now. 'And no one hated Mehmet more than Vlad Dracula.'

'Yes. While the man who had stolen the throne of Wallachia, Vladislav of the Danesti, had fallen out with his mentor, Hunyadi, and was now signing treaties with the Infidel. So the White Knight needed a new protégé. He needed Dracula.'

'But . . . but . . .' the Spatar stuttered. 'Hunyadi had murdered Dracula's father and brother.'

'Almost certainly.'

'I must say,' breathed the Cardinal, 'that you of the

Balkans show a . . . *flexibility* in your dealings that would disgrace no court in Italy.'

Ignoring him, Horvathy continued. 'So Dracula swore enmity to the Turk and eternal amity with Hunyadi and *his* liege lord – my own Sovereign, the Bulwark of Christendom, the King of Hungary. With these men behind him, providing gold and soldiers, by 1456 Vlad was ready to try to take back his throne. And with the jackals inside Wallachia falling out over scraps again . . . well, I do not know those details. I was merely saving us some time.' He leaned towards the confessionals, looked at each in turn. 'Who would speak now of the events of 1456?'

It did not need the Count's raised voice for the scribes to know their cue. They put down the quill with the blue ink, waited to hear whose voice would come, whose colour they would need.

The three witnesses had been eating, drinking, preparing. It had not been easy, to relive what had been hard to live once. Each also knew that, if it had not been easy, it could only grow harder. Yet each, in their own way, was ready.

Ion's whirling mind slowed again. 1456! It was his time. Theirs. A time when he and Vlad did all they'd dreamed of during the wilderness years. Both of them twenty-five years old, with bodies hardened by suffering and trained for war. So now he leaned forward eagerly, as his mind returned to a July day, the first battle in which he'd ever fought . . . and a comet burning through Wallachian skies.

'I will speak of it,' he whispered. 'I will.'

Black ink made shapes across the parchment.

TWENTY-ONE

The Comet

July 1456 — eight years after Dracula's exile began

Vlad found the weakness he was looking for, in the man, in his armour. Dropping suddenly onto his left knee, he wrenched the man's dagger hand down, unbalancing him. At the same time he jerked his own hand free, drove his own dagger up, slipping the point into the slight rent he'd noticed in the chainmail at the man's throat. Rivets gave, burst by tempered steel. Flesh was less resistant.

The man tried to cry out but his voice was lost to blood. Vlad, rising, held him so close that he could see eyes through the narrow visor, terror-filled. Then he looked beyond them, turning the body now this way, now that, as a ward against other enemies. He'd been taught that, when you were triumphing in your own kill, you were most likely to die. Since this was his first battle, he wasn't going to dispute it.

Yet beyond the dying man, his comrades were fleeing. Making the choice seemingly as one, like a flock of birds suddenly turning together in the air. No one called; all realised, turned, fled.

He looked again into the visor, saw the light leave. The man was instantly heavy with death. Vlad dropped him, stepped away, dagger held before — but he had no need of it. The enemy ran down the slight slope, round or over the bodies that had filled the bowl-shaped valley in the three hours it had been fought over, up the equally slight slope opposite. The fastest were amongst their comrades there in forty heartbeats.

It wasn't just the blood in his eyes. It had gotten harder to distinguish individual men across the narrow valley. Soon, it would be night.

He looked sharply to the north-east . . . and there it was. Through the reddening sky, low to the land, the twin-tailed comet burned, as it had every night since his army first set out through the passes from Transylvania. His men had hailed it as a Dragon, a sure sign that his cause was blessed. Yet Vlad was certain that his cousin, Vladislav of the Danesti clan, in the middle of his army on the opposite hill, believed exactly the same.

'Prince?'

Vlad turned to the voice. Grouped behind him, as ever, were his close companions: Black Ilie, the huge Transylvanian, hired during the fugitive years as bodyguard, though for most of them he took his wages in wine and food and often little of either; Laughing Gregor, his face now covered in blood, still split with that permanent, gap-toothed smile; and Stoica the Silent, Vlad's body-servant, a mute who did not need a voice to react to his master's every need. All wore mismatched armour, but it was at least black – like their prince's.

It was Ilie who had called him, the man's voice rumbling from a face so dark it was said he had the blood of Africa in his veins. But it was Stoica who held what he needed: the Dragon's Talon, his father's sword, dropped when an enemy somehow slipped inside his guard and needed to be met with a dagger. He took it, reached up to put it into the sheath he wore over his back, all the while looking all around for the one person he needed most.

'Where's Ion?'

'Here, Prince.'

Vlad frowned as Ion pushed through. 'You are hurt.' He reached out, turned his friend's head. A wound the length of a forefinger ran a fingernail deep from cheekbone to jaw.

'I got careless,' Ion replied. 'I forgot that a man's not dead until he's dead.'

'If I may venture, *jupan*,' said Ilie. 'You're not as pretty as you were.'

'Thank Christ,' laughed Gregor. 'Perhaps the rest of us will have a chance with the tavern girls now.'

Vlad did not smile, his gaze on Ion. 'They fled. And none of our men pursued them?'

'No, lord. I fear the fight's gone out of them.'

'Or the money has,' Gregor added.

Vlad looked along the ridge-line. Aside from his companions, and perhaps five hundred exiled Wallachians, the rest of his army, some six thousand of them, were paid to be there by his backers – the bankers of Brasov and Sibiu, Hungary's King and the White Knight, Janos Hunyadi, Vlad's former enemy, now his ally. Men would fight for gold, even fight fiercely; but only for a time. Many were now taking off their helmets, squatting on the ground, swigging wine. Vlad could see that Gregor was right – they believed they had already earned the gold he'd paid them.

Ion saw the despair in his eyes. 'If it's true of ours it is also true of theirs,' he said, pointing across the valley. 'Just as many mercenaries in the Danesti ranks will feel they have done enough for their wages. They will not come again.' He stepped closer, lowering his voice. 'We can wait till nightfall, then slip away, rally in the mountains.'

Vlad had been looking above Ion, to the comet, brighter even in the few moments that they had talked. He felt that he had ridden its twin tails into the heart of his country. It was still flying towards his enemies. 'Are you so anxious to be a fugitive again? For if we go back now, if we disband this force, that's what we'll be. And our chance may not come again.'

'But it may,' urged Ion. 'While here . . .' He gestured to the field, its dead.

Vlad turned again to it, then looked beyond it to the standard of the Black Eagle on the hill opposite, to the south. Unlike Vlad, Vladislav had not once left its shadow to fight, just sent his men to die.

His gaze shifted to the smaller hill that made up the eastern side of the valley. Other standards flew there. Some of the *boyars* of Wallachia fought for the Danesti. A very few, exiles like himself, served in the ranks of the Draculesti. Many, the most important, had merely watched from that hill, taking no part; eating, drinking, commenting. Amusing themselves with the spectacle of two cousins fighting, not too concerned about the result. Whoever survived they would accept as voivode – until another, more generous leader came along.

'My sight's blurred,' said Vlad, reaching up, wiping sweat from his eyes. 'Who still sits up there?'

Gregor followed the pointing hand. 'Albu the Lard . . . sorry, "the Great". Codrea. Gales. Udriste . . .'

'All the most powerful, Prince,' Ion interrupted. 'Waiting, watching, not moving . . .'

'Wait,' said Black Ilie, stepping forward. 'See who's stirring his fat arse!'

Vlad looked. Horses were being ridden down the slope. One rider carried the bear's head banner of Albu cel Mare. Another a simple white cloth.

'They call for parley,' Ion said.

'To arms,' called Vlad, 'in case of treachery.'

His companions and a few others responded. Most ignored him. The squadron, some twenty strong, rode across the valley and up their slope in moments, then reined in ten paces before them. In the middle of the horsemen, under the two banners, sat a huge man astride an equally vast destrier. He lifted his helmet.

'Albu cel Mare himself,' Ion spat. 'The man who took your army and deserted eight years ago.'

'I don't think I'll mention it now,' murmured Vlad.

The big man reined in. 'Which one of you is Dracul's boy?' he shouted. 'I haven't seen him since he was a puny cub.'

'Here I stand,' said Vlad, stepping forward.

'Hmm.' Albu sniffed, turned aside to a companion and, in a voice not much lowered, said, 'Hasn't grown much, has he?' Then he turned back. 'Dracula *jupan*,' he said, addressing him as 'lord' only, 'it seems this day ends in stalemate.'

'The day is not yet done, Albu *jupan*. Why not join with me and end it?'

'Strange,' laughed the mounted man, 'but that is exactly what your cousin just asked me to do.' He leaned down. 'And I told him what I now tell you: it is just so hard to choose between the spawn of Mircea the Great's line. Why should I favour one until he proves himself?'

'Is this not proof enough?' Vlad pointed at the bodies behind the horsemen.

Albu did not even turn. 'Dead mercenaries? No.' He sighed. 'But war is not good for our land, or our coffers. We need a voivode who has proved himself strong enough to hold the throne.'

'Why not you, Albu cel Mare?' Vlad said softly.

'You know, everyone asks me that.' He scratched his chin. 'Too much responsibility. Too many . . . meetings. I prefer to advise, to influence . . .'

'To stay on my estates and fuck sheep,' muttered Gregor.

Ilie laughed. Albu heard that, not the words, but his face hardened anyway. 'So which of you is the strongest? Dracula or Dan? Vlad or Vladislav? Since you could not lead your armies to prove it, perhaps you could prove it as men.' He smiled again. 'Let God decide. I suggested it to your cousin and he readily agreed.'

'You wish one of us to kill the other for your amusement?'

'No.' The man's smile vanished. 'One of you should kill the other for the crown of Wallachia.'

It was not uncommon to issue a challenge to single combat to the opposing leader. It *was* uncommon to accept. Ion saw his friend's hesitation. 'Prince,' he said quietly, 'do not—'

Vlad's lifted hand halted the words. 'Where and when, Albu *jupan*?'

The smile grew on the large face. 'Since we are all gathered, and there is yet a little light in the sky . . .' – the smile came again to the large face – 'how about here and now?'

Ion wanted to speak, to protest. But his friend's hand was still raised against him.

'What weapons?' Vlad said.

'Well,' drawled the mounted man, 'how about lances to commence? For form's sake. And then, if required' – he shrugged – 'what you will?'

Vlad barely paused. 'Agreed. One condition.'

'Name it.'

'I will not fight him while he wears the crown my father wore. Put that on the side of the field, as prize for our endeavour.'

'Agreed. Shall we say . . .' He looked around. '. . . When the shadow of that oak there touches the stream. Should give us enough time to clear the field of the wounded and the dead, and for you both to prepare.'

'As the *jupan* wishes.'

'Good then.' Albu turned his horse's head, then glanced back. 'You don't look much like your father. Have you half his skill in the lists?'

Vlad smiled. 'That you will soon discover, Albu *jupan*.'

The *boyar* nodded, put spurs to his horse's flanks. As he rode away, the white banner of parley was hoisted three times; obviously a signal, because Vladislav's eagle was raised high once in response. Immediately, some Danesti soldiers descended to the valley floor, to collect the wounded and the dead; others spread along the crest. On their hill, shouts quickly confirmed the news that had already been whispered and Vlad's army began to do the same – tend to fallen comrades; find a place with a better view.

Now Vlad turned, finally lowering his hand. 'Well, Ion?'

'What is left for me to say?' replied his friend. 'You have accepted the challenge before all. Even if you wanted to leave now . . .'

'I don't.' He looked across the valley, then up. 'It ends today. With my Dragon in the sky above me.' He had started to walk back, over the ridge-line; beyond it, Kalafat was tethered and Stoica was already gathering what would be needed for mounted combat. 'Any thoughts, Ion,' Vlad continued, 'beyond your cautions?'

'Not many,' Ion said. 'Vladislav is a noted jouster, has triumphed often in the lists . . .' He broke off.

'While I, you were going to say, have not had time for tourneys and codes of chivalry.' He smiled, raised a hand to halt the apologies. 'But this is not a decorous tilt, fought for a lady's silken favour. We fight for the crown of Wallachia. My father's crown.' The smile left him and he looked once more at the blazing light in the sky. 'And I *will* take it.'

TWENTY-TWO

Single Combat

'The oak's shadow touches the stream. It is time.'

Vlad rose at Ion's voice. Groaned. He shouldn't have knelt, not even to pray. He had fought all afternoon and though he had not been wounded his body was stiff, strained.

He twisted his trunk from side to side, bent over his straight legs, swung his arms, raised them when he was ready. Stoica came, to dress him again in his black armour. It was only slightly better fitting than that of his companions and there had only been time to hammer out the larger dents. At least Stoica had managed to clean off most of the mud. For years, Vlad had not had the coin to buy a better suit and when money came for the invasion, he had chosen to spend it on other things – more soldiers, for one. And, as he was armed, he noted again that he had none of the special equipment required for the tourney. His shield was solid, you didn't scrimp on a shield – a rectangle of riveted, metal-faced wood, its top edge cut in a curve – but it had no recess to rest a jouster's lance. No extra metal reinforced his armour's left side, where the opponent's lance would likely strike. His helmet was the same he'd worn when he'd come from Edirne to take the throne eight years before – a Turkish metal turban, the neck protected in mail, the face open, not closed as jousters' usually were to protect from splintering lances. Stoica slipped it over his head . . . and then he was finished. Armed. It had not taken long. Ion looked at him and could not restrain a sigh.

Kalafat saw him when he was forty paces away and began

to dance, jerking her head up and down, baring her teeth, giving little grunts of welcome. He rubbed at her ears, clicked his tongue.

'Are you certain you won't take mine?' Ion had offered his warhorse before. It was male, huge. The same as Vladislav would certainly be riding.

And Vlad, not the tallest, would look small upon it. 'No,' he replied. 'This is no time to be learning a new horse's ways. Besides' – he leaned forward and kissed Kalafat between the eyes – 'I have ridden her in a tourney before.'

'I wasn't going to mention that,' muttered his friend.

Ilie came forward, cupping his hands. Vlad placed one foot and the big man lifted him into the saddle. He looked down. 'I told you, Ion. I failed then, in my only joust, because it was for nothing. A lady's kerchief. I didn't even know the lady. I will not fail now.' Touching his heels to Kalafat's flanks, he rode her up the slight rise to the hill's crest.

Both armies had been busy in the short time Vlad had prayed and armed. The valley floor had been emptied of bodies. The sun-warmed, blood-steeped soil had disgorged insects, and swallows darted and turned amongst them. Those men who lived had spread around the valley, the armies mingling, for most of them were mercenaries, re-uniting with old comrades. Only a few atop their hill, a few more atop the Danesti's, held themselves loyal and aloof. Mostly Vlad saw men drinking, eating, laughing . . . and he shivered, looked to the hill opposite, just as cheers came from it, as the Eagle banner was pushed forward. Something gleamed underneath it. The valley ran roughly north to south so neither knight would have the setting sun full in their face. But beams still sparkled on the armour that covered both man and horse, making them seem even bigger. He remembered meeting his cousin a few times, the few times there was peace between the clans of Drac and Dan. Vladislav was ten years older, bigger by a head, experienced in joust, in battle. And he had ruled Wallachia for many years now. Of course he had the best armour!

As he stared, trumpets sounded. A squire rode out, bearing the Eagle banner. Cantering to the base of the slope, he raised the flag pole high then drove it into the ground. He turned, rode back, leaving the Eagle to flap in the breeze among the darting swallows.

'Ilie,' Vlad called.

His standard-bearer rode out from the ranks. The Dragon streamed behind him. When he reached level ground he reined in and brought his horse up onto its hind legs. 'A-Dracula!' he cried, before ramming the shaft into the earth.

'Strutter,' laughed Gregor.

On the higher ground to the left, two trumpeters now stepped out and blew a loud refrain. The laughter and carousing ceased as, between the trumpeters, stepped another man. He too bore a flag, folded around a pole, and as he swirled it out all could see it bore no *boyar*'s arms but was all black.

'To the death!' came the mutter from thousands of throats.

As Ilie rode up, smiling, Ion said, 'What other weapon do you take, Prince?'

Vlad gestured to what Stoica already held. 'The Dragon's Talon. My father's sword to reclaim my father's crown.' The weapon was passed over, slid into the sheath across his back. He mounted.

Gregor passed him a lance. 'Your *kebab*, master,' he said. 'Just needs some Wallachian mutton on it.'

Vlad looked at Ion. 'Any last advice, old friend?'

'Yes,' came the grunted reply, 'don't get killed.'

'I will try not to.'

A bray of trumpets. On the opposite slope, a silver shape began to descend it. At a touch, Kalafat moved, too.

'Go with God, Prince,' Ion shouted, stepping forward. 'But fight like your father – the Devil!'

Silence held as the two horsemen descended. The only sounds Vlad could hear were the sharp cries of swallows as they dived, the whispering of water in the stream, the snap of banners in the breeze. But when he was level with the pole and its Dragon, voices did come, shouting and repeating two names.

'Dan. Dan. Dan.'

'Dracula. Dracula. Dracula.'

Then, as if by some accord, the voices ceased as one. Vlad looked at the man a scant hundred paces away. The Voivode of Wallachia. His cousin. His enemy. The setting sun encased him, turning armour to fire.

Vlad glanced back, up, to the east. 'He can have the sun,' he muttered, 'for I ride the comet.'

A shout turned him back. Vladislav had spurred his horse, stolen ground. Couching his lance, Vlad put heels to Kalafat's flanks.

A fast man could have run it in ten seconds. The horses, trained to the instant gallop, met in two. Sunlight flashed off steel armour, off steel lance-tip. Dazzled, Vlad sought a target, tensed for the strike.

He had never been hit so hard. The sound of it was loud, sudden, a shriek as metal point smashed into metalled shield; followed by silence and redness, and everything moving so slowly within it. His own shield smashing back against him then snatched from his grip, gouging finger-flesh through the glove because he was grasping it so hard; his feet leaving the stirrups; his back on Kalafat's haunches, then off them; his feet hitting the ground first so it almost looked like he would stand up; falling, hard, face into the dry earth; toppling slowly onto his side. His eyes never closed, he could see faces on the hill, mouths wide in some shout he could not hear. But he saw them as if through a red, silken veil. Saw the black flag, lifted straight out by a breeze; not flapping, so slowly did it move.

The earth was moving. He felt it, the vibration, as sound

partially returned – distant shouting, a horse's closer snort. A shadow came between him and the sun, something sparkled and he rolled, so was able to watch the lance-tip plunge into the earth where he'd just been. The point gouged turf then was lifted, gone. He felt the vibration of hooves; a clod of mud hit him in the face and somehow that cleared his sight of the redness, brought back the sounds.

'Dan! Dan! Dan!'

No one was calling 'Dracula' now. It brought him onto his knees. He looked at the brightness moving away from him, saw it resolve into man and horse, pausing now beneath the Eagle banner. There the man signalled, and a squire came running down the hill, carrying something, passing it up. Then the man – his cousin – let the something fall and Vlad saw what it was: an iron ball, studded with sharp spurs, an arm's length of chain connecting it to the staff that Vladislav held.

'Ball mace,' Vlad said, aloud. And saying the name of one weapon made him remember another. As his cousin wheeled his horse and began to trot towards him, Vlad reached up and drew his sword from its back sheath; saw, gratefully, that it had not been bent or broken in his fall.

He was still kneeling. Couldn't rise yet, could only hold the sword angled up before him. Vladislav was forced to bend low to strike, swinging the great ball round and round, finally sweeping his arm over in a great downward smash. Vlad could do nothing but slip to the side, sword angled down to avoid the full force that might break it and to guide the blow away from him. The ball drove into the left quillon, bending the hand guard, but not snapping it.

Then Vladislav broke off the attack, circled wide, giving himself room for the charge. He spurred his horse into it . . . but he had also given Vlad a moment. One to get to his feet, plant them solidly underneath him, shake the last of the mist from his eyes and, when the horseman drove at him again, swinging the ball in a great arc, to step in and not away, sword going square above him, tip dropping into his other, gauntleted hand. It was the chain that met it, not the ball that would have snapped the blade; the chain that, because of the force of swing and charge and the weight of the ball, swung round and around the sword. The moment it stopped, Vlad wrenched hard, threw his whole weight down, and jerked the horseman from his saddle.

In the fall, the strap that had held mace to wrist slipped, and the weapon dropped as the man landed. Vladislav was somehow still on his feet, stumbling forward, hand going to his sword. It was halfway from the scabbard when Vlad remembered that he still held his own sword in two hands; and then recalled, from the days of training with a Swabian fight master, one particular stroke. It had been one of the German's favourites. It had a German name.

Mortschlag.

Taking his right hand from the grip, he put it to the blade, just below the wrap of chain. Then, bringing the weapon over in a high arc, he smashed the point of the unbent, right-hand guard into the top of Vladislav's helmet.

A moment of stillness, neither moving. The only thing that did was the chain, unravelling at last from the blade, the ball falling to thud dully into the ground. And only when it had did Vladislav fall also, as if he would sit, his hand still gripping a sword just halfway out of its scabbard.

Vlad's quillon was still embedded in the helmet. Straining, he twisted and finally jerked metal from crumpled metal. Then he reversed the weapon, took the grip again into his hand. The man before him did not move, head lolling forward. Leaning in, Vlad carefully placed the tip of his blade under the man's visor and flicked.

The visor rose. His cousin's eyes were open and Vlad could see that they were almost the same green as his own. He could also see that life was leaving them; and, even as he looked, a gush of blood flowed down the forehead and pooled in the sockets, reddening the green.

At last, the body fell sideways. Vlad knelt, putting the sword-tip into the earth so he could hang from the quillons, one bent, one straight. Only then did he become aware of the chanting, of a name. His name.

'Dracula. Dracula Dracula.'

He looked around. All seemed to be chanting it. His army. His cousin's. He looked up. Swallows still swooped through the sky between him and the comet, careless of man.

Then Ion was there. 'Vlad,' he whispered. 'Vlad!'

Vlad let himself be lifted up. Others came, his close companions. Ilie hoisted the Dragon banner and waved it joyously. Gregor held Kalafat's reins. Stoica handed him a wine skin and he drank deep. When he was ready, he nodded and the group marched up the hill between the two, now silent, armies, to the place where the black banner stood.

Vlad hadn't noticed it before, because it was so small. But hanging over the flag pole's tip was a slim circlet of gold, unadorned save for an emerald the size of a gull's egg in its centre.

'Your father's crown . . . Prince.' Albu cel Mare came forward, spoke in a different tone. The disdain was gone from his eyes. 'Of course, it means nothing until the Metropolitan places it on your head and you are anointed in the cathedral of Targoviste.'

'It means . . . everything,' replied Vlad, reaching, grasping. He lifted the circle of gold high and cried out, 'I claim my father's throne. I claim his title, Voivode of Wallachia.'

Acclamation came, from all around. From both armies; even from the *boyars*, Albu in their centre – at least, from those that remained, for Vlad could see that some had gone when Vladislav died, to offer their allegiance to the next pretender. But he was scarcely aware of the noise. Turning suddenly he buried his face in Ion's chest.

Few could see. They were surrounded by large men. The

cheering went on. In all their time together Ion had never seen him weep. So he just held him, glaring above his head at Albu cel Mare and the *boyars* and, through his own tears, dared any of them to mock.

TWENTY-THREE

Preparations

The Princely Court, Targoviste,
Easter Sunday 1457, nine months later

'Is all prepared?'

'All, my prince. All that I can do without knowing everything.'

'You do not need to know everything, Ion. And I only know a little more than you. For most is in God's hands, and thus unknowable, is it not?'

Vlad grinned, looking again through the grille he'd lifted from the centre of the door. Standing beside him, Ilona looked away from the view onto the Great Hall below, seen through this meshed window and up at him. 'You are merry tonight,' she said.

'Why would I not be?' Vlad replied. 'Has not the Metropolitan of our realm, Supreme Head of the Orthodox Church, crowned me "the Sovereign ruler of Ungro-Wallachia and the duchies of Amlas and Fagaras"?' Vlad pronounced the titles in a perfect imitation of the Metropolitan's nasal squeak, making Ilona laugh. He turned to her. 'And does not the belly of the woman I love swell with my first boy child?'

'You can't know that,' she said, clutching at herself, feeling a kick. 'And you've had only girls so far.'

'Ah, Ion, just because she's lived in a nunnery for eight years she feels I should have lived like a monk.'

She struck his arm. But she didn't care what he had done in their years apart. He had come back to her, something no one would have believed. He was hers again and their time apart felt like a day.

He winced, smiling still, looked through the grille again. 'And here are my friends, the noblest men of my realm, gathered to rejoice with me. In my happiness. In Christ's Resurrection.'

'Friends?'

'Of course. For do not friends help to achieve one's desires? They are gathered here to do so.' Ilona clutched herself again and Vlad instantly guided her into a chair. 'Rest, my Star. Let Ion stand there and count my friends.'

Ion took Ilona's place, joined Vlad to peer through the spying hole. It was another thing that Vlad had borrowed from the Turk, for it was said that Mehmet spied thus upon his council, the Divan. And below, in the Great Hall of the Princely Court, were gathered the members of the Wallachian equivalent, the Sfatul Domnesc, their wives beside them, some with their eldest sons. If they had ever cared that Vlad might be watching them, that time had long past in two hours of feasting, while the Voivode dealt with affairs of state. Their cups were never empty, no matter how often they were drained. Jugglers and acrobats performed. Musicians played ceaselessly, brought from the Draculesti estates of the Arges valley, playing the peasant music of that region on tilinca flutes, the strings of the *cobza*, the deeper tones of the *taragot* trumpet. The *boyars* largely ignored them, preferring their own braying conversations, their loudly declared opinions – when their mouths were not stuffed with food. Platter after platter arrived – songbirds on skewers, whole pike stuffed with parsleyed bulgar wheat; most especially pig in all its forms. Blood sausages, ears shredded in vinegar, snouts filled with sweetbreads, roasts glistening with crisped fat. If ever there was a lull, any hungry *boyar* or mate could go and take a slice of cheek from the boar's head mounted on a stake in the middle of the room.

The noise had grown from subdued murmurs to ceaseless bellowing. Nobles grabbed at serving girls, ignored by their wives who were busy dodging the flying food.

'Friends?' snorted Ion. 'I see none. Only a few who are less your enemies, perhaps.'

'How very cynical you are, Ion. One would think you'd had a hard life.'

Vlad ran a finger up the long scar on Ion's cheek. The finger tipped under Ion's thick hank of hair, slid into the groove of the brand there, before Ion jerked his head away. 'Voivode,' he said, stepping back, smoothing down his hair. He hated it when his prince was playful. It usually meant something was about to happen. Something he would have to react to.

An especially loud shout drew them back to the grille. A man, noticeable for his huge girth and thick neck, had somehow managed to climb upon the table at which he sat, one at the centre of the feast and raised a little higher than the others. He was attempting some steps, for the musicians were playing a peasant dance, the *mocaneasca*. They could hear the wood creak beneath him, even above the roars and laughter.

'Careful, Albu.' Vlad frowned, his face only easing when the huge man, to a cheer, bowed and descended. 'The Great One is enjoying himself.'

'Why would he not? He is better off under your favour than he was under the usurper. When all thought you would kill him, you made him richer.'

'Of course. Albu cel Mare is a power in the land, second only to myself. Such men must be . . .' He broke off, turned. 'How do I look, Ilona?'

Her love was dressed in a doublet so dark most would think it black. But when he turned into the reed torchlight, its flames showed red in the quilted velvet. The garment, fitted loosely to conceal shoulders and chest grown huge from the ceaseless wielding of weapons, reached to mid-thigh, overlapping the hose striped in alternating crimson and black that gave his legs some length. The only adornment was beneath the left shoulder, where a dragon, no bigger than his palm, was worked in silver thread, its scaly tail curling up to wrap around its neck, the cross of St Gheorghe in red along its spine.

The face itself had shed all its boyish softness in the fugitive years, and his hair fell in thick waves over his shoulders and halfway down his back. On either side of the long nose, his eyes were bright emeralds . . . almost dimming the one he lifted now that sat in the centre of a golden star, itself set into a band of exactly three hundred river pearls – which she knew because she had sewn each one to the brim. The cap, made from the same velvet as the doublet, was crested with an ostrich feather plume.

Her eyes returned to his, to the question still in them. 'Every inch a prince,' she said, starting to rise.

He forestalled her by kneeling. 'You know I'd marry you if I could.'

She laughed. 'Me? A tanner's daughter? You can't. Marriage is another weapon for you, to use against *them*.' She tipped her head towards the hall below. 'Rather you should marry the lady who waits for me outside, whom you have cursed me with.'

'The Lady Elisabeta? If I am to marry a horse, I'd rather it was my Kalafat.' They both laughed. 'But a prince's mistress must have a lady from the court to ward her when . . .' He spread a hand over her belly.

'So it is true. Mistress or not, if we are to have a boy child . . .'

'We are.'

'Then he is able to inherit?'

'It is the law of Wallachia. Countless bastards have ruled here.'

The smile was only in his eyes. She laughed for both of them, sighed. 'Then I will have to put up with my . . . horse.'

Vlad looked up. 'Ion would marry you yet. Wouldn't you, my friend?'

Ion nodded. 'I asked her only yesterday. She refused me for the fortieth time.'

'See,' Vlad said. 'You will still have someone when I am dead.'

Her smile vanished. 'Saint Teresa! Do not say that. Even in jest.' She groaned, gripped her belly.

Vlad turned to Ion. 'Summon her woman.'

He made to lift her; she resisted him. 'No, lord. Let me rest here till you have done all you must do here.' She glanced towards the Great Hall, and looked back in time to see the darkness in his eyes. And something else, close to his expression when they came together in love. A different kind of hunger.

'No,' he said, 'I want you safe at your house. By God's good grace, I will join you there tomorrow.'

'Amen,' she said, troubled. It was the first time he'd expressed any doubt about that.

The Lady Elisabeta came in, unable, as ever, to quite keep the disdain from her equine face. 'My prince summoned me?'

'Yes,' Vlad said, rising, helping Ilona to stand. 'Take my lady back to her house.'

'Prince.' She barely curtsyed, then stepped forward.

But Ilona clung to him, leaned close. 'Be careful,' she whispered.

'Always.'

Elisabeta came, took Ilona's arm, moved with her to the door. At it, Ilona paused, looked back. Her love was settling before the other door, adjusting a short, blue-black cape he had donned. Finished, he turned to Ion. 'Open the door,' he said, 'then go to your post. Wait for my signal.'

They looked at each other for a moment. Then Ion bowed. 'My prince.'

Vlad stared at the door before him. Then he nodded, and Ion pulled the three bolts. They were greased and slid open soundlessly. The door opened, admitting a roar of noise, a forge-blast of warmth. Vlad stepped through. Ion shut the door behind him, leaving it unbolted, turned and walked to Ilona. 'I would accompany you to your home . . .'

187

'To your post, Ion,' she replied, controlling the spasms that were starting to shake her body. 'And I will to mine.'

He bowed, then left.

Elisabeta kept the door open, but Ilona did not pass through it. 'Leave me here,' she said.

'But the Voivode's order—'

'I will watch a while and then call you again,' she said. 'Pull the chair over to that door, and leave me.'

'But—'

'Do as I say.'

'As my lady pleases,' Elisabeta said tightly. She picked up the chair, carried it across. Ilona, following slowly, sank into it gratefully. As the other door slammed behind her, Ilona leaned forward and pulled back the little metal plate. At first, all she could see through the grille was a blue-tinged darkness. Then light came, as her prince began to descend the steps into the Great Hall.

— TWENTY-FOUR —

Resurrection

They did not notice him immediately, so silently did he enter, so intent were they on their guzzling. And he knew that few would recognise him instantly anyway. In the half year since the coronation he had only called the Sfatul Domnesc together once, the day after the crowning. He had sent them back to their estates for the long winter with vague memories of a dark-haired young man who drank little and spoke less. He was sure that if they thought of him at all it was only to compare him unfavourably with his father, the Dragon. Ion had repeated the joke that was being told in castles across the land – that Dracul, even without his head, was a good head taller! Twice the man in every way. This youth would be managed. If he proved troublesome – unrewarding – he would be disposed of. In a land where bastardy was no bar to the throne, another bastard could always be found, another puppet to spin in his strings while the great men divided up the spoils.

He knew what his *boyars* thought of him. And as he walked among them, dispensing wine from a flagon he picked up, unnoticed as any slave would be, he thought of them again. This class of men who cared little for their country and nothing at all for their prince. Who bent their knee to God, then violated every one of his commandments. Who believed that the sacrifice Jesus made this day – a life-sized, bloodied representation of which hung above the fireplace – was to give slaves hope and thus keep them quiet while their masters thrived. In former days, Wallachia had been the crossroads of the world and the world's wealth came to the land. No more. Not since brigands and thieves had made the roads impassable to all but small armies. And the chief criminals sat around his table now, faces glistening with pig grease and crimsoned with wine.

They stand between me and my dreams, Vlad thought, pouring another cup, unnoticed still. Tonight I must step over them . . . or not.

He swallowed, suddenly unsure. He looked up to his reassurance; to Ion, appearing at the archway entrance to the smaller hall, where the nobles' bodyguards feasted with Dracula's. Ion was looking at him now, eyebrows raised.

It had to be done. More, it had to be seen to be done. Power, without its demonstration, was power wasted. It was not only the Holy Qur'an he'd learned at the Turkish court. Besides, he thought, running his tongue around his lips, I have waited a long time for this night. I am going to enjoy it.

He looked again at Ion, shook his head, then turned his gaze to the only other man who had been watching him from the moment he entered. He was the *guslar*, the singer of ballads, who also commanded the musicians. Wondering for a moment if a ballad would ever be sung about this night, Vlad nodded.

The music ceased mid-bar. Yet such was the roar of conversation, it took a while for anyone to notice. The Lady Udriste, sat at that one slightly raised table, tired of the conversation her husband was having about boar spears, finally looked up . . . and started. Her father had died the previous year, been buried in red and black, and she had seen his spirit three times since. He appeared to have something he wished to warn her about but she could not hear him. However, when she realised who the man was, she tugged at her husband's sleeve. Irritated, he turned, followed her nod. Whispered to the man next to him.

The roar reduced to a series of whispers, thence to silence. Vlad, standing with head lowered, the slightest of smiles upon his lips, let the silence linger for a few heartbeats before he spoke.

'Welcome, noble *boyars* and fair ladies, bishops of the Holy Church. Welcome, all my loyal countrymen come to share this day with me, this holiest of holies. When Christ rose again in all his glory and gave us the gift of eternal life. Praise him!'

Amens echoed around the hall. Vlad continued. 'I know that we have prayed together this day. I saw you all drink his blood in the Bisierica Domnesca. Praising him' – he gestured to the crucifix, Jesus bloodied upon it – 'asking him to forgive our sins. Praying too for another resurrection – for Wallachia to be once again a strong and powerful land. Free of the lawlessness that impoverishes us, where a man cannot ride a mile from his home without fear of brigands. For justice within our borders and no fear of those outside them who seek to use us as fuel for their war fires. For prosperity that is our right, shared amongst our people, not gathered into a few hands or sold to foreign merchants for a pittance. For one land, united under a strong prince.'

Vlad paused, looked the length of the high table, before adding, softly, 'At least, that is what I prayed for. What about you?' He lifted the flagon, stepped between a nobleman and the lady who'd first noticed him, poured wine into both their goblets. 'Did you pray for all this, Manea Udriste?'

The *boyar*, his thin face poking out of an ermine collar three sizes too big for him, smiled. 'Of course, Voivode. For all these things. And for your continued health.'

'Ah, how loyal of you.' Vlad moved on, poured again. 'And you, my *vornic*, Codrea? Did you pray for your special concern, justice for our land?'

The *boyar*, his jowly, porcine face flushed with wine, nodded. 'As chief justice, my prince, I live by its code.'

'Of course you do.' Vlad moved to the centre of the high table, glanced across it. If the man who'd just answered was corpulent, the one opposite was enormous. He occupied nearly three places, his wife half as much again. It was not only his deeds that gave him his name 'the Great'. 'And you, Albu cel Mare? Were your prayers also as noble?'

'I think they will suffice,' came the reply, the tone bored. 'And I usually get what I want. But you know that, do you not, Dracul-*a*?'

It simply meant Dragon's *son*. But all knew it should have been preceded by a title, heard the emphasis on 'a'. Further down the table, someone giggled. Smiles came, some hidden again, as the two men, young and older, slim and fat, stared at one another.

'You get what you want, Albu cel Mare.' An equally slight emphasis on 'the Great'. 'Of course you do. You recently got the villages of Glodul and Hintea, did you not?'

'They bordered my land.'

'They do now.' Vlad tipped his head to the side. 'And the people who lived in them?'

Cel Mare snapped his fingers. 'Vanished. It was such a surprise.'

'Indeed. Vanished like the gold from the monastery at Govara.'

'Oh no.' The big man leaned forward, his smile broadening. 'That is in my cellar. When the monastery mysteriously burned down it was my Christian duty to give its gold sanctuary.'

He'd glanced up at the crucifix while he spoke, crossed himself. More laughter came, less restrained. And Vlad, looking around the hall, joined in.

Above, shocked, Ilona pressed closer to the grille. Her prince would sometimes smile with her. It was a rare thing, worth waiting for. But he laughed so rarely. And never before others. She curled her fingertips into the mesh and felt a pain push her inside.

Below, the laughter faded to silence. Vlad leaned forward, filled the goblet before him. 'A toast to that then, Albu. To

Christian duty.' The big man did not pick up his wine. 'Do you not drink, my lord?'

Albu smiled. 'I will if you will.'

Vlad pointed at the small metal trees positioned every few paces down the tables. The light from the single candle atop each of them glistened in the tiny pieces of red flesh upon them. 'Do you not trust the fruit of the tree, my lord?'

Albu grunted. 'Snake tongues hung on languiers are one thing. Many say that they can detect poisons. But nothing detects it better than a man drinking what he offers.' He nodded to the flagon in Vlad's hand. 'Will you drink?'

'Of course. What was the toast? Ah yes, Christian duty!' Vlad lifted the flagon, drank, wine spilling round the wide rim. After a moment, Albu took a sip, then put his mug back down.

'Duty,' murmured Vlad. 'I wanted to ask you something. All of you.' He looked the length of the high table, then around the hall. 'How many princes of Wallachia, in your lifetimes, have you pledged your duty to?'

Men glanced away, avoiding his eyes. Only Albu did not lower his. 'Princes?' he said, his voice strong. 'I've lost count. Ten? Twelve? It's hard to remember. They come and they go.'

No one laughed now. 'They come and they go,' echoed Vlad. 'And you remain.' He looked around again. 'All of you remain.' Then he looked back at the man opposite, spoke now so softly that those at other tables had to lean in to hear. 'There's another story I heard about you, Albu. That you were there when my brother Mircea died.'

A hiss of breaths. Everyone stared at the two men, who stared at each other. 'It is not true,' the large man replied.

'No?' Vlad inclined his head. 'Then my informant was mistaken. For he said you were there, along with my loyal Manea here, and my dispenser of justice, Codrea.' He glanced briefly at the two men, who flinched, murmured denials.

'Prove it, Dracula.' Albu cel Mare had pushed himself away from the table so he could look about the hall. But there were no guards to be seen. Only thirty *boyars* and some of their sons, his own included. Each had a carving knife before him. And there was Dracula, alone, with nothing but a flagon in his hand. Albu, seeing all, eased back, smiled again. 'Prove it.'

Behind her grille, Ilona cried out. The pain had come again, doubled, intense. She knew she should call her maid. But she could not leave. Not when she saw her lion surrounded by so many jackals.

'I wonder if I could,' Vlad said softly, laying down the flagon, reaching to the corner of the rich, red damask cloth, one of several that covered the high table, rubbing a gold tassel between his fingers. 'Possibly not. But if I cannot prove who was there, perhaps I could prove another story I heard – the manner of his dying. For I was told that he wasn't beheaded like my father. That Mircea was tortured, had his eyes burned out . . . and then was buried alive.'

'I heard that rumour, too, Prince,' said Chief Justice Codrea, glancing uneasily between the two men. 'I looked into it, as was my duty. Of course, it was impossible to investigate fully because, alas, his coffin was never found.'

'You are right. It never was . . .' Vlad looked across the hall, nodded once at Ion, then looked down again to the piece of cloth in his hand. '. . . Until *now*.'

On the word, Vlad bent and ripped the table-cloth aside. Goblets and cutlery, flagons and snake-tongue trees rose to soak, strike, smash. And then all saw that the noblest of guests had not been dining on a table. They'd been dining on a coffin.

— TWENTY-FIVE —
'Christ is Risen'

All was chaos. The screams of women and men; chairs thrust back hard, bodies tumbling over them; platters and candlesticks crashing to the floor. Cursing *boyars*, many now with knives in their hands, had bunched before their wives. Only Vlad had not moved, stood there still, staring down.

A bull's roar cut through the tumult. 'What do you mean by this, Dracula?' Albu shouted.

Vlad looked up. 'I saw you dancing before, Albu cel Mare. Strange you did not know you were dancing on a grave. A grave you helped to dig.'

'I will not stay to be accused by you,' Albu shouted. He turned to the central archway that led to the other hall. 'Miklos!' he bellowed. 'Bring the men. We leave.'

All, save Vlad, had turned to the archway, so all saw one man walk through it. He was dressed in a white doublet, marked with a bear's head, sign of his allegiance to Albu cel Mare. 'Miklos!' yelled his lord. 'Where are the others?'

The man in the archway didn't answer. Instead he looked from his master down to the front of his pure white doublet. And as he did, it turned red, flooded from within. Something dropped from beneath it, something he tried and failed to catch though he joined it soon enough, collapsing into his own entrails.

More screaming masked the sound of men marching into the galleries above; drowned the sound of bow-strings being drawn taut. All saw them though, how the thirty picked men – Dracula's *vitesji*, as they were called – were dressed in the colours of their master, their black and crimson surcoats emblazoned with a silver dragon. Since an arrow was now aimed at every male chest in the hall, the men there slowly lowered their knives, dropping them onto the floor or table. Only two knives remained in hands – Ion's, dripping red, as he came forward wiping it on his sleeve; and the one Dracula now drew.

'Codrea,' Vlad called.

The *vornic* jerked, shrank back into his wife. 'My . . . my . . . my prince?'

'You said that, had you been able to find my brother's coffin, you would have investigated the crime more fully?' Vlad laid his fingers on the wooden lid. 'Will you help me investigate it now?'

'But . . . but . . .' Codrea swallowed. 'It . . . it is ten years since Mircea's unhappy, uh, disappearance. 'What could . . .' He flicked his fingers at the coffin.

'If it is true that my brother was tortured, his eyes put out, before he was buried alive, there may be some signs of it.'

'S-s-signs, my prince?'

'Shall we see? Your knife, Codrea. No, no, pick it up. Help him, Ion.'

The *vornic*, sweating heavily, was dragged forward, made to grip a knife. Vlad stuck the point of his dagger into the crack of lid and wall. 'You begin that side.'

The nails were gouged out, one by one, Ion doing most of Codrea's share. When all were thrown aside, Vlad looked once around the hall, then placed his fingers under the rim and lifted it, just a finger's width.

There was an immediate breath of something foul. Not rotten, the worms had long since done their work on flesh. But decayed, like improperly salted meat. 'Hmm,' said Vlad, trying to raise the lid further. 'Something's stuck. Ion, Codrea. Gently now.'

The three men lifted. Screams came as the wood rose, something rising with it – two skeletal hands, their fingers joined to the lid as if welded there, as if whoever within was helping to push it up. Then, suddenly, something snapped and the hands fell back in with a clatter of bones.

Standing the lid upright, Vlad looked at its interior. A single finger joint clung there and he reached, touched for a moment, then snapped it off. 'Splinters,' he said, peering closely. 'They must have fused his hands to the wood, especially after his nails kept growing. See?' He held the finger joint higher so all could see the yellowed, curling nail. 'I know Mircea kept the nails of his right hand long, for he was a wondrous player of the lute. Not this long, though.' He turned the joint into the light. 'Strange to think what beautiful music this finger once plucked from a string.' He placed the bone carefully into the coffin, then ran his fingers along the inside of the lid. 'And these lines here, Codrea. Gouging, wouldn't you say? What would you, my Chief Justice, conclude from that?'

The *vornic*'s eyes were wide, his jaw slack. 'That . . . that he was buried alive, my prince. And tried to scratch his way out.'

Vlad nodded. 'I agree. A reasonable conclusion. So,' he said briskly, looking around the hall, 'we now know how he died. But before? What else can you note, *vornic*? Come, you can't investigate from over there. Help him, Ion.'

The man was dragged forward again, one of Ion's hands behind his neck, bending him over the coffin. 'What do you see?' Vlad continued. 'More than my brother did, undoubtedly. For though the jelly has long since melted, this scraping in the eye socket, this flaking bone, this blackening. I would say . . . an iron bar, heated to redness, thrust in, held too long? Is that what you *see*, Codrea? A man blinded before he died?'

'Merciful Christ!' Codrea yelled, trying to jerk away. But Ion was massive, strong, and had him pinned. At his nod, Ilie and Stoica, clad also in black, came forward. Each took a limb.

'Indeed,' said Vlad, moving to the reed torch in the central sconce, placing his knife tip in the flame. 'Christ is merciful. But Mircea Dracula did not receive mercy. And neither will you.'

'No! No! No! No!' Codrea screamed, as Ilie and Stoica bent him over the coffin. The scream rose in pitch as Vlad, quite slowly, slipped the heated knife-tip into the first eyeball, holding it there a few seconds before slipping it into the second.

Two of the watchers fainted, a man and a woman, smashing onto the floor, where Codrea joined them, screaming, palms of hands pressed into what remained of his eyes. 'Take him outside,' Vlad said. 'His coffin awaits.'

No one else moved, as the two men grabbed him by the ankles, dragging him through the central arch. They flinched though, as they heard his head bouncing on every step. The sound carried clear through the hall, easily reached the room above, where Ilona tried to stand and couldn't, couldn't pull her face away from the grille and its view of the man she loved, the man she did not know, her fingers wedged into the mesh, held there as tightly as coffin lid had ever held bone.

The sounds eventually faded. Vlad wiped his blade on his cloak. 'And now . . .' he said.

He was interrupted by another scream. 'No!' It came from Manea Udriste, a short-sword appearing from within his ermine-collared coat. He was three paces from Vlad and he made one of them before the arrows took him, one through the neck, one through the chest. They were shot from ten paces, from a Turkish bow that could send an arrow five hundred and still pierce flesh. These more than pierced his, knocking him backwards, pinning him to a chair where he sat, eyes wide in shock.

Vlad bent swiftly, stared. And Ion suddenly remembered a hunt they'd made as boys, Vlad bending before the boar he'd just stabbed. 'Don't you remember, Ion,' he'd said, in that soft voice. 'You need to look into their eyes as they die.'

His prince didn't say anything now. Just watched the man

till the light left him. Then he stood, murmured, 'A pity. I had something better planned to reward his . . . loyalty.'

Behind her dying husband's chair, the Lady Udriste suddenly knew what it was her father's ghost had been trying to tell her. With a screech, she leapt forward, hands plucking at the arrows that fixed her husband to the chair, that would not shift. Gregor stepped forward, grabbed, lifted. Kicking, the lady was dragged from the hall, her screams finally cut off by his hand placed over her mouth.

'And what do you have planned for me, Devil's son?'

Vlad looked at Albu cel Mare, the huge man staring defiantly at him. Took time before he replied. 'Something worthy.'

'Would you dare to fight me, Vlad Dracula? Here, now, with knives.' He reached slowly towards the dagger at his waist. All heard the bow-strings tauten, until Vlad's raised hand halted them. It stayed up even when Albu drew his blade.

'Dare?' echoed Vlad. 'I might dare. But what purpose would it serve if I killed you that way?'

'It would prove you a man.'

'Oh, I think everyone knows I am that.' Vlad shook his head. 'But it would give you both a chance and an honourable death. When your treason deserves neither.'

Before Albu could reply, Ion stepped in, brought the pommel of his own dagger smashing down upon the fat wrist. The *boyar*'s weapon fell to the floor.

'So kill me then,' howled the *boyar*. 'Chop off my head, why don't you? It was the death I gave your father, the Dragon,' he jeered. 'And he was twice the man that you will ever be.'

'A head for a head,' Vlad replied, 'and so I am revenged?' He nodded as he came slowly forward, paused. 'Yet . . . again, it is too *honourable*, too swift. Besides, vengeance means nothing if it is only for its own sake. Vengeance must say something to the world.' He looked up, from Albu's pain-riven face and around the hall, at the other faces averted from him. 'I cannot make you love me,' he said. 'Men and women love as they please. But they will fear as their prince pleases. And if they fear enough, they will not dare to betray me.' He turned, to the main entrance, to four of his men standing there. 'Bring her,' he said to them. 'Bring it all.'

Everyone heard it, the strange sound in a hall full of men and women, the steady strike of iron on stone, the snort revealing what it was before the horse was led down into the room. 'This is Kalafat,' Vlad said, crossing to her, taking the bridle. 'I have ridden her since my days amongst the Turks. She can be as fleet as the wind and fight like the Devil's child who rides her.' He reached up and scratched between her eyes. 'Yet she can also be gentle and move slowly to my bidding.'

More men were coming down the stairs, bearing rope, pulleys, wood. Others used halberds to herd the crowd back to one end of the hall, while more cleared its centre, pushing aside the table, chairs, coffin, leaving Ion with Albu, Vlad with Kalafat, watching his men proceed with what he had taught them, binding ropes to wood and saddle. When all was ready, he turned to the man Ion held. 'Will you forgive us, Albu cel Mare, if we are a little clumsy? I only saw this done the once.'

And Vlad laughed.

Above, unable to move eye or fingers from the grille despite the agony that was building inside her, Ilona marvelled. Her prince did not laugh. Not like that. *Her* prince did not stand there while Ion took his knife and slit a man's clothes, ripping them from his huge body. Her prince did not kneel between the naked legs of the man – legs that were fat, blue-tinged and mottled – whom his guards had thrown face down.

She could see the dagger descend, could not see through him. But she could hear the terrible scream that grew louder, more terrible, as other men lowered a blunted stake, bent over the huge naked body while Vlad went to his horse's head, whispered in her soft ear. As Kalafat began to move slowly forward, she did manage to close her eyes; but she could not close her ears – to the weeping of men and women, to the deep bellowing of Albu cel Mare that rose, suddenly, to a high-pitched shriek.

'My lady!' It was Elisabeta's voice coming through the sound, horror in it. But her lady-in-waiting was not seeing the blood below, but the blood pooling at the base of Ilona's chair. And then hands were on her, trying to lift her, and she opened her eyes again, saw hands lifting wood below, other hands pulling on ropes. She heard her prince say, 'This is the most difficult part,' as Albu cel Mare rose up, slipped down, his flailing feet caught, held, nailed down . . . and then she fell, slipping through her maid's hands, hoping for oblivion, though it did not come straight away. Not before she heard that voice again, clear, calm, cutting through the screams.

In the hall, Vlad unstrapped the ropes from Kalafat's saddle. 'Do you have it now, Ion?'

'I think so, Prince.'

'Then I will leave you to it. His wife and son will not need a horse. Anyway, for speed's sake, we must learn to use only men. Place them on either side of the Great One. Since he still seems to be living – a rare fortune on my first attempt! – he can watch them die.'

Vlad mounted, turned Kalafat's head, looked back to the crowd, most now weeping on the floor; then past them and the man on the stake, to the man on the cross. Suffering Jesus.

'Christ is risen,' he cried, tapping his heels into Kalafat's flanks, riding from the Great Hall.

TWENTY-SIX

Penance

The dirge filled the room, as heavy to the ears as the incense was to the nostrils. Both came from the priest who stood over the bed, swinging the heavy censer, chanting the song of death.

He wore grey robes, a contrast to Ilona's white shift, the fourth she had worn and the only one she had not stained because, finally, her bleeding had ceased. Too late, her women thought, and summoned the priest. While they'd waited for him, they'd tied her hair back from a face whiter than her garment, clasped the limp hands around a sprig of rosemary and a length of beads.

Now the man sang and swung. Two of the maids wept, though not Elisabeta, the *boyar*'s daughter.

There was a pounding, then boots upon the stair. The door crashed open. The women rose from their knees, huddled, shrieking, at the black-clad, blood-spattered man heaving breaths in the doorway. Vlad gave a cry and staggered across the room, elbowing the priest aside, seizing Ilona's hands, crushing rosemary, rosary and all.

'Ilona,' he murmured, laying his head upon her chest. Then, after a moment, his head shot up. 'She lives,' he cried.

Elisabeta stepped forward. 'She does, Prince, she—'

'Then what pickings does this crow seek here?' Vlad turned to glare at the priest.

'I was summoned and so I came,' the man replied quietly. 'And though I am no physician, I have seen many cross between life and death. This woman hovers at the border and I prepare her for her passage.'

'If you are no physician, then I will not take your word that she is ready to go over yet.' Vlad looked at the women. 'Has one attended?'

'My prince, he came an hour since and left. He did what little he could do.'

'Which I am sure was nothing.' Vlad looked past them, to Black Ilie standing in the doorway. 'There is a wise woman who lives around the corner in Strada Scaloian. Her name is Marca. Bring her.'

The big man bowed, left.

The priest gasped. 'You summon a witch? When I stand here with God's words flowing through me?'

'She is of the Roma people and tells fortunes, yes. That is how I know her. And she heals with herbs and prayer. If that is witchery then I will have it here.' He rose, stepped so close to the priest that their noses almost touched. They were of a height, perhaps of an age, too, though the priest's thick beard made him look older. 'And I tell you, I will make a compact with Satan himself if he helps my Ilona live. So you had best go.'

But the priest did not move. Instead, he said, quietly, 'No, Prince. I had best stay. Someone must remain to defend this child's soul from the Devil's son.'

Elisabeta gasped. Stoica and Gregor stepped closer, the quicker to respond to their prince's certain order to punish this defiance. But Vlad gave no signal, just continued staring, finally spoke. 'Do you know what I have done this night?'

'I have heard. And I can see. Blood is still on your face.'

Vlad reached up, rubbed, studied the brown-red flakes on his fingertips. 'Albu cel Mare's.' He looked at the man before him. 'I could order his fate for you.'

'I know you could command it, Prince. I think that you would not.'

'Would not dare?'

203

'No. But Dracula kills when he needs to. To demonstrate his strength. There is no necessity to kill me. No strength would be proven.'

Vlad leaned back, the better to study. 'You think you know me.'

'A little. I have watched you. I marched in your army last year, when the comet was in the sky.'

'A soldier *and* a priest?'

'Just a priest now.' The man closed his eyes. 'What I saw on that campaign made me one.'

'Lightning on the road to Damascus?'

'No, Prince,' replied the man softly. 'Just too much blood.'

Vlad stared a moment. 'What is your name?'

The man hesitated. 'I am now called . . . Brother Vasilie.'

Below, the street door opened. There was creaking on the stairs. 'You interest me,' Vlad said, turning away. 'Stay.'

Ilie pushed an old woman into the room. Her dress was a dazzle of overlapping cloths in different hues, and her head-scarf, woven through with silver thread, glittered with tiny mirrors. A wealthy one then, rewarded for her skills of prophecy, the reading of fate. And for other skills, the ones she was summoned to practise now. She was followed by a girl, similarly but less richly dressed. Both bobbed a curtsy to Vlad, crossed themselves when they saw the priest, before the elder moved stiffly over to the bed. There she lifted Ilona's eyelids, put a hand to head and heart, bent close to sniff her breath. Then she turned to the maids, babbled a question in her own tongue. The youngest, darkest one there obviously had some Roma blood. She answered, pointed, and the woman rose, went to a pail in the corner of the room, lifted its lid, studied what was inside. Replacing the lid, she said something to the young girl, who nodded and ran down the stairs.

Vlad blanched, pointed. 'What . . .' One of the maids began to sob. 'What? Tell me!' Roaring, he crossed the room, seizing Elisabeta by the arm.

She cried out as his fingers dug into her. 'Prince! It is . . . was your child.'

Vlad released her, sagged as if struck. Brother Vasilie passed him, bending swiftly to lift the pail. 'I will take this. That gypsy has seen it. All know that the Roma use the fat of unborn babies in their hellish potions. I will—'

Vlad reached out, held him. 'Let me see,' he whispered.

'Prince . . .'

Vlad looked at him. 'I will see what Ilona and I have made. What God has taken from us.' He nodded. 'Open it.'

With a sigh, Vasilie did. Both men stared. After a long moment, Vlad nodded. 'A son,' he said. 'With the black hair of the Draculesti.' He glanced across to the prone figure on the bed. 'I told her that this time I would have a son.'

'This time?' The priest slid the lid back onto the pail. 'You have committed this sin before?'

Vlad looked back. 'Sin?'

'You have other children?'

Vlad, his eyes glazed, nodded. 'Two daughters. That is all that I know.'

'And you were not married to their mothers? Nor to this woman?'

'You know that I am not.'

'Sins.'

All waited for the storm to lash upon the priest's head. It did not come. 'You think that this is the punishment for my sins? When so many sin thus daily, yet gather their bastards around their knees?'

Vasilie shook his head. 'I cannot claim to understand the will of God. Whom he chooses to punish and why. But perhaps a prince is held to a higher standard.'

'Sins,' murmured Vlad, looking again at Ilona. Then he raised his eyes again to the priest. 'And if I were to *atone* for my sins? Would God spare this woman's life?'

'You do not bargain with God.'

'Really?' Vlad shook his head. 'I think we do exactly that

each time we pray. We say, "I will give up this, Lord, if only you will give me that."'

'Prayer is only a part of it all. You must confess, do penance—'

'Confess?' Vlad interrupted, stepping forward. 'Yes. I have not had a confessor for years. So I appoint you my confessor.'

The priest stepped back, shock clear on his face. 'Prince, no. I am not . . . equipped. I am new, inexperienced. I have my parish . . .'

'And you may remain there. You just have a new parishioner.'

'But . . .' The priest shrugged helplessly. 'Why me?'

'You are a former soldier. You have lived a man's life. You will understand a man's sins. Besides . . . no one has spoken to me as you just did since I was a student at the *enderun kolej*.'

'I cannot . . .'

Below, the door opened again. Footsteps sounded. Vlad's face drained of colour, of light. Darkness returned as he looked at the bed. 'Enough,' he said. 'It is decided. I will confess to you and I will atone for this sin. And even if God is not to be bargained with I swear this to Him – and He knows how I keep my oaths – if He lets my Ilona live, I will have no more children out of wedlock.'

The girl came in, bearing a small pail. Steam issued from beneath its lid. The older Roma took it from her, went straight to the bed, sat. Lifting Ilona's head onto her lap, she raised the pail to her bloodless lips, mumbling the while. Most of the liquid spilled. But Ilona gagged, swallowed.

Vasilie sighed. There was nothing more he could do. 'Let us pray,' he said, 'for a prince's word, given to God. And for the life of this poor woman, in His hands.'

All there knelt, except for the priest, who set down the other pail behind him and picked up his censer again. Swinging it, jerking the chain to a sudden halt to force out the sweet-smelling smoke, he began to intone, the others responding. Somewhere close, a church bell tolled the six.

They were still kneeling, still praying, when seven bells began to strike. But only three had sounded when a groan came from the bed. In a moment Vlad was up, across, kneeling again, taking the deathly white hands. 'My love?' he said softly. 'Come back to me.'

Her eyes fluttered open. 'My prince,' she sighed. He saw light in them before they closed again.

Vlad stared at her for some time, then turned to the old gypsy still cradling Ilona's head. 'Will she live?'

A shrug. 'If you will it so, Prince.'

The priest stepped closer. 'She is in God's hands.'

'And in mine,' said Vlad, clasping tighter.

TWENTY-SEVEN

The First Confession

'Father, I have sinned against heaven and before you.'

'Prince, rise up!'

'No. Upon my knees – here, now. This first time at least. I cannot guarantee we shall always have this luxury – a quiet chapel, a carpet to kneel upon. But now, this first time . . .'

'Then I will kneel, too. So we can pray together.'

The two men faced each other at the doorway of the altar screen. The church was empty now, the congregation had come, chanted, partaken of the host and the mystery, departed refreshed, renewed in faith and hope. Vlad had not tasted the holy wafer, the holy wine. It had been too long since his last confession. And there were sins to discuss first.

Upon the walls, frescoed saints gazed down in various stages of beatification or martyrdom. Behind the priest and the screen, above the altar, Christ hung on the cross, agony rendered in colour and sculpted in plaster upon his face. Before him, incense smoke rose in a steady plume. Beside the censer stood a gold communion cup that Vlad had presented to the church only that morning.

'Prince,' said the priest, 'before you begin I must ask you again – is it me you want? Surely the Voivode requires no one less than the head of the church in Wallachia, the Metropolitan, to be his confessor? Someone who understands high matters of state, the context of your supposed sins? I am but a simple man . . .'

'Who was once a soldier?'

'Yes.'

'A sinner?'

'All men are born sinners.'

'But you are one who has killed?'

'May God forgive me, I have.'

'Loved a woman?'

'Yes. I have committed most of the common sins. And some uncommon ones.' He coughed. 'I hunted with hawks.'

'You think that a sin?'

'It is when you do it obsessively. When you give up everything to find the right bird.'

'Then we are more alike than ever. And we are of an age, are we not?'

'Close, I think. But—'

'I do not need an old man who has forgotten a young man's urges and ambitions. Who thinks mostly of eternity. I need one who lives now. And as for the context of my sins, it is simple.' Vlad leaned forward. 'I must rule.'

'You do.'

'No. I sit on the throne. It is placed at the centre of the most lawless land in the world. And I have been placed upon it to change that. That is my *kismet.*'

'I do not know that word.'

'It is a word of the Turks. It poorly translates as "unalterable destiny". Given by God at birth.' He closed his eyes. 'There is a saying of Mohammed, one of the *haditha*, "Every man's fate we have tied upon his own neck."'

'Are you saying you cannot help what you do?'

'Yes.'

'That is not the teaching of our Church, of your faith. Each man has a choice, to work good or evil.'

'Then perhaps I stray from the Orthodox in this point. Because I know what I am destined to do and how I must do it. I cannot do other.'

The priest licked dry lips. Both men could see an argument on doctrine before them. And there were many rumours about Vlad and who he worshipped. The Devil was not only in his name, some said. Others whispered that his mother had been of the hated Roman faith and so he only pretended to be a good son of the Greek Church that was the faith of his land. While still others whispered of an even greater heresy – that he had been forced to come to Allah before the Turks gave him an army.

But doctrine was not why they were there. And the Voivode was now kneeling in a Greek church. 'What is your *kismet* then?'

'To serve God.'

The priest frowned. 'But that is everyone's. Every farmer believes the same, or should.'

'True. But being born Dracula, my destiny is different from every farmer's. I cannot just praise Him in words and till my fields. I must be God's bright and shining sword. And to do that I must first hone my own.'

'How?'

'In three steps.' Vlad came up onto his feet, then squatted down in the manner of the Turk. 'First I must return justice to our land. And I must begin with those who threaten me most – the *boyars*.'

'Was justice what Albu cel Mare received last night?'

'Of course. He admitted the murder of my father and brother. He deserved to die.'

'That way?' The priest shuddered. 'You choose it to humiliate, to take a man as a man takes a woman, to prolong suffering . . .'

'No. Yes! But that is merely one of its purposes.'

'What are the others?'

Vlad leaned forward. 'I was taught a phrase once, by people who knew their business: "You torture others so they cannot torture you."'

'So you dispose of an enemy horribly, before he disposes of you in the same way?'

Vlad nodded. 'Yes. And at the same time you offer people a simple choice: obey God's Anointed or be punished. Moreover, punished in such a way that you are given a glimpse of the torments that await you for all eternity if you sin.'

'But did our Saviour not speak of love as the only sure footing on the road to salvation?'

Vlad closed his eyes. Had to reach a hand down to the carpet to steady himself – for the last word had brought with it a vision of one who had spoken it – the only word he had spoken, with Vlad the only one to understand him, in the courtyard of Tokat, just before the stake was inserted. Vlad swallowed, opened his eyes again. 'He did. But I cannot control men's love, only their fear. Love changes. Fear is as constant as a star.'

'So you would have your people live in fear?'

'I would have them live in certainty. To know their place in God's kingdom. To obey, without question, the laws I make in His name.' Vlad nodded. 'And to know that if they fail to obey, they will be punished in a way that will make others pause before they sin, or not sin at all.'

'For what crimes will you apply this punishment?'

'All.'

'All? What if someone steals a cow?'

'He is impaled. You chop off his hand, you have a former thief who is now a beggar that can't work. But for his time upon the stake, he is an example.'

'Rapine?'

'Impaled. Taken as you took.'

'Coining? Conning? Riot?'

'Impaled. Impaled. Impaled.'

The priest came off his knees, sat and sighed. The confession had been lost somewhere. 'You mean to do this?'

'I *will* do it. Wallachia was once the crossroads of the world. Now the world considers us all to be brigands and takes their wealth elsewhere, impoverishing us, limiting my power to rule – for what power does a bankrupt prince possess? But see that gold chalice upon your altar? Within five years I will place one far richer, studded with jewels, upon the town well of Targoviste for the use of all . . . and no one will steal it.'

'That will not happen.'

'I vow to you, here, before Christ, that it will.'

For a moment the priest just stared, seeking bravado, or a fanatic's gleam, in the green eyes before him. But he only saw certainty. 'And yet,' he continued, 'if you have your order here, there are things – people – you cannot control. Like those beyond your borders who want you to fail. How do you deal with them?'

'Same rule. Same punishment. A thousand times the example.'

'You mean . . .'

'I mean to confront the Saxons who control Transylvania from their walled cities there – Brasov, Sibiu and the others. If they continue to choke off our trade – impaling, by the way, any Wallachian merchant they find trading in their domain . . .' Vlad nodded. 'Oh yes, priest. Impalement is a German punishment, part of the Law of Iglau, and applied there long before I brought it to Wallachia. The Turks learned it from our fellow Christians.'

'Whoever practises it, it is still an abomination.'

'True. And if the Saxons of Transylvania continue to give refuge to every rival to my throne and plot to thwart the fulfilment of my destiny, I will descend upon them like Hannibal upon Rome and ravage them with sword, fire and a thousand blunted stakes.'

Silence again. Each man stared at the other until the priest found some moisture to speak. 'And then? You have pacified your land. Restored order and law – by whatever means. Quelled the Saxons who strangle its trade. Made Wallachia wealthy again. Have you fulfilled your destiny?'

'No,' Vlad replied, light in his eyes, 'I have barely begun. The sword is honed but still sheathed. God's sword and the Dragon's Talon, one and the same blade. For when I finally draw it, I will make such a stroke that any sin I have committed will be cut away, leaving only redemption.' He raised a hand, forestalling the question. 'I know! If my *kismet* is unalterable, how can my actions alter it? It is a contradiction. But then,' he said with a smile, 'so am I.'

'But the sweeping away of all sins . . . there is only one way for a knight to gain such total forgiveness.'

'Yes, there is.'

They said it together: 'Crusade.'

Vlad nodded. 'Holy War. I will place Christ's cross again on the altar of Santa Sophia in Constantinople.'

The priest gasped. He had looked for bravado, fanaticism in the green eyes. How had he missed insanity? 'It is impossible.'

'Is it? They said Constantinople would never fall, yet Mehmet took it.'

'But tiny Wallachia against . . .' He broke off. 'It is said the Turk can field armies the size of our entire population.'

'Not quite. But though you might fear it, I am not mad. Wallachia will be the tip of the spear, as ever. But all Christendom will be the shaft and the thrust.'

'And this is your destiny?'

'Yes.' Vlad stared at a point above the priest. 'I have known it from my days as a hostage. Since I received the . . . blessings of their education.' Darkness didn't quite extinguish the light in the eyes. 'And I know Mehmet, the man they now call "Fatih" – "the Conqueror". He is vain beyond imagining. Because of that, he can be beaten, as Hunyadi beat him last year at Belgrade.' The darkness deepened. 'He has my brother still. But, with God's good grace, one day I will have him a sword-length away. And then . . .' He broke off.

'Then?'

'I will die, happy in the moment of fate fulfilled. Die a

crusader, with all my sins wiped clean. Die in the arms of God.'

Silence again. Both men staring now, beyond walls and words. Then the priest leaned forward. 'You came here to confess. And the purpose of that, in our faith, the one true faith, is so that you can go forward, with all your sins remitted. To cleanse you for your . . . purposes.' He shuddered slightly. 'Perhaps when you have felt God's grace, when you have been shriven, done penance, tasted again of the body and blood of our Saviour, you will think differently about your . . . methods.'

Vlad looked up, beyond the priest to the crucifix upon the altar, to the suffering Christ. Finally he spoke one word: 'Perhaps.'

'Remember Luke: "No one who puts his hand to the plough and looks back is fit for the kingdom of God."' The priest swallowed. 'So let me hear of the sins you have committed. So we can look forward.'

Vlad shook his head, a slight smile coming. 'Where to begin . . .'

Noise from outside, footsteps approaching the church's door. Vlad turned towards the sound. 'I am summoned.' He came again onto his knees. 'But come with me, priest. You may sit in judgement on me over a flagon of wine.'

'It is not I who sit in judgement, Vlad Dracula,' the priest said severely as he rose, 'but God.'

'True,' said Vlad, still smiling. 'But I cannot drink with Him.'

'Blasphemy, Prince?'

'Yes.' The smile grew. 'Forgive me, father, for I have sinned against heaven and before you.'

The church door opened. Ion stood there, blinking into the gloom. At last he noticed the figure, kneeling at the altar door. 'Voivode,' he said, coming forward, 'it is time.'

Vlad looked up. 'I am coming, Ion. And my confessor will come, too.'

'Confessor?'

Vlad turned back. The deeper gloom beyond the altar screen was deserted.

'Never mind,' said Vlad, rising. 'He will be there when I need him.'

— PART THREE —

Crusade

'First Moloch, horrid king, besmeared with blood
Of human sacrifice, and parents' tears.'
— PARADISE LOST, John Milton

TWENTY-EIGHT

The Goblet

Targoviste, December 1461, four years later

They had walked for hours through the alleys and thorough-
fares of Targoviste, leaving the city by its eastern gate, crossing the small bridge over the River Lalomita, stopping to
warm themselves for a while at the caravanserai set up there
for travellers and merchants who had not been able, or
chosen not, to make the city before its gates were barred for
the night. The innkeeper had barely noted them, beyond the
richness of the clothes beneath their cloaks; and that was just
business, to serve them better wine, charge them a higher
price. They were not unusual, for his inn had a good reputation and many wealthy merchants stayed there. It was near
full tonight, even on this chill December evening. The
blessings of peace, the prosperity it brought, had made him
as wealthy as many of those he served. Remembering to
thank both Christ and Saint Nicolae, patron of pawnbrokers
– for it was the profits from that trade he'd pursued, in the
bad days before Prince Dracula, that had allowed him to
invest in the tavern – the innkeeper pocketed the gold coin
they left and blessed both.

If he'd known that the two men had been discussing the
best way to end that peace, he might have prayed more
fervently to the Virgin.

Vlad and Ion crossed back into the town, the gates opened
for them as they would be for no one else. As they crossed the
square before the cathedral, the Bisierica Domnesca, the door
of one of the taverns burst open, smashing against the
building's wall. Shouts and drunken shooshing followed,

then the sound of staggering. Vlad pulled Ion into the shadows of the great well.

'The *boyars*, Prince,' Ion cautioned.

'They have waited this long for us. A little longer will only make them even more . . . amenable. Besides, I like to hear what is said.'

Squatting, Turkish-style, thigh to calf, backs to stone, the two men listened.

The first voice came to them thickened with wine and by the guttural timbre typical of his land; a Bulgar, beyond doubt. 'Horse dung,' the man exclaimed. 'It's just another of the many lies told of him.'

'Truth, master.' A second man spoke, not as drunk, a higher-pitched voice and in the accent of the town. 'One year since it was placed there, and there it remains.'

'Horse dung,' the first man repeated, spat. 'Where?'

'There.'

A moment's silence, a fumbling. 'Christ on a carthorse!' the Bulgar exclaimed.

'Can you see it, master?'

'Well enough, even by moonlight . . .' He whistled. 'Solid gold, you say?'

'Yes.'

'And what are these . . . pearls? Huh. But these others? I cannot tell what they are.'

'There are rubies, sapphires, an emerald . . .'

'An emperor's goblet! And he leaves it here for peasants to use.' The man gasped. 'Heavy, by the Mother. And not chained.'

'Drink from it, master. The well water's sweeter than any wine we've had tonight.'

'I will.'

The sound of slurping came to the listening men. Ion gestured for them to be gone. Vlad stayed him with a hand.

The voice came again, softer, slightly less slurred. 'I could buy a palace in Sofia for the price of this.' He grunted. 'You say it has never been stolen?'

'I said it has never been kept. It has been stolen twice. The first time, a day after the Voivode placed it here. A week later it was back on the well wall – with the thief and his entire family spitted on a dozen stakes beside it. The second time it was back in a day. His own father turned the thief in, so only one stake was required.'

The voice dropped to a whisper. 'But how would he know? I could be gone tomorrow, as soon as the gates open.'

'Shake it, master.'

'Eh?'

'Shake it.'

The man did. A faint chime came. 'What's that?'

'There. In the stem. A silver bell in a golden cage. It is said our Voivode can hear it every time it is raised. That he could follow its sound wherever it went. And that he would bring a stake to wherever the bell led him.'

The man shook it again, his voice awed. 'Does he love impaling so much?'

'Perhaps, master. But what is certain is that he hates crime. And so there is none in our land. All pass freely, safely. Trade and all its benefits have come again to Wallachia. It is even better than the time of his father, the Dragon. And it is why you are here, is it not?'

The awe was still there. Gold shimmered as it was lifted into a shaft of moonlight. 'Who made this?'

'The Goldsmiths' Guild of Brasov. It was part of the tribute the Saxon towns sent, when our Voivode forced them to a peace. They freed the Wallachian merchants they'd imprisoned and let them pass freely now. They paid a fortune for an army to guard the trade routes. And they sent this for his table.'

'And he gave it to his people.' The man spat again. 'What did the Saxons get in return?'

The other man laughed. 'He stopped impaling them by the thousand.'

Again Ion signalled that they should go. Again, Vlad waved him down.

The Bulgar spoke. 'What if I just slipped it under my cloak? Left at dawn?'

'You'd be looking down on it from a spike by noon.' The man laughed again. 'Drink deep, my friend, of the emperor's goblet. Then put it back for the peasants.'

The waiting men heard the chink of metal on stone. 'I want no more filthy water. Give me more wine!' His voice was angry now, as if somehow he'd been humiliated.

'Of course, master,' said the man from Targoviste. 'And perhaps over it we can discuss how I can further help you with the copper mines. The owners are notorious . . .'

The voice trailed away. A door opened and the noise of the tavern spilled out once more, cut off by the door's closing.

Vlad and Ion rose, walked round the well. Ion lifted the cup, filled it, handed it across. 'A loyal son of Wallachia. Or do you think he knew someone was listening?' he said.

'Of course he knew.' Vlad drained the goblet, shook it. The faint chime came. 'For I always am.' He set the vessel down upon the stone. 'Now, Ion, to other sons of our land. Less loyal, perhaps.'

Walking briskly, the two men crossed the square, and made for the Princely Court.

In the Great Hall, the fires had not been lit. The breaths of the *boyars* plumed the air. Despite their furs, their wool-lined boots, every member of the Sfatul Domnesc sat in their high-backed chairs and froze.

'Perhaps I *should* have heated the chamber,' Vlad said, staring down through the mesh of the grille. 'I cannot talk to lumps of ice.'

'If they were warm,' Ion replied, 'they might argue more.

As it is, they will assent to what you say just to get before their own fires again.'

Vlad leaned back so his friend could also look. 'And who will argue most?'

Ion squinted. 'The three great *jupans* – Turcul, his brother Gales, and Dobrita – have most to lose if the war goes badly. They have the biggest estates.'

'And so the most to gain if it goes well. The other senior men?'

'Buriu, as Spatar, commands the cavalry – and what is a knight without a fight? Cazan, your chancellor, will worry about who will pay for it all . . .'

'He will be relieved when I tell him of my plans for plunder. The rest?'

'They are all your men, sworn.'

'And him?' Vlad pointed.

'The Metropolitan?' Ion sighed. 'You promise him what a churchman should most want – Holy War. Yet he has larger estates even than Turcul *jupan*, and monasteries that would be sacked if the war went against us . . .' Ion shrugged. 'Yet he is a devout man and hates the Infidel. He could lean either way.'

'Well,' said Vlad, stepping back, 'bishop or lord, they are all men. And will be bent to my will by the usual means.'

Ion lifted Vlad's short cloak, draped it over his shoulder. 'Which are?'

'Greed and terror.' Vlad spread his arms wide. 'How do I look?'

Vlad was wearing a black silk doublet under the cloak; light Turkish *shalvari* swathed his legs. Ion shivered. 'You make me even colder just looking at you.'

Vlad smiled. 'Good.'

Unlike at a certain Easter, this time Vlad did not enter his hall silently but clattered the door outwards. Ion followed. The men below started, rising hurriedly as their Voivode descended the steps and moved rapidly to his chair at the table's end. 'My lords, loyal *boyars*, Holy Father . . . I apologise for keeping you waiting. Some messengers came with hot news I needed to hear, and you must hear it, too. Please sit.'

They did. 'What news, Prince?' It was Turcul who spoke, his tone testy. 'I hope it will be hot enough to shrink the piles I have grown sitting on this chair.'

'It may do.' Vlad nodded. 'A fire has been lit to heat us all.' He leaned forward. 'The Crow flies south in the spring.'

Men gasped, looked at him, at each other. Ion studied their reactions, a blend of desire and dread. If the King of Hungary was coming to their aid, bringing his army through the passes at first snow melt, then they would have no choice but to fight. Indeed, as their Voivode had already urged, they would have to begin that fight.

But Ion also knew that Corvinus had actually promised no such thing.

'This was the news we were waiting for, wasn't it, lords?' Vlad continued. 'While other princes in Germany, Poland, Venice, Genoa and Italy hesitate, Hungary moves. With that force behind us, we can beat the Turk.'

Far behind us, Ion thought. Sat in Buda waiting for Vlad to fan spark into flame. Only then would Matthew Corvinus, the cunning Crow, decide if he would stir from his nest or not.

'And so, lords, I say again, yet with more urgency: it is time for war.' Vlad, who had not sat, bent forward, resting his fingertips upon the table. 'Mehmet Fatih has now dealt with the White Sheep Uzbeks in the east. It was their rebellion that made him agree a treaty with us two years ago, one he had no intention of keeping. Now he demands what was agreed: the gold tribute we must pay as his *vassals*.' The tone was mocking. 'And, worse, he has reinstated the *devsirme*. Fifteen hundred of our finest, strongest, most gifted boys must be sent from our lands to be trained as the Sultan's warriors, to live as the Sultan's slaves. I would prefer them to be Wallachian warriors . . . and free!'

There was a murmur of assent. The boy levy that most vassal states sent to the Sublime Porte sucked lifeblood from the land. 'I have never sent it. I know what is learned under their . . . tutelage,' Vlad went on quietly. 'Most succumb. Some, a rare few, do not.'

'And you were the Dracula who did not, Prince, is that not right?' It was another *boyar*, Dobrita, who spoke. 'While your brother Radu knelt and offered his arse to the Sultan's pleasure?'

A low laugh came. Vlad straightened. 'My brother is still a prince of this realm, Dobrita. Any of the blood of the Draculesti must be treated with respect.'

The *boyar* flushed red. 'I . . . I . . . I meant no disrespect, Prince, I . . .'

Vlad cut him off. 'It does not matter. My brother will ride at Mehmet's side. Many of the enemy will not be Turkish but what of that? They have bowed before the Crescent, seek now to plant their horsetail standards on our walls and erect a minaret above the dome of the Bisierica Domnesca as they have over the Hagia Sophia. So we must be the first to answer the call to crusade. For our land, our people, our faith.'

'Which faith, Voivode?' It was the Metropolitan who spoke now, his voice deepened by a lifetime of chanting his faith. 'This crusade was called by the Bishop of Rome.' He spat out the title. 'And what do we in the Orthodox Church have to do with him? What do you?'

All turned from the prelate to the prince. It was a question all had asked. But only the Metropolitan, who was not appointed by Vlad, who controlled wealth and resources nearly as large, dared ask it aloud. There had always been rumours about Vlad's beliefs.

He replied softly. 'You know that I believe as you do, Eminence. That until they recognise their errors, the two faiths must remain separate. I believe the Romans are learning, slowly.' He nodded. 'But the Pontiff's call at Mantua cannot be answered slowly. Hear what he said.' Vlad lifted a paper from before him. ' "Mehmet will never lay down his arms except in victory or total defeat. Every victory will be for him a stepping stone to another until, after subjecting all the princes of the West, he has destroyed the Gospel of Christ and imposed the law of his false prophet upon the whole world." '

He lowered the paper, looked up. 'However the Bishop of Rome might err in doctrine, he is right about the peril all Christianity faces. The Gospel of Christ, however we interpret it, is what Mehmet seeks to destroy. He will raise the Crescent on our sacred Mount Athos *and* in Rome. Each country between is but a stepping stone along the way. And little Wallachia is the first he would stand on.'

Vlad left the table, walked to the dormant fireplace. On its mantel the crucifix still stood, as it had that Easter almost five years before, Christ's ordeal clear in the figure upon it. 'We have a choice, lords,' Vlad said, staring up. 'Do we call ourselves Mohammedans? Or do we fight?' He turned back to them. 'Mehmet has summoned me to meet his ambassadors at his fortress of Guirgiu on the Danube – the fortress my grandfather Mircea built. There to bring his tribute in boys and gold. I have a mind to answer with men and steel. And then to cross beyond Guirgiu into the Bulgarian lands the Turk rules and begin to destroy my enemies there. To take gold, not give it. To slay his boys before he enslaves ours.'

Reaching up, he lifted the crucifix from the mantel. 'Who will join me for the glory of Christ? For the redemption of all sins? For Wallachia?'

Half the men stood, cheered, though the cheers were not full-throated. So, lowering the cross, Vlad reached to the other side of the fireplace and lifted what was there – a stout ash pole as tall as a man, and half again. It was stained red and brown. Its end was blunted. Hefting both cross and stake, he shouted, 'Who would not follow his prince to glory?'

No one, it seemed, for the remaining men rose, the three *jupans* cheering as loud as any. The shouts soon settled on one word, becoming a chant.

'Crusade! Crusade! Crusade!'

TWENTY-NINE

Farewells

After the *boyars* had been dispatched to rouse their followers and the Metropolitan to gather gold, Vlad and Ion sat on in the Great Hall but close to a hearth now blazing. They planned, studied maps and rosters. Messengers were summoned, dispatched. It was deep in the night before they could sit back and talk of other things.

Ion poured wine into both their goblets. 'You never told me which illustrious representative Mehmet is sending for us to grovel before?'

Vlad had picked up his wine. Now he lowered it, unsipped. 'Hamza *pasha*.'

Ion whistled. 'Our old teacher? The falconer? And a *pasha* now? He has risen in the world.'

Vlad stared into the fire. 'He was always much more than a falconer, though his skills were great. Mehmet made him High Admiral at Constantinople, during the siege. Since then he has undertaken a dozen embassies for the Sublime Porte. Become a *pasha*. It is rumoured he'll be Grand Vizier one day. Second only to the Sultan.'

'An eminent man. What an honour for little Wallachia!'

Vlad shook his head. 'It is a move on the chessboard. Mehmet sends someone who I . . . will remember.'

Ion looked up, catching something in Vlad's voice, not understanding it. But his prince and friend still stared into the flames. 'Of course. You were more than just his pupil, weren't you?'

Now the eyes came to him, flame in them still. 'What do you mean?'

Ion flinched. 'I . . . mean nothing. I just remember you talked with him in a way that no one else did. And . . . didn't you make something for him?'

'A hawking glove.' Vlad's gaze returned to fire.

'That was it. And didn't he rescue you from Tokat?'

'No,' Vlad murmured, sipping at last. 'He came to fetch me. It is different.'

There was something his friend was not saying, although that was not unusual. 'Do you think Hamza comes with treachery in mind?'

'I do not know. It may be that Mehmet expects me to kiss his ambassador's feet, to give over what is demanded. It is what most people in my position would do."

'Yet he probably still has your *jereed* mark upon his back. I am sure he remembers your nature.'

'True. And even if he does not plan to kill me, why would he not do what his father did to mine at Gallipoli? Chain the Dragon to a cart wheel for a month. Take his sons as hostages.'

'You have no sons to take.'

'No. I do not.' Vlad stared for a moment then stood up swiftly. 'Ilona,' he said. 'I promised I'd visit her this night.'

'Prince,' said Ion, following him to the stairs, 'you must rest a little, if we are to ride at sunrise.'

Vlad pushed open the door to his chamber. He looked back, the darkness gone from his face. 'After all this time, you are still trying to keep us apart?'

Ion looked down, mumbled, 'Of course not. I—'

'Thirteen years she has been my mistress. Yet you still love her?'

Ion looked up, spoke softly. 'I would marry her tomorrow.'

'Ah.' Vlad reached for his riding cloak. 'Might not the fact that you are already married interfere with that?'

'I'd get it annulled.'

'On what grounds?'

Ion frowned. 'Non-consummation.'

'I see. And your three daughters?'

'Virgin births, each one. You know how hard my Maria prays to her namesake.'

Both men laughed, Vlad laying a hand on Ion's arm. As the laughter faded, he kept it there. 'You know, there are times when I wish she was yours, not mine. I think she would be happier.'

'No.' Ion shook his head. 'From that first look upon the dockside at Edirne, there was no one in the world but you.'

Vlad squeezed his friend's arm. 'If all . . . all goes wrong at Guirgiu. Afterwards. You will look to Ilona, won't you? The *boyars* hate her. They think my love for her prevents me marrying one of their horse-faced daughters.' He smiled. 'Maybe they are right.'

'I will kill the man who harms her. Be he ever so high.' Ion placed his own hand on top of Vlad's. 'This I swear, my prince.'

'Good.' Vlad stepped past him. 'For whether I am in heaven or hell I will hold you to that oath.'

Candle-light bewitched her. There was something in dancing flame that soothed, freeing her mind, letting it move where it would around the aura of yellow, the core of blue. Her life moved there, as it had been, as it might have been. As it was.

Her life was this. Waiting for him, for his increasingly infrequent visits. She had lost count of the number of times he said he would come and didn't. She knew he was busy, knew also that it was not purely with affairs of state. He had another mistress, perhaps more than one.

What her life might have been. Meeting someone like . . . Ion, who would love her, perhaps even only her. She would have had his children, raised them in some quiet corner of the realm . . .

She blinked, dissolving the vision. No, she would never have met a *boyar*'s son. Raised in her remote village, a tanner's daughter, she'd have married the tanner's apprentice at fourteen, borne the brute a dozen children. If she'd survived them, by now she'd be bent-backed, grey-haired, fat. Not sitting in her own house, still pretty enough, her hair still all hazel, dressed in rich damask. Though she was thirty now, she did not look it. No children will do that. No children and an easy life.

She waved her hand, saw the flame lengthen sideways, changing the story. She would never have met the tanner's apprentice. Because she was pretty she'd been enslaved and prepared for a life as a concubine. Mehmet would have visited her even less than Vlad, what with his many wives, his other girls, his boys. She'd have lived her life in the indolence of the *saray*, first in Edirne, later in Constantinople until such time as she either bred or was given as wife to some provincial official or soldier.

The flame lengthened again. Somewhere in the house, someone had opened a door perhaps. She shivered, pulled a rug around her; then leaned forward and blew out the candle. He would not come now. He had forgotten . . . or chosen to go elsewhere. Chosen someone else over her.

Then her door opened and there he was. She could not see his face with the candle out and the fire banked low, but a reed torch lit the corridor beyond and his silhouette was clear against its light.

'Ilona.'

'Prince.'

He did not come from the door, held there by the coldness of the title. 'I am sorry,' he muttered, 'I . . .'

'Let me get a light,' she said, snatching a taper from the table, going to move past him into the corridor. But he grabbed her arm, held her in the doorway. A little light spilled onto his face and immediately she regretted her coldness. 'Let us stay in the dark,' he whispered.

'But I have food for you, wine . . .'

'Nothing,' he said, drawing her in. 'Nothing but you.'

As he drew her to the bed, her anger flashed again. Did he not have whores he could use thus? But when he laid her down and lay beside her she realised that she had mistook him. 'Ah,' he groaned, 'praise God for the softness of goose down.'

'Does my prince require nothing more than feathers for his back?' she asked, her tone amused.

'A pillow, perhaps?' He stopped her hand as she reached for one. 'No. Here,' he said, lifting his head. She slid under him and he lowered himself onto her with a sigh. 'And praise God for the softness of a woman's thighs.'

'Any woman's?' she enquired, raising the fingers that caressed his forehead, flicking them hard down.

'Ai!' he yelped. '*Your* thighs, I meant. Only yours, Ilona.'

She decided not to point out that this might not be true. But perhaps he felt his cushion harden. 'Only here, lying thus, do I have peace, my love. The only place in this wide world.'

'Flatterer,' she said, her hands returning to run through his thick hair.

'Truth-teller,' he murmured.

She stroked and listened to his breaths lengthen, felt his body ease on her. After a while she thought he must be sleeping. Then she watched his eyes slowly open.

'You know I leave tomorrow. Today. In a few hours.'

'Is it to be war, then?'

'It is to be crusade.' There was a tremor in his voice. 'The triumph of the One Cross over the Crescent. The Dragon perched on the horsetail. Mehmet bent under my sword.'

'And of all of these, is not this last the greatest?'

'Perhaps.' He smiled. 'As Christ's warrior I know I should only be a conduit for his glory. But I seek my own. I am ardent for it. To conquer the conqueror.'

'And can you?' she said softly, moving his hair to one side. 'Is the Turk not too powerful?'

'Powerful? Yes. Unbeatable? No. As Hunyadi did, at Belgrade, at Nis, as Skanderbeg does again and again in Albania, I can do here. With a little help.'

'From Hungary?'

'Yes. I can start the war, prosper for a while. But if Corvinus does not start to use all the gold the Pope has given him to fight . . .'

'Then?'

'Then we are doomed.' He looked up. 'You understand it is only to you, here, I can say that?'

'Yes.'

She stroked. He breathed. After a while she called, 'Vlad?' but he did not stir. She took off his boots and, after a moment, her dress, leaving only her shift, then pulled a soft Olteni rug over them both and curled into him.

She didn't think she slept. Yet she opened her eyes to a faint glow beyond the shutters. Quietly, she slipped away from him, opened them a crack. There was indeed a lightening in the east.

'Is it the dawn?' he called, his voice drowsy.

'No, love,' she said, closing the shutters, coming to his side again, 'just Targoviste in flames. Go back to sleep.'

'Good.' He breathed again, then said, 'You jest, yes?'

'Yes. Go back to sleep.'

After a moment, he said, 'Could your feet be any colder?'

'They are hot coals compared to my hands. Feel!' And she slipped a hand inside his *shalvari* and wrapped her fingers round his cock.

'Jesu!' he yelled, rising up, falling back. 'What do you do to me?'

'This,' she said, moving her hand upon him. 'And . . . ah! You don't seem to mind.'

'Ilona,' he groaned, turning towards her, his hands moving, too, sliding up under her shift.

'Whose hands are cold now?' she laughed, clutching him harder.

'Do you mind it?'

'I mind nothing you have ever done to me. Nor ever will.'

'Truly?'

'Truly,' she replied. 'I am yours, in any way you want me. Here. Now. For ever.'

'Here and now will do,' he said, and ripped the shift from her body.

He had come to her in many moods. They had made love in many ways. But she liked it best this way – lost in the heat of it, with him most lost of all. He never was anywhere else, with anyone else, she knew that. He always needed to show some face to the world but not here, not with her. That he lost himself in her excited her beyond measure. For in his abandon, she could be abandoned, too.

They moved, above, below, cold to hot, getting hotter. The faint light grew stronger beyond the shutters and she dreamt that Targoviste *was* in flames, devouring flames that would take them both. Then she felt him tense, the first time in an age and she knew, as he tried to pull back, as he had done ever since he made a vow to a priest to have no more bastards in exchange for her life. And she knew also that now, when she might never see him again, she could not let him go. 'No, my prince, stay,' she whispered, wrapping her legs tight around him.

'Ilona . . .' he groaned.

'It is safe, my love, safe. I know my times.'

'You are certain?'

'I would never lie to you.'

'No, you would not. The only one who would not. It is why you are my sanctuary.' He smiled. 'Then thank God,' he cried, easing down again.

The pause gave them a moment, which extended. Cries came, their flesh, meeting, mingling.

*

They lay joined, pressed together, feeling hearts slow and breaths ease. His eyes were closed again, his face calm. Hers were open to study him. He looked almost like the boy he'd been when she'd taken off the veil of coins and seen him properly that first time.

She knew the stories. There had been many in the court all too willing to recount his deeds – her maid, Elisabeta, daughter of Turcul *jupan*, the most eager until she stopped her. But those she knew – of cruelty, of hideous punishments – did not tally with the man who lay in her arms. He did not talk of them there, nor of anything like that; had never revealed to her the source of the darkness that could flood his eyes in an instant. Those words were for the confessor it was said he went to, and for God, not for her. He called her his sanctuary. She would not violate the one place he felt safe, no matter what it was said he had done.

A horse came down the street. Pass by, she prayed, but it didn't. A voice came softly through the shutters. 'Prince?'

She pressed her hands over his ears but he heard anyway. 'I come,' he called.

The horse moved away. Not far. He tried to rise and she held him still. 'My love,' he said, placing his hands on top of hers.

'Stay.'

'No longer,' he said firmly, 'God calls.'

'Strange that God speaks in Ion's voice.'

He laughed, slipped her grip, rose, dressed swiftly while she watched him, studying each curve of muscle, noting every scar. There were none new to add to the map she carried in her head.

He turned, one boot on, seeing the intensity of her regard. 'What is it? he asked.

'Come back to me,' she whispered.

He pulled on the second boot, sat upon the bed. 'I shall,' he replied, 'and if I do not then Ion has sworn—'

She put a finger to his lip. 'I know. But I suspect that if you do not come then Ion will not, either, for I cannot see him live if you die.' He tried to interrupt but she went on. 'I will be safe. I will dress once more as a boy and get myself to the nuns at Clejani whose cloisters you have so generously endowed. It is the ending place for every royal mistress, is it not?'

He smiled at her sudden temper, pulled her fingers away, kissed them. 'Somehow I cannot see you in a wimple.'

She did not smile. 'If you do not come back I will shave my head and wear one till I die.'

He reached for her thick hair, lifted it from her shoulder. 'If for no other reason then,' he said. She laid her head in his palm. He bent, kissed her eyes closed. 'Keep them shut,' he whispered. 'And when you open them I will be here again.'

She obeyed, as ever. She heard her door open, then the one on the street below, a murmur of voices there. As the horses were ridden away, she kept her eyes shut still, despite the tears that squeezed through. He had never broken a promise to her and, for as long as she could, she'd believe he never would.

THIRTY

Night Cries

It was the cry that woke him. At first, Hamza was not sure if the hawk's call had come from within his dream or without it. If within, then he heard it in the place of dreams, the sand dunes beneath the walls of Laz. If within then, perhaps, he could return there, to his birthplace on the shores of the Black Sea, in the brief time he had left before the *muezzin*'s call to prayer. A few moments of heat, of brightness, before he rose to the chill and dullness of Guirgiu castle, where the piles of furs and sheepskins under which he lay failed to prevent the river chill seeping into his every bone.

If the cry was without, it was most likely the saker he'd brought with him. Though his title of *cakircibas* – chief falconer – was largely honorific now, so busy was he with affairs of state and the Sultan's commands, every man had still to labour at his trade when he could, against the day of disaster. Mehmet himself was to be found in his gardens, trowel in hand. Often, actually, such was the Sultan's love of all things that grew. Every emissary was ordered to seek the rarest plants in the lands they visited.

This embassy was a good chance for Hamza to ready a hunting bird for the spring and Mehmet's fist. But it was an eyass, stolen from its nest too early, so nervous and bad-tempered. His kindness had failed so far. It would soon be time for harshness.

He was awake now, dreams of a warm sea beyond reach. In a few moments he would be forced to his knees, his prayer *kilim* scant protection from the flagstones. Though the Turks held it now, Guirgiu had been built by the Franks years before and they did not seem to care about the cold.

Another cry, but this time more of a giggle and close by. Hamza turned to see the outline of a head upon the pillow, the prized and styled hair a red halo around it. He could guess the sort of dream the man beside him was having. It would involve pain, inflicted.

Thomas Catavolinos. Though after the fall of his city of Constantinople, he had converted to Islam in order to serve the Sultan, and taken the name Yunus Bey, Hamza still thought of him by his former name. The man had made little other concession to the faith, kept the clothes, the uncovered hair, the Greek delight in all things devious. And he had risen high because of certain skills . . .

Hamza sighed. He knew why Mehmet had yoked them in the harness of this embassy. As a falconer, he had often used a blinded rat, tethered near a saker's nest, to trap an adult bird. He was that rat, to lure the one they were to meet. While the man beside him had been sent for his special talents. The Sultan's orders had been clear – once the Prince of Wallachia was taken he was to be broken. As with his falcon, Mehmet did not have the time to make his enemy biddable himself. He only wanted to enjoy the results. And no one was more skilled at breaking men than this Greek.

Hamza shuddered. It was not something he would be involved in, praise be to Allah, Most Merciful. He remembered how hard it had been to break the youth. How much more would it take, now he was a man? A man who had ruled, and of whom . . . disturbing stories were now told. A part of him hoped the prince would not come, that the lure of his own reassuring presence would not be enough. Yet, what choice did Vlad have? Hamza had spies in every court in Europe. All told him the same thing. That though Vlad might itch to face his enemy, every other monarch was looking the other way. Hungary alone was actually mustering. But Corvinus had taken too much papal gold not to put on a show. Hamza was certain he had no intention of going to war.

Vlad would know this. Indeed, his spy at Targoviste, a *boyar* named Dobrita, had told him how isolated the prince was, even in his own land. He would have to come, bring tribute in coin and boys, bend his knee. And it would achieve him nothing. Mehmet had decided that the throne of Wallachia needed another, more compliant, occupant – his lover, Vlad's brother, Radu 'cel Frumos' – 'the Handsome' – more beautiful now than when he was a pretty boy, and still in Mehmet's heart. Often still beside him on his divan.

Another noise, a groan this time. Hamza looked again, in disgust. He'd been unable to refuse his fellow ambassador the comfort and warmth of Guirgiu's only bed, since they were of equal status. He supposed he could have chosen to sleep in the stables himself. But the winter had bitten hard.

Their first night in Guirgiu, he had suspected the Greek would attempt to seduce him, had lain tense, ready to fend him off. But in their week in the fortress, he had come to realise that the man was interested in neither men nor women – in that way. Only in pain. And truly, Hamza knew, his own appetite for men had never been strong. In his life, he had simply . . . loved. His four wives, especially his first, Karima; Murad, the old Sultan, when he was his cupbearer. For a time, the one they had been sent there to take. And the green-eyed youth was the only man he sometimes still thought about, at night.

Hamza shivered. Perhaps he will not come, he thought.

And then it came again, the cry that had woken him, and it had him off the bed in a moment, despite the frosted air, the freezing stone. For the bird that gave the cry should not be there! Only a heron or a rough-legged buzzard should be hunting the Danube delta in December. Not a goshawk. That bird should be snug in the forests of the north, awaiting spring.

Someone must have brought it there.

He found slippers, a robe, and climbed the stairs that led from the room to the turret platform above. In the last light of a waning full moon, the Danube glistened silver on the three sides of the island the fortress was built upon, those that he could see. Yet it was not to the water that Hamza looked now but to the land, the flood plain rising gently in banks of mace reed to a stand of white willow about two hundred paces from the narrow bridge that joined island to shore. The moonspill etched the trees in silver, around cores of darkness.

And then a shape separated from the willows, stepped to the side of them so it was silhouetted against the coming dawn. When an arm was raised, Hamza knew he was looking at a man, not a beast, one as black as the darkness he had come from. A cry came, the same call that had woken him; slightly different because this one came from a human throat.

'*Kree-ak, kree-ak.*'

It was only because the moon was yet bright, his eyesight good and he was staring so very hard that he saw the fast-moving shape swoop down, saw the man bend to absorb the velocity of the goshawk's landing. The man straightened and, for a moment, all was still. Then he vanished among the trees and Hamza, who had been holding his breath, let it out on one, slow word.

'Dracula.'

'Voivode? Where are you?'

Ion's harsh whisper was lost beneath the willows. His prince had been beside him a few minutes before. And then he had gone, soundlessly, and the next noise he'd heard was the hunting cry of that cursed hawk Vlad had insisted on bringing! Ion shared his friend's passion for falconry. But was this the time and the place?

'Voivode,' he hissed again.

'Here.' Vlad slid in beside Ion as silently as he'd left.

'What have you been doing?'

'Hunting.' Vlad raised his left fist. 'But my beautiful Kara Khan has had no success.'

'Of course not,' Ion said, exasperated. 'What sort of fool flies hawks at night?'

Vlad's teeth glinted in his smile. 'This kind.' He gave a low whistle and immediately his falconer-servant, Stoica the Silent, came from the shadows, moonlight reflecting off his bald head. 'Take her,' said Vlad, and the man nodded, the only reply he could make since the priests had taken his tongue for blasphemy. He pressed his gauntlet to Vlad's, luring the bird with meat from a pouch, then retreated to the darkness again.

Ion was not satisfied. 'Are you not worried that you were seen?'

'At night, this distance from the castle?'

'Someone might have seen you. Recognised you even. And if they did, they might tell Hamza *pasha*.'

'He already knows I am coming. We have hardly made it a secret.'

'But he might be concerned that none of his men has warned him of our nearer approach.'

'He might.' Vlad grinned again. 'Have you the clothes?'

Ion shook his head, sighed. 'Stoica has them here.'

Vlad whistled again. 'You worry too much, my friend,' he said as his servant, birdless, came forward bearing clothes and armour. Vlad took the breastplate, held it up to his chest. 'Good,' he said. 'I was worried we might not find one that fitted. Is it possible that the Turks are growing taller?'

He began to pull off his black clothes, Ion holding what was discarded, Stoica passing what replaced it. 'We got this from one of those we killed tonight,' Ion said, watching his prince transform into a Turkish warrior. He stripped to his loin cloth, then put on two cotton robes, topping them with a knee-length woollen *capinat*. Over this he pulled the mail-coat that covered him from shoulder to shin. The breast-and-back plate was slipped over, a skirt of steel links dropping to mid-thigh. As Stoica moved to tie the straps, Vlad looked at Ion. 'Come, Ion *bey* before you split a gut. Say what you wish to say.'

'Well, since we are using Turkish titles . . . Hospodar,' Ion snapped, 'I think this is madness.'

'And have said so often enough. Though never in front of the men.' He glanced at Stoica who kept strapping. 'Even dumb ones. But I have told you before: I need to make sure of the castle. It will be my base for all that is to follow.'

'I understand that. What I don't see is why I cannot be the one to take it.'

'With me safe in the camp, you mean?' Vlad shook his head, as Stoica knelt and began to fix greaves to his shins. 'After all this time, have you not learned? I can never, will never, lead from behind. My *kismet* is already fixed. If I am to die this day then there is nothing I can do about it.'

'Maybe you won't die. Maybe you'll be recognised and taken,' Ion grunted.

'What? In this cunning disguise?' As he spoke, Stoica tied a silk scarf around his face, then offered him the turban helmet. When Vlad had slipped it over his head, and spread the metal mesh that hung from it over his shoulders, only his eyes shone, their greenness pale in the early dawn light. He gestured at them with two fingers. 'Besides, if anyone does note these – and Ilona assures me they are my best feature – I hope they will be using their own to look at you.'

Ion sighed. 'You are merry, my prince.'

'Of course. I am about to start killing Turks.' He stepped back a pace. 'How do I look?'

Ion considered. 'Like a sodomite donkey,' he said at last.

'Excellent,' replied Vlad. 'I should blend right in.'

Stoica had gone back into the bushes. He returned, holding an armful of weapons. 'Ah!' said Vlad, his hand resting for a moment on the Dragon's Talon.

'Prince . . .' Ion warned.

'You are right, my friend. They may not know my eyes but

a *yaya* with a hand-and-a-half, marked with the Dragon . . .'
He sighed, looked to the heavens. 'Soon, Father,' he murmured, releasing it, picking up the Mamluk sabre with its slightly curving blade and hilt, cutting the air with it, swinging it hard down. 'Good balance but . . . no,' he said, 'for where we are going I think this mace' – he hefted the heavy club with its four-fluted head of iron – 'and a falchion.'

Slipping the long-bladed dagger and club into his belt he turned and began to move through the trees, the crust of ice on the shallow stream cracking beneath his feet. Ion followed and soon they had come to a bowl-shaped pool, surrounded by willows, its banks thick with reeds. Sitting among them were twenty men dressed just like Vlad. Dangling from branches were the same number of men, stripped naked, their black tongues protruding from swollen lips.

The soldiers rose as Vlad and Ion entered the circle. Their leader took his time to look each man in the eye and nod. They had been with him a while, these *vitesji*, selected men who had helped him regain his throne and hold it. Thirty of their comrades were back in Targoviste, keeping the *boyars* in hand. Those here, nearly all Wallachians, had been chosen because each had spent time among the Turk – as soldiers and slaves both – and spoke the tongue.

Vlad beckoned one of them forward. 'So, Ilie,' he said to the man standing beside him who seemed to be twice his height and inordinately dark, 'have you mastered it yet?'

'No, Voivode.' The man's voice was as dark as his face. Now he held out what he had in his hand. 'There's something wrong with it. It cannot be pulled all the way.'

'Cannot?'

Ilie gripped the string, inhaled, then drew. But it reached no further than his chin. After a moment of shaking, he relaxed the string. 'See?' he grunted. 'Broken.' He looked around. 'Everyone has tried.' His gaze came back, met Vlad's. He tipped his head and held out the bow. 'Except you.'

Vlad looked up into the man's black eyes then around at

the rest of his men; all silent as Stoica now, staring back. Only Gregor smiled, as he always did. Ion shook his head very slightly. He had also tried the bow, and failed, and was reminding Vlad that the Turkish bow was a very particular weapon. To draw it required a skill possessed by few men who had not practised with it since childhood. For it did not take mere strength but focused strength. And the head-shake was also meant to remind Vlad of something else – soldiers were always looking for favourable signs before they went into battle. Their leader failing to pull a bow, even if all had failed before him . . .

So Ion shook his head. Don't, his eyes said.

Vlad took the bow. Saw immediately that one of the men who dangled behind them must have been wealthy, for the weapon was of the finest kind. The wood was certainly maple, the sinew stretched over it undoubtedly buffalo. It looked old although it was hard to tell with a Turkish bow. The best, it was said, could last for two hundred years.

Vlad reached back, not turning. Stoica placed his arrow ring in his hand. He had had it since Edirne, when a bowyer had fitted it to his finger with sealing wax. Slipping it on, he took one of the long pine arrows his servant held, ran his finger down the swan-feather flight. He looked up once more into Ilie's black eyes. Then, fitting the arrow, he drew, paused for a moment where Ilie had halted, string to chin, breathed deep . . . then pulled it all the way to his ear; held it there a moment before he loosed the shaft. The arrow whispered between the willows towards the river beyond.

Vlad lowered the bow. 'I'll keep this if I may.'

'Yours, Voivode.' Black Ilie grinned, bowed, stepped back.

'So, let us follow the arrow,' Vlad said, and as men bent to pick up their weapons, he turned to another man, dressed in the clothes and armour of a Wallachian, his commander of cavalry. 'You know the signal, Buriu. Keep Stoica before the trees so he will be clear.' He nodded at the dumb man. 'And when you come, come fast.'

'Voivode,' Buriu replied. Then the two men bowed before disappearing into the reeds, to join the second, far larger party of men, hidden in a small valley beyond.

His *vitesji* stood in two files. He took a step towards the front.

Ion's hand restrained him. 'Prince . . .' he said.

Vlad placed his hand over his friend's. 'In one hour, Ion. In the castle my grandfather built. It begins.'

And then he was gone, the files following. The gap was narrow between two willows, and the two men hanging there were spun opposite ways by the passing shoulders. When the last soldier had moved through, Ion stepped up, stilled the spinning, hands to naked feet. 'Go with God,' he murmured. Then he set about his own tasks.

THIRTY-ONE

Troy

To Hamza, the scenery around Guirgiu was as dull under the sun as it had been by moonlight. The endless banks of reeds still waved in the Austru, the frigid south-easterly wind. The Danube still moved, sluggish and grey, between them. On the crest of the small hill the willows and poplars were skeletal, even more barren now that their leafless branches could be seen.

At least there was some life now, some movement. On the water, boats set out ceaselessly from the Thracian shore bringing supplies and men. He had seen at least two boat-loads of soldiers. Though it was yet early winter, Mehmet was already preparing for war and this frontier fort must be reinforced.

A war that might not take place if Vlad Dracula is part of the other movement, the one on the land, he thought, and wondered at the different ways that made him feel.

'Is that him?'

The voice startled, for the Greek had come on slippered feet up the stone steps to the battlements. Pulling his beard three times – a gesture he was annoyed to find had become a habit – Hamza looked at Thomas Catavolinos for a moment, then back to the party of men beginning their descent from the trees, the twelve horsemen and three carriages, the last a black-draped *palanquin*. 'Perhaps,' he said. 'The two wagons could contain the tribute. And the prince sent word he was sick, remember? So he could be in that last carriage.'

'But where are the boys?' Thomas said, leaning forward on one of the crenulations.

'They will follow. Our spies say Prince Dracula has been recruiting in every village.'

Hamza studied the man beside him. He had been about his toilet, for his hair had once more been tamed into red spirals that fell to his shoulders. And the eyes he now turned to Hamza were subtly shaded in crimson.

'You must be so excited, *enishste*. To be seeing your old lover again.'

Hamza grunted, looked away to the water, to the boats now docked and disgorging their cargo of soldiers. He hated that others knew of his life, especially the man beside him. But he had told the old Sultan, of course, about Dracula's final taming. Murad had told his son and Mehmet had told the Greek. Since the fall of Constantinople, the Sultan had taken more and more of the conquered noblemen into his inner circle. It was hard these days to find anyone in the Divan who spoke fluent Osmanlica.

'Is it true that this Dracula studied for a time at Tokat?'

Hamza nodded. 'He did. Reluctantly.'

'And so did I. Not reluctantly at all.' He clapped his hands delightedly. 'I am sure we've added some refinements since his time. I shall be pleased to demonstrate them to him. On him.'

He laughed again and Hamza shuddered. He knew the commands of his Sultan must be obeyed without question. He had seen what happened to those who failed Mehmet. But it didn't mean he had to like his role. And he still was uneasy as to its fulfilment. The Vlad he remembered was far from stupid. He would know how Mehmet still felt about him. And he had surprised them in the past. Radu had told the astonishing tale of the abduction of a concubine in the streets of Edirne.

Perhaps he would surprise them now. Perhaps he *would* be lying in the black-draped *palanquin*, fighting the fever that was said to have seized him. And in case he was . . . Hamza gave a final glance around the courtyard. Men were everywhere, of course, moving about their tasks. But many – his men – were still; watching and waiting. This was particularly true of the main tower of the gatehouse, almost a separate fortress within the larger one. He looked up to its battlements. Every crenel had a soldier in it. Yet Hosnick, his commander, had obviously decided to put even the arrivals to use, for a party of new men was approaching the tower from the direction of the dock.

All was ready. It was up to Dracula now to surprise them or to disappoint. Tugging his beard three times, Hamza was not certain which he would prefer.

He looked to the road. The Wallachian party had passed through the huts clustered around the approach road and were now reforming to cross the narrow bridge that led to the island fortress. Though it was not Vlad, there was something familiar about their tall commander. 'Shall we go and greet our guests?' he said.

They descended the stairs, preceded and followed by their ceremonial guard of six halberdiers. They reached the floor of the castle yard, just as the first of the horsemen came through the gate. Hamza did not need to look to see that his men were ready. He could hear the slight creak as scores of arrows were notched and bow-strings pulled back. Then there was a sudden, louder noise, someone dropping armour in the tower above. Startled, he looked up . . . but there was Hosnick, leaning through a gap of stone, a hand raised.

The party ahead halted. All were dismounting or climbing down from the wagons. Hamza stepped forward. 'May Allah, Most Exalted, be praised for your safe arrival,' he said.

The leader of the Wallachians handed his reins to one of his men. Taking off his helmet he turned and spoke. 'And may the Most Holy Father bless this reunion of friends.'

Hamza halted, a half dozen paces away. 'By the beard! Ion? Ion Tremblac?'

'The same, Hamza *pasha*. Your most stupid student,' replied Ion.

Both men made the obeisance – head to mouth to heart, hands opening in welcome.

'It is not true, Ion. Sometimes the strongest tree grows from an unpromising sapling. And look at you – a fine Wallachian oak indeed.' Hamza, who did not consider himself small, found himself looking up into Ion's eyes. He sought Mehmet's *tugra* beneath the fringe of long, fair hair, but the brand was hidden. 'Forgive me. My fellow ambassador, Yunus Bey.'

The Greek made the same obeisance, then stepped closer. 'Before Mehmet Fatih, most glorious, lifted the scales from my eyes and brought me to Allah, most merciful,' he said, 'I was called Thomas Catavolinos. And I used to greet my fellow Christians thus.' He held out his hand. 'Is it not so?'

'Indeed, sir.' Thomas took the hand, surprised by the strength in the womanly man's grip. 'I am honoured.'

'As am I.'

The hands dropped. All three looked at each other for a moment in silence until Hamza spoke. 'And my other student? Your prince, Dracula. Is he well?'

'Alas, *enishte*,' said Ion stepping back, 'he is still weakened by the fit that took him. But he would not be left behind.'

'He's here?'

'Yes.' Ion swallowed, glancing up. Then he took a step, the others following. He led them along the line of the covered wagons, past the dismounted soldiers who, Hamza noted, were armed with nothing more than the daggers agreed upon in the preliminary letters. As he walked Ion spoke. 'These two wagons contain, not only the 10,000 crowns of gold but also certain gifts – for both of you and, of course, for the Sultan.'

'Most pleasing,' murmured Hamza.

'The *devsirme* follows. You know how slowly boys walk. Fifteen hundred of our finest youth.'

'Gratifying,' said the Greek.

They had drawn level to the *palanquin*. Ion began to untie the straps that held the black cloth down. Immediately there was a sound from within, a rustling. 'Easy, Prince, easy,' murmured Ion. His fingers shook as he untied.

Hamza frowned at the placating tone of voice. This illness that had taken the prince? The tales from Vlad's court had become increasingly strange. It was said that in his fits he would do the most terrible things. Indeed, many spoke of a man who had lost his mind. Yet, in the Abode of Peace, the insane were treated with respect for, having forsaken the holds of this world, they were thought to be one step closer to paradise. So, as Ion managed to undo the last of the straps, as he began to throw back the cloth, Hamza prepared himself for a vision. Not only of an old love, but of one of God's lost beloved.

And saw a hawk. In the centre of the otherwise empty carriage was a perch. A goshawk was tied to it, a tiercel by his size. He raised his pale blue wings, fluffed out his black and white belly feathers, and let out a shriek of outrage – '*Cra! Cra! Cra!*' – at his sudden exposure to the light.

Ion had put on the gauntlet that rested inside. Now, making soothing sounds in his throat, he undid a latch in the *palanquin*'s latticed wall, opened a small door, reached in, untied the jesses and drew the bird gently onto his fist. The tiercel shot its head down, biting hard on the thick leather of the thumb. Yet despite its surprise, it settled swiftly. Beautifully trained, Hamza could instantly see.

Thomas, obviously not a falconer, had stepped away fast from the shrieking bird. Now he peered around Hamza. 'What's this?' he said.

'A goshawk. And a beauty.' He reached a hand forward and the hawk eyed it, seeking prey. Hamza withdrew it, smiled. He'd decided not to show any surprise. 'No doubt a gift from Dracula to me?'

Ion did not answer. But another voice did, calling from above them. 'No, *enishte*. The Black Prince is mine.'

The Turk, looking up, saw two things. The first was Hosnick, his throat fountaining blood, tumbling feet over head to thump into the courtyard's floor. The second was the man who had spoken, his face hidden by a scarf, thrusting out a gauntleted fist.

Ion stepped away from the wagon and threw out his arm. Kara Khan, the Black Prince, took off fast. It took him only four beats to reach the other hand. He stayed there only a moment, though, before he was launched into the air again.

'Good hunting,' Dracula cried, as the world went mad.

THIRTY-TWO

The Taking

On top of the gatehouse, every crenel was now filled with a Wallachian, each drawing their bows to full stretch, the shorter men standing on the bodies of the Turks whose throats they'd slit, to get more height.

Vlad had tipped his step-stool into the courtyard. So he jumped up into the gap, balanced there, drew and shot. The halberdier to Hamza's right was clutching an arrow in his chest as he fell backwards.

There was no need to command. Each of the *vitesji* knew exactly what to do. So Ion just wrapped an arm around Hamza's throat. 'Move and you die,' he hissed, resting the point of his dagger in the man's ear.

Frozen, Hamza stared at what was happening. At other arrows felling the remainder of his guards. At the Wallachians in the courtyard running to the two wagons, ripping back covers, pulling out swords and shields. At those shields lifting over and around them, him and Thomas at the centre of a barricade of rising, steel-ringed wood, their backs pressed to the *palanquin*. Ion, to take a shield, had to release Hamza's throat. And the Turk knew that, if he was captured – if Dracula captured Guirgiu, for that was what was happening, it was clear – he was a dead man. Prince or sultan would see to that. So, the moment before Ion's shield closed to cut off the world from sight and sound, he screamed, 'Take them!'

The strange silence that had held for the few moments since Hosnick fell, which had only been filled by the creak and thrum of bow-string and arrow and the sigh of men suddenly dying, was shattered by the cry.

Everyone in the castle began screaming at once, everyone but the Prince of Wallachia and his men who were shooting arrow after arrow while they had the chance. Many fell. But Vlad knew it was a garrison of three hundred – and that they were Turks, the conquerors of the world. He knew their officers would have recognised the old Roman tactic of the *testudo* that was temporarily protecting Ion and his prize. That many would also have noted an older story – the Trojan Horse. Twenty men did not take a fortress. But they could take and hold a gatehouse until an army stormed in.

As the first Turkish arrow bounced off the crenulation before him, Vlad stepped back, moved to the side of the tower, saw there what he'd expected – officers already rallying men at the west tower along the battlements. There would be a similar rally to the east.

'Swords, to me!' he cried. Half the men joined him. 'There!' Vlad pointed and his men loosed shaft after shaft at Turks beginning to run along the battlements towards them. Many fell, others tripped over the bodies. But most kept their shields high. And Vlad could also see that some held a battering ram in their midst.

The other side, another flight of arrows, another charge damaged but not stopped. It was time. Shooting a last arrow, he did not even pause to see if it had found its mark. 'Now!' he shouted, and his men followed him, leaving only 'the Bows', the six best archers, to stay and harass.

He'd glanced once to the landward side. Kara Khan must have found Stoica's hand because riders were emerging from the tree-line, moving slowly as they must so as not to turn a leg in the streams and pools hidden in the reeds. It would be some minutes before they reached galloping ground. Minutes that the drawbridge must be kept down.

The four men he'd left in the mechanism room had done the best they could. Barrels, boxes and rope coils had been piled against the barred wooden doors, east and west. Now, seven men faced each door, Vlad turning to the one from which the first thump came. From the sling at his belt he drew his mace. From its sheath his falchion. He'd been correct as to his choice of weapons for, like all such rooms, there was little space around the giant winch that would pull up the drawbridge. His bastard sword would have been unwieldy.

He glanced at his men as the second thump came. Most had made the same decision, dropped the Turkish swords that had been a part of their disguise, held small axe, short spear and dagger. Only the huge Black Ilie carried a weapon to match – the pole axe, with its cutting blade, spear-point and hook. He grinned at Vlad, and tipped the blade in a salute.

And then the eastern door fell in. It was held up for a moment by the barrels piled against it. Then it was lifted, shoved in. Vlad and his men stepped aside to avoid it as the first Turk came through the door. He stumbled on a coil of rope and Vlad drove the man's helmet into his skull with one swift swing of the mace.

Many more waited behind him. '*Allah-u-akbar*,' the Turks cried, surging forward.

'St Gheorghe,' yelled the Wallachians, stepping up to meet them.

Vlad was right in the middle. It was always thus for him. Battle made everything simple, reducing the world to single, clear sounds – the scrape of steel on steel, the snap of bone, the shrieks of rage, pain, terror. He felt neither anger nor fear, only the craving to take another enemy's life. A hundred or one, it was the same to him. Someone who wanted to prove himself stronger, failing to do so.

As these did, coming one after the other, dying one after the other. But Wallachian success – and his men were killing as many as he – was also their problem. The body mound grew but it was a moving barrier, forcing the defenders back.

And then a huge Turk, roaring his fury, ran over the bodies of his comrades, knocking Ilie aside with a swung shield, bringing down his sword in an unstoppable arc towards Vlad's head. There was nowhere to go but back. His foot hit the winch platform, the slice missed his face by a finger, the force causing the blade to bite into the floor, the wood holding it there just long enough for Vlad to punch his falchion straight through the Turk's throat.

Yet the doorway beyond him was clear and where one had got through, three came now. 'With me,' Vlad cried, sheathing his falchion, snatching up the man's shield. He hurled it into the face of one man, ducked the swung blow of a second, smashed his mace into the knee of a third. Blades passed him on either side, driving the Turks back.

'Voivode,' came the scream from behind him. Vlad turned to see the other, western door, the two men he'd left there stepping away from it as the axes, whose thudding Vlad had heard somewhere in the mayhem, reduced the last of it to splinters and broke the crossbar in half. His two men killed the first two of the enemy who came. But others loomed in the doorway. Many others.

'Hold here!' Vlad commanded. 'Gregor! Ilie! Gheorghe! With me!'

At a glance he could see that his fourteen men had been reduced to ten. Five for each door. Is it over? Vlad thought, with the same clarity, the same dispassion. He snatched up another shield, looked over it at the first of his enemies, a huge bearded brute, hesitating in the western doorway. It would not be for long. The Turk never hesitated for long.

And then the man's lips parted, his eyes opening wide – shocked, no doubt, by the arrow head sticking a hand's breadth out of his throat. For a moment he looked down, crossing his eyes to see what protruded. Then he fell and men either side of him were leaping clear of his body, flinging themselves off the battlements before the door, preferring a fall to the arrows coming at them from the walkway behind them. Vlad saw an arrow pass through the space where a head had just been, and miss him by a nail. He turned to see an enemy trying to pull it from his eye, giving up, sinking down. Beyond him came Ion and his *testudo*, locked shields battering the Turks from the walkway.

Vlad felt tired. He knelt as did the men around him.

'Are you hurt, my prince?'

Ion crouched beside him. Vlad shook his head. 'The castle?'

'Nearly ours. A few groups holding out; most are fleeing. Buriu's killing them.'

'Hamza?'

'Safe. Stoica has him, and the other, the Greek.'

'And my Black Prince?'

'Back on his perch.'

He offered an arm and Vlad hauled himself up. 'Good,' he said, 'he'll be hungry.'

THIRTY-THREE

Messages

Vlad knew it was midday because, surprisingly, the *muezzin* had begun to issue the call to prayer. His men had thought this inappropriate in what was now a Christian castle and had used the imam as target practice for a while. He must have died happy, despite the intrusion of arrows, a martyr assured of paradise.

Vlad had just finished issuing his orders. How many should be slain and in what manner; how many mutilated and sent out into the world. The strongest of the prisoners would be marched back to Targoviste for they would survive the longest on the least and, if things went well, they could be exchanged later for those few Mehmet would spare. If things went badly . . . well, that would be judged then.

'Voivode,' said Ion, coming into Guirgiu's main hall, slipping around the scaffolding that shrouded the door; the Turks had been re-building, workmen's tools scattered all around. 'Do you want them now?'

Vlad looked down, considered. Under normal circumstances there was a decorum to such embassies, a protocol to be observed. One didn't usually greet ambassadors with the blood and brains of their servants on one's doublet. But that, of course, made them abnormal circumstances.

'Yes, my friend. Bring them in.'

The four were held by his sword-and-bow men, all now dressed again in their black uniforms. They were brought up to the raised dais and its table covered in maps, lists, scraps of bread and meat. Vlad studied them, noting the bruise on

Hamza's face; the extraordinary red profusion of the Greek's hair. It was unhindered by a turban and Vlad suspected that, despite his conversion to Islam, such glorious hair was rarely concealed. Hamza's turban had been knocked off, perhaps in the same blow that had given him the bruise. Vlad was surprised at how grey his hair had become. The other two ambassadors still wore their turbans, albeit somewhat askew.

He looked at the table before him. Because of the breeze coming through one of the great stone arches, he'd weighted down his papers with a mallet and nails abandoned by some fleeing workman. He slid one of the papers out, studied the names of those before him. Abdulaziz he half remembered, a minor official under Murad, risen now. Abdulmunsif, the younger of the two, he did not know. Taking up his quill, dipping it, he hesitated a moment, before putting a line through one of the names. Then, without looking up, he said softly, 'Is it not customary to remove your hats in the presence of a prince?'

He raised his eyes. All four men were staring at him, wondering who was being addressed. He decided to specify. 'Abdulmunsif. It means, "Servant of the Just", does it not?'

The man swallowed, nodded. 'Yes, lord.'

'And no doubt you emulate your master. So deal justly with me. Does one not remove one's hat in the presence of a prince?'

The man blinked. It was Hamza who replied, his voice roughened with shouting. 'You know the reason they do not, Prince Dracula.'

'Because of the example of the Prophet, in the presence of Allah, most merciful.' He stepped down from the dais, stood before it, hands clasped. 'But while we are certain the prince is here, how certain are we that God is? Here, now?'

Hamza licked his lips. 'You blaspheme. It is a sin in your religion as in ours.'

'Ah, but I am not sure I do. Perhaps God, however we name him, is elsewhere right now. Busy with other sinners.'

258

He stepped up to Abdulmunsif. 'Would you render me justice, just one? Would you remove your hat?'

The Turk began to quiver, looking at Hamza, who had lowered his eyes again. '*Effendi*! Lord Prince! I . . . I cannot. Allah forbids it.'

Vlad nodded, smiled. 'You are as brave as you are just.'

Abdulmunsif was not a small man. But Vlad lifted him easily by the collar of his robes up onto the dais before the table. Nodding to his men, two of them came forward and pinned the Turk by his arms. Vlad picked up one of the long nails. 'I admire courage,' he said, 'and I will help keep you steadfast in your faith.'

Then, snatching up the mallet, he placed his knee on the Turk's neck, forced his head onto the table and, with one strike, drove the nail through the turban and into his skull. The man's cry was short. His legs thrashed for longer as the men held him. When they finally stilled, Vlad picked up three other nails and drove them in too with single strokes. Then he stepped away. 'Abdulaziz,' he called.

'No, master, no! See? See?' The smaller, older man was on his knees, the turban ripped away, revealing his baldness. 'I beg you. I pray . . .'

Vlad nodded and two of his men grabbed the weeping man, dragging him to the table, throwing him down there. Vlad bent, spoke gently. 'Abdulaziz?'

Still the man did not react, his eyes shut, babbling prayers. So Vlad tapped him lightly on the temple with the hammer. The whimpering stopped. 'Good,' he said. 'Now listen. It is not your *kismet* to die this day, but only the one of God's choosing – if you do exactly as I say. You will be escorted across the river and a little way along the road. You will then continue to your master. You will not be quite alone for your companion, the just one's servant, will be with you, exactly as he is now.' He stooped, laying the hammer against the man's skull. 'But listen to me well. No, Abdulaziz, open your eyes and your ears and listen to me.' The man stared up. 'If you do not deliver Abdulmunsif to Mehmet exactly as he is, I will hear of it and then . . .' He drew back the hammer, struck with a light but distinct *thok*. '. . . Then I will find you. And at that time, you would pray for nails. Do you understand?'

'Yes, *effendi*. Yes, Prince. Thank you! I . . . yes . . .'

Vlad raised the hammer, halting the flow of words. 'Take him,' he called. Two men lifted the Turk and half-dragged him from the hall. Two more brought the other, after a little difficulty in prising him from the table. Vlad waited till the doors closed behind them all before he spoke again. 'Thomas Catavolinos?'

Swallowing, the Greek watched Vlad walk forward. 'I am hatless, Prince Dracula.'

'Of course you are.' Vlad smiled. 'And besides, such a joke is truly only funny the first time.' He stopped before the kneeling man. 'I hear you were at Tokat?'

'A fellow graduate.'

'Yes. Though I am sure you were there willingly.' He glanced at Hamza, who did not look up, still knelt, eyes downcast as they had been since the hammer's strike. 'So I would be interested in your opinion on impalement. I believe I have made a few improvements. Sped the whole thing up. Practice, eh?' He smiled again. 'Ion, take our handsome friend to the courtyard. Make sure he is in a good place to see everything.'

Ion came forward, grabbed the Greek's hair, jerking the yelping Catavolinos to his feet. 'And him?' he said, nodding at Hamza.

'Leave him with me. The rest of you, go.'

Ion frowned. 'I'll leave two guards . . .'

Vlad shook his head. 'No, my friend. My old teacher and I have so much to talk about. Best we do it alone. And Hamza *pasha* is not the killing type.' He looked down. 'He lies. He . . . corrupts. But he gets others to do his killing. Go.'

They did. Soon the hall was clear except for the two men, one kneeling, one standing. Vlad returned to the table, lifted a flagon there. 'Some wine, Hamza? No, of course! You were one of the few men at Murad's court who did not drink.'

Hamza raised his head, cleared his throat. 'Men change.' He rose, joined Vlad at the table.

'They do indeed.' Vlad filled two goblets, held one out.

Hamza paused before taking it, staring at Vlad's hand. 'Not even shaking. Has it become so easy for you to kill a man that you do not even quiver at it?'

Vlad handed him the cup and gestured him into a chair that Hamza took. 'Why would I? If I ever did, that time was long ago. Before my lessons began. And you were one of my first, my best teachers, Hamza *agha*.'

'I did not teach you that. I tried to teach you other things.'

'Such as?'

'The philosophies of love. Of compassion. As expressed in our Holy Qur'an and in your own Bible. In the verses of Jalaluddin and Hakim Omar Khayyam. Do you not remember them?'

'No,' said Vlad leaning closer, his voice soft. 'All I remember now is the lesson you taught when you bent me over the cushions . . .'

'Stop,' said Hamza, leaning away. 'It wasn't like that, Vlad. We . . . shared . . .'

'How is my brother?'

Hamza blinked at the interruption, the sudden switch. 'Radu . . . thrives. He is held in great estimation by the Sultan.'

'I am sure he is. Are they still lovers?'

'I . . . do not believe so.'

'No. Radu is twenty-five now. Mehmet would be seeking younger company.' Vlad refilled Hamza's goblet as the wine had been gulped down. 'And how *is* my old schoolfellow? They call him "Conqueror" now, after Constantinople. Mehmet *Fatih*. But conquering can be as compulsive as wine.' He raised his goblet. 'Will his desire for it ever be sated?'

'I do not—'

'I hear he calls himself the new Alexander. That he will not stop until he has an empire as far-flung. And here am I. Me and my tiny country. In his way.'

'There is yet time, Prince.' Hamza set down his goblet. 'Do not take him on in a war you cannot win. Submit. Send the tribute, the boy levy. Do not provoke him further.'

'I think we are beyond that, teacher,' replied Vlad, folding a piece of parchment, using it to divert a stream of ambassador's blood that had been coming towards him. 'I will cut off the noses of his people and send them to him in bags. I will burn his crops, kill his cattle. I will impale his soldiers and, if people get inured to that, I will devise new and ever better methods of slow murder.'

'But . . . why?' Hamza swallowed. 'Why this . . . excess?'

'To do exactly what you say I should not – to provoke him. To make him come for me before he is fully ready.' Vlad nodded. 'Do you know what they used to make us chant at Tokat? "You torture others so they cannot torture you." It was the motto of the place.' Vlad smiled. 'And was not that what Mehmet had planned for me? I could have brought you all the gold in Wallachia and ten thousand prime boys and I would still have been in a cage by nightfall and the Greek would have tried to break me on the road to Constantinople. Ready for Mehmet to have . . . easier amusements. True?'

There seemed little point in denying it. Hamza nodded.

'Of course. You see, we understand each other, Mehmet and I. We send each other messages.' Vlad leaned across. 'It sounds so glorious: the New Alexander. But history no longer tells us how many died horribly so the Macedonian could build his empire. And this Fatih – how many were slaughtered when Constantinople's walls were breached? How many boys and girls were raped that day on the altar of Santa Sophia?' Vlad stood. 'If I were to follow anyone's example in history it would not be the Macedonian but the Carthaginian.'

Hamza stood, too. His legs felt weak and he leaned against the table. 'Hannibal? Why? Wasn't he the cruellest of all?'

'*Because* he was the cruellest of all. He took on Rome, a nation five times stronger, and beat it again and again. Less than a hundred years ago, a shepherd from the east, Timur-i-leng, did the same, smashing the Turks, killing their Sultan.' Vlad's eyes glowed. 'I make no claim to be Alexander. But I may be Hannibal. I may be Timur-i-leng.'

'No, Vlad,' Hamza said, stepping up, taking the younger man's arm. 'You will be what they already call you – Kaziklu Bey, "the Impaler Prince". Is that the name you wish to be remembered by?'

'Hamza,' Vlad said, lifting the other man's hand, holding it for the moment, 'if I succeed, I will only be remembered as the man who freed Wallachia.'

They stared at each other for a moment, then Vlad dropped the hand, stepped back to the table, reached for the mace that was lying there. When he turned back he was smiling. 'Do you not think it strange that I am known by a skill I acquired almost at your knee? But if you have a reputation for something, you may as well preserve it.' He moved towards the door. 'Come. I have something to show you.'

Hamza did not follow. 'I have already seen impalement, Prince.'

'You see, you become known for one thing . . .' Vlad shook his head ruefully. 'No, Hamza *agha*. I was going to show you other fruits of your teaching. You are still chief falconer, are you not?'

'I am, in title. But I have little time for birds.' Hamza began to follow. 'Do you sew?'

'Alas, time is as chary with me.' He opened the door. 'Do you still have that glove I made for you?'

'With me. I never travel without it.'

'Indeed?' Vlad tipped his head. 'I am honoured, *enishte*.'

They passed into the courtyard. Hamza looked around.

On the western side, those of the garrison who had not been killed in the assault or managed to flee had been gathered. Wallachians, with arrows notched, watched them. Others stood by horses. Ropes were coiled. Shafts of wood leaned in bunches, like hay ricks on Wallachian farms. No one was moving. Hamza shuddered.

Vlad had not looked. He walked on, through the door of the eastern tower, up the circular stair to the room that Hamza and Thomas had lately occupied. The Turk saw that their possessions were gone. In their place was a trunk with a silver Dragon embossed on the lid.

They did not pause in the room, went straight up to the turret. 'You saw my beautiful Black Prince but you did not meet him,' said Vlad. He went to the perch set up there, pulled on a glove, reached and untied the bird's jesses, took it onto his hand.

'A beauty, indeed,' Hamza murmured, admiring the goshawk tiercel again. 'Passage or eyass?'

'Passage, praise God. Taken last year. Already about five, wouldn't you say? See the touch of red in the eyes?'

Those eyes were darting, seeking meat. Vlad reached into a pouch that hung there, passing a morsel across. 'A fool had him, tried to train him. Failed. I didn't.' He bent his head to the bird, cooing softly. 'Still mostly training sakers, Hamza?' he asked, his eyes still on the bird.

'In fact I have one . . .' He broke off. There was something in Vlad's eye, a flash of red, almost like the hawk's.

'Would you like to see Kara Khan hunt?' said Vlad. 'He's a true cook's bird. I've seen him take ten rabbits in a day, three hares, pigeons . . .'

'Pigeons are hard,' Hamza said, uneasily, though he didn't know why.

'And uncommon this time of year. I wonder what we could . . .'

Vlad let out a sudden, sharp whistle. And in the gate tower along the battlements, a shutter was flung outwards. From the gap issued a bird and, from the way it flew, Hamza knew immediately it was a saker. His saker.

'Kill,' Vlad said, throwing out his fist.

It wasn't a long chase. The saker was fresh from the mews, disoriented flying over new ground, ground the goshawk had already traversed. Yet the saker saw the other coming, in those five beats, that glide. Tried to climb higher, faster, use its larger wings. But a goshawk loves an underbelly. Five more beats, a flip onto its back, into the glide. Talons reaching, sinking in.

The two birds spiralled down. Just before the ground, the goshawk flipped again, spinning around to get on top, releasing the other bird that was possibly already dead but was certainly so when it smashed into the frozen ground before the little bridge. The Black Prince settled, one foot planted, its feathers riffling in the wind off the river. He looked around once, then plunged in his beak to rip and tear.

Hamza made sure he had control of his voice before he spoke. 'He flies well. Are you not going to call him back?'

'No,' said Vlad, taking off his glove, laying it down. 'Let him feed.'

He turned, crossed to the castle side of the turret. All the men there were looking up. Bound prisoners. Guards with ropes, pulleys, wood. Waiting.

The silence was complete. Vlad raised one arm . . .

THIRTY-FOUR

War

July 1462, seven months later

The twilight was affecting Ion's eyes.

Every time he looked at one of his companions, the man's face would shift, features sliding into other features. Black Ilie would be sitting there, then his dark features would change, his nose lengthen, his eyes sink, his hair change, lighten . . . and Gheorghe would be in his place. Gheorghe, who had taken an arrow through both lungs trying to halt the enemy at the ford over the Dambovnic. He'd spent three nights coughing blood yet they'd carried him as they retreated before the enemy, committing his recovery to God's mercy. But when, on the fourth day, God had shown none, Ion had received the man's blood-choked blessing, then slit his throat. He could not go further. And they left no one to the Turk.

Which was why he should not be here now. Why Ion had grown certain that Gheorghe had become a *varcolaci*, one of the undead, his black Dragon coat turning to wolf skin, his desire clear in his so-pale face: to be avenged on the one who'd slain him. Why, when Ion reached to his belt now, it was not to feel the comfort of sword but of crucifix.

He stared; the features realigned. It was Ilie sitting opposite him again, Ilie who said, 'Are you well, *vornic*?'

Ion nodded, laid his head on his knees, closed his eyes. When had he last slept? Truly slept? When had any of them? Most nights were spent doing everything possible to slow the enemy. Burning any crop that already stood in the field in July. Emptying the farms, both peasant's small-holdings and *boyar*'s estates, of anything that could be eaten or drunk. Driving the people before them with what little they could take, slaughtering the animals they could not, throwing the corpses down wells or using them to dam the streams to poison all water. At least if they did not sleep, they ate well, and drank before they poisoned. The Turks, in the hottest summer in anyone's memory, slaughtered their dogs and camels, as well as the horses that died of thirst, and roasted the flesh without the aid of fire upon their searing breast-plates.

And during the days, they fought. Not in battle, not since the Danube when they'd first tried to stop the enemy and had slain so many the river turned red. The Wallachians fought in raid, bursting out from beneath beech and oak to attack any who strayed from the column in their desperate search for drinkable water. They fought in ambush, in the gorges, rolling trunks down to crush, using arquebus to shoot, the gunpowder explosions terrifying man and beast. They fought with disease, sending the sick dressed as Turks into the enemy camp, martyrdom their reward if they died, gold if they somehow returned alive. And each of these coughing men and women Vlad kissed before they left, kissed hard on the lips as he blessed them. When Ion tried to dissuade him from the act, his prince had said but one word: '*Kismet.*'

Yet, no matter how they fought, how many they killed, the Turk came on. It was rumoured that ninety thousand had crossed the Danube. The Wallachians never numbered more than twenty thousand. And even if the enemy was reduced by battle, sickness, starvation and terror, at least half of them still marched relentlessly towards Targoviste. While Ion knew that the retreating Wallachian army now numbered less than five thousand.

Ion looked up again, had to or he knew he would sleep. Saw the officers of that shrinking army sitting in concentric circles around the bowl of the small glade. Over its lip, the rest of the army had drawn tight, on Vlad's orders before he'd gone out three days before. 'I will return before sunset on the third night, Ion. Keep them here,' he'd said before he left, dressed as a Turk and accompanied only by Stoica. And somehow Ion had held them, in eyes for ever open, with threat, with promise, with the call of loyalty to their prince and their love of the True Cross. But if Vlad did not return this night, only God would be left. And He would not be enough to hold them together.

A voice forced his head up. '*Vornic*,' said another man opposite him, 'the sun sets. He will not come.'

He had spoken softly. But any sound carried in the bowl of the glade and all two hundred officers looked up. 'There is still light in the sky, Gales *jupan*. Our Voivode deserves a little grace.'

'Not much,' muttered Gales, loudly enough to be heard.

Ion studied him. He was a short, round man, whose fat the privations of campaign had done little to diminish. One of his eyes was wooden, painted. He claimed he'd lost the other fighting for Dracul years before, though most believed the rumour he had lost it falling onto a fence stake when drunk. Ion often wondered why Gales had stayed, one of only two *boyars* to remain with the army; the second was Cazan, Dracul's chancellor, and as loyal to son as to father. The other five had deserted quietly, leaving papers behind detailing various excuses, taking their men with them. But Gales was the brother of Stepan 'Turcul' – and Stepan 'the Turk', named for his time as a war prisoner, was the greatest of the *boyars*, the second man in the kingdom. Ion supposed that until Vlad was completely beaten, or preferably dead, neither brother dared to defy him.

It looked as if Gales was preparing for defiance now. And Ion knew that if he didn't stop him, at least half the officers sitting there would leave with him. Yet exhaustion held his tongue. What words could he speak?

And then he didn't have to. For Black Ilie, sitting on the *boyar*'s right, reached over and laid a huge hand on the man's arm, squeezing. Gales gave a little yelp, his one eye fired in pain and protest. But he didn't speak more and Ion smiled. A few years before, any peasant who even touched a *boyar* would soon be hanging from the nearest branch. But Ilie was dressed in black and wore the silver dragon; he was one of Vlad's *vitesji*, his chosen men. They did anything their Voivode ordered. Gales had seen what that meant, and he subsided now.

Ion glanced up to the west and it was the first time he did not need to shade his eyes. The sun had half-sunk below the lip of the bowl. Soon it would be night. Vlad had not come.

Then something moved in that last flash of sunlight. Ion saw a familiar silhouette there – an enemy's turban. He was about to cry out that they were surprised by the foe, when the figure stepped out of the sunflash, below the ridgeline, and Ion saw who it was.

'All rise for the prince,' he called.

Men leapt up, brushing dust from their clothes, looking every way, trying to see in all the movement a particular one. The man who moved through them was not conspicuous and most were looking for their black-clad Voivode. Instead, man by man, they finally saw someone dressed in the simplest of Turkish clothing. Not a *sipahi* warrior, not even an *akinci* scout. An artisan wearing a grey turban, a stained yellow robe, baggy *shalvari* and rope-soled sandals. But behind him, dressed in uniform black, walked a shadow, Stoica the Silent, carrying the Dragon's Talon. Men knew the master by the man – and the weapon.

Ion bowed low, as did everyone when they realised. He took the proffered arm and Vlad pulled him close.

'Still here?' Vlad whispered, taking the water skin Ion handed him, drinking deep.

'Only just,' Ion replied.

'Good,' Vlad said, stepping away. He reached up, removed the turban, and his long black hair cascaded down his back. Then, with arms spread wide he turned a full circle, displaying himself. 'Countrymen,' he cried. 'I bring good news from the Turkish camp. They all want to return home.'

Cries of wonder, of joy. Then Vlad added, 'We just have to give them a little push.'

'How little, Voivode?' came a cry from the slopes.

'Nothing much,' replied Vlad. 'All we have to do is kill their Sultan.'

Gasps, some laughter. The same voice came again. 'Then can we get him to come here, Prince? My horse has the squits.'

Louder laughter. 'Then you'll have to borrow one, Gregor. For we must ride to him.'

There was no humour in Gales's voice. 'What plan have you conceived, Voivode?'

Instead of answering, Vlad turned, passed Stoica his turban and drew the sword his servant held from its sheath, raising it high in the air. Gales stumbled back but Vlad did not move towards him. 'Come close,' Vlad called, 'so all may see.' Then, with the tip of his blade, he carved the circumference of a wheel in the sand of the dried-up stream bed, the diameter twice the height of a man. Then he began on the four spokes.

By the time his men had gathered into three tight circles, the nearest and tightest being *vitesji* and the two *boyars*, Vlad had finished. Now he walked to the centre of what he'd fashioned. 'Mehmet,' he said quietly, driving the blade down. He stepped away from it, the twilight casting a moving crucifix upon the ground.

'The sword is the Sultan's *tug*. It is raised before his pavilion at the centre of the vast camp that is made each night. Here Mehmet sits, surrounded by his army. Here he sips his sherbets while his men thirst. Here he entertains his . . . friends. Here, he has forty thousand reasons to believe he is safe.' Vlad looked up. 'He is not safe.'

He walked to the edge of the circle, bent and snatched up a handful of pebbles. 'These lines,' he said, 'are the four main roads in. Though all around is a web of ropes holding up a city of canvas, these must be kept clear. For messengers. For Mehmet, who might suddenly decide to ride out and hunt or hawk. These roads are his ways out.' He smiled. 'They are also our way in.'

He began to walk around the circumference, dropping stones. 'On the outer rim dwell the conscript masses, the *yaya* infantry of Anatolia. Also his *akinci*, those scouts and raiders from the mountains of Tartary who are unleashed ahead of the army.' He smiled. 'We have been slaughtering *them* in their thousands.' He began to walk down a line towards the centre, scattering stones. 'Here, the *belerbeys* from the provinces pitch their pavilions, surrounded by the *sipahi* warriors they have brought – from Anatolia, from Rumelia, from Egypt and the shores of the Red Sea.' A stone landed in each quadrant as he named them.

Ion, seeing his prince empty-handed, fetched more. Vlad took them, continued throwing and naming. 'Here, closer in, are the *orta*s of the janissaries, and here those who are even more select. To the right of the *tug* – Mehmet's right, for his tent faces Mecca – is planted the red oriflame of the right wing of his household cavalry. To his left, the yellow standard of the left.'

Vlad leaned now on the quillons of the Dragon's Talon, the left one for ever bent so all would note it and remember his triumph in single combat over his cousin Vladislav. He let the final stones drop now. 'Here, at the very heart of the camp, surrounding the two pavilions he uses – one for sleep, one for his Council – are the Sultan's closest men.' Drop. 'The *muteferrika*, with their halberds.' Drop. 'His *peyk* guards, the spleenless ones.' Drop. 'Here the *solaks*, these who draw their bows with their right hands, here those who draw with the left, so he is always covered.' Drop. Drop. 'And here, at the very centre, is Mehmet.' Vlad placed the last stone against the metal and let it slide down. 'One man.'

Vlad stepped back, waved his hand along the southern

road. 'We will ride in here, with the full moon at our backs. I know that the *akinci* here are grudging in their service. The *sipahis* beyond them are from the east and suffered most in the last war against the White Sheep Uzbeks. All is not well beneath the yellow oriflame of the left wing. Mehmet had their veteran commander strangled with a silken bow-string last year and his successor has tried to buy love with raki, which they drink now instead of the water they must save for their horses.'

A murmur was building under his words, a buzz of wonder. He raised a hand to quell it. 'And here stand the *peyk*. The removal of their spleens may have made their dispositions more conciliatory. But it has also made them less fierce. And in the end, they are all that will stand between me and Mehmet. One man.' Vlad straightened. 'Does anyone wish to ask a question?'

Gales, the *boyar*, stepped forward. But it was Black Ilie whose deep voice broke in first. 'Voivode, some of us have visited Turkish camps. Some of us have even lived in them. But how, by the giant balls of Samson, do you know all this?'

When the laughter died down, Vlad smiled. 'That's easily answered, Ilie. There was a tear in Mehmet's tent wall. I repaired it.'

Vlad let the gasps and murmurings continue longer than the laughter had, then went on. 'You all know that the Turk has two camps – one that is built, one that is struck, each leaping over the other so the army can progress smoothly. This morning, I walked into the one they were building. I spent the day walking around it, talking to servants and slaves. Then I was asked to sew Mehmet's tear.' He turned to Ion. 'It seems I have not forgotten all the skills I learned in Edirne against the day of disaster. Though I did not do the work well. You never know when you might want to leave a tent by its walls instead of its door.' He looked around the circle. 'Other questions?'

It was Gales who spoke. 'I am not certain I understand this, Voivode. How many men are in their camp?'

'They will have raiders ranging wide. Forces have been detached to seize different places. I estimate they will have close to thirty thousand around the *tug*. More or less.'

'More or . . .' The *boyar*'s mouth opened wide. 'And you plan to ride in with the four thousand we have left?'

'No,' said Vlad. 'There will be two thousand with me from the south. And, a short while later, you will bring the other two thousand from the north.'

'I . . . I . . .' Gales spluttered. 'But even if your way to the Sultan is blocked by feckless, drunken . . . spleenless men, there will still be close to ten thousand of them in that quarter alone.' The thought removed his fear. 'Have you lost your mind?'

Men hissed. Vlad was not one of them. 'And have you lost your heart?' he said, stepping close. They were of a height, their gazes level, locked. 'You have seen what Mehmet has wrought upon our land. You know what he will still do if he is not stopped. We cannot beat him in the open field. We can only slow him with raid and destruction.' His eyes gleamed. 'But we can stop him with a single sword-thrust. In the terror of the night, in the chaos of their camp, a few men who know exactly what they are doing can end the war. They can save their country. Perhaps they can save Christendom.'

He had spoken to the *boyar* but every man there heard him. He turned to them now. 'Crusaders,' he called, his voice ringing beyond the glade, carried by the rising slopes to the soldiers who had gathered on the far side when word of his return had spread, 'our destinies hover at the point of our swords, raised under the cross of Christ. If we die in this Holy War, we die as martyrs and we go to heaven to sit at God's right hand, all our sins forgiven. If we triumph, then we avenge Constantinople. We conquer the Conqueror.' Snatching up the sword, he held it aloft, his voice rising to a shout. 'So will you follow the Dragon's son to victory or to Paradise?'

The cry had travelled far over the glade. Now the sound crashed down, from the officers within, from their men beyond: 'Victory!'

Vlad let it roll on for a while, then raised a commanding hand. 'Go to your fires. Hone your blades. Feed your horses, eat what you can, sleep if you can. Make your peace with God and your fellow man. Gather at the eastern edge of the forest two hours beyond midnight. And prepare to ride to glory, in this world or beyond.'

It came again, one shout: 'Victory!'

The officers turned, scrambled from the glade.

One remained, his one eye rolling wildly. 'Tonight? You attack tonight?'

'*We* attack, *jupan*. Or must someone else lead the forces of Amlas and Fagaras?'

The one eye centred. 'I will lead them, Prince. As ever.' Then he turned and followed the others up the slope.

Vlad and Ion watched him go.

'He will not come,' said Ion.

'I think he will. He knows what will become of his family and himself if I succeed and he has failed me. But if he doesn't . . .' He turned, handed his sword to Stoica, who sheathed it, bowed and ran ahead. Vlad began to follow, walking slowly up the slope towards his own encampment. Ion could see how weary his friend was, now the course had been set. 'If he doesn't, then you will be there to kill him and lead his men yourself.'

Ion stopped. 'Me? I shall be guarding your back as ever.'

Vlad halted, too, looked back. 'Not this time, old friend. I need your sword in Gales's back or through his throat. I need the second attack to happen.'

'Then why not let me lead it?'

'You will, truly. But Gales must be seen to lead it. The other *boyars* are wavering. In Targoviste especially. If Turcul *jupan* sees his brother still fighting by my side, they might hold firm a little longer. Then my back truly will be safe.'

They had reached the ridge. Paths furrowed the ground within the thick oak and beech forest of Vlasia, hiding the Wallachian army from Turkish eyes. One led, in a few short steps, to Vlad's tent.

And to the two men standing before it. Ion could not see their faces at first, so swiftly had the gloom taken the woods. He hurried forward, preparing to shoo them away, whatever their news, for his prince must rest if he was going to lead his army into battle in a few short hours. But then he saw who they were, and he could not speak.

THIRTY-FIVE

Vows

Vlad saw them, too. 'Your Eminence,' he said, kneeling to kiss the Metropolitan's ring, 'what make you from Targoviste?'

The churchman was tall, and lean with it, taking his spiritual role of God's Appointee far more seriously than many who had grown fat on the profits of the position. His serious face was troubled now. 'I have news, Prince. And I could trust no one else to bring it.'

'I see. A moment.' He turned to the other man, who stood in battered armour encrusted with dust, his face so filthy it was barely distinguishable. 'And you, Buriu, most loyal of my *boyars*? Could you trust no one with your news, either?'

'Alas, my prince,' the man replied, 'I had no one left alive to trust.'

Ion flinched. Vlad had been forced to send Buriu east with half his army to defend the key fortress of Chilia. Not from the Turks. From his own cousin, his former fellow fugitive, Stephen of Moldavia, who had chosen this moment to betray him, and Christ, by trying to seize what he most desired. That Buriu was here again, alone . . .

Vlad must have realised the same. 'Inside, friends. And speak quietly, I pray you.'

The old *boyar*'s news was spoken quietly enough and swiftly. There was not much to tell.

'My scouts failed to return. I knew I must proceed with speed, lest that accursed Moldavian seize the fortress. But it must have been him who warned the Turk . . .' Buriu's voice cracked. 'They waited for us in reeds either side of a bridge. They let half my men across then attacked from both sides. They had five times our numbers. I . . . was with the rearguard. I still don't know how I escaped, why I was spared . . .'

The older man began to weep. Vlad sat beside him, put a hand on his shoulder. 'You did not die, Spatar, because I needed you beside me, Dracul's oldest friend.'

The man looked up, wiped his eyes. 'Is it true what I heard? That you ride this night against Mehmet's camp?'

'It is.'

The old *boyar* rose, every joint creaking. 'Then I must go and knock the dents out of my armour.'

'My lord.' Vlad rose, too. 'You have done enough. Rest this night.'

'When the Dragon banner flies against the enemy?' A little smile came. 'Your father would never forgive me.'

He stooped under the tent flap, was gone. Stoica entered, with bread, meat and wine. Vlad turned. 'Will you pardon me, Eminence, if I . . . ?'

The priest gestured him down to his truckle bed. 'You will need sustenance, Prince, for what you attempt tonight. And, alas, for what you must hear.'

Vlad sat, drank and chewed. 'Go on.'

'You know that when you took the throne, I was uncertain of your intentions. I thought that perhaps you were just another in a line of voivode, seeking power only for your own glory.'

'And now?'

'I have seen what you have wrought. I may have questioned some of your methods . . .' – the prelate swallowed – '. . . but I have seen the results. A land free of brigands, where men and women can live without fear of another man taking their little. A land where the Church flourishes, for you have been a keen benefactor. And what you are about now, this crusade . . .'

Vlad interrupted with a sigh. 'Your Eminence, I am glad you approve. I have always tried to follow the Church's dictates – with a few personal adaptations.' He glanced at Ion. 'But in hours I will face my greatest enemy and all my work may be undone if I do not succeed. And the look in your eyes fills me with fear. I do not need that. So please, tell me why you have come.'

The older man nodded. 'Then hear this: the *boyars* plot against you.'

Vlad smiled. 'You could have saved yourself the ride from Targoviste. Every time a crow caws in the forest they sing me that same song.'

'But now they believe they have a weapon to use against you.'

'What weapon?'

'The woman, Ilona Ferenc.'

Ion stepped forward. Vlad rose. 'She is well?'

'My lord, she is with child.'

Vlad closed his eyes. For a moment, he was not there, a prince preparing for battle. For a moment he was back in her house, on her bed, a lover only, and Ilona was promising him release, with no consequences. '*It is safe, my love, safe. I know my times . . .*'

She'd lied. The only one who never would, had.

The priest stared at his prince's quivering eyelids. He glanced at Ion, swallowed, went on hurriedly. 'And the *boyars*, who have always hated her for her hold on you, for the fact that you will marry none of theirs while she lives, see this as a chance to hurt you.'

Vlad, eyes still shut, nodded. 'Because of my vow.'

'Yes. Your vow to have no more bastards, spoken to your confessor, re-affirmed to me before the altar of the Bisierica Domnesca. They think you still will not marry her. That you will break the vow, dishonour her and yourself. Most of all break your covenant with God just when Wallachia needs Him most.'

'I see.' Vlad lifted his head, listened. Beyond the canvas, an army was preparing for battle. The whistle of steel being honed on the whetstone. The strike of mallet on armour as dents were hammered out. Somewhere close a man was singing a *doina*, a sad lament of a shepherd's lost love. Vlad listened for a moment to the plaintive tune, waited for the harmony . . . which came, beautifully, from a higher, boyish voice. Then he nodded, accepted God's Will and called out, 'Stoica!'

His servant appeared. He carried an arming doublet. Vlad began to strip off his Turkish garb. 'Your Eminence, when we gather, you will bless the host and kiss the banner of the Holy Cross. Then you will return to Targoviste and make preparations for my wedding.' Stripped to a long shirt, Vlad held out his arms and Stoica slipped the arming doublet over them, immediately beginning to cinch the leather cords. 'One week from now, at midday on the Feast of the Saints John and Simeon, I will come to the Bisierica Domnesca. I will either be in my coffin or on my feet. If the first, let a mass be sung for my soul, for I died a warrior Prince of Wallachia. If the other . . . well, let the wedding bells ring.'

Stoica, his initial task complete, picked up the first pieces of steel, the sabaton and greave for the lower leg. Vlad stared at the black armour piled to the side. A fortune paid for it, to the craftsmen of Nuremberg. Very different from the borrowings he'd worn to take the throne.

Such a long road since, he thought. *So many sins.*

He stayed Stoica's reaching hands. 'Hear my confession, Your Eminence?' he asked, kneeling. 'Though I do not know if I have time for any penance.'

For the first time, the Metropolitan smiled. 'Bring the head of Mehmet Fatih to your wedding feast, Prince Dracula, and you will have done penance for a lifetime.'

'I am not so sure. I have much to atone for. With more to come.' Vlad crossed himself. 'But I will try. For God's love, for all my sins, I will try.'

They gathered just inside the canopy, on the long ridge-line where forest gave way to sloping meadow. In the clear sky a full moon turned the contours of the land silver, lining them in black. It looked as if a hundred thousand stars were reflected in the centre of the plain far below. But it was the Turkish camp, its four roadways a dark cross within the circle.

Vlad nudged Kalafat forward, Ion and Gales following. 'It will take us two hours to ride around to the southern side. Then, with the moonlight near behind us, we will charge down that road. Gales *jupan*, ride to the crossroads of the blasted oak. As soon as you hear the fight begin – and I think the wailing of the enemy will carry clear to you there – charge in along the northern road. With God's good grace, we will meet again beneath Mehmet's *tug*.'

'How will we recognise your men in the fray, in the dark, Voivode?' Gales said. 'Your own fine armour is, of course, so distinctive. But many of our men have picked up the enemy's armour along the way.'

'I have prepared for that.' Vlad raised his voice and it carried clear along the canopy's edge. 'Let each man dismount now and, kneeling, ask for a remission of his sins, paid in Infidel blood. And let each man tie the white ribbon, symbol of Maria the Holy Mother's purity, to his helm.'

The word spread to those who hadn't heard. Soldiers dismounted, came beyond the tree-line, knelt on the slopes. Priests in tall mitres, carrying the staffs of the faith, moved among them, uttering blessings, dispensing white, silk scarves, which the men affixed to their helmets.

Vlad and Ion knelt side by side, were blessed by the Metropolitan, rose and returned to their mounts together. Each began checking straps and weapons. 'You know who will likely be there, beneath the Sultan's *tug*?' Ion asked quietly.

Vlad nodded. 'For years I have dreamed of freeing my

brother from Mehmet's embrace. I only hope that, when we meet again, Radu remembers that he is also the Dragon's son.' He reached for his Turkish bow, the one he'd carried since Guirgiu, which no other man there could pull, and slipped the bow-string over his head, making sure the weapon rested easy on his back. Then he turned. 'So, Ion. I will see you there.'

Ion's reply was soft, for one man only. 'Right in the middle of the fight, Vlad. As ever.'

His prince smiled, then watched as the white banner with the red cross was waved a last time before being brought back into the forest. Vlad waited for Christ to have His moment. Then he turned to his left side and the huge, dark man there. 'Now,' he said.

Black Ilie bowed, then urged his horse forward, halting twenty paces before the forest. Clear to all those within it, he rose in his stirrups and began to swirl the tall pole he held, unwinding the cloth upon it. When it was free, he leaned back, brought the banner shooting forward. Lit by moonlight, the silver dragon soared. 'Dracula!' Ilie cried in his huge, deep voice.

'Dracula!' came the echo from four thousand throats. And on the cry, with the Dragon flying before them, the host of Wallachia swept down the slope.

THIRTY-SIX

Kaziklu Bey

They had ridden in an easy canter, swung wide around the Turkish camp, paused to re-group at the head of the valley that gave onto the plain. Now that they were again riding downhill, drawing closer, they began to gather speed, though not yet at full gallop. The contours of the land, narrowing down, forced them together, a phalanx of men and horses. When the valley ended and they were on flat ground, his men spread to either side of Vlad in ranks of two hundred men, ten files deep.

Closest to him were his *vitesji*, the fifty who were left of the original hundred, and closest still his bannermen: Black Ilie, Laughing Gregor, Stoica the Silent. All fifty were armed, like their leader, in finest, blackened Nuremberg steel, the lightest and strongest that could be bought. Behind each of them rode a squire – armoured, too, if not so finely. Each of these younger men carried a pitch torch, lit before they began the descent, the flames bent back by the speed of their passing.

All had seen the twin-tailed comet that had torn through Wallachian skies the year the Dragon's son took back his father's throne. It was said then that Vlad had ridden it to his triumph. To those who followed now, it looked as if that comet flew again, their prince once more astride it.

The valley floor was as parched as all the land, a few tufts of grass clinging to the dust that rose up and followed them in a great, roiling cloud. It was this the first of the enemy saw, taking it to be a storm cloud, the flames within it the first flashes of lightning, the sound of hooves the growl of thunder. When they saw it, even the Dragon could be explained – for these nomads of Tartary knew that dragons dwelt on their mountain peaks and would descend to suck the bones of men. They did not even reach for weapons, for no mortal's blade could kill such a beast. The safest thing was to wait unmoving beside their horses and hope that another was chosen to sate the beast's hunger. Some died waiting, falling not to a Dragon's claw but to the arrows that Vlad's companions shot. Not many. There were more important targets ahead.

It was a *yaya* from the plains of Anatolia, a poor farmer waking from a dream of crops and the cool water in his own well, who was the first to realise the truth. His brother had disappeared into the dungeons of Tokat, never to return, and he had lived in dread of the punishments practised there ever since. So when he woke and saw the Dragon banner he knew it was neither beast nor storm but something far worse.

'Kaziklu Bey,' he cried, giving out Vlad's title in his own tongue.

Impaler Prince.

They had swept in from the side, because there were more guards at the outermost end of the road. But they were through the outer lines now, past the *akinci*, who slept beside their horses in the open air, and the *yaya*, who slept in huge tents that could be avoided. Ahead, though, the tents grew smaller and ever closer together, their ropes a snare for flying hooves.

Black Ilie was watching him closely, riding nose to haunch. So when Vlad swerved right, the Dragon banner swerved with him and the phalanx of men followed, heading towards the road.

It was time. Vlad did not need to look for Stoica. The little man rode on his other side, his sturdy tarpan horse almost at full gallop to keep up with Kalafat. Everywhere Vlad looked now, flame edged up to the elbows of his *vitesji*, who all imitated him now – unshouldered their bows, felt in their quivers for the arrows with the cloth heads wet with oil, drew them out and, in one flowing movement, passed the tips through fire, before notching them to strings, swiftly drawn back. The targets did not require much in the way of aiming. All arrows found their marks: the pavilions of the *sipahi* horsemen. Their pitch-caulked canvases were afire in moments.

'Kaziklu Bey!' The cry coming from many mouths now, the terror clear.

'Do you hear me coming, Mehmet?' Vlad whispered. His visor was still raised and his eyes moved constantly, seeking targets for his normal, bone-tipped arrows; seeking most for the change in tents that would tell him where he was.

It came. Beyond the smaller pavilions of the *sipahis* were rows of camel-hair cones that swept up to a larger, single pavilion. A pole stood before it and, in the moonlight, Vlad was able to see the flag upon it, the elephant rising on its yellow and green background. He could even remember – for as a student he had worshipped these men – the *orta* that the flag represented.

The 79th, he thought, and remembered the last time he had seen that elephant, outside the tavern in Edirne, when he had stolen Ilona. The thought was there, then gone as he yelled, 'Janissaries!' then drew and shot, drew and shot again. An arrow struck him, the first he'd received, glancing off the fluted planes of his breastplate. He pushed down his visor. His mount wore little armour, for Vlad did not wish to restrict Kalafat's nimbleness. But she had a thick, quilted hide coat, studded with small metal plates, and a steel shaffron to protect her head and muzzle. This, with its sharpened spike, the length of a man's forearm, thrust out above her eyes, transformed her. It was a unicorn the Turks saw, a black devil on its back, galloping beneath a silver dragon.

Waves of shrieking men had fled before the storm, knocking over tent poles, gouging out ropes. Vlad saw them crashing into men trying to rally, saw these janissaries slicing the deserters down. Someone was thumping the great *kos* drum; and soldiers, some in helmet, some in breastplate, most in neither, but all with weapons, were scrambling to the elephant standard.

His desire was to fight and kill only one man that night. But these janissaries were the heart of the enemy army. And they stood between him and the road to Mehmet.

'To me,' he cried, though there was no need, for his men were still tight with him, his black-armoured comrades closest. There was time for a last flight of arrows. Then bows were slung and, in the next instant, swords unsheathed. 'Dracula,' they screamed, and charged into the rallying janissaries.

There were perhaps three hundred janissaries, perhaps more. They were scythed like wheat, the *vitesji*'s blades dipping, rising, a harvest of blood.

And then Vlad was through, most of his men with him, and the road was gained, wide enough to take twenty men abreast. After a little jostling, horses and riders settled, increasing speed, a flaming spear driving straight into the heart of God's enemies.

Theirs was not the only flame. The avenue was lined on both sides with lanterns, oil-soaked rags burning within them. The speed with which he was moving now made it seem that the lights were moving too, fireballs streaming towards the road's end – Mehmet's pavilion.

A hundred men could lie toe to head along its front. He could see the walls he had helped to stitch only the day before; make out the two-tiered gate that was its entrance. He was far enough away yet that he could only see the flagpole, not what topped it, but Vlad knew that the *tug* had six horsetails, the golden crescent of Cibele and a thousand, chiming silver bells. And he could see that men had gathered at its base. Perhaps one of them was the one he sought.

Two, he reminded himself, as arrows flew from the side

and he lowered himself beside Kalafat's head as he had once lowered himself playing *jereed*. Where Mehmet was, Radu would be, the brother he'd been unable to rescue. Another surge, the space consumed by Kalafat's speed, and he would be upon them both.

And then his view changed. Where there had been only a few frantic figures between him and the *tug*, now his way was blocked by horsemen. He could see moonlight glint on breastplate and helm, men who had been forewarned enough to arm, at least partly. He could not tell the colour of their standard but he knew it would be yellow – the silken oriflame of the household cavalry of Anatolia.

He'd told his men they were disaffected, unhappy with their commander, probably drunk. He had not needed to tell them that they were still fine warriors, among the most elite of Mehmet's guard. And behind them, also rallying, he saw infantry clutching halberds – the spleenless ones, the *peyk*.

There was no moment to pause, to be daunted. Vlad levelled his sword beside Kalafat's head, offering a parallel steel thrust towards the enemy – unicorn's horn and Dragon's Talon.

He rode at one man, an officer by his crested, feathered helm. His foe held a lance and so outreached him – but there were ways around that, especially as the man only now began to ride and Vlad was still moving fast. When they closed, he feinted right to glance the lance-tip off his rising shield; swerved suddenly left, letting the weapon slide under his shield arm; dropping that suddenly, as he brought Kalafat to an instant halt, pinning the man's weapon to him, pulling the Turk forward, off balance. He'd dropped the pommel of his sword low, the point angled up. Inserting it between chain-mail and chin, Vlad thrust up.

A twist of blade, an enemy falling, seeking another as he turned back into what had become a mêlée. Beside him, Stoica shoved his still-burning torch into the face of a huge Turk who screamed and fell, beard aflame. Behind him he saw Gregor laugh as he crushed a warrior's metal turban with his mace. The Dragon flew forward in the thrust of the spear-tipped standard Ilie bore; another Infidel dead, gladdening God's heart. And then the next wave of Wallachians crashed through, and the Anatolians of the left wing were swept aside.

Men on huge warhorses passed Vlad. A touch of his heels and Kalafat was catching up to her bigger, slower brothers. But though Vlad was not in the first wave that smashed into the *peyk,* he could see the havoc wreaked by axe-headed halberds – their side hooks dragging men from their saddles, the rear hammer crushing helmets, the points thrust through visors. Yet the enemy ranks soon disordered into a series of individual combats, and Vlad's *vitesji* had not lost sight of him. They and many more now followed Dragon's son and flying Dragon, threading through the fight.

Into open ground and moonlight and Vlad now close enough to see the horsetails of the *tug,* the men rallied before it. Recognised *solaks* there, the janissary archers of the guard, among mounted and dismounted *sipahis.* As Vlad and his men broke clear of the mob, a thousand points of steel were levelled against them in arrow, spear and sword.

He looked beyond them – and there, at last, were the two men he sought, the purpose of all this death. Mehmet, in a violet night-robe of gold and silver brocade, his great, gilded helmet surmounted by an ostrich plume, stood with a sword in his hand. While beside him, dressed just like him, clutching a bow, was a man Vlad had last seen as a boy. His brother, Radu.

Water came into his eye. He raised his visor to wipe it away, looked left and right at his men. Some were still engaged at points along the way. Some had fled. Many were dead. Of the two thousand who had begun the wild ride, there were perhaps two hundred reining in beside him now. Yet somewhere beyond the Sultan's pavilion, by now Ion should be bringing two thousand more.

He could not wait to find out. He looked at the men he'd

sought, and the men before them. It was not quite a silence, fighting and fear precluded that. But the killing had slackened just enough for Vlad to make something else out – the faintest chime of silver bells.

It lasted but a moment – then the great cry came. '*Allah-u-akbar*,' the Turks roared, beckoning the Christians forward.

The response came easily to men who had seen what it did to the enemy. 'Kaziklu Bey,' the men of Wallachia cried, and followed the Impaler Prince into the charge.

But Vlad and his *vitesji* had sheathed their swords. Once more bows were in their hands. As bone-pointed arrows began to fall upon them, a score of arrows flew back. These, though, were again flame-tipped, sinking into the Sultan's pavilion, crisping the lavish silks that decorated the walls in an instant, streams of fire flowing along tarred ropes. As soon as Vlad shot he slung his bow, drew his sword again, lowered his head as if into driving rain, not driven bone. In an arrow storm all he could hope was that the costliest armour in the land would guide death away from his flesh.

A blow to the chest knocked him into his saddle-back. He regained his balance. Kalafat stumbled, surged on. Then they were through the storm, into the enemy ranks, too close for arrows to fly. It was time for other ways to kill.

The charge had taken him deep into the press. He brought Kalafat up onto her rear hooves, her front ones flailing. He was aware of his men beside him, then he was aware of little but the blows that came, which were pushed aside, the ones he returned.

He was killing. It was something he'd always been good at.

Then, within the blood-flecked mist into which he'd sunk, he remembered why he was there, and looked beyond the mêlée to see Mehmet a dozen paces back, *solak* archers and a few halberdiers around him. The beard was longer, a deeper red. The eyes were more sunken, the lips even fuller. But it was the same braggart he'd known in his youth, the same bully. The man who had come to his land to destroy him.

Who had perhaps destroyed Vlad's brother. Fury came but it did not blind him now. Instead, in that instant, he remembered how he had beaten this man once before, upon the *jereed* field. So when two of his *vitesji* broke from the press and charged, he followed, using them as a screen, as he had once used Ion and Radu.

Two bodies fell either side of him. Two horses shied right and left away from arrows and blades. But Vlad came through the middle and smashed into the enemy. Their ranks imploded, archers with no armour fleeing flailing hoof and swung steel. Those who did not scatter died, while his men, seeing the ranks break, followed him into them.

Vlad had lost sight of his targets. Now he saw them again, the Sultan screaming defiance, being dragged back by the last of his bodyguards, Radu still at his side.

'Mehmet,' Vlad shouted in joy, tapping Kalafat's flanks. Five strides and he'd have him, as Kara Khan took his prey in five beats and a glide.

But Kalafat didn't move. Her front hooves landed on the ground, then seemed to sink into it. She knelt suddenly, coughing blood between bared teeth. Sliding out of the saddle, Vlad saw what he had not seen before – the hedgehog quills of arrows that bristled in her hide chest-coat. Most had not penetrated it. Three were sunk in deeper and the last had pierced her heart. As he stepped away, Kalafat rolled onto her side and closed her eyes.

There was no moment to mourn, none to think. Only to react, to the two men running at him with curving Mamluk sabres. Placing his left hand halfway up his own blade, Vlad ducked and leapt inside the upraised arms of the first man, jabbing the point into his throat, just a little, just enough. The man screamed as he fell but Vlad stayed close, moved his body into the path of the other man who struck over his dying comrade, missed. As he raised his weapon to strike again, Vlad placed his other hand beside his first and, holding the flat of the blade fully now, brought it over and down like an axe, the heavy pommel smashing down, driving the man's turban into his head. He had once killed a prince of Wallachia that way. It worked equally well on a slave.

Before either man had reached the ground Vlad had moved on, towards the raging enemy being dragged into his pavilion. It was burning, but the main canvas had not caught. Anyway, as he slipped under the two-tiered gate Vlad saw that the bodyguards had no intention of pausing there. The rear, lesser entrance was open, and the group was rushing to safety.

'Where is Gales?' Vlad wondered for a moment. Then two men were beside him – Little Stoica, Laughing Gregor – and the three of them swiftly caught up with the group ahead. There were eight guards, armed with sword or pike, and they fought them in the very centre of the pavilion, before the raised bed, as fiery, tarred ropes fell around them. Eight to three but the three in armour and the eight with half an eye on the raging, striking sultan in their midst.

Laughing Gregor died, still laughing, his mace so embedded in a skull he could not withdraw it to block the thrust that took him. Stoica went down, a pike haft to the head, killing the man who struck him, even as he fell. There were two more guards before Vlad and, double-handed on his bastard sword, he took one high, one low.

And then there were just two.

They faced him, one Wallachian and one Turk, both dressed as Greeks in purple, gold and silver robes. He had not seen his brother since he was a boy of eleven. The angel's face had matured into one from the myths, an Athenian hero's. 'Cel Frumos' they called him, 'The Handsome', and he was, his eyes the turquoise of the Bosphorus, his styled brown hair falling thick to his shoulders, his beard exquisitely trimmed. Beside him Mehmet, with his sharply curved nose, his full lips and thick beard, looked coarse and as cruel as his reputation. Both men held the slightly curving swords of the

Turk in fighting stance, blades behind them, hands thrust forward.

From beyond the blazing, smoke-filled tent came the sounds of a battle raging on. The great *kos* drum was being beaten. Then a trumpet sounded – Wallachian – urging the recall, the retreat. No trumpet announced another charge. Gales had not come. But it did not matter. Not with his greatest enemy a lunge away.

Vlad pushed up his visor, stepped forward. The men before him stepped back. 'Brother,' said Vlad, his voice thickened with sudden grief for all the lost years, 'you are free at last. Let Dracul's remaining sons join together and slay the tyrant.'

Radu swallowed, stared.

It was Mehmet who spoke. 'He is my brother now, Vlad Dracula. Yours no longer. And I am giving him the throne of Wallachia.'

'It is not yours to give, Mehmet Celebi,' Vlad said, turning to him, using an old name. 'And my brother still has Dragon's blood, however you have corrupted him.' His voice broke. 'I know what you have been,' he continued. 'So I do not ask that he kills you. Only that he steps aside while I do.'

At that, Radu did step to one side. Mehmet glanced, looked back, snarled. 'While you try, Kaziklu Bey. For I am every part the warrior you are.'

'That we shall see,' said Vlad, dropping his visor, lowering his sword before him, stepping forward.

He was so focused on the man he hated that he did not see the sword flashing down until it was almost too late. He lunged backwards, his own sword rising . . . but one guard was bent, never straightened, in memory of his triumph over Vladislav. So it was not there to stop Radu's Damascene steel slicing through his gauntlet, severing the little finger from his left hand.

It fell to the carpeted floor. All three men looked at it.

'Radu . . .' Vlad gasped.

'No!' screamed his brother. 'You never came for me. You left me . . . to them. Well, I am theirs now. And the throne of my father will be mine.'

Mehmet was moving towards him, smiling. Vlad still held his double-handed sword in his right hand. He raised it now, though it seemed twice the weight as before. 'Radu . . .' He coughed. And then a huge strip of burning canvas rolled down from the ceiling, passing between them, dangling there for a moment before falling.

Sight was lost in smoke and flame. Shapes moved, voices yelled, men rushed in. There was no going forward, or back. Dragging his sword, slick now with his blood, he stumbled to the side of the tent that was smouldering but not yet aflame. He had no breath; his mind, already numbed, was sinking towards oblivion. Then he saw a flap panel, poorly stitched; recognised it as his own work. Choking, he kicked at it till it gave and he could crawl out.

Eyes blurred with smoke and tears, he looked up to see his men, his *vitesji*, still fighting. Once more a Wallachian trumpet sounded the rally, the recall to the Dragon banner that yet waved. He stumbled towards it. But Turks were rallying, too, some turning towards him. He tried to lift his sword.

A cry to his right, from behind what was left of the Sultan's tent. He turned to where two thousand fresh warriors should be charging in and saw one, riding between two *orta*s of rallying janissaries.

'Ion,' Vlad screamed, and somehow his friend heard him, saw him, turned his horse's head and rode to him.

'Vlad,' Ion shouted. But janissaries were running at them now and they could not pause. Grabbing the arm that was thrust down, Vlad, with a scream of pain, scrambled up behind Ion.

Ion looked at the hand that had clasped. 'My prince! You bleed!'

'Ride,' whispered Vlad, laying his forehead against his friend's cool armour.

'Did you—'

'Ride,' he said again, and closed his eyes.

Ion drove spurs into his horse's flanks. It surged forward into the conflict. At its centre, Black Ilie was swinging a huge sword with both hands. He had driven the Dragon banner into the earth to do so. Snatching it up, Ion cried, 'Wallachians! To me!'

Few could have heard him. But the sight of the Dragon flying away was plain, and those that could followed it. A far smaller phalanx swept back the way they'd come. Since most had fled from their coming, few made any attempt to halt them now.

THIRTY-SEVEN

Moloch

'Vlad,' she called, trying to rise at the opening of the door.

'No, Ilona. Only me.' Ion crossed to her, laid a hand on her shoulder. 'Rest.'

She tried to resist even the gentle pressure. 'It must be time. I should . . .'

'It is not time. And you would have to stand out there. The heat is terrible in the church. It is cooler here and you are yet weak. Rest.'

'I am better,' she lied, sinking down. 'A little longer and then I must . . .' She placed her hand on the one that still lay on her shoulder. 'He will look for me first when he comes, as he always does. I would not want to disappoint him.'

'If he comes,' said Ion, sitting, leaning on the table to place his head in his hands. He had been tired for months. Ever since the Turks crossed the Danube.

'If? Have you heard anything more?'

He looked up at her fear. 'No. Only the same rumours.'

She looked away. 'The ones that say he is already dead.' When he didn't reply, she closed her eyes. 'Tell me again.'

'Ilona—'

'Tell me. Of the last time you saw him alive, a week ago. When you speak of it, I see him, here.' She waved her hand across her shut eyelids. 'And then he is still alive, here.'

Ion sighed. He wished he could lie to her. But in all the years they'd known each other, all the time they'd spent together – time that Vlad could not spare – he'd never been able to tell her even one comforting lie. 'The Turk came after us. *Sipahi* knights. *Akinci* raiders. We had to fight our way back to the Vlasia forest. For a while, despite it all, I thought Vlad slept, so silent was he upon my back. But then, on the edge of the trees, five paces from safety, one of his *vitesji*, Nicolae, took an arrow in the throat, fell dead from his horse beside us. And Vlad stirred, leapt, was on that horse. He had pulled his right-hand gauntlet upside-down onto his left, to try to stem the blood. But I could see it dripping . . .' Ion broke off. It had to be the exhaustion. Telling no lies did not mean telling everything. 'He shouted at me, "Ride to Targoviste." And then he turned back, to fight, to kill, to bring in the rest of his men. And I obeyed.' He swallowed. 'I left him.'

Ilona still had her eyes shut. She looked as if she were studying something inside them, leaning forward slightly, her vision of Vlad keeping him alive. ' "Ride to Targoviste",' she echoed softly. Then her eyes opened. 'And there is fighting still. The rumours speak of that.'

Ion nodded. 'The Infidel comes on again, but much more slowly. The night attack has made them edgy. And if Turks are still being slain, then I believe it is our prince who is slaying them.'

'I believe it, too. And the night attack? It nearly succeeded?'

'Nearly. If Gales had come, not fled to some hole. If I could have stopped him . . .' He shook his head, glanced to the door. 'But nearly is not enough. Not for those jackals out there. To them "nearly" is a defeat.'

She reached forward, squeezed his hand. 'And that is why he sent you to Targoviste. That's why you had to obey, to leave him. To keep the *boyars* loyal.'

He placed his other hand on top of hers. 'He sent me for a wedding too, Ilona.' He smiled. 'Vlad understands one of the main lessons of statecraft: to unite a people all a prince needs is a war . . . or a wedding. And look here . . . we have both!'

It had to be the exhaustion. Suddenly they were both laughing, hard. It lasted for five heartbeats then, as suddenly as it had come, it was gone. Startled by the darkness in her eyes, he tried to keep her hands, but she pulled them away. 'Vlad commanded it,' he said, 'because he loves you.'

'Oh, Ion.' Her laugh was bitter now. 'He commanded it for his vow, made to God, not to me. God, whom he needs now more than ever. The Voivode of Wallachia would never leave his crusade to marry a commoner were it not for that vow.' She pointed towards the church. 'And he would still leave them hoping that he would choose one of their daughters, bring one of their families closer to the throne.'

Ion shrugged. He'd never been able to lie to her and he couldn't begin now. They had tried so hard to keep her out of the chess game each voivode played with the *boyars*. They had failed. And Ion knew that, even if a miracle happened and Vlad did come to marry her this day, she would never be a queen, ever a pawn.

She closed her eyes. 'He would have come by now. He will not come.'

He could not tell if it was hope or dread in her whisper. 'As long as I have known him, Vlad has never arrived early for anything. He only ever arrives exactly on his hour.' He smiled again. 'It drives me mad.'

She stared at him, hope – and dread – clear on her face, which was whiter than the dress she wore, whiter than any statue. And then a bell sounded. Three tolls. 'It is a quarter before noon,' she said. 'I must go.'

'Ilona—'

'No,' she said, struggling to rise. 'Give me your arm or stand out of my way, Ion. For I will go to greet my prince.'

Ilona swayed. Once again, Ion's hand reached, held her till she steadied.

'Let me fetch you a stool,' he murmured softly. 'All will understand.'

She would not. Could not. If she sat, she knew she'd never rise again that day. If she sat, she feared that the blood, seeping now, would flood. That no matter how many layers of thick, white linen made up her dress the stain would press through them. Badge of her sorrow, colour of her shame.

He must not see that. Not here before the altar screen of the Bisierica Domnesca. Not on her wedding day.

She closed her eyes, summoned breath to battle her nausea, grateful for Ion's grip on her arm. The wave passed. She opened them again, narrowing against the glare of flame in candelabra and sconce, against the sun burning through the great stained-glass windows that dappled her in blues, reds, greens, yellows, as if her dress were a rainbow and not the purest white.

She wished she could narrow her nostrils, too, tried to breathe only through her mouth. The cathedral was the coolest place in Targoviste and the heat there nearly overwhelmed. Sweating men in their court dress, sweating women in theirs, the stench sicklied over with potions and the sweetness of sandalwood, myrrh and lavender, wafted in smoke from the priests' swung censers. It did nothing to dissipate the foulness. Rather, by the contrast, it enhanced it.

The glare forced her eyes away; to Ion beside her, ever faithful, holding her up. Behind him were such of her family as had made the journey from Curtea de Arges. Uncles, cousins, all artisans, all sweating as much as any nobleman; more, perhaps, unaccustomed as they were to such rich cloth. But her prince had raised them up and they had to sport his favours.

She looked to where the others bunched. The *boyars*. All avoided her eyes, avoided looking anywhere near her in case they might meet her gaze and be sullied by a peasant's glance.

How they hated her. Though she had done nothing, desired neither their titles, nor their status. All she wanted was to be left in peace, to wait for those rare times when her love would come to her.

There! One did look back. Turcul *jupan*. The second man of Wallachia. His brother, Gales *jupan*, who had ridden back from the war with the worst of news, was not present. Gales had deserted his lord upon the battlefield and undoubtedly Vlad would kill him on sight, wedding day or no. But her prince still needed the other *boyars* and Turcul, the wealthiest, most of all. And of all the nobles, Turcul hated her the most, even if he had given his daughter, Elisabeta, to be her maid. She stood beside him now, whispering into his hairy ear. And as Ilona looked, Elisabeta glanced over. Not at her face. Lower.

Despite the heat, Ilona flushed cold. She felt a surge of blood, as if it were summoned by their regard. She leaned more heavily on Ion, closed her eyes again to the rainbow glare.

Perhaps he will not come. Sacred Jesus, let him not come. Sacred Maria, let him not come.

And then he came.

She did not know which metal she heard first, the tolling of the great bell in the tower, or the striking of his horseshoes on the cobbles of the square. They alternated thereafter, iron and iron, until one finally ceased, leaving the silence to be broken only by the twelfth and final toll.

The echo faded among the huge stone columns of the cathedral. Then metal struck again – the pommel of a sword, banging on wood. Three times it came, the space of a breath between each. Priests scurried. The two great doors of the church swung open.

He'd leaned against the door before he struck it. The dozen steps had sapped him, and drawing his sword seemed impossible. Unless he was going to use it to kill. It was the only time he felt awake, when the Infidel was under his blade. The rest was a dream of life through which he staggered.

When had he last slept? He could not remember. He'd forgotten how it was done. He'd close his eyes . . . but that was not enough. For behind his lids it was still daylight. And they would come.

Kalafat, his beloved horse, closing her soft brown eyes as she knelt so slowly, so he could step from her back before she died; Hamza, roped to a saddle, stumbling in the road dust; mostly the same two men – Mehmet, so close Vlad could smell the ginger and musk, and Radu, beautiful Radu, that beauty twisted by hate. Radu bringing the sword down from the high plane . . .

His eyes would open to blood, real blood, his blood. The wound where his finger had been would not remain staunched. He'd been told to rest it. He had laughed. He killed with the Dragon's Talon, and it needed both hands.

Yet it was not his own blood or the blood of others that tormented him the most. Not even the cruellest cut, of brother on brother. It was the moment just before that. The one when Mehmet the Conqueror stood a sword's length away and all their fates gathered. He'd talked all his life of *kismet*, of his destiny. That single moment was it. But then . . . then instead of lunging, striking, slaying he'd . . . paused. Someone else struck.

He fought still, killed still. But now it was not others' deaths he truly sought. It was his own. And *kismet* denied him even that.

Vlad opened his eyes, moving from that single moment to an oaken door. He heard a horse snort behind him, turned. His men, his *vitesji*, stood at their mounts' heads, looking up at him in silence. Stoica, who had somehow escaped the Sultan's burning tent and rejoined him; Black Ilie; the rest. There were just twenty of them left now and their armour was as smashed and filthy as his, as stained with blood.

He sought an answer in their eyes. Why was he there? Were there not Turks still to slay? What door was this?

Then he remembered. He was there for a wedding. His wedding. And, amidst all the betrayal, another. In some ways, the worst.

She'd lied to him. Yet he'd made a vow. He drew his sword.

There he stood, silhouetted in sunlight, the Dragon's Talon stretched out to his side.

Dracula. Her prince.

He was not the tallest of men. But he was broad and strong, and his sable armour made it seem that a black giant stood at the entrance of the Bisierica. And when she saw him, her heart, as it always did when they had been parted for a time, beat faster, her breath caught. And, as always, she remembered the first time she had seen him – dappled by Turkish sunlight, through the slats of a litter. She'd seen him again through a string of golden coins as he rescued her; but finally and clearly only when the boat was pulling away from the dock. And in that last look, her life's course was set. *Kismet*, he called it.

His men came in behind him, each bending stiffly, crossing themselves before spreading out at the end of the nave.

Silence held for a long moment. Broken when Dracula sheathed his great sword and began to move down the central aisle. He walked slowly, staring straight ahead, ignoring peasants and *boyars* prostrating themselves as he passed. As he drew closer, she could see the weariness in him, the black bruises under his eyes, startling in that so-pale face, as black as the dust-shrouded armour. Closer he came, and closer. Beside her, Ion squeezed her arm and she looked up, saw his smile that his prince was alive. Ilona was happy he would give her away, since she did not have a father. It was only her one friend and her one love that kept her standing. Ten paces and Dracula would be beside her. Only ten . . .

He never took them. A man moved between her and her love.

'You have come, Voivode,' said the *jupan*, Turcul. 'We did not think you would.'

The reply took a while. His voice was ever low, and here it came through road dust and the ravages of exhaustion. 'Should a man not come to his own wedding?'

The words were for the *boyar*. But his eyes, those great green eyes, were for her alone.

'Yet can such a wedding take place? To *her*?' All heard the contempt in the last word.

The eyes changed. The chill that could sweep away all warmth took them and, for the first and only time in her life, Ilona pitied the *jupan*.

'To her?' There was no tiredness in the voice now. 'Of course. Only to her.'

The *boyar* swallowed. He was a powerful man, second only to Dracula himself in the whole kingdom. But he *was* second. 'My prince,' he mumbled, 'I seek only to preserve your honour.'

'If only that were true.' The words came on a whisper, but loud enough to carry. 'Tell me what you mean, *jupan*. Now.'

The *boyar* hesitated. But he was too far in now. And seeing how much the man was prepared to risk, Ilona realised, for the first time, the true extent of her danger, and shivered in the heat.

'She has brought you here falsely, my prince. To trick you into this marriage.'

'*Trick* me? No one tricks me.' A sudden shout. 'No one!'

'Never the less . . .'

There was a blur of movement, a shadow passing through sunbeams, a gauntleted hand seizing a throat. Turcul was a head taller but he was lowered like a doll so that Dracula could look down on him.

Other nobles stirred. Each man there had a sword at his side. None reached for them. Perhaps it was the sound of black-armoured men notching arrows to bow-strings.

The whisper again. 'Tell me what you mean.'

A gurgle came. Metalled fingers eased enough to allow out sound.

'She lied. For she is not with child.'

'Lied?' The word echoed off the stone. 'Ilona never lies.' He looked around. 'The only one who . . . who . . .'

All saw it, how he faltered, stumbling forward, the man slipping from his grasp.

'Then ask her, Prince,' Turcul wheezed from the floor. 'Ask her.'

His gaze came back to her, a darkness in the eyes she'd seen bestowed elsewhere, but not on her. Never on her. She felt all her breath leave her, as if she'd forgotten how to breathe. 'One word, Ilona. End this with a word.' His voice dropped again. 'Do you carry my child?'

She nearly fainted then, in the heat, in the sudden surge of blood below, in the terrible darkness in his eyes. 'My prince . . .'

'One word!' He shouted now. 'Do you carry my child?'

She felt it. In the emptiness inside her. In the look Turcul's daughter had given her. In the soiled linen at her belly. In the tiny shift of Ion's fingers on her arm. She was in a rainbow and then she was slipping into darkness. But she could not go there again until she had answered him. He'd asked for one word. She always obeyed him.

'No.'

The word hung there, like a dust mote in a coloured sunbeam. And all could see the effect it had on Dracula; how he sagged, as if within his armour his flesh shrank away, contracting from the metal touch. 'No,' he echoed. Then, he closed his eyes and whispered, 'Another lie.'

Dragging himself up, Turcul went to stand with the other nobles, a phalanx surrounding him. 'And how will you deal with this, my lord?'

The beckoning darkness held off. 'My lord?' she wanted to shriek. He is your prince. But she knew what Turcul did. He was reminding Dracula that he was truly only *primus inter pares* – the first among equals – that he owed his crown to them.

'Deal with?' The weariness was back in his voice, in his body. 'You ask me this now, with the Turks a day away from Targoviste?' A murmur came at that. 'You ask me this, you, who should, even now, be gathering your men, buckling on your armour, to follow me?'

Another voice, a different noble. 'How can we follow someone who allows this treason to pass? Who will not do what must be done?'

Other voices joined, with the courage of the pack.

He silenced them with a raised fist. And she noticed then how the smallest metalled finger was twined to the one next to it. It glistened in the torch-light and the twine was red with blood.

His words took a long while to come. 'What must be done.' It was an echo, infinitely weary. But it was not a question.

And then Dracula was moving, as fast as he'd moved to Turcul. Faster. Seizing Ilona by the arm.

'No!' Ion had released her, stepped forward, tried to get between the man in the black armour and the woman in the white dress. 'Prince! Vlad! No! She—'

The hand that had crushed a noble's throat now smashed into Ion's face. He was flung backwards, crumpling onto the stones. Then Vlad dragged Ilona through the screen door, up the two steps to the altar, flinging her down before it. No one else entered the space before the screen, not the Metropolitan whose realm it was, not the *jupan* Turcul and the other nobles. They crowded both doors, but did not cross the threshold.

For a moment, Dracula stared up at the crucifix on the high table, at the figure of the tortured Saviour upon it. For a moment, he paused. Then he closed his eyes . . . and drew his stiletto, the thin-bladed weapon crowned with the same Dragon as his sword, its edge as keen. Raising it on high, its blade and guard paralleling the cross before him, he cried out, 'Moloch!'

The cry echoed around the great stone vault of the cathedral. All knew what it meant – the men crowded at the rood screen door, the congregation in the nave, the man spitting teeth and blood upon the stones where Vlad's blow had thrown him.

It was the Canaanites, throwing their children upon the fire.

It was the sacrifice of what one loved most.

The dagger fell. Not into flesh. Not yet. It sank into white linen, slitting, in one swift movement, the dress from hem to neck. It parted like a Bible, opening.

Their faces were so close she could have kissed him. She lay there, not struggling, frozen by the eyes of the man she loved. In them was something she'd never seen before. No, not something. An absence of something. Of life.

He was so close, only she could hear him. 'Do not move,' he whispered. 'Not a hair's breadth.'

And then he jabbed the tip of his stiletto into her breast.

THIRTY-EIGHT

A Single Tear

Poenari Castle, 1481

'Enough! Surely this is enough!' Petru shouted, leaping up.

It brought the Count of Pecs suddenly, forcefully, back to the hall of Poenari Castle, to the three curtained confessionals and the tale of a man emerging from them. He had not been there for a while, lost, as all of them had been lost, in the last confession of Dracula, as told by the three people who had known him best. He had even been lost to his reasons for listening to these horrors . . . until this last horror proved too much for a young man who, Horvathy now remembered, had a young wife upstairs, heavy with her first child.

'Peace, Spatar,' he said, rising from his chair to grasp the younger man's arm. The touch silenced the knight, though Horvathy could feel how the silence cost him in the shaking under his fingers. 'We all feel your disgust. But, in the end, we are not here to feel. We are here to consider. We are here to judge, are we not?'

Horvathy's words were spoken to the Spatar. But they were meant for the other man there, the one still sitting. For it would be up to Cardinal Grimani, the Papal Legate, to make a judgement; then to advise the Pope whether to permit Christ's Crusader to emerge from these tales and thus allow the Dragon Order to rise again, uniting the Balkans under its banner in Holy War. And if he judged thus, if Dracula's sins were to be forgiven, then . . . perhaps Horvathy would be able to forgive himself.

The Count turned now to Grimani and, as he had

attempted from time to time as the tale unfolded, tried again to read something definite in the Italian's face. Yet, as ever, there was little he could tell. Horrors had been described, yet even with this last one, this desecration, Grimani's expression had scarcely altered. His lips remained parted in what could have been a smile. His eyelids still drooped, as if he would sleep. Beneath them, though, the eyes themselves were bright as ever, and moving.

'Judge?' cried Petru, pulling his arm from the Count's grasp. 'There can be only one judgement after this! He was the Devil himself, not just his son. Before the high altar? It was blasphemy!'

'Perhaps.' The Cardinal's quiet tone shocked as much as the shout had.

'Perhaps?' Petru blurted. 'You, a man of God, can say this?'

'I am a man of God,' replied the Cardinal. 'I am also, in my way, a warrior for Christ. I know what it is to have the Infidel kicking at my gate. But to have him about to burst through my door?' He shook his head.

'Are you calling this obscenity a necessity?' Petru turned. 'My lord Horvathy, I appeal to you.'

The Count had been watching the Italian, hope rising in him. 'As I said, I share your disgust, Spatar,' he said, 'but His Eminence is right. Consider the threat Dracula faced. Have you ever seen what happens when the Turk sacks a town?' He shivered. 'This obscenity, as you call it, would be swiftly lost in the thousands that followed.'

'That cannot justify—'

Horvathy raised a hand. 'Dracula was a pragmatist, Spatar. He needed the *boyars* to raise their forces and follow him. Men will rarely do that for love. Not even always for God.' He closed his one eye. 'But I have witnessed, often, how they will do it for terror.'

'But are we not missing another point, my lord?' the Cardinal said. 'In many parts of Italy, we have the Feast of Fools, when madmen are given licence for a day to behave

306

according to their madness. Do you not have the same in Wallachia? From what we have heard, Dracula was maddened, then at least. Should we not give him licence?'

'Surely you cannot have it both ways, my lords,' Petru whined. 'A mad pragmatist does not sound a likely combination.'

'On the contrary, young man. Most of the princes I know in Italy have *exactly* that combination.' Grimani laughed, continued. 'There is something I am curious about, though. Like some of these other horrors, I had heard a version of this one before. But it told of a mistress's *murder*.' He turned to look at the middle confessional. 'Yet here she is, telling it herself. What are we to believe?'

All now looked at that confessional. Within it, Ilona had not really been listening to their talk but rather to the fall of Ion's tears within his. Hearing them, she remembered others. Her own, that day, from the agony, from the grief. The two times she had cried since. The first, after the cutting, on the way to the convent, when she'd realised exactly what he'd done and why, and how she would never, could never, be allowed to see him again. And the second time when she'd been proved wrong, and did see him. A part of him, anyway.

Yet the Cardinal had asked a question only she could answer. So she did. 'Believe this, so you know it all,' she said softly. 'He slit me from breast to breast. Then he completed the crucifix by cutting from my throat down, all the way down . . .'

'Blasphemy on blasphemy!' Petru stepped before her confessional, arms spread wide as if they could stop the words. 'Enough! What more is there to know?'

'Only this.' Her voice grew stronger, for what she had to tell now had sustained her through every night of her darkness. 'When he placed his knife . . . there, when he cut me there, the pain was . . .' She sighed. 'But, in the end, it was not the blade that ravaged me. It was the single tear that dropped onto me. The only one I ever saw him shed.'

Silence, a whisper of flame the only sound, even the scribes' quills stilled. After a moment, she spoke on, but softly now so that all had to lean closer to hear. 'He called me his sanctuary. In that one tear were all his goodbyes. A farewell to the only peace he'd ever known.'

'You *forgive* him?'

'Is that not what God's children are meant to do, Your Eminence?'

'But . . . that?'

How could she make them understand? Wasn't it so simple in the end?

'I loved him,' she said, 'and I have never stopped.'

'It is impossible,' Petru whispered. 'No one who received such wounds could have lived.'

Another voice came – Ion's, rough with grief. 'Only he could have inflicted them and *let* someone live. He had learned the lessons of Tokat too well. He knew, better than any, the border-land between life and death. He dwelt astride it. God forgive me, I helped him straddle it often enough.'

A silence again, longer than any one before. And the cry that finally broke it did not come from within the room, but beyond it.

'*Kree-ak, kree-ak.*'

All who could, looked up at the hawk's call. Through the opaque, beeswax cloth that blocked the arrow slit, the faintest of lights came. They had talked and listened for a day and half a night. Yet no one there felt tired.

The Count gestured to the tables. Petru, forcing down his disgust, turned and ordered his servants to take food and water into the confessionals. Horvathy crossed the room, helped himself to wine. Grimani joined him, walking silently on slippered feet. The Hungarian's good eye was turned away from the Italian, who studied the other, puckered socket before he spoke, softly. 'My lord,' he said, as Pecs started, turned. 'Before we go on, I have something to ask you.'

The Count took a sip. 'Ask.'

Grimani glanced over his shoulder. No one was near, but his voice dropped to a whisper anyway. 'You have made clear your desire to see your Dragon Order restored to glory. You judge that such an outcome would be vital to the success of the crusade we hope to launch against the encroaching Turk – leaders throughout the Balkans united under the Dragon banner. You may well be right.' He leaned closer. 'But I see something else, Count Horvathy. Hear it in what you say and how you say it. Hear it perhaps most in what you do not say.'

The Count remained silent. Grimani went on. 'There is a yearning in you, for something beyond the dream of a restored brotherhood. Greater maybe even than your love of God? And I can see this yearning is rooted in pain.' He squeezed the other man's arm gently. 'Am I not right?'

The one eye was turned fully on him now, reflecting reed torch-light. 'Perhaps.'

The Cardinal reached out, laid his hand gently on the taller man's arm. 'My son, I am a priest as well as a judge. And you are a true child of our Holy Church.' His voice was honey. 'Before we proceed further with Dracula's confession, do you wish me to hear *yours*? Relieve you of the weight I see you carry.' He tipped his head to the confessionals. 'We can clear everyone from the room, sit within one of these. Without the need for any of it to be set down on paper.'

Horvathy slipped his arm from the other man's grasp. 'I will speak of it when the time comes. It will not be long, now. And I will speak of it for the record, so all may hear. So all may judge my sins. You. The Holy Father. These people.'

'Very well.' Grimani's voice hardened. 'Then, by the merciful Christ, let us proceed swiftly. For all this sitting is aggravating my arse.'

Horvathy nodded, swallowed another gulp of wine. Setting down the goblet, he strode back to the dais. Grimani joined him, the half-smile gone, settling into his chair with a grunt. The Count waited for Petru to sit, then spoke. 'So, who will proceed with this tale? My young friend here has said what all must feel – that what you have just described is blasphemy as well as cruelty. Is there worse? Or was this the ultimate?'

It was a voice less frequently heard that spoke now. 'Not the ultimate, my lord,' the hermit said. 'Not even close.'

Horvathy nodded, sat. 'Speak then.'

'I will.'

THIRTY-NINE

The Wedding Feast

When he had finished cutting Ilona, Vlad stood and ripped the white cloth from the altar. He threw it over her and immediately the blood shot through it in the lines of a ragged crucifix. For a moment he stared at it. Then he slowly turned, dagger still in hand, to look at the horrified faces of the *boyars* crowded at the altar screen's doors.

'To me,' he cried, as he would in battle, and the noblemen were jostled aside as his twenty companions rushed to his side. He leaned into Stoica, whispering. A nod, and the little man bent, effortlessly lifted the blood-stained cloth and body, and carried it into the priest's room behind the altar.

'Now,' cried Vlad, striding to the altar screen's doorway, 'are we not here for a wedding?'

Two hundred faces looked up at him in horror. Not all had seen. But all had heard the screams, the witnesses staggering back, white-faced, vomiting.

'Come!' Vlad stepped forward. 'I seek a bride. Is that not what you all wanted? Me to marry one of yours? Well, here I am!' He threw his arms wide, laughing. 'Who will have me?'

Everyone looked everywhere else. He descended to the nave floor. 'You, lady?' He pointed with the bloodied dagger he still held at one woman. 'No. You are already married. And yet . . . is that your husband, my visitier, Iova, cowering behind you? Come, shall I make you a widow first and a bride straight after? You demure? Very well.' He passed on up the nave. 'You? No, too old. I need sons, so that the Draculesti will reign in Wallachia for ever. You?' A *boyar's* daughter, screaming with fear, buried her face in her father's shoulder. 'No! Too young. I have certain . . . tastes and no time to teach them.'

He stopped, swung in a circle till his gaze rested on one man. 'Turcul *jupan*. So, you got what you wanted, eh? I have not married my mistress. You must be happy. How can I make you happier?' He moved towards the *boyar*. 'Who is that you shelter with your bulk? Could it be . . . ?' He darted round the man. 'Elisabeta! Of course. Ilona's maid, who always hated her. Perfect!' He grabbed her arm, jerked her forward.

'My prince! Please!' Turcul grabbed his daughter's other arm. 'Please. You cannot—'

'I have shown you what I can do, *jupan*,' Vlad said, his voice ice. 'You have seen my sacrifice to Moloch. Now love is dead and only duty remains. Yours to me. Mine to God. Would you stand between me and Him?'

'Prince . . .' Turcul said brokenly.

But he let his daughter go, and Vlad dragged the weeping woman forward, throwing her down before the altar screen, at the feet of the Metropolitan. 'Marry us,' he said.

'I . . . I . . . cannot.' The old man thrust the crucifix he held forward as if he were warding off the Devil. 'After this . . . desecration!' He gestured to the screen door, to the thin stream of blood running from behind it, staining the carpet red.

'What?' yelled Vlad. 'Concerned by a little blood? What of Christ's blood? What of His suffering, His sacrifice? Christ knew all about Moloch.' He knelt, pulling Elisabeta down beside him. 'And now you do, too.'

'Prince! I . . . I must not . . .'

'Marry us,' replied Vlad, in a low voice that still carried to every corner of the church, 'or I will burn the cathedral around your ears with all of you inside it. I will abandon God and become for ever who you all say I am . . . the Devil's son!' His voice rose to a shout. 'Marry us!'

It did not take long. Vlad dismissed any pomp, cut short prayer and blessing, allowed only the minimum required. He made his vows, confirmed that the tear-wracked choking that came from Elisabeta were hers. As soon as the Metropolitan had placed the groom's golden wreath of oak leaf and ivy on his head, the prince was up and turning to the crowd.

'The Turk is a day from Targoviste. I must stop him. No . . . we must, since we are all now united. Is that not right, Father-in-law?'

Turcul gave a slow, numbed nod.

'So buckle on your armour, gather your retainers . . .' A murmur came. '. . . But do not fear. I do not plan to lead you in another night attack. I have a different plan now. Moloch has inspired me!' He turned back to the sobbing Elisabeta, still sunk upon the floor, laid his hands again upon her already blood-streaked hair. 'We must have a wedding feast. And my bride must have her gift.' His eyes gleamed. 'Five thousand gifts.' He straightened. 'Ion?' he shouted.

No one moved. No one came. At last Black Ilie stepped forward. 'Voivode,' he said softly, 'the *vornic* is gone.'

Vlad swayed, Elisabeta crying out as his hand stayed in her hair. Then he steadied. 'You must do this, Ilie. This is my command. Raise the garrison. Empty all the gaols. Every Turk we hold. Every deserter, every criminal, man or woman. All.'

'And where shall we take them?'

'To the Field of the Ravens,' Vlad replied.

'My prince.' Black Ilie bowed, turned, signalled half the *vitesji* to follow, and strode from the church.

Vlad slid his arm around Elisabeta, holding her up. He smiled down at her, then turned again to the crowd. 'Come, one and all!' he cried. 'Come to the wedding feast!'

To the Field of the Ravens, before the gates of Targoviste, the tables were carried. Vlad had them arranged with the precision of a Turkish camp but in a crucifix, not a circle. The high table was placed in the centre, where the altar would have been if it were a church. The spaces between, the areas around, were left clear.

The food was hardly sumptuous. The guests, all those who had been at the cathedral, ate what the army ate – every part of the pig, meat that had been boiled, roasted, minced, skewered. The largest boar's head had been baked, so that slices could be taken from its fatty cheeks. To make the delicacy accessible, it stood at the crossway of the crucifix, mounted upon a stake.

It was only the first.

The paucity of the wedding fare scarcely mattered. Only the bridegroom and his soldiers really ate anyway, with the appetite of men on campaign who had seen little food in weeks. The other guests sat almost motionless, clutching implements they didn't use, eyes fixed ahead, as if salvation lay only in the face opposite.

They stayed like that until the screaming began.

The prisoners came. First, there were the Turks, mostly soldiers, taken from the day Guirgiu fell and whenever there was time in the war of raid and ambush that followed. These proud men, warriors of the Crescent, attempted to march, to revile their guards – until they saw what they were being herded towards. Then prayer replaced curses.

Those of Wallachia followed – men and women, serfs and gypsies – criminals who had sat in their prison cells, suffering certainly – but with a little hope. For since the day Dracula was crowned, justice had always been swift, sinners executed the day they were condemned. Yet not one had been killed during the seven months of the war. So their pleadings now were of the usual kind – for the food they could smell, for the water they craved.

Their cries changed when they saw the stakes. These were laid out in rows, their bases touching the holes dug just behind the tables, running the entire length of the cruciform shape, three ranks deep.

If the wedding guests could close their eyes, they could not close their ears. To the screams. To Dracula, rising now, a skewer of meat in one hand.

'There are two kinds of impalement,' he declared, 'and the lie that is spread about me is that I use only the one. It suits to have my enemies believe this of me. But the reality is that true impalement – the "*trusus in anum*" . . .' – he poked the skewer forward – '. . . like any difficult skill, takes time, manpower, expertise. It is for the lazy hour. And with the Turk less than a day's march away . . .'

He lifted the skewer high, looked the length of the crucifix and the teams of men standing behind the tables. They were grouped in fours, two men holding a prisoner's arms, two now raising between them a sharpened stake, looking up to their prince. Behind them, other soldiers with pikes con-trolled the weeping, praying unfortunates who waited their turn.

'Still,' Vlad said, 'we will just have to make do.'

He dropped his arm. Then, along every face of the crucifix, pairs of men ran forward and drove their stakes through the prisoners' bodies.

'The problem with this method is two-fold,' said Vlad, raising his voice above the screams, the retching, the wailing of prisoners and wedding guests. 'The first is that most die instantly – as you can all witness. The second is that once the stakes are fixed in their holes . . . yes, like that one there, a flagon of wine to you and your men, Black Ilie, for being the first! . . . the bodies start to slip down. With a smooth pole a corpse might follow the entrails to the ground in an hour, which would spoil the effect.' Vlad lifted a goblet, drank, then continued. 'But our carpenters have solved the problem by trimming all the branches but only down to the height of a man. See how the sinner is caught upon them? Look, wife, that one, who wriggles but can only wriggle so far? No, no, do look!'

Dracula bent, pulled Elisabeta's hands away from her face,

his other hand turning her head. Sobbing, she looked, then wrenched away, vomiting.

She was not the only one. Up and down the lines women and men were doing the same. 'Yes.' Dracula nodded, glancing left and right. 'You are all so grateful I have restored law to Wallachia. That the roads are cleared of brigands and beggars, that you can ride in safety from the Fagaras mountains to the Danubian plain. But none of you has ever considered the price. Until now.'

Another wave of prisoners was dragged forward, dispatched; a third. On the field, a forest grew, of wood and blood and flesh. Vlad sat, silent now, staring ahead at nothing while the screaming grew, peaked, ebbed, finally ceased. There was still weeping, retching. But something close to a silence had come by the time Black Ilie stood beside his prince, stooped and whispered.

Dracula nodded, rose, continued talking as if he hadn't stopped. 'But how could I deny you a glimpse of what has made me so . . . famous. Why you all call me Tepes behind my back. Why the Turk calls me Kaziklu Bey.' He smiled. 'So I have reserved three special prisoners. Here they shall be placed, right here, at the centre of the crossroads and the cross.'

He signalled, and servants came to clear away tables and chairs, everyone forced to rise, stagger back, though the hedge of stakes prevented anyone leaving. The wedding party stayed closer, held in by a semi-circle of *vitesji*. Only Dracula remained where he was, eyes downcast.

An entrance had been left at the base of the cross. Now a man was brought through it, dragged forward, thrown down before Dracula, who bent and lifted his face so all could see and gasp when they did.

It was the *boyar*, Gales.

'Yes, your brother, Turcul *jupan*. The one whose whereabouts you said you didn't know? Someone did, and dug him from one hole . . .' He gestured, to three servants rapidly digging. '. . . To bring him to another.'

'Prince, I beg you . . . mercy . . .' the kneeling man whined.

Dracula ignored him. 'This man deserted me upon the battlefield. When victory was in my grasp he snatched it away. He betrayed not only his country and his Voivode but God Himself, whose anointed I am, whose cross I carry against the Infidel.' He looked around at the *boyars* and their families, at the long line of them stretching down the crucifix made of wood and flesh. 'Some of you once saw the fate of Albu who called himself "the Great". It appears you didn't learn the lesson. So it must be repeated.'

Gales was sobbing. His brother stepped forward, knelt. 'Prince, I beg . . .'

'A place beside him, Father-in-law? Of course. It is there, if you crave it so.'

Turcul rose, staggered back, jerking the edge of his robe from his brother's despairing grasp. Dracula nodded to Ilie. Six men came forward, all in black armour. Skilled men. They bore a longer stake, ropes, pulleys. One led a blinkered farm horse.

He had to speak louder to be heard over Gales's screams, as his men began. 'You see how long it takes? How much effort?' He looked around, at all the averted faces, then bellowed, 'I command you to watch. To watch and to learn the price of justice.' One by one the whitened, wet faces were lifted to him. He gestured and all jerked their gazes to the prisoner. 'Good.' Dracula nodded, looked himself. Only when the stake's butt end was raised, then lowered into the hole, when the nails had been driven through feet into the wooden step, did he step forward, look up. 'Dead,' he murmured, 'it happens.' He turned, his voice gentle now. 'Ilie, try to take a little more care next time.'

'My prince.'

A second man was dragged in. Thomas Catavolinos'

exquisite red hair was a morass of indeterminate colour, full of the muck of whatever cell floor he'd been lying on for the previous seven months. His fine robes were in shreds. Yet in his besmeared face, his eyes were defiant.

Dracula looked into them. 'Do you have something to say, Ambassador?'

'Only this, Impaler.' The Greek leaned forward, sniffed exaggeratedly. 'There's a dreadful smell just here. And I think it emanates from you.'

There was a gasp. Dracula merely nodded. 'It must be hard for you, used as you are to the perfumes of the east.' He squinted into the sunlight. 'There's sweeter air up there, I'm certain.' He turned to his waiting men. 'Fetch a longer stake.'

He was obeyed. His men took more care and Thomas's eyes were open as the wood was lifted high, though whether fresher air reached his nostrils, above the stake protruding from his mouth, only he could tell.

'And now,' said Dracula, turning slowly, 'at last.'

Hamza had been better treated than the other prisoners. Vlad had commanded it and Ion had seen to it, visiting their former *agha* on occasion, staying to talk, bringing better food, clearer water. The robes he'd been taken in at Guirgiu were tattered but relatively clean; his beard was trimmed short, his pale blue eyes were clear. He looked around – at the Wallachians who stared back. At the thousands of dead who didn't. At his fellow ambassador high above them all. Finally at his former pupil.

'Is it time, Vlad?'

A shocked whisper went down the lines of the watchers. The prince simply nodded. 'It is time, Hamza *agha*.'

'And yet,' Hamza said, running a tongue around his lips, 'I would not die today.' He looked up again at Thomas Cata-volinos, then hastily away. 'You know the way of these things. What use is this . . . example . . . if it is not reported? Let me return to my master. He listens to me. I can persuade him . . . perhaps to end this war? To leave you in peace? He listens to me,' he repeated, his voice weakening. 'Please. Let me go to Mehmet.'

There was a silence. A breeze had sprung up, but there was no coolness in it. It ruffled clothes soaked in blood, lifted sodden hair. Finally, a raven broke it, settling on Thomas's stake before letting out a harsh croak.

Vlad glanced up at the cry, stared for a moment. Then he looked back. 'No, old friend,' he said, stepping away. 'It is better that Mehmet comes to you.'

His men came forward, stripping, turning. As they threw him face down, Hamza cried out, 'There, Prince! Folded into my belt! There!'

Vlad raised a hand and his men halted instantly. He stooped, felt through the discarded robes, then stood straight.

In his hand was a falconer's glove.

'Do you remember when you made it for me?' Hamza said, craning around, trying to see Vlad's eyes.

'Yes.' Vlad turned the gauntlet over in his hand. 'I was good at my trade, was I not?'

'You were. And do you remember the verse?'

Vlad nodded. Softly, he read it aloud. ' "I am trapped. Held in this cage of flesh. And yet I claim to be a hawk flying free." ' Vlad smiled, then knelt beside the prone man. 'Jalaluddin was our favourite, wasn't he? The poet of mystics and falconers.'

'Like us.' The men had released Hamza enough so he could turn fully, could look up into the green eyes of his former pupil. 'Spare me, Vlad,' he pleaded. When the prince did not move, did not blink, he went on in a whisper. 'You said you loved me once.'

Vlad stared for just a moment longer. Before his eyes focused and he said, 'I did. I do. Die well.'

Then, leaning back, he slipped the glove over the stake's blunted end.

FORTY

The Traitor

Ion wept as he rode. For his devastated country. For his prince, gone to hell. For himself.

Mostly, he wept for Ilona.

He was still weeping when the *akinci* found him. They were Tartars, mounted on their shaggy-coated, un-shod ponies. They came from nowhere, surrounding him in a moment. They debated whether to roast him over their fire. They did roast his horse, having no use for the big destriers the Infidels rode. But it was ordered that all prisoners were to be brought alive to the Sultan's camp. They might have disobeyed had they not so feared the All-Seeing Eye that Mehmet was said to have borrowed from a famous djinn. And were it not for the gold piece that was offered in exchange for the most valuable prisoners. Ion looked valuable, judging by the armour they stripped from him. They liked gold; it could be exchanged for good horses, unlike this one whose bones they sucked before they tied Ion's thumbs to his toes with wet rawhide and threw him over the back of a donkey.

Ion lay staring at the woven beauty of an orchid in the Izmerian carpet. They'd cut the thongs from his thumbs so he had not lost the use of them. Still, he could not feel them, only the new bonds that yoked his wrists to his ankles behind him.

It was quiet in the Sultan's tent. The men who had bought him from the Tartars did not think he spoke Turkish, or did not care, for they talked openly about how their master was out hawking, not so much for the sport as for his pot. Kaziklu Bey may have devastated the earth and water of Wallachia before the advancing enemy, leaving little for the cooking pots – including the Sultan's – but not even the Devil's Son could lay waste to the air, and Mehmet was setting all his sakers against grouse and pigeon.

Maybe Ion slept, maybe he didn't, but he was looking at the orchid again and acclamation was growing steadily louder. Then there was horse harness jingling, laughter at the entrance, swiftly cut off, and he was surrounded by slippers, the cuffs of the *shalvari* above them covered in road dust. He closed his eyes.

'Do you know him, my heart?'

The sound of Mehmet's voice was not one Ion would ever have forgotten, strangely high for such a big man, strangely gentle for such a cruel one. But Radu's voice had gone from boy to man since last they met.

'His name is Ion Tremblac,' Radu said, 'and he is the Impaler's right hand.'

'He needs a whole one now, since you took one of his fingers,' Mehmet laughed. 'That he has lost this, too . . .' He bent to study. 'You know, I remember this one. He studied at the *enderun kolej*. He rode with you at *jereed*.'

'Just so, beloved.'

'Wait!' Mehmet knelt, pushed the hank of sweaty hair away from Ion's forehead. 'I thought he was the same! See how he still bears my *tugra*?' He let the hair fall again over the branding, stood, wiping his hand on his shalvari. 'So what makes he here?'

Ion craned up to meet the Sultan's gaze. 'I come to offer myself to Dracula . . .' He faltered. '. . . To Radu Dracula. Will you free me so that I may kneel before him?'

A surprised grunt from Radu. Mehmet smiled. 'My great-grandfather, Murad the First, may his memory always be blessed, was killed by a Serbian in his tent after the first battle of Kossovo. I am sure there are Wallachians who would do the same. Still, you were brought in by Tartars who would have stripped you of everything pointed.' He looked up. 'Cut his leg bands.'

He was obeyed. After several attempts, Ion managed to roll up onto his knees. Mehmet was now sitting on an ornate purple couch. Radu stood beside it. With eyes lowered, Ion began.

'I offer you my everything, Prince Radu. I will guide your army through the marshes the Impaler has created in your path. I will show you the pits that have been dug for your horses to fall into. I will take you past all the poisoned wells, to the hidden ones where the water is sweet. I will bring you to the gates of Targoviste. He does not plan to defend it, nor the Princely Court within. Neither is built for a siege. But if they are even closed against you I will throw them open and lead you to the cellar where he has hidden the throne of your fathers so you can be crowned upon it.'

Radu regarded him for a long moment before he spoke. 'And why will you do all this, Ion Tremblac? You, who have stood beside him while he committed the worst sins—'

'Who committed them at his side, joyfully.'

'Then why? Why now? Is it because he is beaten?'

Ion shook his head. 'He is not. And if he were, I would have stood beside him as ever, guarded his back as ever, taken any death meant for him on myself.'

'Well now,' said Radu, coming forward, bending, 'what ever could my brother have done to forfeit such loyalty?'

Finally, Ion raised his own eyes, looked into the ones before him.

'He has murdered the woman I love.'

The murdered woman groaned.

A face loomed over her, one from her nightmares. Bald, soundless, he clicked in his throat and was replaced by another horror – the Roma woman with the colourful scarf who had tended her when she had lost Vlad's first child. She lifted Ilona by the neck, raised a bottle to her lips. The liquid spilled, as the carriage lurched over a pothole. Some went down her throat. She groaned and the gypsy, thinking she cried from pain, made her swallow more of the lulling liquid before laying her carefully down.

Yet it was not the pain, reduced to dullness by the elixir, that made her groan. Nor the bleeding, which had stopped not long after the cutting was over, for he had not scored the cross too deeply anywhere in her flesh.

No, her sorrow came from memory – of a teardrop and a word.

'Goodbye,' he had said, just before the teardrop fell, before the last thrust of his stiletto.

She moaned again. Through wet eyes she saw the mute, Stoica, tap the gypsy's shoulder, appealing with his hands; saw the shrug in response. All they could do they had done. Dressed her wounds, spirited her from the city of death towards the unknown.

Her lover was gone. He had said goodbye, in a tear, in a word, in blood. And she wept now, not from pain, but because she knew she would never see him again.

They had seen the shape of the cross from the ridge. Its perimeter had been marked by torches spaced every dozen paces. But midnight darkness shrouded the rest until they were close to it.

The *akinci* scouts had reported back, told of a forest of the dead before the gates, a deserted city beyond them, its gates swinging wide. But since, in such situations, they tended to speak in the language of myth, of demons and ghosts, they were hard to understand. Veteran officers of the household had ridden down and returned, white, trembling, struggling to distinguish facts from horror. Impatient as ever, Mehmet had waved away their mutterings, spurred his horse forward, Ion and Radu at his side, *solak* archers surrounding them.

Beyond the spill of torchlight, the advanced guard of the Sultan's army, five thousand of his fiercest warriors surrounded the crucifix five rows deep. They faced outward, weapons drawn. Ever since the night attack, the shock of an enemy so close with a blade, Mehmet had found sleep hard, and surrounded himself with men who rarely slept themselves.

The ranks parted, just enough to admit the three of them, and one archer each side. They entered at the bottom of the cross. Its sides were made up of nothing but the dead, in three ranks. Most were impaled through the front and were now bent over, arms and legs hanging. Occasionally, for variety, someone had been pierced through the back, a reverse dangling of limbs.

The torches had been placed within the cross, so torchlight could reflect in dead eyes . . . those who still had them. Only the ravens moved and they did so slowly, bloated from the gorge. A few cawed as the horsemen passed, their protests as listless as their movements.

It was mainly Turks who hung there, and both Mehmet and Radu gave out several groans of recognition. But Wallachians hung there, too; traitors, thieves, the luckless, some women among the men.

After initial glances left and right, Mehmet kept his gaze fixed forward, to the middle of the cross and the greater illumination there. Ion looked, counted, gave up counting. If the press was as thick upon each side then at least five thousand had been impaled upon the Field of the Ravens.

The press was less thick at the centre of the cross. It consisted of just three stakes, the middle one set at the uppermost. Ion recognised the man on the right as the *boyar*, the deserter, Gales. To his left, he saw the frayed finery of a Greek robe. Finally, he looked at the last stake, its occupant. Like those beside him, he had been impaled in the traditional way.

The chief falconer's eyes were open, unpecked. They did

not have the glazed look of the dead but seemed to be staring at what protruded from his mouth. Yet unlike the men beside him, it was not the familiar, blunted, bloodied piece of wood but a hand, five fingers stiff with blood, that jutted out there. As if someone had reached all the way through the Turk's body and pushed out his guts.

Ion turned to the Sultan. He knew him to be a man used to cruelty, who had killed, often with his own hands. Yet now Ion saw something working within Mehmet's usually calm face. And his voice, when it came, was as harsh as any raven's.

'Hamza *pasha*,' Mehmet cried.

At the cry, the body twitched. All looked up, saw the slew of clotted blood that cascaded down the stake. Saw eyes that had been staring straight ahead, swivel down. No sound could come from that throat. None was needed.

'No!' Mehmet shrieked, spooking his horse, who danced towards the three stakes until the Sultan jerked the reins back. 'No! I cannot . . . I will not . . .' He turned till he was facing Radu. 'This is not just a blasphemy against your God,' he screamed. 'This is a blasphemy against humanity. I cannot . . . will not . . . I will return to my palace, my *sarayi*, my gardens . . .' He was raging now. '. . . And if you want this terrible place so much, you can take it.'

'Beloved—'

No!' Jabbing his heels into his horse's flank, charging down the avenue of the dead, Mehmet was gone.

His archers followed, leaving the two Wallachians. They looked after Mehmet, then back at each other. Anywhere but up. Neither spoke. Finally, all Ion could do was raise a hand and gesture past the last three stakes, to the gates of Targoviste beyond them, gaping wide.

As they rode from the flesh crucifix towards them, a raven screamed.

FORTY-ONE

Last Stand

'Does Corvinus come?'

It was the question he had first asked in June on the banks of the Danube as he watched the huge Turkish army afloat and seeking a landing place. He had asked it again many times as he retreated across his country, slowing the enemy any way he could – with fire, plague, starvation, thirst, gunpowder, arrows and blades. With terror. The Turk had paid for every mile of scorched Wallachian soil, and each mile held was ten more that the Hungarian army could gain, marching to the succour of their fellow crusaders.

Now Vlad asked it again, at the end of August, in the main hall of his fortress, atop the mountain called Poenari, on the far side of his realm. From the castle he could look back at his land down the valley of the River Arges. He could also see, to the north, the Fagaras mountains. Beyond them lay another province – Transylvania, land of his birth.

Vlad looked down the long table, at the twenty men who sat at it, the debris of a simple meal before them. When he'd first asked the question he'd commanded twenty thousand men. Now he had these twenty, some of whom still wore a last few pieces of black armour. These, and thirty more soldiers above patrolling the walls, were all that remained. He'd built Poenari Castle so it could be held by fifty men. Now he was going to prove it.

If Corvinus was coming.

Every face Vlad studied was a mirror for his own. If he had scarcely slept in months, his *vitesji* had not slept much more.

It showed in eyes sunk into holes, in flesh that was grey beneath the burn of a still-fierce summer sun. Yet he knew they would go on fighting for him, as long as he could give them a little hope. It was why he asked the question aloud that he usually only asked himself. It was not advice he sought. It was not truly a question any more. But these men, these last few at the extremity of their country and their strength, had to be roused for a last stand. Had to be asked to believe one last time.

He had built Poenari to be held by fifty men. But they had to fight.

The question, which was not one, hung there like smoke from the cooking fire. Now Vlad leaned down, resting his fists on the table. 'He does. He must. He raised the banner of crusade as we did, and would be dishonoured if he folded it again without striking blows. My last report placed the King at Szeged three weeks ago. Still in his own realm, yes. But my messengers would have told him of our peril. If he has acted on their word, an advance of horse could be through Transylvania and approaching the Fagaras now. He could be here within the week.'

Silence for a moment. Then a question came. 'And will he, Voivode?'

Vlad was staring now at the table-top, as if through it down into the depths of the mountain. Another silence came, grew. Men began to shift in their seats, to look at each other. They had all seen their prince stare like this, for minutes at a time. Sometimes more.

'Voivode?'

'Yes, Ion?'

The big, dark man looked around uneasily. 'It is Ilie, my prince. Ion's . . . gone.'

Vlad's eyes focused on the man before him. 'Yes, Ilie. Corvinus will come.'

*

'Here's to the Crow, Corvinus,' Turcul bellowed, 'and his clipped wings.'

A cheer, a dozen hoisted goblets. Ion drank with the rest, laughed with the rest, carefully.

'Where was he, Voivode, at your last report?' Turcul resumed.

All looked to Radu, Prince of Wallachia, who sat at the head of the table. He smiled. 'He squats on the border of Hungary yet, *jupan*. His side of it.'

'So if he ever intended to fight, he's left it too late?'

'He never intended it,' Ion said, and all men stared. 'He will use the Pope's gold, not for crusade, but to buy back the crown of St Stephen from the Emperor and secure himself upon the throne of Hungary.'

'So what will he do now, Ion Tremblac?' Radu asked.

'He will cross into Transylvania. It is his fiefdom and he will reinforce it in case we decide to push north. If we do not, he will go home to Buda and tell of how Vlad failed both him and God.'

Radu leaned forward. 'How do you know he will do that?'

'Wouldn't you, my prince? Isn't that what all men do when a cause is lost? Distance themselves from the loser?'

'As you have?' Radu smiled as Ion coloured, before going on. 'And what will the Crow do then, do you think?'

'Make peace with the victor. With you, Voivode. Just as soon as you return the army the Sultan lent you to conquer your country.'

Radu frowned. 'My army is Wallachian, too, Spatar.'

Ion nodded, stayed silent.

Another man spoke – Mihailoglu Ali Bey, the Turkish commander. 'And Mehmet Fatih, blessed be the name of the Conqueror, only keeps us here to do God's work. To rid our brothers' suffering land of the beast.'

Turcul banged his goblet upon the table. 'And what will we do if we take that beast alive?' he said, his eyes afire.

'His head must go to the Sultan,' said the Turk.

'Of course,' replied the *jupan*, grinning, 'but it does not have to be separated from the body immediately.'

'That must go on a stake!' yelled another *boyar*.

There was universal assent to this, with further refinements added, suggestions shouted out. As each was expanded upon, Ion studied the face of the other Dracula. Its beauty revealed nothing. Radu listened to every mutilation to be visited upon his brother's living body or ravaged corpse, and he didn't even blink.

At last, he ended the discussion with a raised hand. 'It still remains for us to capture him,' Radu said. 'And it is now time to reveal how we will begin to do that, even on the morrow.'

'Surely our allies will just run at the walls and build a bridge with their bodies, as they did at Constantinople,' Turcul guffawed. 'Do they not all seek a martyr's death?'

'Yes,' said Mihailoglu Ali Bey, rising, 'but not a fool's one.' He reached across the table, picked up Turcul's cup and tipped the contents onto the table, splashing his doublet. 'And you have drunk too much if you think you can mock us and our faith.'

Turcul went white, gaped, looking up the table at Radu. 'My prince, I . . . I object . . .'

'Be quiet, Turcul, before you confirm the Bey's opinion of you.' As the *jupan* sank back, Radu continued. 'And there is no need for martyrdom when we have betrayal.' He glanced at Ion, who looked away. 'When my brother chose Poenari, he chose well, built well. The slopes are too steep, the walls too high to take by simple storm. But there is one weakness, knowledge he shared with one man. Tell us, Ion Tremblac, what that weakness is.'

This was part of the punishment for his betrayal – a public acknowledgement of it. Ion accepted it, spoke. 'There is only one hilltop adjacent to Poenari that might command it. There is but one path up to it, its entrance concealed by thorn bushes. The path is so steep that only goats ascend there; so thickly wooded that it would take an army to widen it into a trail.' He sighed. 'But where a goat can go, a man can follow. And if enough men go there, and you don't mind losing a few, they can drag cannon. If an army cuts a path first.'

And then, as if by command, there came the distinct sound of a single axe biting into wood. Another came, then another, until it was clear that there *was* an army out there, wielding axes.

'We are working by torchlight, burning some trees down, hewing others,' Radu said. 'We will have cleared a trail by dawn, and a field of fire by noon. The bombardment will begin then. The walls are tall and thick, but they are, after all, just brick over spill. Only the donjon is granite, and once the outer walls are down, well . . .'

He broke off, smiling. It was Mihailoglu Ali Bey who finished for him. 'With so much firewood chopped, we will pile it around the donjon walls and roast the Impaler alive.' The Turk stood, lifting his goblet. 'By this time tomorrow night we will be looking at his charred body or hoisting him onto a stake. Perhaps both.'

Men rose, goblets in hand, cheering. Ion was one of them, though he could not find a voice, so thick was his throat. He looked across, at Radu, smiling broadly now. Raising his cup, Ion toasted him, even smiled before closing his eyes.

The cheers, the laughter, the toasts went on, the men moving away from the table, bunching into a crowd. Ion cheered with them, laughed. But something was working in his stomach, beyond the surfeit of wine he'd drunk to convince himself that he was where he should be, doing what was right, beside the right Dracula. When he was sure no one in the drunken, boisterous crowd would notice, he slipped from the tent.

He made for the riverbank, stepped onto the sand, doubled over, vomited, a series of retches that went on till his stomach was empty and his mouth filled with bile. It was bitter – the very taste of his treason, it seemed – so he let it sit on his lips and did not wipe it away.

He hated Vlad. Hated him with a totality only possible in one who had once loved. And hate had replaced love in an instant, in that one moment when he lay on the flagstones of the Bisierica Domnesca, and heard Ilona's death scream, the whispered horror of what was happening beyond the screen. It did not matter that she had never been his, would never be his. He had loved her. If Vlad stood before him now he would stab him in a heartbeat, with joy.

And yet . . . these fat-faced traitors, these all-conquering Turks, that beautiful brother, all preparing to torture his prince to death? His Vlad, whose life he had saved in alleys and on battlefields, who had saved him in return and had the scars to prove it. They had fought each for the other, countless times.

He looked up. The forest and the folds of mountain hid the peak from the river. But Vlad was up there, with the rest of Ion's former comrades.

Ion wiped the bile at last from his mouth. He hated the man who waited up there. He would be the first over the wall to kill him if he could. But he could not stand by and watch him be torn apart by jackals.

He went to his tent, wrote. Then he grabbed his Turkish bow and set out to climb the mountain.

FORTY-TWO

Arrow in the Night

It was a normal sound, an axe driven into wood. An army needed timber, for fuel, for defence, especially if they were building siege lines. It was less customary to chop at night. Then, when there were two axes, ten, fifty, countless, he went to the arrow slit, stared out, tried to gauge where they were falling, and why.

He must have dozed. A moan woke him and he turned sharply, hand on dagger hilt. But it was only the woman on the bed, and one of her nightmares. He stared at her for a moment, then turned back to Turkish axes on a mountain-side.

A knock turned him again. He went to the door. 'Who's there?'

'Ilie.'

Vlad lifted the heavy beam, set it aside, drew his dagger, stepped back. 'Come.'

The door creaked open. Ilie stood there. Vlad was about to say that he had heard the axes, that there was nothing to fear, when he noticed shadows behind his man. 'Who is with you?' he said, holding the weapon before him.

'Men,' Ilie replied. 'Villagers from Arefu.'

'How did they . . . ?' Vlad began, stopped. The people of Arefu were *his* people, the closest he had to supporters. They had loved the Dragon. They loved his son. It was one of the reasons he had built the castle where he had. So there was no need to ask how they had come here through a besieging army. This was their mountain.

'They have been searched?' A nod. 'Then bring them in. And stand here beside me, with your sword drawn.'

Three men were shoved in. The first two were undoubtedly brothers, probably twins. Shepherds, a life spent in toil, they could have been any age from thirty to seventy.

Behind them, a shadow in the shadows, stood another figure. He was dressed in a monk's plain, brown robe, the hood drooping over his face. Yet as Dracula stared, the hood suddenly lifted . . . and the prince's knees gave. He cried out, staggered back into Ilie, the big man steadying him.

Dracula's breaths came fast. Eyes shut, he tried to steady them. When he was ready, he looked again; but now the cowl was lowered, the face hidden. Still, he knew what he had seen – his father's eyes, just like his own, the same Draculesti green.

He had seen his father sometimes, in the sleepless nights of constant war, in the pain of his wounds and the potions taken to try and relieve it. Had even talked with him, just as he had done in the cell at Tokat. But he had never seen the Dragon when others were around. Until now.

Ilie still had a hand on him. He murmured something and Dracula looked across at the shepherds, their startled faces. Breathing deeply, making sure he looked only at them, not their shadow, he spoke. 'Greetings, fathers,' he said, 'what do you wish of me?'

The two men came forward, knelt, kissed the Dragon ring, touched their foreheads to Vlad's slippered feet. The figure in the cowl did not move. 'We come not to ask but to offer, Prince Vlad,' said one of the men, in the guttural accent of the region. 'To offer you salvation.'

'I have a confessor for that,' Vlad replied, 'though I seem to have mislaid him somewhere along the way.'

'It is not your soul we seek to save, Voivode, but your body,' said the second brother in an identical voice. 'We can take you out of the castle the same way we came in. There is a path, known only to us. It runs from a cave below your walls to the river below.'

Vlad swallowed. He tried to look only at the shepherds before him, not the silent figure beyond. 'I know this mountain well. There is no path.'

The second man licked his lips, looked at the first. 'Forgive me, lord, my sin of contradicting you. But . . . there is. You may trust us on that. Trust also that we will see you down it and that we have a dozen horses waiting with other guides to take you over the Fagaras to safety.'

'I am safe here.'

'Perhaps not for long.'

'I will not need long. Corvinus comes . . .' He saw the look that passed between them. 'Do you know anything?'

'Nothing . . . ce-ce-certain, Prince,' stammered the first man, 'we just heard his coming is in doubt.'

'Well, it is not,' Vlad said, loudly enough for listening ears beyond the room.

'God grant it so, lord,' said the second man, more calmly. 'But what *is* certain is that we can get you out, tonight. After tonight . . .' He shrugged, glancing out the arrow slit.

Vlad stared at them for a moment. 'It is dangerous for you to offer this. Why would you?'

'We have ever loved your family, Prince. And . . .'

'And?'

'And your family has loved us. Your father granted us the rights to ten mountain tops around about, sheepfolds for our summer flocks. He . . . died before he could authorise the grant. And now Turcul *jupan* claims they were never promised. If you were to . . .' – he glanced at the Dragon seal ring upon Vlad's hand – '. . . then we . . .'

He left the promise in the air. Vlad looked around – out of the arrow slit to the Turkish firelight and the sound of axes; to the beams above. Back to the men. At last, when he was sure he was ready, beyond them. Then, drawing his dagger, he crossed the room in three strides, seized the robed figure, flung back the hood, and raised the knife to strike . . .

Elisabeta on the bed shrieked. Both shepherds took a step forward – but Ilie hissed at them, sword lifted, and they stopped. All just stared at Dracula . . . and a young man bent before him, whimpering beneath the raised blade.

And then both Ilie and Elisabeta gasped.

'Who are you?' Vlad whispered.

One of the elders took a half-step forward, remembered Ilie, halted. 'Prince, this . . . this is your son.'

Another cry from the bed. Elisabeta raised herself to stare. The boy, whose eyes were shut against the blow he thought was coming, opened them at the softness in Dracula's voice.

'Who was his mother?'

'Her name was Maria Stanctu. She died when he was born.'

'I do not remember her.'

'No, my prince.'

Slowly, Dracula lowered his weapon, sheathed it, reached down, took the boy's chin, gently tilted it up. The face was a youth's not a man's, with a youth's softness; but it was also almost a mirror – and a return to his past. The same cheekbones, the same high forehead, the same long nose, the same black hair and eyebrows. Only the eyes were different, the shape of them not so deep-set, though just as green; and, seeing them, Vlad nodded.

'I remember her now,' he said, and did. He'd come here during his first, brief reign in 1448, fourteen years before, to visit the Dragon's people, and the donjon his grandfather had built. A pretty shepherdess, a lonely young man, one night. 'What is your name?' he asked, still holding the chin.

'My mother asked that I was christened Nicolae, after her father,' the youth said, his voice warring between boy and man. Then something came into his eyes and the voice deepened. 'But *I* have always called myself Vlad. After mine.'

Silence in the room. All became aware again of the fall of

335

axes, the shouts of labourers. And then a different sound. Sharp, sudden and ending in a scream.

An arrow had passed through the slit window and stuck in the headboard of the bed, a hand's span from Elisabeta's face.

Ion rubbed his eyes and lowered the bow. He had always been good with it, nearly as good as Vlad. There was no wind. But this was a night shot, at two hundred paces, hilltop to hilltop, and he was aiming at candle flicker within an arrow slit. He had missed the first two times, he knew; and he'd only written the note three times, the number of the Holy Trinity, of salvation.

One for God, one for Man . . . and one for the Devil, he thought as he raised the bow again, for the last time, and sighted. Thought of this last shaft with the paper wound round it, carrying Dracula's fate. He breathed out, loosed . . . and a woman's shriek came almost immediately. He had found a target. Fate had chosen which one.

No more cries came, for which he was grateful. They would remind him of another's, and he had already forgotten how to sleep.

Vlad knew the hand. He and Ion had learned to write together when they were seven.

'What does it say?' whispered Elisabeta, her voice quavering.

'Read it,' he said, handing it to her. 'Aloud.'

She did. ' "The Crow sits on his nest. Axes clear a meadow to be sowed with cannon and they will bloom with the sun. They are blunting a stake for you. If you can, go." ' She looked up. 'What will you do?'

They all stared at him. He looked back at each in turn – the shepherds, Ilie, his son. He didn't look again at his princess. 'I will go.'

Ilie had taken the note. 'Voivode, this is the *vornic*'s hand.'

'Yes.'

'Then . . .' The big man hesitated. All the remaining *vitesji* knew better than to speak of Ion and his treason. Yet . . . 'Might not this be a trick?' He looked at the shepherds. 'All part of the same trap?'

Dracula thought for a moment, then shook his head. 'Ion Tremblac would cut out my heart if he could. And perhaps he will try to, one day. But he would not stand around and watch others do it. That I know.' He crossed to the old men. 'A dozen horses, you say?' On their nod he turned to Ilie. 'I will take you, Stoica and eight others. Let the rest of the *vitesji* draw lots.' He turned. 'And I will take my son.'

The boy gasped.

Ilie nodded. 'And the rest?'

'They must man the walls till we are well clear, then take their chances with the Turk.'

'And I?' Elisabeta came forward, her voice shrill. 'Must I take my chances with them, too?'

Vlad gestured for everyone to go. His son lingered last but Ilie pushed him out of the door. When all were gone, Vlad slipped the heavy bar onto its brackets and began gathering what was essential, speaking without looking up. 'Your father is out there, lady, waiting to glory in my fall. My men will wait a while and then try to flee, or surrender. If you are lucky and the enemy grants terms, I am sure the *jupan* will be happy to have you back. For as we both know, your virginity is still for sale.'

'If I am lucky . . .' She echoed him, wonder in her tone. 'Do you hate me that much that you would risk seeing me raped to death by Infidels?'

Still Vlad did not look up. 'Hate you? I have not thought of you enough to hate you.'

'You truly are the Devil,' she cried. And then she ran for the stairs that led to the turret, ran up them. Vlad continued packing . . . until the screaming began. Then he took the stairs two at a time.

'Father!' she screamed. 'Turcul *jupan*! Help me!' The axes

ceased falling. In the silence that followed her voice rang clear. 'Father. The Devil seeks to flee. Help me! Help—'

A hand went round her mouth. 'Silence, lady. My escape will be hard enough without . . .'

He could not stifle the yelp of agony. She had grabbed his other hand, jerked it. It only had three fingers and was never without pain. Gasping, he released her.

She broke clear, circled to the other side of the turret. In the faint light that penetrated under the wooden roof, a blade now glittered. 'You know,' she said, her voice all bitterness, 'I think that is the first time you ever touched me.'

She was on the far side of the turret now so she began to scream past him, towards the Turkish lights. 'Help me, Father. He comes tonight. Dracula flies . . .'

He lunged at her and she threw herself back, fast, too fast, her feet catching in her long gown, tripping her, plunging her into the gap between two stone buttresses, her force carrying her through them.

He grabbed an edge of her dress . . . but three fingers and a thumb could not hold her. She fell. The donjon was the height of six men but it was built against the edge of the sheerest precipice of the mountain and she did not hit rock, or cease screaming, till she was halfway down it.

Vlad stared down into the darkness in the long moment between the wail's ending, and the axes beginning to fall again. Then he turned and went swiftly down the stairs.

The packing took but moments. He remembered how little a fugitive needed and took it, kept all that truly mattered on his body – the Dragon's Talon slung across his back; the Dragon's Ring upon the one little finger left to him. Below, in his saddle-pack, Ilie would already have the Dragon's banner folded.

A postern gate gave onto the north-facing side of the mountain, a slope so sheer no tower had been built to cover it. Hand over hand, a man might climb up. Or down.

Far below the River Arges curled, a sliver of silver in the moonlight.

Vlad looked down, then up to the battlements. Those who were not coming peered over them. They obeyed him entirely – for fear, for love, for all the reasons in between. They understood why only the ten who stood around him now could go. And Vlad knew that their oath of allegiance ended when the fugitives reached the valley floor; that they would make their own arrangements. Some, perhaps most, would live. The Turk prized slaves and tended them well, like their flocks – though Vlad was not sure if that would be true of the Wallachians who also waited beyond, hungry for vengeance.

He looked around at his chosen ones, at the shepherds who would lead them; lastly at his son. The boy's eyes glowed within the mirror of that face. And in it Vlad saw himself as a boy – proudly riding beside his father to meet a Sultan. Like his son before him, Vlad had not been fleeing then, but riding towards an unknown fate. Towards his *kismet*. And in that mirror he realised he still was.

To the fall of axes, and the bark of ravens, men and boy slipped and slid down the slope. The worst steepness ended in a cave and from there a ribbon of a path descended to the river. On its banks, horses were tethered. Not warhorses but tough tarpans from the mountains. Their hooves were wrapped in cloth, so they did not clatter on the pebbles of the river's bed as they were led along it by the men of Arefu.

There was a point where the river began to bend. Before them, other mountains shrouded the valley in black. Behind was a last view of the castle. Vlad reined over, letting the others go ahead, then looked up. The moon was a Turkish bow, resting its tip on the battlements. When he'd been not much older than the boy who had just passed him, he had first held the throne, first lost it. He had sworn an oath of return, then. A young man's oath. Now that he was older, he promised himself and God precisely nothing.

With a jab of spurs – the horse was not Kalafat – he followed the others into the darkness.

FORTY-THREE

Betrayal

Brasov, Transylvania, six weeks later

'How do I look?'

Stoica and Ilie shrugged. One could not speak, one dared not. But the shrugs told their thoughts clearly. That the Voivode of Wallachia should meet the emissaries of King Matthias and the Council of Brasov dressed splendidly, as befitted a prince. Both men knew he had a beautiful suit made of black silk, ordered the day he arrived in Brasov five weeks earlier, delivered a week later, paid for by the Brasovians. They had not dared deny him, considering what he'd visited upon them only three years before, in fire and wood.

But this day the suit hung in the wardrobe. Their prince had donned his armour. He had not even allowed Stoica to hammer out the dents, nor wash away the mud, the traces of blood that looked like rust.

Vlad smiled at the eloquence of the two shrugs. Yet he knew what they did not – the workings of men's minds. If he went before the Council and Hungary's ambassadors dressed for the court he would appear as just another pretender, begging arms and gold to take back a throne. Dressed in well-used armour he was a warrior still; most importantly, a warrior with a war still ongoing, merely paused.

It also reminded them of something else. What he did best. Kill.

He turned, stared at the door. Remembered another time, another door, the one that led down into the Great Hall at Targoviste. He'd stood before it that Easter when he'd been about to descend and overthrow the *boyars*. He'd asked Ion how he'd looked. Ion had told him, and would now, sparing him neither praise nor insult.

His smile died. Ion was not there. Vlad was alone, save for these two, loyal, disapproving. All the others had gone. Yet in a few hours, he should have the beginnings of an army and the gold to pay for it, for the war that was merely paused.

'Sword,' he commanded.

Stoica brought the Dragon's Talon, went to fasten the belt across his prince's shoulder. Vlad delayed him with a raised hand, his maimed left one, lifting it to run his three fingers over the emblem in the pommel, over the Dragon that flew there. Thinking of the other Dragon that waited, in the Goldsmiths' Hall, among the Council of Brasov.

Janos Horvathy. He had known him a little, when Vlad had been an exile at Corvinus's court. One of dozens of 'new men' around the new king – for Matthias distrusted the old nobility, wanted men loyal only to him, lesser nobles who sought to rise. Horvathy, to have been sent on such an important embassy as this, must have begun that rise.

Yet it was not the oath Horvathy had sworn to his king that made Vlad smile now. It was another oath – sworn to the brotherhood to which they both belonged.

'Brother Dragon,' Horvathy had said a week before when first he'd greeted Vlad. There had been warmth in the special handshake the Count of Pecs had given him, in the kiss of welcome, in the smile. He had negotiated hard in the following days, on behalf of his sovereign. But Vlad knew that behind the Hungarian's insistence on Hungarian terms lay a loyalty as deep. Deeper in many ways and bound by the most sacred of oaths.

'Brother Dragon,' murmured Vlad.

Stoica, not hearing or not understanding, thought he was commanded and lifted the sword-belt again. This time Vlad let him fasten it over his shoulders, across his chest. The great weapon's tip reached almost to the floor.

Vlad touched the grip at his shoulder. He could have it

drawn in a moment. But it was there only to complete the impression of ready warrior. He would not need it. Not when a Dragon waited for him in the Goldsmiths' Hall.

'Let us go,' he said.

Janos Horvathy rubbed his eyes. It did nothing to clear the blurriness. Only sleep would and he'd had little enough of that during the week he'd been negotiating with Dracula; and none at all, in the three days since his master, Matthias Corvinus, King of Hungary, had decided that the negotiations were over. However, it wasn't the further arrangements, detailed though they had to be, that had kept his eyes open at night. It was the memory of an oath.

'Count? Did you hear me?'

Horvathy started at the voice. He'd forgotten that Jiskra was there. Now his eyes began to focus at last, on the details of the old warrior's face: the nose, skewed by some long-forgotten blow, trailing left; the pink-hued skin, flaking, so he was spotted as if with flour; the thick, unkempt grey beard; the small, shoved-together eyes. Detail cleared the blurriness at last. 'What did you say?'

'I said that it was time, Horvathy. All is ready.'

'The Council?'

'The members have taken their seats in the chamber.'

'Your men?'

'In their places.'

'You are sure you have enough?'

Jiskra snorted. 'Why, by the bleeding Christ, is everyone so frightened of this Wallachian? Because he has had some success against the Turk and has used some . . . harsh methods?' He laughed. 'Well, I was killing Turks – harshly! – when Dracula was sucking his wet nurse's tit. Besides, he only has those two with him always. And I know my job.'

'I am sure you do. It is only . . .' The Count paused. 'Do you not regret the necessity?'

'Regret necessity? What stupidity is that?' the older warrior spat. 'A man acts on what is decided. Our king has decided that this Dracula is an embarrassment. He is! And a fool! Demanding that the Crow honours his promises?' He jeered. 'Kings don't honour promises, not unless it suits them. They act on expedience. It is not expedient to go to war against the Turk, and the Crow never truly intended it. He has other uses for his soldiers, to the north. And better ways to spend his gold. He will not sit safely on the throne of Hungary until the crown of St Stephen sits on his head. The not-so Holy Roman Emperor demands eighty thousand crowns for its return. The Crow could buy a small war with that, with all its risks. Or he could get his crown out of pawn.' He turned, cleared his throat noisily, spat into the fireplace. 'Furthermore—'

'I know! I know!' Horvathy raised a hand to halt the flow of words. Jiskra, once started, would talk for days about the 'realities of politics' if he was allowed. 'I only truly regret that it has to be this way.' He gestured to the three rolled parchments on the table.

Jiskra shrugged. 'What are a few more lies amongst the many? This Wallachian is causing a fuss, with his appeals to the Pope, to other sovereigns. He must be proved to have betrayed the cause, so we can dispose of him.'

'Betrayed? Who is the betrayer here?' Horvathy murmured.

'Man!' Jiskra shouted, looking up at the ceiling. 'You are meant to be one of the coming men, whom Corvinus is raising up. *His* men. Isn't he going to get your castle out of pawn, like his crown, when you do this? Well, I tell you – you will not last a week in the snake's nest of Buda's court if you try to keep your conscience clean.'

'But it is not just to the King that I owe loyalty,' the Count replied, angered now. 'For Dracula and I are both members of the same brotherhood – the Order of the Dragon. Formed to fight the Infidel. Sworn to aid each other. I took an oath—'

'Fuck your oath,' Jiskra bellowed. 'I belong to no orders. I serve one God and one man and take oaths only to them. It keeps it simple.' He straightened. 'So it's them I obey now. Their enemy must be accused and arrested publicly, so all may witness his treason, know of his disgrace.' He leaned forward. 'Are you ready to do what must be done? Or would you rather hide up here with your oaths and your conscience while I do the dirty stuff?'

Horvathy stood, reached for his sword. 'No, Jiskra. I will do what I must. I have no choice.'

'You do not.' The door opened. A soldier appeared, nodded. Jiskra turned back. 'And Dracula's here.'

The door to the Goldsmiths' Hall opened. Instantly, the members of the Council of Brasov, seated in ranks on either side of the main floor, hushed, turned to it. Horvathy, on a dais at the hall's end, looked, his sight blurred again, this time by sunlight. Then the dark figure stepped beyond it and the Count was able to see the man clearly, to note the battered armour and the stained cloak. He smiled for a moment as he realised what Dracula was saying, then remembered that what Dracula said there that day meant nothing.

He shifted his gaze, looked to either side of the hall at the members of the Council, their rich cloaks and rounded forms a contrast to the lean, stained warrior now striding to the central table, flanked by his two guards. Most stared at him in disgust, in fear, for he had forced them to a settlement three years before, with flame and the stake. Now he was there as supplicant. Horvathy could see, on the faces of those few it had been necessary to tell, a scarcely concealed triumph.

Vlad did not look to either side. He strode to the middle of the chamber, halted at the table there that bore the Council records in heavy, leather-bound tomes. Beside these, symbols of the Guild's wealth as well as samples of their prowess, stood two gold objects. One was a golden moon, wreathed in vine leaves. The other was a hawk, its wingspan as wide as a hand, stooping on a hare, both beasts rendered in exquisite detail.

Vlad studied the craftsmanship for a moment, the expression of hunter and prey. Then he looked up at the councillors who had caused them to be made, saw the smiles on some faces that men did not bother to hide; looked across the table, to the raised dais, the man sitting there; saw the sadness in the Count's grey eyes. Watched as Horvathy glanced left, followed the glance. To Jan Jiskra, beckoning. And he knew.

The dozen men came fast through the sunshine, some with swords, some with cudgels. Black Ilie saw steel, tried to draw his own. Clubs fell – on hand, to stomach – and he was down. Stoica had a blade to his throat, his own dagger swiftly removed. Only Dracula was untouched, though blades were levelled at him. Probably because his arms were raised high in the air in the unmistakable gesture of surrender.

He let the hubbub settle before he spoke. 'Why?' he said clearly.

The Council had risen but Vlad was not addressing them. His question was for the Hungarian, standing ten paces away at the other end of the long table.

Horvathy took a breath, made sure his voice was steady before he replied. He intoned, speaking slowly, for scribes were placed around the room and needed to note down all that was said. 'Vlad Dracula, former Voivode of Wallachia, it is with great sadness that we have learned of your treachery. That you, who claimed to be a warrior for Christ, and a loyal vassal of our good King Matthias, have proved a traitor to both.'

Vlad's voice, when it came, was calm contrast to the quaver in the Hungarian's. 'Proved? How have I proved so, when my entire life has proved the opposite?'

'We have the letters, Dracula.'

'What letters?'

'These.' The Count gestured to the three rolls of

346

parchment before him on the table. 'One you wrote to your equally traitorous cousin, Stephen, Voivode of Moldavia. A second to the Grand Vizier of the Turk, Mamoud. The last to the Sultan himself, the man you claimed as mortal enemy. All three testify to your treasonous plans. That you would take the forces my mighty sovereign was going to lend you and turn them against His Majesty. That you would use the gold offered by Brasov to corrupt loyal men. And finally, and most heinously' – Horvathy reached forward and picked up one of the papers – 'that you planned on kidnapping King Matthias and delivering him, naked and bound, to the Turk.'

The councillors had started to murmur under the Hungarian's words. At this last many shouted, cursed the traitor. Brave now, some even leaned in to spit. Vlad stood still, ignoring them, looking at one man.

That man raised his hand to halt the noise, then continued. 'It is all written here, signed with your name, sealed with your seal. This will be entered into the records of the Council of Brasov. And pamphlets will be printed and distributed so that the world knows of your infamy.' Horvathy lowered the paper he held when he noticed that his hand was shaking. In a quieter voice, he said, 'Do you have anything to say?'

'Only this.' Vlad leaned down, placing his hands on the table before him. Though his movements were slow, soldiers still stepped a little closer, swords raised. 'I know why the men of Brasov would do this, for they have long hated me. I also know why Hungary's King would do this, for his throne is not steady beneath him and he needs the Pope's gold, which he took for crusade, to shore it up.' He raised his eyes. 'Yet I do not know why *you* would do this. Or allow it to be done. For you must know, *Brother Dragon*, the disgrace these forgeries will bring upon the brotherhood. That is the real betrayal, and it will damn all Dragons and blunt, perhaps for ever, the lance-tip of Christ, just when it is needed most.'

Horvathy felt his knees weaken. He bent, held the table,

too, stared down it at the man opposite, joined to him by wood. 'I do what must be done, Dracula. For the realm. For my king . . .'

'And for yourself. I am certain that by delivering me in this manner, you will rise higher, faster, in the court of the Crow. But I also tell you this, Janos Horvathy . . .' And then Vlad straightened, thrusting his maimed hand out before him, three fingers and thumb spread in a warding gesture. '. . . You will never find contentment in your rise. For my curse will be ever with you. I curse you. I curse you and your family – for eternity! And you will learn, soon enough, that my curse is as real as these lies are false. That I am not called the Devil's son for nothing!'

The curse had risen to a shout.

'Seize him!' Jan Jiskra cried. A soldier came, and Vlad ducked beneath the outstretched arm, took it, snapped it and flung the howling man back into the second who followed. Then, in the moment he had, Vlad snatched up the golden hawk on the table before him and hurled it the length of the table. The golden beak, poised to tear a hare's flesh, sunk into Horvathy's left eye. He shrieked and staggered back, as soldiers fell on Dracula, silent now, powerless at last.

PART FOUR

The Last Crusade

'I acknowledged my sin to You, and I did not hide my iniquity . . . then did you forgive the iniquity of my sin.'

— PSALMS 32.5

FORTY-FOUR

The Exile

Poenari Castle, 1481

'And he was proven right.'

Silence, at last, in the hall of Poenari. Horvathy had stopped speaking, for the first time in a while. And the interjections that had come occasionally from the hermit in his confessional had ceased, too. But as he concluded his story, Horvathy had been speaking increasingly fast, and the scribes now took the chance to ease their cramped fingers, and trim another quill.

And then he spoke again.

'This,' he said, touching the puckered scar that was his left eye, 'was the least of the curse. Dracula was right, for I rose swiftly, and Pecs grew from an impoverished shambles into the foremost fiefdom of the land. While I stood behind the throne and helped Matthias become the mighty monarch he is. Yet as I rose, the curse accompanied me.' He closed the other eye. 'My wife, dead at twenty-five. Our two sons lost, one to war and wound, one to plague. Our daughter killed by the first child she tried to bear, who died with her. I am, and will be, the last of the line of Horvathy.'

Silence again, for a moment, until another voice came. 'A lesser man would have succumbed to his sorrows, Count Horvathy,' the Cardinal said, softly. 'Yet here you are, still striving to keep your oaths to your king, and to God.'

'No, Cardinal Grimani. I serve them in what I do here, perhaps. But I strive for another oath. The one I broke to a fellow Dragon. The one for which I am cursed, for which I have never been forgiven.' He opened his eye, looked at the

Italian. 'Yet perhaps here, in what has been heard – in what, I remind you, you are still to judge – the curse may be lifted and forgiveness follow. Forgiveness – and the raising of the Dragon banner once more.'

Grimani turned away, from the one eye and its appeal, revealing nothing. 'That we have yet to decide. And soon,' he said briskly. 'For it seems this confession is nearing its conclusion. I suggest we proceed with pace' – he glanced at the arrow slit, the light growing outside it – 'so I can be gone, with my recommendations to the Pope, before another sunset. Yet . . .' He paused. 'I am curious about some inconsistencies in the telling.' He looked at the end confessional. 'Where *were* you, priest?'

The hermit's croak came. 'Where?'

'Yes. When you just reported Dracula's words, you said the Voivode "mislaid you". Where?'

'I . . .' The hermit coughed. 'When I heard what had happened in the cathedral, I joined the thousands who fled Targoviste at the Turk's approach.'

'So you did not see the . . . wedding? Nor the impalement outside the gates?'

'I did not.'

'Yet you have helped these others describe them in some detail.'

The Count leaned forward. 'Your point is?'

'Only that even this witness, who seems sometimes to know Dracula's very soul, is often speaking second-hand.' Grimani pointed at Ion's confessional. 'While that one even chooses to speak for the Turk, Hamza *pasha*.'

'I knew him,' Ion protested. 'I visited him often in his cell.'

Both men ignored him. 'And therefore?' Horvathy asked.

'Therefore,' replied the Cardinal, 'his testimony, all their testimonies, must be treated carefully.'

'Have we not been doing just that? Getting three opinions to agree on a combined one?'

'Indeed.' The Cardinal sat back. 'I merely state it. For the record. People's opinions are just that, in the end. So,' he said with a smile, 'the conclusions we draw can therefore be our own.'

Horvathy nodded. 'The ones we need them to be.'

'Indeed.'

Petru, less versed in the ways of politics, had a belief in simpler truths. 'But this man was his confessor! He speaks what he heard. And even if it is a sin that he betrays those confessions now, still, we must believe the truth of them. A man does not lie to his priest in confession.'

'Doesn't he?' The Cardinal shook his head. 'I have known men exaggerate their sins greatly, thinking that when they are then forgiven it gives them a certain licence. The worst is pardoned, so if a lesser sin is committed later . . .'

Petru was outraged. 'This may be true of the Church of Rome—'

The Count intervened. 'It is true of men anywhere, Spatar. I am sure within their own rituals the Turk has a way of doing the same. Forgiving himself for what he still must do.' He cleared his throat. 'But the point is made. The record states it. And I agree with His Eminence. Let us proceed swiftly.' He turned. 'And I am also unclear about something, hermit. When did you re-join Dracula?'

The croak came. 'I went to his prison. To Visegrad.'

'Caged again,' murmured the Cardinal.

'It is hardly Tokat,' the Count commented, 'more palace than prison. The windows are not barred. The gardens are beautiful and in the Italian style. And the country beyond! Full of game for hound and hawk.' He nodded. 'A man could live content there.'

'Content?' blurted Petru. 'After all the killing he had done, all he had striven for in ashes, his throne lost, his love . . . mutilated . . .' He swallowed. 'His best friend a traitor, who sits before us trying to excuse his betrayal.' He shook his head. 'Are you saying he was content to live the life of a . . . a provincial gentleman?'

Horvathy grunted. 'Content? I do not know. Perhaps he raged for a time. But in the end what choice does the songbird have but to sing? The world had shifted. As you say, Dracula had lost everything – throne, power, support, the love of those he loved.' He glanced at two of the confessionals. 'He already knew the life of the fugitive. And now he had ten thousand more enemies lurking in alleys with knives, lusting for revenge. Remember, a cage keeps others out, as well as someone in.'

'And could he not simply have been tired, my lord,' the Cardinal said. 'Even Dracula. Tired of blood?'

'Well.' Horvathy licked his cracked lips. 'That we have yet to hear.'

Petru looked up, to the arrow slit, to dawn's earliest light there. 'Shall we recess? We have talked a day and night through. Perhaps the last could be heard after a little sleep?'

Horvathy looked at the Cardinal. 'No, I agree with His Eminence. Let us hear the last of it. It will not be long till you are nestled in beside that pretty young wife of yours again. And we will be gone, to trouble your sleep no more.' He raised a hand. 'But let me, at least, speed the process. I know something of what happened next. For I sat in Corvinus's court, and heard the tales we have just heard re-shaped. Read the pamphlets' – he gestured to the pile on the table – 'that damned the name of Dracula throughout the world. And, may God forgive me, I furthered my damnation, and that of my brotherhood, by helping to spread some of the stories.' He rubbed at his forehead. 'But time passed. Soon enough we had other ogres to focus on. Christian took on Christian again, while the Infidel sat back and laughed.'

'As it ever was,' murmured the Cardinal. 'And then?'

'Then, about four years later,' continued the Count, 'with eyes everywhere else, Dracula was quietly brought from Visegrad to Pest, across the river from the King's palace at Buda. He was given a house. More, he was given a cousin of the King as wife.'

'What?' Petru gasped. 'Why?'

'He was still on a leash, but a loose one now. For Corvinus fought Dracula's cousin Stephen of Moldavia – whom, you remember, betrayed the prince at the very height of his crusade, forcing him to divide his tiny army. So Dracula was once again a threat . . . to be unleashed perhaps. Then, when the two Christian monarchs settled their grievances and looked again at the Infidel, it suited them to keep Dracula as just that: a threat.'

The Cardinal leaned forward. 'Did you see him?'

Horvathy shook his head. 'No. The King spared me his rare visits to court. He was paraded sometimes, usually when an embassy came from the Sultan. It amused the King to see the Grand Turk's emissaries spot him, and hasten to remove their turbans.' Horvathy laughed, but there was little humour in the sound. He continued. 'But you can only make a threat for so long before you must use it.'

'Indeed.'

'So what happened?' Petru leaned forward.

'What happened?' the Count echoed. 'The world shifted again.' He looked at the confessionals. 'Which of you would like to tell us how?'

— FORTY-FIVE —

Sleeping Dragon

Pest, Hungary, February 1475,
thirteen years after Dracula's arrest

It was dusk when Ion reached the villa on the outskirts of the town. He had meant to be there much earlier, so he would be able to deliver his message and return to the King's palace in Buda before dark. No one travelled alone at night anywhere near a city.

The frustrations of the journey, which had begun a month before with blocked passes in the Transylvanian Alps, had continued to its end. The bridge across the river that divided Buda from Pest had recently burned down. This would not have been a problem for the ice was usually thick enough to support man and horse across. But a sudden early thaw had rendered it thin and dangerous, yet still too thick for boats to push through. He'd had to go downstream, to a narrower section where a passage had been cut, pay twice as much for the ferry, ride up the opposite bank. This last delay meant it would be necessary to spend the night in a Pest inn, for he would not spend a night beneath the roof of the man he'd come to see.

That roof was identical to those to its left and right, grey slate rising sharply to sturdy timber gables. The houses were solid, square; an arched entranceway in each that was wide enough to admit a small coach; shutters rising two levels up the ochre-daubed walls, all shut firmly against the winter air. The dwellings were unremarkable. No doubt some merchant or town burgher lived in the two on either side.

A month it had taken him to get here and now Ion sat on his horse, unwilling to dismount, despite the mist that thrust chilled fingers under his furs and poked his myriad scars and re-set bones. Each winter was harder, stiffening him, greying the hair that still hung thick over his brow, still concealed the brand Mehmet had given him nearly thirty years before, its edges purpled now, blurring into the wrinkles of his face.

He reached up, ran his fingers over the flesh that stood slightly proud. Why was he hesitating now, when he had not paused, except when forced to, in the entire journey that had begun four weeks previously in Stephen cel Mare's court at Suceava?

He dropped his hand. He knew why. He had not seen the man who dwelt within these dull walls in thirteen years. Since a very different day, one of terrible heat, in Targoviste. If he'd had his choice, he would never have seen him again. But a king and a prince wished it otherwise. And God, too, he believed. Had to believe. Otherwise he would not be able to walk his horse to the wooden doors, dismount before them, raise one hand to the great iron hoop, lift it . . .

He never let it fall. Because, beyond the door, he heard familiar sounds: metal striking metal; men crying out. Someone was fighting inside, fighting hard. With a soldier's instinct, Ion had his horse hitched and his own sword drawn in a moment. Pressing his ear to the grille, he heard running footsteps, a yelp of terror.

Ion had not ridden all that way to speak to a dead man, however much he hated him. Perhaps one of his many enemies had found him out. Turning the iron ring of the handle, he was surprised when the door gave. Opening it wide, for he did not know how fast he might have to come out, he stepped into the darkness of a short tunnel. Shouts came down it and at its end light dazzled him, for the courtyard beyond was brightly lit by torches. Shielding his eyes against the glare, Ion saw two shapes run across. Both held hand-and-a-half swords. One was desperately parrying; the other striking high, low, wide, close.

Ion advanced cautiously, letting his eyes adjust, sword held before him. The men were fighting now in some other part of the courtyard, their blows and cries echoing off the stones. He wrapped his hand around the archway's inner edge, took a breath, leaned in . . .

As Ion watched, one of the men stepped under an overhead cut, his own sword high. Blade screeched on blade, the pair locked, grappled, almost still now as they wrestled for dominance, and Ion was able to see them. One was clad in a black leather jerkin, a full helmet obscuring his face. The opponent, turned away from Ion, was naked to the waist, long black hair flowing down a thickly muscled back that steamed in the chill night air.

He did not know what to do. Who was fighting, and why? He was about to call out, step in, distract . . . when the grapple ended, the visored man bending at his knees, straightening fast, throwing the other one back. The barechested one stumbled around the table, then turned, his sword rising . . .

The man who turned was Dracula.

Ion gasped. It could not be! For this was the prince he remembered. The bull's body, the midnight-black hair and moustache. Each scar was livid in the torchlight, and Ion could have named the weapon that made them, the alley or field where it had cut. Yet the man before him was no older than the one he'd last seen in Targoviste. Worse! If anything, he was younger!

Ion began crossing himself, again and again, mumbling a warding prayer. There were many who had said that his prince was kin to another, that the Devil's son was more than a name. He had not believed it . . . until now. The proof was clear before his eyes. Dracula had made a pact with Satan. He had exchanged his soul for immortality.

'Holy Father, protect me!' Ion cried.

The fighters, who had charged like bulls into another grapple, heard. Still holding each other's blades high they turned, as one. Then Dracula released his opponent's hand, disengaged his blade, began to step away. And the other, whose faceless helmet had turned also, now turned back. Dropping his blade, he cocked his wrist and stepped past the naked chest, moving between Ion and Dracula, who shrieked now in agony. Then Ion saw why – across the taut, muscled stomach a thin red line had opened and immediately pulsed blood.

With another yelp, Dracula dropped his sword, clutched his stomach and staggered backwards, falling onto a wooden bench. The helmetted one leaned down to him, reaching up to the straps at his chin, beginning to untie them. He spoke softly, but in a voice that carried, 'Will you never learn? You do not stop fighting, whatever the distraction, while a man has a blade near your throat.'

'You've cut me,' Dracula screamed.

'I have,' said the other man, beginning to lift off his helmet, 'and the scar it leaves will remind you and perhaps save your life one day.'

The helmet came off . . . and Ion plunged deeper into his nightmare. For the head that emerged was identical to the one beside it . . . but only if it had suddenly been lit by lightning on a dark night. All that was black in the one man was white in the other – the moustache, the eyebrows, the thick hair shaken loose, now tumbling down the back, all as white as a bleached skull. And then, as Ion gasped again and looked closer, he saw that they were not identical; that the features of this older man were a corruption of the younger's; the eyes sunken, the nose thinner, the flesh looser. And he recognised him, even before the elder man turned and spoke.

'Welcome, Ion,' said the true Dracula. 'I have been expecting you.'

After brief introductions, the younger man was dispatched to the housekeeper. The cut, as both could see, was nothing to men who had had metal stuck into them. It was as if finely cropped parchment had been run across the skin.

The two men watched him go.

'I wanted him to be a priest,' Vlad said, 'but he insists on being a warrior. So I train him to fight – and remind him always of the cost.'

'Your son,' said Ion. It was not a question. 'I didn't know you had one that age. How old is he?'

'Twenty-six. A gift from Arefu. Came to me the night I left the castle. When you missed me with your arrow, Ion.'

Ion stiffened. 'I don't know what you are talking about.'

'Indeed?' Vlad studied him a moment, looked away. 'I have other sons, two of them. Small.' He looked back. 'And you? How many sons have you?'

'None. Five daughters.'

'Five? Your house must be noisy.'

'As yours is quiet.'

Vlad nodded. 'The boys are around. My wife hides them when we train. There's usually blood. Sometimes even mine, for I am getting slow.' He took Ion's arm. 'You'll stay for supper?'

Ion looked down at the hand that held him. Three fingers and a stump. 'No. I am ordered to deliver a message. But I eat where I choose. With whom I choose . . . my lord.'

The crippled grip tightened. 'My lord? I am still a prince, Ion Tremblac.'

'Not mine,' Ion said. 'I serve another now.'

Vlad did not move. But his face flushed with colour, startling in the whiteness of the surround. 'I heard. My cousin, Stephen of Moldavia. "The Great" they call him now, because of his victories over the Turk and the Hungarian. Stephen cel Mare,' he whispered. 'While my victories are forgotten and I am called Vlad Tepes – the Impaler. Remembered only for a tool of justice I once employed.'

'Oh, you are remembered for many things, *my lord*,' Ion said, jerking his arm from the other's grip.

Vlad stared, taking in the bitterness in the taller man's voice, in his eyes. Then he nodded, spoke briskly. 'Well, I do not receive embassies with sweat still on my body and my throat a desert. So you'll stay and eat, or return another day . . . Spatar.'

Ion paused. 'I will stay.'

'Good.' Vlad clapped his hands. 'You remember Stoica?'

A man emerged from under the balcony. Unlike his master, the small, bald servant did not appear to have aged much. Only when he stepped a little closer into a pool of torchlight did Ion see the fine lines around his eyes. 'Of course. How are you?'

The mute shrugged, waited.

Vlad continued, 'You'll recognise more faces in Pest. Half a dozen of my *vitesji* live nearby. Black Ilie lives here, still my bodyguard, though he has a wife and family in the town.' He turned to Stoica. 'Take his horse to the stable, his things to a spare room.'

'I said I would eat with you,' Ion protested, 'I said nothing about staying here.'

'You won't want to walk the streets alone at night. This is not Targoviste in 1462. Still, that choice can be made after supper.' He nodded; Stoica bowed, withdrew. Vlad was already walking away, slipping into the shadows. 'You'll be fetched when eight bells toll,' he called, and was gone.

Another servant came, beckoned. Finally sheathing his sword – he had forgotten he still held it – Ion shivered and followed.

FORTY-SIX

Persuasion

Dracula was alone. He sat at one end of a short, rectangular table. As Ion came in he didn't look up, just continued to stare into candle-light. Only when Ion sat in the chair held for him at the opposite end of the table were those green eyes lifted to fix on him, though there was no recognition in them, no acknowledgement, nothing. Unnerved, Ion accepted the goblet of hot wine the servant handed him before he withdrew; but he did not drink.

To escape the stare, he looked at the table. It was uncluttered. There were two pots, both steaming; one held the wine, heady with the scent of juniper; the other gave off a whiff of stew, game probably, the hint of rot that went with a hare or rabbit properly hung. There were metal bowls, knives, spoons, two candelabra and a languier. The metal tree was an oak in winter, the fissured bark and barren branches skilfully crafted. Flame-light flickered on the snake tongues that hung there.

Finally Ion looked up, met those expressionless eyes. He pointed at the languier and spoke, over-loudly, to end the silence. 'You still fear poisoning then?'

Dracula stirred. 'I fear nothing,' he replied, his voice low, 'but I do not believe it is my fate to be murdered thus. So I call upon the snake to detect any poisons for me. And the unicorn.' He raised his goblet, turning one side towards Ion and the light. 'I have a piece of its horn here. As do you.'

Ion looked down, saw the striations of the horn embedded in the silver mug. 'Expensive,' he said.

'My wife's.'

'Does she not join us? She and your son?'

'My son has gone into Pest to carouse with his friends and show off his latest scar. I hear he has not bought a flagon in years, for all pay to see the Dragon's claw marks on his skin. That is a lot of wine, for the boy is easily distracted, as you saw.' Dracula lifted his goblet, drank. 'And my wife will visit but not eat. One of the other boys is sick and she will not leave him long . . . and here she is.' Vlad stood, smiling. 'Come in, my dear, and meet an old . . . friend, Ion Tremblac. Ion . . . this is Ilona.'

That name! It had hardly been out of his mind since he first set out; as if he felt her beside him every step, her wounds crying out for a vengeance he could not take. So he couldn't help the slight stagger as he rose, as he turned towards the impossible.

Yet no ghost stood there, just a woman. Her face was as white as the snow beyond her walls, dark eyes bright within it, her nose long, her cheekbones sharp. She had no eyebrows, as was the custom in the court at Buda, and her forehead was high under a coif where a hint of her black hair was held. The contrast to the other Ilona, the one for ever in Ion's mind, was marked. Yet if she was not beautiful, as she came forward into the candle-light, Ion could see the kindness in her eyes.

She stretched a hand before her. He bent, kissed. 'You are welcome, sir,' she said, Hungarian words in a warm voice, 'I have heard much of you.'

Ion, rising from the kiss, was disconcerted. What had her husband said of him? Ion had told his own wife little of the man he'd once loved, and it was often shouted out after too much wine, or from the depths of sleep, hate-wracked and vile. 'I . . . I wish I could make your better acquaintance, lady.'

'I hoped it, too. Soon perhaps. But I have one sick child and one . . .' She reached behind her and suddenly there was a face at her hip, with hair and huge eyes the colour of hers, of night, a boy of about four. He peeped around her, staring up at the stranger, before his glance darted to the table, the snake tongues upon it, and then onto his father.

'May I touch them, Papa?' he whispered.

'Yes,' said Dracula. 'But mind! They may still bite.'

His son crept around, reached up, flicked a tongue, laughed. His father stretched a hand past him. 'Aiee!' he yelled, jerking his hand back. 'Look! It has taken a finger!'

He thrust one hand out, stump foremost. The boy squealed delightedly, as his father mussed his hair, then ran behind his mother once more.

She clutched him, smiled. 'You will come and see Mircea?'

Vlad nodded. 'I will come. Later. When my business here is done.'

'Business,' she echoed, a frown coming. 'Do not . . .' She broke off, turned to Ion. 'Do not keep my husband too long, sir.'

'I will not, at your request, lady.' He bowed.

She inclined her head, and left the room, shooing her reluctant son before her.

Vlad, still standing, looked after her. When he spoke, he reverted to the language of their land. 'She is a wise woman. Her words, the ones she does not speak, caution me.'

He gestured to the soup pot and a servant came and filled the two bowls, handing one to each man. Dracula pointed to the door and the man left. Then he sat and immediately began to eat.

Ion sat. 'Caution you against what?'

'Against you. And what you would persuade me to do.'

Ion had picked up his spoon. Still, he did not eat. 'And how would she know what that was?'

Dracula snorted, took another mouthful. 'She is the King's cousin. A Szilagy of Corvinus's own family. So she is my wife and a Crow, too. And she knows what crows do – let someone else do their killing for them, then show up to feast on the scraps.' He looked over a full spoon, paused before his mouth. 'And are you not here to ask me to provide Corvinus with a supper?'

Ion still had not eaten. Now he laid his spoon down. 'I do not serve King Matthias,' he said, 'but Stephen of Moldavia.'

Dracula slurped. 'Whom Matthias hates and loves, and fights and embraces depending on the wind from Constantinople. And now the Great and the Crow need each other again. And between them they have decided that they also need the Impaler.'

'I do not think you understand—'

'I understand everything,' Dracula shouted, his face thrust forward, green eyes bright between the dangling frames of bone-white hair. 'Remember, I have been Corvinus's prisoner for thirteen years, ever since he betrayed me, betrayed the crusade, by failing to march to my aid; since he ordered letters forged claiming that *I* was the betrayer. And used a man I thought was a brother in that betrayal.' He threw his spoon into the bowl. 'Four years I was at Visegrad, an embarrassment, waiting for my murderer to come. But then the wind changed. Crow fought the Great, fought the Turk, and the Impaler was useful again. Not to use his *speciality*.' A half-smile came. 'Just to threaten it, against whomsoever Corvinus chose.' He waved a hand. 'My prison changed. He even gave me a companion for my cell. Kept me close – but not too close, across the river – to be trotted out, exhibited like a monster, a grotesque at a country fair.'

He rose, crossed to a chest, threw it open, delved within. 'I'll show you something.' He moved back to the table, and flung down a packet of papers. 'Pamphlets,' he said. 'First made by my enemies in Brasov and Sibiu after my fall. They had good reason to hate me, those Saxons, after the way I broke their hold on Wallachian trade. And the Hungarians – some of them even my brother Dragons – helped spread these pamphlets throughout the world to justify their betrayal.' He lifted one, held it under Ion's nose. 'Have you read any?'

Ion pushed the paper away. 'They are in Prince Stephen's court, as elsewhere.'

'So you know what they say of what we did. What *we* did, Ion.' He slapped a pamphlet down. 'This tells of the thirty thousand I impaled at Brasov. Do you remember how long it takes to impale a man?'

'I rememb—'

'Thirty thousand! I'd be there now, still hefting wood.' *Slap*. Another pamphlet thrown down. 'This talks of the mothers whose breasts I cut off, their babies' heads thrust into the holes. Remember that?'

'No, I—'

Slap. 'And this one tells how I cut off *boyars*' heads and used them to grow cabbages. Cabbages!' he yelled. 'I don't even like cabbage.'

He was standing over Ion, breathing hard. Then he leaned on the table, used it to support him as he walked back to his chair. He did not sit, just rested there on his knuckles before continuing, quietly. 'I know I did many . . . questionable things. I also know that many things were done in my name. For all I had to do was slip the leash and let the beast run free.'

'The beast?'

' "Who is like unto the Beast? Who is able to make war with him?" ' Dracula leaned forward. 'The Book of Revelations. I read it constantly. For it tells us that if the Devil runs free, thousands follow him, imitate him, even seek to exceed him. The Devil . . . or the Devil's son.' He pointed. 'And all who have damned me with these writings for their own ends know this also to be true: when the Cross of Crusade is raised above the host, the beast comes and shelters beneath it. And then everyone does things that others might . . . question.'

He laughed, the sound harsh. 'So I have become a tale to amuse fat burghers over their suppers, and to hush their children with terror when they will not sleep.' He lifted his goblet, drank, set it down. 'All I did, all the measures I took for Wallachia, against thieves and traitors and Infidels, come to this.' He jabbed a finger at the pamphlets. 'Me, reduced to a blood-sucking monster.'

Finally, he sat, stared before him. Ion watched him, uneasy now. This was not the man he remembered. Not even the one he hated. Dracula, for all his myriad sins, had been a man who justified nothing that he did and never blamed others who acted in his name. Who was this . . . this white-haired husk, railing against a world that didn't understand him?

He was about to speak, to provoke, to test if there was yet some core to the man, when Dracula spoke again. 'And now you have been sent to ask what my cousins the Great and the Crow have already asked and I have already refused – for the monster to be released from his chains. Again.' He picked up his spoon, began noisily to swallow soup. 'For what? So they can write more lies about me to frighten their children?' He raised his white eyebrows to the room. 'This is all the kingdom I need now. I read, I think, I watch my sons grow. I have five servants, two horses and one beautiful goshawk, who provides our supper this night. Everything I want, I control. Out there . . . I can control nothing.' He glared. 'So tell me. Why would I give that up? For what?'

Ion had been warned. By Stephen before he set out; by Matthias when he arrived. The Impaler had grown old, and tired of blood. He looked down at the pile of pamphlets. They were, in the main, as Dracula had said, sensational exaggerations. But they were based on truth – the truth of innumerable sins. And sins, as both men knew, could be forgiven – if they were atoned for. One sin, especially.

So Ion leaned forward, spoke softly. 'I will tell you, Vlad Dracula, why you will do this. You will do it for Ilona.'

Dracula's eyes, which had opened wide with his questions, his justifications, now hooded. He sat back. 'Ilona?' he muttered.

'I do not mean . . .' Ion waved a hand to the door.

'I know who you mean,' Dracula said sharply.

A silence came between them as both men stared, and remembered. It ended when a snake's tongue, too close to flickering flame, crisped and fell from its metal branch.

Then Ion spoke again. 'Do you still go to confession?'

'My confessor is here. I keep him still . . . nearby.' Dracula was staring down at the table. 'But I only talk. I do not, cannot confess. What penance could I do? Walk barefoot to Jerusalem? I would not get a mile before someone stuck a knife in me. No, there is nothing. No forgiveness for my sins.' He met Ion's gaze. 'That one, or any other.'

Ion shook his head. 'You are wrong about penance. There is one, there always has been.'

Something flickered in Dracula's green eyes, in his voice. 'What penance?'

'Crusade.'

'Oh,' said Dracula, slumping back. 'I've tried that. It doesn't work. To crusade is not enough. You must either win or die. I failed to do either.'

'But this time we *can* win.' Ion stretched out a hand. 'Moldavia and Hungary are united as never before. Corvinus *will* come this time. More, he will lead. And Wallachia will thrive again, under the Dragon banner.'

Vlad shook his head. 'You forget that it already does. For my brother rules, and he is a Dragon's son, too.'

'But this is the news I bring, Prince.' He used the title for the first time and deliberately. 'For your brother rules no longer. Your brother is dead.'

Dracula blinked. 'Who killed him?'

'God.' Ion shrugged. 'He had lost most of the land you ruled. To *boyars*, Turks, pretenders. All he had left was Guirgiu, the fortress you took by stealth and courage. He drew up the drawbridge, safe from his enemies.' He swallowed. 'But not from God. The disease that had been visited upon him years before ate his flesh, destroyed the beauty that had once lured a sultan. An apt punishment for the fleshly sins he committed with Mehmet. In the end, Radu the Handsome had no nose, no ears, half a jaw . . .'

Dracula lifted a hand. 'Enough! I know you see a sinner, punished. But all I see is a brother, whom I loved, dead. Horribly dead.' He brought his half hand to his mouth, kissed the stump, whispered, 'Radu.' Then he raised his eyes again. 'So who rules now in Targoviste?'

'Another of your cousins, Basarab Laiota. Stephen wanted him on the throne and your brother gone. But now that has happened, the puppet refuses to dance for the puppeteer. He has signed a treaty with Mehmet. He sends him gold, boys . . .'

Dracula tipped his head back, looked at the ceiling. 'And so it goes on and on and on – the Danse Macabre. The dead join hands with the living and gambol on the grave of the Dragon.' He looked down. 'And you want me to join in the dance again? To meet the same fate as all my family? Dracul beheaded, Mircea buried alive, Radu . . . rotted?'

'No, my prince,' Ion replied, less hesitation on the word. 'This time, with this alliance, we can take and hold the Dragon's land, expel the usurper, finish what we began. Make Wallachia safe again, strong again.'

'We, Ion?' Dracula thrust his head forward into the candle-light. 'You, who hate me more than anyone, would stand again at my side? Why?'

Ion could not hold the green gaze fixed upon him. He looked down, at snakes' tongues and cooling soup, and spoke softly. 'I would do it for my land, which deserves better than to be ruled by dupes and tyrants. I would do it for the cross of Jesus, raised in triumph over His enemies. And I would do it for the expiation of innumerable sins. Mine own . . . and yours, too.' He breathed, deeply. 'And if God *can* forgive so many, then perhaps . . . perhaps I can forgive one.'

'Forgive me for Ilona,' Dracula said clearly, loudly.

'Yes,' replied Ion, meeting his gaze again. 'For Ilona.'

For a long moment the two men stared at each other. Then

Dracula slumped back, reached for his wine, drank deep, finally spoke in a low voice. 'Well. It is much you offer. More than any prince has done. But forgiveness? I am not sure there can be any for either of us, Ion, this side of hell.' He rubbed his eyes. 'And I tell you this – even if I wanted too, how can I do what you ask? I am not the man I was.' He shook his hair forward till it almost covered his face. 'Look at me! An old man should be content in his own little kingdom. Content with what he can control.' He sighed. 'I fear the Dragon has slept too long to be roused now.'

'You are my age, my prince,' Ion protested, 'forty-four. Why your father—'

Vlad pushed the hair back from his face. 'Old,' he interrupted, picking up his spoon again, sipping soup. 'Crusading is for the young.'

Ion stared at the man opposite him. He wanted to speak, to urge, to use some final, unanswerable argument. But if the man would not do it for country, for God, even ultimately, for Ilona . . .

Silence. Another snake tongue crisped and fell. And then the silence was ended by the loud banging of metal on wood and by shouting. Silent still, both men rose and reached for their swords.

FORTY-SEVEN

Invasion

They descended to the courtyard. It was bright with flame-light, for several of the strangers carried torches – apart from the huge man who stood at their centre whose hands were occupied in throttling Stoica.

They stepped from the shadows under the balcony. Immediately, two crossbows were levelled. They raised their blades flat before them, in defence. 'Peace,' called Dracula.

'If you want that,' yelled the big man, 'then put your weapons down now. Now!'

They slid them onto the courtyard table, pommels towards them. 'And now,' said Dracula, 'will you release my steward?'

'Eh?' The officer – they could see his chain of office from the city of Pest hanging at his chest – looked down as if he'd forgotten what his hands were about. Still he didn't release the gasping man. 'He tried to deny me entrance. Me! Then he wouldn't answer any questions.'

'He's mute.'

'Oh,' grunted the officer, dropping Stoica as if he had some disease. The bald man rolled backwards under the table, clutching his throat. 'Well, you're not. Do you order your servants to deny entrance to the King's men?'

'This is my kingdom,' Dracula replied. 'It is customary to treat for admission.'

The man tipped back his head, roaring with laughter. 'Kingdom, is it? You Pest merchants. Think you're all princes.' He scratched his thick beard. 'In the week I've been here I've seen more conceit than in most of the courts of Europe. And I've seen a few.'

'Never the less—'

'Quiet, old man!' He was very tall, with a huge chest, and he made Dracula look small as he leaned down and thrust his face close. 'I am not here to "treat" with you. I am here for a thief.' He straightened, looked around at his men. 'Find him!'

'You must not—'

'I said, quiet!' The officer raised a gauntleted hand, and flame-light glimmered on metal studs. 'Unless you want some of what your servant got.' He turned. 'Search!'

Ion looked at his former prince. He had never seen anyone speak to him this way, not *boyars*, not Turks, not kings. Yet Dracula did nothing, showed nothing, just stared. Ion sought, as he had at supper, for some flame within the eyes; but he saw only its reflection. And its absence confirmed what he'd begun to suspect – that he had ridden hard, for four weeks, for nothing.

'Whom do you seek?' Dracula asked, as the Watch spread out among the rooms.

'Hmm?' The officer dropped into one of the courtyard chairs, laid his long, booted legs upon the table. 'Oh, a notorious thief. I am doing you a favour, old man. This villain has robbed half the houses in Pest. The local law was helpless. That's why they sent for me.' He struck his bulging chest. 'Janos Varency. Thief-taker!'

'Janos *Horvathy*?' Dracula said softly.

'Eh? No, *Varency*. Are you deaf?' The officer took off his gauntlets, pressed fingers to his nose, leaned to the side and blew it. Wiping his fingers on his jerkin, he smiled up. 'You must have heard of me. I am the best there is.'

'This thief,' said Dracula, staring down, 'why do you think he's here?'

'A tavern rat warned us that he was to rob the house next door tonight. We waited out there – Jesu, it's cold enough to freeze the balls off a plaster Christ, isn't it? – until we spotted

him. But he spotted us, too, hopped onto your roof and . . .'
He spread his arms wide. '. . . Here we are.'

The sounds of banging doors, opened shutters and chests
came from all around. Somewhere a plate smashed, followed
by laughter. 'My wife and children are upstairs. I doubt they
sleep now but I must go and reassure them.'

Varency brought his legs off the table. 'You'll go nowhere.
They will be brought to you.'

'No,' came the soft reply. 'They are not allowed to see
blood spilled.'

Ion, who had been looking down, contemplating failure,
now looked sharply up. So did the officer.

'There'll be no blood,' Varency said. 'Well, maybe a little.
But the town wants this pig fucker alive so they can boil him
in oil in the town square next Sunday as an example.'

'It was not his blood I was talking about,' said Dracula.

'Eh?' Varency's brow wrinkled. Then the shouting began,
of triumph, of despair. Two of the Watch appeared from the
kitchens, a third man thrust before them.

'Gotcha!' Varency smiled, rose, as the thief was thrown at
his feet. He lifted his chin with the toe of a boot. The thief
wore a soiled, padded coat, thick woollen leg coverings, boots
that gaped. Greasy brown hair fell around an angular face. He
was not much more than a boy. 'This him?' Varency's nose
wrinkled in disgust as he studied what was on his boot, as
if he'd brought it in from the open sewers outside. 'This
worm?'

He had put his studded gauntlets back on. Now he bent,
grabbing cloth, jerking the whimpering youth up till his
toes barely touched the ground, pulled one hand back, made
a fist, and drove it into the youth's face. The whimpering
ceased as the body sagged.

Varency dropped him. Wiping blood and skin onto his
coat, he called, 'Drag him out by his heels.'

Two of his men rushed forward, grabbed a boot each.

'Wait!'

No one heard Dracula, apart from Ion, who had been listening for a word, hoping for a word. So he said it again, louder, stepping forward to grip the shoulder of a crossbow-man about to leave.

The man tried to shrug off the grip, was surprised when he couldn't. 'Sir?' he called.

The officer, who had already taken a couple of strides towards the tunnel, stopped, as did the men doing the dragging. He looked back. 'What is it?' he said.

'I know your name, Janos Varency. But you do not know mine.'

'Why would I care? Oh, and let go of my man,' the officer replied, coming back, his hand going to the sword hilt at his side.

He obeyed, releasing the man, taking a step towards the table. 'You should care,' he said. 'For my name is Dracula.'

The other men in the courtyard paused, sucked in breath. One whistled. Varency laughed. 'What, as in the Impaler?'

'That is one name I am known by, yes. But another is Prince of Wallachia.' He looked around. 'And when I said that this is my kingdom, I meant exactly that. This is a piece of Wallachia while I stand upon it.' He pointed at the semi-conscious prisoner. 'And he sought sanctuary here, in my country. So it is up to the prince to rule whether you may have him or not.'

'May have him?' Varency echoed in wonder. Then he bellowed, 'Are you stupid as well as deaf? I am the law in Pest.'

'I have just told you. This is not Pest. This is Wallachia. I am its prince. So I am the law, here.'

Wonder had changed to fury. 'Well, I wouldn't care if you were the fucking Pope,' Varency said, stepping closer. 'If you *are* Dracula, you're little more than a prisoner, too, of the king I serve. Now,' he continued, jabbing his toe into the youth's side, drawing a squeal, 'when I deliver this filth to the town gaol, I get a bag of silver in return. Quite a large bag.

And no so-called "Prince of Wallachia" is going to stop me, understand?' Turning to his men, he bellowed, 'Take him out,' and as he did, he drew his sword.

'Now that,' said Dracula softly, 'is an act of war.'

'Oh, go shove a stake up your arse, Impaler,' Varency said, the last thing he ever said.

Ion doubted he saw much, as Dracula moved so fast. His own sword was on the table, then it was in his hands and he'd jumped, for Varency was a tall man, and swung at the same time. And then Varency's head was on the ground, though the body stood above it for just a moment longer before it also fell.

Ion had picked up his sword, too, as a precaution, but none of the other men reached for theirs. They simply began walking slowly backwards into the tunnel. Then, as if by a signal, they all broke and ran.

The thief was still prone on the ground, conscious now, eyes wide and gazing into the surprised eyes of Janos Varency. He looked up as Dracula leaned down. 'Find another town to steal in,' he said, nudging him with the tip of his sword.

The youth was up and gone in a heartbeat.

Vlad stooped to stare into the severed head's still-open eyes. He straightened, beckoned Stoica from under the table. 'Fetch me a pail. With a lid,' he commanded.

The mute left the other two men to silence until he returned. On his prince's nod, he lifted the head by the long hair, dropped it into the pail, lowered the lid.

'Corvinus may wish to see his officer,' said Dracula, sheathing his sword, 'and we must see him. Now. Tonight.' He turned to Ion, eyes bright within the frame of his white hair, and smiled. 'For it seems I am the same man after all.'

The Crow was nothing like his nickname. He was tall, thin and fair, not squat and black; his hair was a mass of blond curls, and his face was pocked with old scars and new spots.

These stood out now in a face flushed with both the heat of his recently vacated bed, and his anger.

A trembling servant was failing to tie a cord around the waist of Corvinus's nightgown. After the third futile attempt, the King of Hungary slapped his hand away and did it himself, his eyes never leaving the two men who stood before him. 'Well, cousin,' he said, his voice hard, 'I hope you have a very good reason for dragging me this early from my bed.'

Ion studied the King. He had met him several times before, on embassies. Most recently only the previous day when he arrived with messages from the court of Moldavia and the details of his mission. Corvinus was a decade younger than the two of them, and looked twice that. It wasn't just the adolescent's skin that made him so. He was more plotter than warrior, ever cautious, and had spent his life in palaces, rarely in army camps, unlike his father, Hunyadi – the White Knight had slept little in goose-down beds.

'A very good reason, Majesty,' Dracula said, bowing. 'I thought you should hear two pieces of news, from my own lips and not from others.'

'News that could not wait till the morning?' Corvinus replied testily.

'Apologies, but . . .' Dracula shrugged. 'First – did you know an officer by the name of Janos Varency?'

'The thief-taker? Of course I know him. I sent him . . .' He broke off. 'What do you mean, "did"?'

'I regret to inform you, Majesty, that Varency is dead.'

'Indeed? And how did he die?'

'He committed suicide,' Dracula said, and pulled the lid off the pail.

The colour left Corvinus's face as he looked. He struggled for control, managed it. 'That seems unlikely,' he said, through his teeth, 'since his head has been chopped off.'

'No, no. Suicide, sure,' said Vlad. 'He did it by invading the home of a monarch. I merely . . . aided him.'

The Crow raised his pallid eyes. 'Aiding suicide is still a sin, Prince,' he said.

'For which I will do penance . . . King.'

The two men looked at each other for a long moment. Ion watched Corvinus's face. Watched as a smile came, followed by a laugh.

'Cousin,' the King cried, 'you are incredible as ever.'

'I am pleased to please Your Majesty.'

The smile vanished. 'That we have yet to learn.' He stepped around the pail, pushed between the two men, went to a table. There he poured three goblets of wine, turned, beckoned. He gestured that they should choose a cup, lifted the one left, then drank. 'The rest of this tale we shall hear in more detail,' he said, of the severed head. 'But what I need to know is of the success of this man's embassy.' He glanced at Ion. 'Do you rally to the Cross, or no?'

Dracula nodded. 'That is my second piece of news, Majesty. Eclipsing this other. I do . . . rally. On certain conditions.'

Corvinus set down his goblet. 'Name them.'

'I fight in your name, and in my own, under the banners of Hungary and the Dragon. But I will not be commanded by anyone but Your Majesty. Not my cousin, Stephen of Moldavia.'

'And since I will, aside from some banner raising, be largely here, you know that you will command upon the field.'

'And all my commands will be obeyed. All. For I know only one way to fight. Without mercy. Mercy is for the time of peace. It has no place in war.'

The King, glancing into the still-open pail, shuddered. 'Are you already sharpening stakes as well as swords, Vlad Dracula?'

A slight smile came. 'Your Majesty has misheard. Stakes need to be blunted.' The smile disappeared. 'But I will do any and everything to triumph in our crusade. Only victory matters and if it is achieved, nothing that was done to achieve it will be remembered. It never is.' He looked at each man in turn, then thrust out a closed, maimed fist. 'Is it agreed?'

'It is,' said Ion, folding his hand over Dracula's, 'on behalf of Stephen of Moldavia, I vow that we shall do all that is necessary to triumph, even unto death.'

Corvinus laid his hand atop the others. 'And I vow, upon the Holy Cross and in the name of all Christendom, that you will command the forces you need to reclaim the throne of your fathers, kill the usurper and throw the Infidels back across the Danube. You will make Wallachia again into the bulwark it should always be against the Turk.' He brought his other hand up beneath, sealing the other three. 'I vow I will do all that is necessary, even unto death.'

'And I vow the same,' Dracula said, glancing at Ion, 'for the redemption of all my sins.'

'Then go,' said Corvinus, raising all the hands, holding them high for a moment before releasing them, 'take my armies, and help my enemies to their . . . suicides.'

The King returned to his bed. Vlad and Ion stepped outside the main gates of the palace. The east was lightening and both men looked towards it, through the mist that rose off the thawing river.

'Well, my prince,' Ion said. 'Do we loose the chains of hell?'

Dracula shook his head. 'No, Ion. We unfurl my father's banner. We hoist the Cross of Christ. And we watch the beast come and crouch beneath them both.'

FORTY-EIGHT

Danse Macabre

Bucharest, December 1476, twenty-two months later

From the battlements, Ion watched the last man ride through the gates. The Hungarian raised his arm but Ion did not remove his own from the warmth of his thick woollen cloak to return the salute. It was too cold, for one. For another, he had done everything in his power to make the man, and his soldiers, stay. He'd be damned if he'd wave him farewell!

As if sensing the displeasure, Stephen Bathory, Voivode of Transylvania, shrugged and turned his attention back to his horse, spurring him through the gates to catch up with his bodyguard. The rest of his army had set out the previous day for the mountain passes, which were still, almost miraculously, clear of snow. It was this near miracle that had decided the Hungarian to return to Buda and his king's court for the Feast of the Saviour's birth. Why he had decided to take his army as well was unclear. Maybe he'd decided that what was good enough for Stephen cel Mare, who had departed for Moldavia a few days before with his, was good enough for him.

'You are awake early.'

The voice came from behind him. He had no need to turn to it. 'As you are, my prince.'

'I?' The man stepped in beside him. 'I have not slept.'

Ion turned now, saw that Dracula was dressed as he had been the night before at the farewell feast, his leather-faced clothes as black as his hair. It had been his first act of crusade, to dye it, along with his eyebrows, though the moustache would not take the colour so he had shaved it off. His son had immediately emulated him and shaved off his.

The dyeing was not vanity. The prince had none. However, he was no longer merely a man, he was a leader who had to inspire, one who knew that soldiers followed greybeards reluctantly.

Ion stared. Lack of sleep made him dull, made him feel old, each re-set bone and old wound pulsing. Yet Dracula appeared to be getting younger with each day. The colouring was the least obvious sign. The puffy flesh, the sunken eyes, the grey pallor had gone, sloughing off like some lizard's skin. War did that, for those who excelled at it. And since the Dragon banner and the Holy Cross had been hoisted in Buda a year and a half before, it had been all war, the crusaders sweeping through Bosnia, slaughtering the Turk wherever he was found, with Dracula for ever in the forefront. Ion had tried to caution, even to chastise, saying that it was vanity to expose himself so often to Infidel swords, that the commander's task was more to lead than to fight. He had said it first before Srebrenica, when his prince had stood before him, folding his hair into a turban, once again donning Turkish armour, preparing to infiltrate the town and surprise its garrison. Dracula had picked up his bow, the same Turkish bow that only he could pull, and smiled. 'I am in God's hands, Ion. My *kismet*, as ever, already written.'

'I have been hunting,' Dracula said now, stepping up to lean on the battlements. 'That sick goshawk we found at Kuslat? She has recovered and makes her early flights. Does so best when there is only a little light in the sky.'

Ion turned away, shivering slightly. It was not all they had taken at Kuslat, at Zwornik, at Srebrenica, and a dozen towns and battlefields since. They had taken lives, by the thousand – Turkish, Bulgar, traitorous Wallachian. The passage of the Cross was marked, as usual, in blood and stakes. Leading here, to Bucharest, a town Vlad was now favouring over Targoviste. He said it was because it was closer to the Danube and provided earlier word of the enemy. But Ion believed it was because it was a newer place and held fewer memories.

The fortress gate, which had scarcely closed, was opening again. For a moment of hope, Ion looked to see the Hungarian, Bathory, returning, acknowledging the present danger, agreeing to over-winter in Wallachia. But the hope was false. The gate admitted another Dracula. He fell through it, he and three giggling, staggering companions.

'My son is still celebrating our victory over the Turk, I see.'

Ion grunted. 'We never celebrated the triumph of the Cross with whores.'

Vlad smiled. 'You are getting old, my friend.'

'Well? We didn't, did we?' Ion said, his mouth sour with words and stale wine.

'I had no need. I had my love . . .' He broke off. 'Who did you have, Ion?'

I had your love, too, Ion thought, but didn't say, his stomach instantly churning.

They watched the younger Dracula stagger across the courtyard. Suddenly aware that he was observed he stopped, looked up, gave an exaggerated bow, laughed, stumbled on. He had fought well, within his limitations. He was not his father and he loved his indulgences too much – but he had scars now that the elder Dracula had not inflicted. He had grown older as his father had seemed to grow younger. It was almost as if they met in the middle.

The two of them did not watch alone. She had been mentioned and, in the rare times that she was she always stood between them, bringing back a memory of love and Ion's hate. When they were about the things they had always done together – hunting, fighting, ruling – it was as if nothing had changed between them, since their days at the *enderun kolej*, since before. And then she would come, in a word, in the shadow within an eye, and she would bring his hate with her, full force, unassuaged. Like the finger Radu had once taken from Vlad, the wound would not be staunched. Yet even that cruellest cut had eventually healed over. Ion's wound never had.

It was as if Dracula sensed the broil within, felt her presence as Ion did. And here, now, for the first time, he chose to speak of it. 'Ilona,' he said, clearing his throat. 'There's something you should know.'

'Do not . . .' Ion said, looking back sharply. 'I have warned you. Do not try to excuse, to explain, to—'

He got no further. The gate interrupted him, banging open for the third time. This time, a single horseman was there. As they watched, he slid off his horse, leaning against it for a moment, exhausted.

'He has ridden hard,' Ion said, speaking past what blocked his throat. 'He must bring urgent news of the usurper.'

Dracula stared at Ion for a moment, then looked down again before he spoke. 'Let us go and hear it.'

They descended to the main hall, to hear news that was not news. The messenger reported what their spies had seen and heard – Basarab Laiota was issuing calls to the disaffected *boyars* of Wallachia to rally to him; his Turkish allies were mustering troops at the Danube to support him.

'You see?'

'It does not mean he will cross it, Ion. He threatens to keep us watchful, distracted, as I would do.'

'Never the less, we should not have allowed the Hungarians and Moldavians to go.' Ion thumped the table. 'If he does come . . .'

'Then we will deal with him.' Dracula broke off a piece of bread, dipped it in the warm wine before him. 'And how could we have kept our allies on the strength of such rumours? They would celebrate the Feast of Christ's Birth with their own families. You should do the same. Go back to Suceava and your five daughters.'

'And you? You do not go back to Pest.'

'You know I cannot.'

'And you do not send for your family to join you here.'

'No. But . . .'

Ion threw himself back in his chair. 'Then I am going nowhere either.'

'You know this is not the fighting season. Armies rarely attack in winter.'

Ion snorted. 'Like we didn't at Guirgiu? Like you didn't last year in Bosnia?'

'Well . . .' Vlad shrugged. 'We are in God's hands, as ever.'

'Yes. But that's no reason to sit on our own.' Ion rose. 'As your *logofat*, I have much to organise. The first is to send to all the *boyars* who have sworn their loyalty to you to prove it by sending men and money, now.'

Vlad threw down the crust he'd been chewing. 'I also have letters to write. The Saxons of Brasov and Sibiu are still withholding the gold they promised for crusade.' He rubbed his hands. 'And then I will attend to my hawk. She's loused, and Stoica just found a store of mercury for me to smooth onto her.'

Ion shook his head. 'Is this the time for hawks, Voivode?'

Vlad smiled. 'It is always time for hawks, *logofat*. Don't you know that by now?'

More news came a week later. News that was news.

Ion found him, as ever, in the mews within the stables, the hawk on his fist. When Ion burst in it jerked up to the limits of its jesses, flipped upside down, wings wide, screeching.

'Easy, my jewel! My beloved, easy,' Dracula crooned.

'My prince!'

The un-gauntleted, maimed hand waved Ion down. 'Peace,' Dracula said, using the same tone he used to calm the bird. 'And wait!'

Ion stood, hands clenching and unclenching. He glanced behind the prince . . . and started, as he saw Black Ilie and Stoica both there in the darkness, Dracula's constant shadows. The big man nodded, the smaller just stared at him. The last of the *vitesji*, neither had welcomed Ion the traitor back to their prince's side. He had not cared. Neither of them had his cause.

The bird was gentled, with soft words and raw meat. Soon, she had settled, bending to the meal and to the finger that rose up to scratch between the eyes.

'Softly, now,' Dracula said.

Ion realised he was being spoken to. 'They have crossed—' he blurted.

'Softly!'

Ion closed his eyes, breathed deep, unclenched his fists. When he spoke, it was more quietly. 'Basarab Laiota has crossed the Danube.'

'With how many men?'

'Reports vary. At least three thousand.'

'Not so many. And the *boyar* I set to watch and delay the enemy? Gherghina, who swore such oaths of loyalty to me at my coronation?'

'Gone over to the usurper.'

'I see. No, easy, my pretty, easy!' He did not look up. 'And the other *boyars* you summoned to meet us here for the Feast of the Saviour's birth?'

'I received many assurances of their setting out. I have not heard of any who have actually done so.'

'Really?' A little smile came. 'One would think I had a reputation for poor hospitality.'

Ion flushed. 'You are taking all this very calmly, my prince.'

'What would you have me do?'

'What you must.' Ion dragged a stool over, sat, leaned in. 'I have ordered the troops here, such as they are, to muster. We will be ready to march in an hour.'

'Where?'

Ion frowned. 'Where? To Targoviste, of course. If at least some of the *boyars* rally to us there, and the usurper is not reinforced, we can defend the Princely Court until the Hungarians can be called back. If we get no more support –

and I fear we will not – we can retreat further, to Poenari. You said once you could hold it with fifty men. I think we have five hundred left so . . .'

'Five hundred?' Dracula looked away from the bird at last. 'And Laiota brings three thousand? That's one to six. Good odds. Wallachian odds. We were one to twenty when we rode from the Vlasia forest and stormed Mehmet's camp.'

A chill gripped Ion. 'My prince . . . we lost that day.'

'Only just.'

'You only just lost a finger,' Ion said, loudly, brutally, 'and it is still gone.'

In the shadows, Black Ilie stirred, took a step forward. Dracula calmed him with a raised hand. 'So?' His voice did not rise. 'It was a chance we took and we failed. Another chance and there could be another outcome.' He gestured with his hand to prevent interruption. 'No, Ion. I will not crawl again along the same old, dreary route. Targoviste to Poenari to Pest. A fugitive, soon an exile, and then, once again, the poor relative of a king; a monster to be brought out to frighten the guests at banquets – until they have learned to laugh at me. No.' He looked beyond the bird. 'You know, *someone* once asked me, in such a situation, whether I would be a lion or an ass. Well, being a lion all the time is tiring.' He shook his head. 'I have tried all my life to break free of the strings with which a Wallachian voivode is bound; tried not to dance to the touch of sultan or king but only to my *kismet*, as dictated by the will of God and my own actions. But I am tired of taking the throne to lose it, taking it to lose it, taking it . . .' He broke off. 'At some time, that circle must be broken. So I will go and take a look at Basarab Laiota and his three thousand Turks. And I will kill him if I can.'

Ion's voice was as soft as his prince's. 'And if he kills you?'

'Then I am dead. And my sorrow is ended.' Dracula clicked his tongue to lull the bird, whose feathers lifted at the sound. He loosed the jesses from his fingers, swiftly re-tied them onto the perch, took out a piece of raw meat, lifted it to the beak. 'But let us not speak of my death but of his. We will send again to Bathory and Moldavia. We will urge the *boyars* to our side – and if the Cross does not draw them, the stake might, eh?' He smiled. 'Believe me, I do not seek an ass's death, only an ending to this . . . Danse Macabre. Will you seek it with me? For a little longer, at least?'

'Do I have a choice?'

Dracula, who had turned and beckoned Stoica forward, turned back, something else in his eyes. 'A choice?' he said, handing the bird over. He looked up. 'Do you remember, that time in Edirne, when I offered Ilona a choice?'

The name burned him. The fury, as ever, was instant. 'What choice did she ever have?' he shouted.

'The same one we all have, Ion,' Dracula replied. 'To stay or to go. The same one you have now.' The green eyes darkened. 'That you took once before, remember?'

Her name, her fate, the memory Dracula drew up now of his treason. The reason for that betrayal ever between them.

Something shifted in him, rising in bile and blood, and he reached, grabbed the other man by the collar of his coat, jerked him close. Behind Dracula, Black Ilie stepped forward with an oath but the prince instantly halted him with a raised hand. 'Wait!' he said, then looked straight into Ion's eyes. 'What is it?' he said softly. 'What is it you want to say that you have always wanted to say?'

For a moment, Ion couldn't speak. Then he did. 'I vowed to you once that I would kill the man that ever hurt her. It is yet another oath I have broken. But I tell you now, *Vlad* . . .' He coughed, found his voice again. 'Never . . . never speak of her to me again, you . . . fucking . . . whoreson,' he whispered. 'Never talk of her, or try to claim you ever loved her. For if you do, I will leave you again. This time, for ever!' He pressed his face even closer, till nose touched nose. 'But before I go, I will watch you die!'

He threw Dracula back and he stumbled, Ilie moving to halt his fall. They hit the perch and the bird upon it lurched and began to scream, wings spread wide. Ion turned and ran from the stable, slamming the door. But it did not shut out the shriek of the hawk, nor block the green gaze that bored into his back.

FORTY-NINE

The Last Stake

Ion stumbled up the hill, snow-blind. The storm, with winds that swirled now this way, now that, had taken most of his senses. His horse had refused to move; he'd had to blinker and lead her, one hand trailing on the bridle, the other flapping, feeling with a frozen hand for the smooth trunks of beeches, whose leafless limbs provided no shelter to the white onslaught. Sight was useless; he'd long since wound his scarf completely over his face from the helmet down. His only hope was that the trees still delineated the path that Dracula had brought him up on a clear, sunny, snow-free morning five days before to peep at the enemy camped on the opposite hill.

Laiota's army had been there a week, obviously awaiting reinforcements before making the final push on Bucharest. Ion had been dispatched in one last attempt to rally re-inforcements of their own. He'd failed. All he'd brought back was his frozen self.

And then his only other working sense warned him of danger. The crack of a stick and his own horse's sudden snort had him drawing his sword. He'd been gone three days and the enemy could well have moved onto this hill as well. If they'd discovered he was there, Dracula did not have enough men to hold it.

He ripped the scarf clear, peered into whiteness. 'Friend?' he called, but the wind shredded the soft word. Shrinking to place his back against a trunk, he tried it louder.

'Friend of whom?' came a deep-voiced reply and he

started, wondered what to say. When he'd left the skies had been clear, the air warm for December. They had not thought to arrange words of recognition for the blind. Ion lowered himself to a squat, his blade raised in a square guard above his head. 'Friend of the Dragon?' he said, wincing against a blow.

'*Logofat?*' It was a voice he recognised, a Moldavian called Roman, one of the two hundred Stephen cel Mare had deigned to leave.

'Yes. It is I,' Ion said, rising. 'Is the Voivode still here?'

'I'll take you to him. Give me your hand.'

He sheathed his sword, reached, clasped. With one hand stretched behind him still pulling his horse, he was led between the trees, up the hill. His sight cleared a little and he realised that here, higher up, there were pines among the beeches and they blocked some of the snow. Then the ground flattened suddenly and he stumbled to his knees, losing the guiding hand. Looking up, he saw the flicker of firelight.

'Come, *logofat*,' came the voice. 'Dracula is within.'

It was a cave, a big one Ion could see straight away, for at least half a dozen fire-pits crackled into the distance and their flames reflected off walls at least twenty strides apart. The roof he could not see at all, only columns of smoke spiralling to some natural fissures or holes. A dozen paces in and his face was warm, the snow on his eyebrows melting. He realised, as he followed Roman deeper, that it was not just the fires that caused the heat. He had to watch where he placed his feet, such was the press of men lying on either side. He knew that the Wallachian army consisted of no more than five hundred. Most of them had to be crammed into this cavern. And there, on a raised shelf, like a dais above the cavern's floor, before his own fire, crouched Dracula.

He rose. 'Welcome,' he said, then held up his hand when Ion made to speak. 'No words yet. Sit, eat, drink. Get warm.'

Gratefully, Ion sank down. Stoica came forward with two bowls, dipping one into each of the small cauldrons that swung from the metal trellis. He handed the first across and Ion gulped hot wine, choked, gulped more. The second bowl contained some kind of game stew, and Ion swallowed it with a sigh. 'My prince . . .' he began, but Dracula raised his hand, halting the words.

'Eat. Drink. Get warm,' he repeated.

Gradually, the rest of him thawed and he was able to use fingers that worked again to unclasp his cloak, undo his helmet, lay both down beside him. When his bowls were empty, Dracula hushed him with a finger, then rose, beckoning him to follow. They withdrew beyond the circle of firelight, to crouch under the sloping walls at the furthest extremity of the cave. A draught came down here from one of the hidden fissures and Ion started shivering again.

It was simply, swiftly told. Dracula nodded. 'And so not one of my *boyars* will come.' It was not a question.

'They send messages that they will, Prince. They even make a show of mustering, it is said. But none had ridden from their halls when I left Bucharest.' Ion sighed. 'And with this foul storm, our messengers may not even have caught up with the Hungarians, nor yet have made the court at Suceava.'

'The storm is passing with the night,' said Dracula. 'Can't you smell it?' He raised his nose, sniffed. 'And we are on our own, as ever.' He looked back into the cavern. 'Good.'

Ion followed the gaze. 'You do not think to fight?'

A low laugh came. 'I never think of anything else.'

Ion turned back. 'But if they get their reinforcements—'

'They already have. Two thousand more Turks crossed the Danube two days ago. We caught a few, killed a few. Most made it here, to their rendezvous. They will set out today, for Bucharest.'

'And we?' said Ion faintly, already knowing.

'We will stop them.'

It was probably useless but he had to try. 'Prince, they have five thousand men now. We have five hundred . . .'

'Four hundred and ninety-nine.'

'What do you mean?'

'Black Ilie's gone.'

'Dead?'

'Deserted.'

'Ilie?' Ion stopped. The big Transylvanian was the first of the *vitesji*, he and Stoica. And the last. He was the standard bearer, had stayed through it all, through the worst of everything. Ion looked at Dracula. 'What did you do to him?'

'I gave him a choice. Stay and die. Go back to his wife in Pest and live. He chose life.'

Ion looked back towards the fire, to the small, silent man. 'And Stoica?'

'Stoica has no one to go to. But you do.' Dracula leaned in. 'You should do the same.'

Before Ion could reply, Dracula stood. 'See who comes.'

It was the younger Dracula who was hurrying towards them, his cloak and helm covered in melting snow. 'You asked to be told.'

'Yes?'

'The enemy have started to break camp. And the storm's clearing.' He flicked slush from his brow, smiled. 'Do we attack, Father?'

'We shall go and take a look at them. Tell my captains to rouse the men.'

A salute and he was gone, calling loudly, excitedly.

'He is mad,' Ion said.

'Of course,' said Dracula, striding away. 'It's in the blood.'

They stood just inside the forest's fringe, shadows within its shadows. The dawn sky loured grey, full of the snow to come, the snow it had given shrouding every bush and tree stump on the slope to the valley floor. There, the enemy were assembling for their march: *akinci*, the Tartar ravagers, wrapped in camel hide, their heads huge globes of wool; *sipahis*, armoured but with thick quilted coats over their plate and mail. Yet most of the men who gathered on the snow-concealed Bucharest road were not Turk. Bulgars, Serbs, Montenegrins, Croats – and Wallachians, dressed like the Wallachians who watched them, with wool, leather and cloth thrust into any gap that might admit the wind flowing from the distant, frozen Danube.

Ion looked from below to their own men and suddenly remembered another tree-line, a very different time, men who would have ridden naked to ease the terrible heat were it not for the blades they rode against. But that day, in the Vlasia forest, just before they stormed Mehmet's camp, he had been unable to see to the end of the crusader ranks, just knew that four thousand men awaited the command. Here he could see the end of the single rank clearly, even in this dawn's dirty light. A mere five hundred waited there. Fewer, as had been pointed out; even fewer now, as he saw some of those on the very end slip back, heard the muffled crack of stick beneath snow as some men fled between the trees.

He looked again, impatiently, at the two men beside him, the Draculesti, father and son, in their matching black armour. But where the younger one was shivering hard and muttering curses, the elder was immobile, silent. An icicle had started to form at the tip of his long nose.

It is time, Ion thought. Time to follow the example of the wisest men furthest from the centre and retreat quietly through the forest.

'My prince?'

Dracula stirred, his eyes focusing. He reached up to wipe away the icicle. 'Is it time?' he muttered, still staring down.

'Yes. If we circle ahead of them we can take the road to the city first. Collect the garrison, move on to . . .'

He stopped. There was something in that bone-white face, in those green eyes, that stopped him. Then Dracula spoke. 'It is not time to retreat, Ion,' he said softly. 'It is time to attack.'

'No, my prince.' He gestured to the hill opposite. 'There are too many.'

'Up there, yes. But down there . . .' He leaned slightly forward. 'Infidels to kill.' He turned to his son. 'Whisper the order: arrows first, from here. Then swords.'

'Wait!' Ion reached forward, seizing the younger man's arm. He looked back at the elder. 'Do not do this now. A few more dead, it will make no difference.' The eyes did not change. 'Prince, think of your country, under the usurper again. Think of your family . . .'

'I do.' Dracula's voice was ice. 'I think of my father, decapitated by traitors. I think of one brother, his eyes gouged out, buried alive. Of another brother, his face eaten by a disease given to him by a sultan.' He pointed. 'Down there, I can avenge all that, again and again. Down there, Turks and traitors will die.' He reached, jerked Ion's hand from his son's arm, repeated, 'Give the word. Arrows, then swords.'

The younger Dracula moved away, whispering. The first man nodded, headed the other way, did the same. Men began to pull bows from leather covers.

Ion shook his head. 'Why do this?'

'Because it is a time of choice, Ion. For all of us.' Dracula leaned in. 'I have chosen. Have you? Do you ride?'

Ion swallowed. 'To our deaths?'

'We are riding to them every day. Maybe yours is down there. Maybe mine. Both.' His green eyes moved between Ion's, seeking. 'So choose.'

'I . . .' Ion paused. And in the pause, the world shifted.

'Too late.' Dracula leaned back, looked away. 'I have chosen for you. I dismiss you from my service. Go to your wife, your daughters. Die in your bed.'

'N . . . no,' Ion stuttered. 'I will . . .'

'Do you not understand?' Dracula turned back, certainty in his eyes now, fury, too. 'I do not want you here. Why should I let a known traitor ride at my side?'

Ion gasped. 'That was—'

'Because of Ilona. The name I must not speak. You left because of your love of Ilona.' His voice turned to a sneer. 'And I will tell you now of Ilona, what you have refused to hear. How . . .'

'Do not . . .'

'. . . how I killed her . . .'

'I . . . know . . .'

'No, you have heard what I did. You glimpsed the result before you ran sobbing to my enemies. But how I did it . . .' He laughed. 'I stuck my dagger point into one of her exquisite breasts. The right one, actually. And then I . . .'

'Stop it!' Ion tried to turn away, his voice rising, but Dracula stepped close, one arm wrapping around Ion's chest, one hand going over his mouth. Ion could have fought him, could have burst free perhaps. But the eyes held him, the green eyes, glowing now, that voice, coming in a whisper.

'I ripped it across, breast to breast, then placed the point at her chin, ripped down, down . . .'

'Stop it,' Ion pleaded from beneath the hand.

But grip and voice and eyes were unrelenting. 'And when I'd done, I laughed. Because it was no different from when we made love. I enjoyed hurting her. She enjoyed being hurt. Being hurt by me.'

The groan came, denying. Still he could not break free.

'It is true. Haven't we always spoken of choice? Well, that was hers. To stay with me, be hurt by me, when she could have married you, been loved by you. She chose me, chose pain. How I laughed as I hurt her! Again and again, and never more than when I finally reached the place of betrayal, where my bastards had slithered out, half-formed . . .'

'No!'

Ion broke the bonds then, of hand, eyes and voice. But the prince reached and lifted him easily, slammed him onto the ground, then bent till their noses touched. The terrible whisper came again. 'It is over, Ion Tremblac. All love, all loyalty, all truth. There is only death. Ilona's, the Infidel's. Mine. I go to it. I embrace it as I once did my lover. I will die now, if God wills it.'

'God?' Ion hissed. 'He will have nothing to do with you. You, of all men, will burn in hell for ever.'

'Well.' The green eyes didn't waver. 'Then I will await you in the flames.'

Dracula surged up, lifting Ion, shoving him back towards his horse, turning away. Cursing, sobbing, Ion fumbled beneath the blankets for his sword, undid the ties, drew it, took a step back. But he had to pause to wipe water from his eyes and when they were clear, he saw that Dracula had already mounted, and was heeling his horse beyond the tree-line.

The sword slipped from his grasp. He could only stagger forward, brace himself against a tree, watch the men of Wallachia ride silently out to join their Voivode on the slope. He looked down into the valley, saw a Turk glance up, look down again, look sharply up, cry out.

'Kaziklu Bey!'

Then the Impaler raised his bow, one of near five hundred that rose. 'Shoot! he cried and loosed, a little before the rest. Found his mark, the first Turk to acclaim him, falling, trying to pluck an arrow from his eye. Then the grey sky was further darkened with shaft and feather, the bows pulled and loosed until quivers were empty and men and beasts wailed as one upon the valley floor.

'Swords!' yelled Dracula, dropping his visor over his face, as his son did beside him. But he himself did not draw, just leaned to the side and snatched up a boar spear standing butt-end in the earth. Cloth was folded around its length, yet with five great, two-handed swirls he unwound it, the wind off the Danube spread it, and the Dragon flew once more.

'Dracula!' he cried, echoed by his men. Then he spurred his horse down the hill.

Most on the valley floor, those that lived, were trying to flee towards the hilltop camp. But men were pouring down from it, too, and many fugitives escaped death only to meet it under their comrades' hooves. The enemy was ready. And though they charged down in separate squadrons, Ion could see that they came in their thousands.

Still, the Wallachians had the momentum, the shock, the terror. Those who had not fled, who tried to rally, were swept aside. The first of the charging enemy were smashed into, driven back. Then the Turk's main body arrived and the mêlée swirled into hundreds of individual fights. All Ion could distinguish, amidst the mass of men in hide and wool and steel, turning snow to mush and mud under their hooves, was the Dragon dipping, jerking, rising again to fall, until finally it was thrown high, caught and held, and Ion glimpsed the Dragon's Talon, Dracul's sword, aloft for just one moment.

Then a new body of the enemy, all heavily armoured *sipahis*, charged straight in from the side, making for the standard. They carved a way through the crowd, felling friend and foe, aiming straight and, in the widening gap, Ion could see that their leader was a huge Turk swathed in white, from his turban helmet and face scarf down to his spurs. He was holding a giant war axe, and he drove at the black-armoured figure, suddenly alone under the Dragon banner. Axe met sword, knocking it down, but Ion saw Dracula thrust back, up. Then something happened to the blade, it slipped under the arm of the white-clad warrior, who twisted horse and body around and wrenched the weapon free. For a moment, Ion saw Dracula, unarmed, looking up at an axe raised on high. Yet even as the axe began its fall, the mêlée closed again, snatching away sight, banner, Prince and all.

'No!' Ion screamed. In a moment he had mounted and was charging down the slope. He had not even stopped to pick up his sword. He did not have the time.

He got close, fast, because he did not pause to swap blows.

And the fringes of the fight were already thinning, as Wallachians who had seen the standard fall began to flee, those that could; those that were not unhorsed now, on their backs, squirming as four soldiers held each one down and thrust daggers through their visors.

He got close. But then men were turning to him, one had his horse's bit, using his weight to drag it down. Someone else sliced at his mount's legs and she crumpled with a scream, fell, throwing him forward. He hit the ground, his helmet, which he had not had time to secure, pitched off and a Turk struck down with a halberd; but Ion was still rolling and the blade missed him. But the haft didn't, wood hitting hard, driving him face down into mud and mush. He knew he was going, could see that same halberd raised again, waited for it to fall, the cutting edge this time, in a world turning to shadow . . .

. . . and then, beyond it, he saw something else, something that held him in consciousness, someone . . . Dracula, rising from the earth, long black hair like a veil over half a face, the half that was smashed. The other half was clear, unblemished, its one eye wide, gleaming, green, staring; staring straight at him. And then the rest of him came in sight, the little there was – a neck, a bloody line across it; nothing more. And as the light faded, as the halberd fell again through the gloom, Ion saw one last sight . . . Dracula's head thrust down upon a stake, then hoisted high.

FIFTY

The Shroud

She was dreaming of him. He was touching her, gently, as was his way . . . and she felt the ache for him she always felt. But she wanted him to be rougher. In the house on the Street of Nectar she'd been taught ways to deal with that, a role to play, tricks to increase her master's pleasure. But she knew that if she did them right, they would increase hers, too. She did not want his sadness now; she did not wish to be anyone's sanctuary. She wanted to be taken hard, fast and cruelly, to fill her emptiness, her yearning. She wanted him to turn her, spread her legs, pull her head up by the hair, bend to bite her neck as he barged into her. If she could she'd nip his hand, his wounded hand, give him pain for pain, and then decide which, of a thousand and one tricks, she'd try next.

A cry woke her. Not of pleasure, nor of pain selectively applied. It was a whimper of terror, and Ilona, instantly awake, thought that perhaps she had attacked her bed companion again. It happened rarely, but often enough for some to protest that they did not want to share her bed – for the nuns doubled up in winter or they would freeze to death in their cells. In her instant wakefulness, Ilona realised it was Maria beside her – chatty, chubby Maria – and she hoped she had not hurt her. She was fond of her. And the laughing farm girl was the warmest in the convent.

Maria was not laughing now, but whimpering. Caught in a dream herself perhaps. Ilona reached out to gentle her. 'What is it, child?' she whispered.

'Did you not hear it, Sister Vasilica?' The girl's skin was covered in goosebumps and her voice quavered.

Ilona listened. The storm had passed; the wind no longer shook the trees outside the convent's walls, nor whistled in the chimneys. She heard nothing now but the muffled silence, knew that the world beyond was shrouded in white. This first, late, huge snowfall had sealed them up completely. They would live on the little they had till the road to Clejani opened again with the first thaw.

And then she heard what Maria had heard and flushed cold, too.

Three blows struck upon the convent's great oak door. And when the silence came again it was not total. Both clearly heard the snort of a beast.

'*Varcolaci*!' Maria wailed, thrusting her head under the covers.

Ilona petted her, murmuring gentle words. Some of the other young nuns had been whispering terrifying tales, after prayers, of the night stalkers – the undead who sleep in their graves with eyes open and walk under a full moon to steal babies from their cribs and suck their blood.

It was not that Ilona did not believe in those who walked at night. But there was something in the rhythmic quality of the knocking that made her think it was made by a living human, not one risen from a grave. The convent was remote, even without the snow. Only those in great need sought it out on the clearest of days. For someone to come through a blizzard, at night . . .

Need touched her. It always had.

'I will go and see,' she said, sliding from under the thick wool blankets.

'Shall I come?' Maria's voice still quavered.

Ilona smiled. 'No, child. Keep the bed warm.' Lowering her feet upon the flag-stoned floor, she reached for her habit.

*

Old Kristo, the gatekeeper, and the only man who dwelt within the walls, was standing before the oaken doors. His eyes were filmy with sleep and the effects of plum brandy. 'I told whoever is out there to go to the stables and wait till dawn, Sister Vasilica,' he mumbled, his toothless mouth thick with saliva, 'but he made no reply and . . .' He gestured, as the measured knock came again.

'How many?' She pointed at the grille in the door.

'One. I only saw one. But others could be hiding.' He scratched his stubbled chin. 'Shall I wake the Abbess?'

Ilona shook her head. Mother Ignatia was old and hard to waken; also, she was deferring decisions more and more to 'Sister Vasilica'. 'No,' she said, stepping up to the grille, pulling it open, 'I will, if I have to . . .'

The face halted her words, stopped her breath. Stoica had grown older in the fourteen years since he had delivered her to her first convent, his eyebrows now grey, the lines of his face multiplied. But the blue eyes and the bald head were exactly as she remembered. As was the way he nodded as he also recognised her, despite her own great changes.

She slammed the grille shut, leaned her forehead against it, welcoming the searing chill of slatted metal on her skin. It was real, the pain, unlike all the thoughts that hurtled though her mind. The convent was remote but news came to it eventually. She'd learned he was married a year after the event; knew he'd become a father, too. When he'd invaded Wallachia earlier that year, defeated his rival in battle, sat again upon his father's throne, requiems were sung in his praise, even at the Convent of Clejani. Before the snow began to fall, a woodcutter had brought news with his logs – that the usurper was coming again at the head of a Turkish army, that the Voivode would ride out to meet it. She had said her own prayers then. For him. For herself. For somewhere in those whirl of thoughts a tiny hope had lingered. He would not need a mistress. Her glorious auburn hair had long-since been scythed to grey stubble, she walked stooped from her scars, and all the flesh that was not cut now sagged. He would not look at her and see a trace of the young concubine, not even of the mistress he'd kept in Targoviste. But he had always called her his sanctuary. Perhaps, beset by so many enemies, he would need her for that again? And Stoica being there? It could only mean that her prince still knew where she was, had kept track of her as she was moved from convent to convent, till all who knew her as anything other than Sister Vasilica were left behind. No one ever saw her scars. But he had remembered them . . . and her.

Taking a breath, filling with air and sudden hope, she gestured at Kristo to open the doors. He shot the bolts, lifted the heavy bar, laid it aside, bent to pull. It opened, and knee-high snow tumbled in. She did not need the torch the old man proffered, for the full moon rode high in a sky newly clear of snow clouds. Hitching her habit, she stepped eagerly over the snow mound.

Stoica had bowed and stepped aside, his arm passing before him to point her towards what waited – a donkey, standing up to its withers in snow. Her heart beat faster as she thought how she could not come this moment, in the night. There were supplies to get for the road, furs to put on against the cold. And yet, perhaps his need was so pressing . . .

Then she saw the donkey's burden.

It was a cone of hide and cloth, lashed to the saddle. She stopped. 'What . . .' she whispered.

Stoica passed her, peeled back the icy canvas. She saw the naked feet, blue, stiffened. There was a stone trough before the gate, its water frozen within it. She sank upon it and the ice creaked but did not crack. 'Is it him?' she said softly, then remembered that Stoica was mute and looked up.

He nodded, once.

'Did he ask . . .' She swallowed. 'Did he ask that I prepare his body for the grave?'

Another nod.

It only took a moment for her to realise that her wish had

been granted. Her prince did need her, one last time. 'Then that is what I shall do,' she said, wiping the water from her eye, her joints creaking as she rose and beckoned Stoica through the gate. He halted her with a raised hand, pointed to the far side of the animal, led her there, raised the stiff cloth again.

The first severing was the hand, the left one, the one that should have had just three fingers – taken, no doubt, for the Dragon ring that would have been upon it. The second was worse, of course, because one of the last things she'd hoped to do was to kiss his lips, however cold. But the head was gone, the ragged hole there a mass of congealed, frozen blood.

'Oh, my love,' she sighed and laid her hand upon the shoulder, her fingertips on a scar she thought she remembered. Then Stoica took the bridle and together they walked Dracula's corpse into the convent.

She tended to him alone. Stoica had gone as suddenly as he'd arrived, leading the donkey back into the night. Other nuns, when they heard of the body they assumed to be one of Sister Vasilica's relations, offered to help. She let them boil water in a vast cauldron and bring it to an empty cell close to the kitchen, allowed them to tear sheets into a hundred cloths. But then, she sent everyone away. She had dreamed so long of being alone with him again. Now she would be.

His body was a little different than she remembered it to be, aside from the freezing of both winter and death. But it was fifteen years since she had held it; she knew how she had changed in that time. There were scars she recalled, ones she'd once traced with finger and tongue-tip; new ones that had come. A life of struggle carved onto flesh. Ended now.

He was curved like a bow, rigor mortis holding him in the shape he had taken over the donkey's back, so she had to leave him on his side. As she dipped the first cloth in the water, as she touched it to his bloodied skin, she began to sing. In Edirne, she had been taught a thousand and one songs to please a man. But this was a song from her childhood, from the village of her birth; a *doina*, lullaby and lament.

She took her time, starting from his feet, working slowly up, wiping, singing. Remembering the time when *she* was washed, the day he came to steal her. Turning him was hard but, for all her age and ills, she was still strong. When all the blood was gone and the cauldron's cooling water rosy pink, she began to sew, closing the slashes that covered him, drawing the flesh together as well as she could. The gaping wound of his neck she covered with a linen cap, stitching it into the shoulder. Then she took an oil fragranced with sage and bergamot and rubbed the length of his body again until he glistened in the lamplight. He'd been anointed as prince and now he was anointed again, for death.

She was tired by the time a square patch of pale winter daylight was falling upon him. But there was a last thing to do, a last effort. She took a sheet and, after a struggle, managed to roll him onto it. Then she folded over the edges and, with thick twine, sealed him into his shroud.

She stepped away from the table, rubbing at the small of her back. The murmur of voices had been building at the door. Now she would accept help.

'Come,' she called.

They sang prayers as they bore him back through the gates, Ilona preceding, six of the younger nuns following with him behind, the rest of the convent trailing. There was a tree a little way along the path, down the hill, and the men from the gardens and stables stood underneath it, shovels to hand. They had cleared away the snow, lit a fire to warm the earth, though only the surface had been frozen solid, such was the suddenness of winter's coming. A hole had been dug, and she saw that it was longer than required for he was never the tallest of men and now . . . she couldn't help her smile. It was

403

the sort of joke her prince would have appreciated. She almost heard him then, that rare laugh, so doubly wondrous when it came.

They laid him down at the hole's edge. She could see acorns in it, for the tree was a red oak. She knew he would like that, dissolving into the soil of his Wallachia. From him, other trees would grow.

As the plainsong grew stronger around her, she knelt and laid a hand on his chest. His head may have been missing, but his heart was still there, she knew. 'Rest in peace, my love,' she whispered. Then, alone, she reached beneath him and tipped Dracula's shrouded body into his grave.

FIFTY-ONE

The Shriving

Poenari Castle, 1481

It was told, the last of it, for her at least. It ended when the body was covered in earth. No marker was ever raised. She always knew exactly where he lay, for a red oak did grow from one of the acorns that lay with him. It was five times the length of a man's forearm now, one for each year. Soon, she knew, the younger tree would be striving for space with the elder from which it sprung. It was the way both of trees and of men. She had no doubt that, with her prince's blood to feed it, the sapling would prevail.

All this Ilona thought but did not say, as the quills traced her last words, and Dracula's last fall, in ink upon the parchment. Then there was silence within the hall, though beyond it the noises of the day came. The storm that had come, bringing the last big snow, had gone. Sun had returned to the land, warm enough to start the melting. All in the room stayed silent for a while, listened to the drip, heard a huge icicle drop from a turret and shatter on the rocks beneath the walls.

It was the Count who broke the silence. He turned to the Cardinal, seeking some reaction, some hope. But the Italian's jowly face was as impassive as ever. Horvathy swallowed, made sure his voice was even before he spoke. 'Is there anything more you need to hear, Your Eminence?'

'Dracula is dead,' the Cardinal replied. 'It was interesting, though, to hear what became of his body. But perhaps I can give the last detail required for the record?' He smiled. 'His severed head, as all know, was sent to Mehmet. I heard it was the one time the Great Turk was delighted to receive something other than an exotic plant for his gardens. So much so that he kept it beside him for a week before he allowed it to be spiked and placed on the walls of Constantinople.' He rose, stretching his back. 'So now – his last confession is over. Though *I* must confess to being a little curious – and the scribes need not note down my curiosity – of how our three witnesses survived. And how they have lived these five years since.'

Silence again, till Petru leaned forward and shouted, 'Answer!'

Ilona spoke again. 'You know, because it was your men that brought me here. Where I was a sister, now I am Abbess of the Convent of Clejani.'

'And what secrets our habits conceal, eh, Reverend Mother? Though your scars are perhaps more interesting than my own.' The Cardinal turned to face the confessional on the left. 'And Dracula's friend? We could only assume from your tale that you'd been killed. Yet, obviously not so. What became of the worthy traitor?'

Ion's mind, which had drifted like a leaf ever since he spoke of the last stake, drifted back now at the word. 'Would I *had* been killed. But such was not my fate. Mine was to become Laiota Basarab's prisoner, buried at the same time as Dracula – but buried alive, as his brother once was! Yet, unlike Mircea, with air to breathe and so allowed the barest form of life. Forgotten in my living grave until this day. And would that I had been forgotten there still.' His voice broke and he sobbed, 'And if there is any mercy in you, you will return me there now, and torment me no further with these memories!'

Count Horvathy, impatient now, faced the last of the confessionals. 'And you, his confessor? We have heard little enough of you this last hour. Can you satisfy His Eminence's curiosity and let us leave this place?'

The hermit's voice rasped clearly. 'What was there for me

to tell? I was left behind in Pest. And Dracula left for war without seeking absolution. So I heard nothing of his final thoughts.'

'But then, after his death, you journeyed here, to the cave upon his mountain, did you not?'

No reply came.

'Tell it swiftly!' Petru barked. There was a last task he had to perform and, after a night of sitting, he was eager to be about it.

'I came here.'

The Cardinal, rotating his fleshy neck, looked down. 'A special curiosity among the many. Why would you do that?'

'Because I thought that perhaps here, in this place he loved, his final thoughts *might* be heard.' A laugh came, the first he'd given, a strange sound. 'And was I not right?'

'Enough,' snapped the Count, rising. He turned to the man beside him. Horvathy was as exhausted as he had ever been; yet he knew his only hope for a sleep without ghosts lay in the gift of the man beside him. 'I ask again, Your Eminence – is there anything more, beyond the satisfaction of your curiosity, that you need to hear?'

The Cardinal looked back into the Count's one, hope-filled eye. 'No,' he said.

Horvathy hesitated, looking down at the smaller, rounder man, his unreadable face. Then he swallowed. 'And can you tell us what your conclusion might be?' He lifted his hand, rubbed the socket of that one eye. 'I know we have heard a tale of horror here tonight. But we have also heard of a crusader prince, Christ's Warrior, slaying His enemies under the Dragon banner. Dying finally, under that banner, still killing Infidels. With the exoneration of the Pope, and our gold to counteract the lies that have been told – and to mitigate the worst of the truth – the Dragon's son could rise again. Then, so could the Dragon and all its brood.' He paused, searched the eyes before him for some sign. When none came, he blurted, 'Well, Grimani? Does my Order rise or fall?'

The Cardinal looked up at the Count, then across at the younger man, whose hope shone as clearly upon his face; finally down at the three confessionals. 'Neither,' he said, then overrode the gasp that came, 'for now.' He stepped off the dais, moved towards the door. Stopping before it, he turned. 'Really, Count Horvathy, you cannot expect a decision based on such tales and after such a long night, in a moment. And you know that it is not, finally, my decision to give. I represent authority, but I am not its highest voice. I will read again all that has passed here tonight. Then I will talk to the Pope. From that conversation' – he looked again at the confessionals and made the sign of the cross – 'a shriving must come. Or not. Only the Holy Father can forgive such a sinner as Dracula from such . . . spectacular sins.'

Horvathy approached him. 'May I hope? For myself? For the sacred Order of the Dragon?'

'Well,' replied Grimani, 'there are precedents. So ready your gold for your Order. And hope for yourself.'

Horvathy nodded. He had done all he could. 'We will collect the confessions. We will mark all three with our three seals. Then you may take one with you. I will take one to Buda, for secret printing. And we will leave one here, where the tale was told.'

'Good.' Grimani glanced again at the three confessionals. 'And, uh, the other business?'

'We will deal with matters here, Your Eminence,' Horvathy replied, looking at Petru.

The Cardinal stared back at them for a moment. 'Of course you will,' he said softly. 'Each to their own skills, eh?' He raised two conjoined fingers. '*Dominus vobiscum*,' he intoned, making the cross.

'*Et cum spiritu tuo*,' Horvathy said, bowing.

With a slight inclination of the head, Cardinal Grimani left the hall.

The wiry frame of Bogdan, Petru's lieutenant, replaced him in the doorway. He raised his eyebrows and Petru nodded. Bogdan turned, beckoned two soldiers; one young and eager, the other older, edgy.

Behind the guards came another man. He was dressed quite differently, with a leather apron covering him from nape to ankle. His face was streaked in soot and he held a sword. The hilt of the weapon was level with his chin while the blade's tip rested on the ground.

Horvathy smiled. 'The Dragon's Talon,' he said. 'I had forgotten that it was being re-forged.'

He beckoned the smith forward, took the sword in both hands, lifted it high. 'What a weapon!' he marvelled, turning the blade to catch a beam of sunlight that came through the arrow slit. It played on the pommel and made the Dragons on each side seem to fly. 'You know, Petru, those who have never held a bastard sword think it must be heavy, because you wield it with two hands. But it is forged so exquisitely that it is light, can be lifted again and again. Can kill again and again.' He threw it up, caught it, sighed. 'With this alone I feel I could take back Constantinople.'

'My lord?'

Horvathy looked at Petru. The younger man held out his hands. When the Hungarian did not lower the sword, Petru said, 'It is the sword of Wallachia, my lord. It belongs to my prince.'

The Count's one eye narrowed. Then he shrugged, brought the weapon down, handed it across. Petru took it and held it for a moment before laying it flat across the arms of the centre chair. Then he waved the blacksmith out, closing the door behind him.

The Count breathed deeply before stepping off the dais. 'The testament,' he snapped, and immediately the curtain on the priest's side of the first confessional was drawn back. The monk within blinked up at the brighter light of the hall. He had already rolled and ribboned the papers. Horvathy took them. 'Thank you for your work. You will be rewarded.' He nodded. 'Please step out and wait over there.'

The monk rose, stretched, walked over to stand before Petru and his men. The Count approached the second and third confessionals, where the same actions and words were repeated. The three monks, like the prisoners, had only been allowed out twice in the proceedings, and they looked tired and hungry. Petru gestured to the smaller table at the other end of the room. 'Food and wine are provided. Help yourselves.' Eagerly the monks, shadowed by the soldiers, moved to the far end of the hall.

Horvathy clutched the three rolls of testimony to his chest with one hand. With his other, he slowly drew back the first of the remaining curtains. Ion blinked up, raising a hand to shelter his eyes from the glare. In his short time out of his cell, his eyesight had come back a little bit more. He could even see the features of a face, an oval above him, etched in brightness.

Without a word, Horvathy moved on, drew more material aside. Ilona did not look up, did not open her eyes. Her mouth moved, but whether in prayer or in the lament she had recently sung, as she had sung it over Dracula's body, Horvathy could not tell.

In the last confessional Dracula's confessor did not raise his head. Within the hood, all the Hungarian could see was the man's shadowed mouth and chin, his lips, like those of the Abbess, moving silently.

He hesitated for a moment, then he swallowed, turned away, laid the testaments on his chair. He took Petru's arm, leading him to the door. 'Do what must be done,' he whispered.

'I . . .' The younger man looked back, ran his tongue over his lips nervously. 'I only regret . . . the woman,' he muttered. 'It seems a sin.'

'You have heard her confession. *Her* sins are innumerable.' The Count squeezed his arm hard. 'And remember this – all *our* sins will be forgiven in crusade. When the Dragon and the Cross fly side by side again and sweep the Infidel from the Balkans.'

Petru swallowed, nodded. 'What must be done,' he echoed. Horvathy reached for the door handle – but Petru put his hand against the door. 'You will not stay, my lord, and bear witness?'

Horvathy looked in the younger man's eyes; saw duty there, some apprehension. But there was hunger, too. Petru had scrupulously, loyally carried out his Voivode's strange wishes – but Horvathy knew he also aspired to be inducted into the Order of the Dragon, if it were allowed to rise. And indeed, if it did, if all they had done there that night were successful, then it would be no bad thing to have a Dragon commanding such a valuable frontier post as Poenari in the crusade that would follow. The young Spatar had shown organisational ability. But could he kill? It would be worth knowing.

Horvathy took his hand off the door. 'I will stay. But be quick!' He lifted the rolls of parchment he held. 'These must be signed and sealed before Grimani takes one to Rome. And the Italian is anxious to be gone.'

Petru nodded, shot the bolt on the door, then turned to gaze for a moment at the confessionals and their three silent occupants. Then he looked to the other end of the hall, where monks feasted and soldiers watched them. 'Bogdan,' he called, and when the man looked up, he raised his hand.

It was done quickly, without too much suffering, Horvathy judged. He was watching the confessionals, to see if those within reacted to the sudden noise, the gasp, the peculiar suck of metal on throat, the gulping. None seemed to hear, just carried on with what they were doing – muttering, mouthing, staring sightlessly. When he looked again, the guards were standing over two, still-twitching, bodies while Bogdan was lowering his in order to raise the flagstone near the wall by the metal ring set into it. Petru and Hovarthy watched him bend, drag, shove. The first monk's body disappeared fast. The man whose confession they had heard told tonight had built the sluice out over the precipice for the clearing of filth. No doubt it had also been useful to get rid of bodies unseen. It still was.

When the last body disappeared – an arm flailing as if waved in farewell – the soldiers joined him. 'Come,' said Petru, his voice cracking on the word as he moved to the confessionals. 'Come,' he said again, more firmly. 'You have done well, all three of you. Food awaits at the end of this hall, and a comfortable place to lie for a few days. Then you will be returned to your abodes. Though you, Ion Tremblac, will now have an honoured place by a hearth in Suceava.' The lies soothed the speaker, his voice growing stronger. He even smiled. 'You have been about God's work this night and day. Come.'

In his confessional, Ion appeared not to have heard, to be gazing at shapes within his eyelids. At Petru's nod, the young guard reached in and pulled him out. He hung there, his weakened legs not supporting him, so the soldier let him slide onto the floor.

Ilona rose unaided, stood before the confessional, turning to see the man beside her for the first time. His voice, his weeping, his mad laughter had prepared her a little – but not for the wreckage she now saw. 'Oh, Ion,' she murmured, kneeling, winding her arms around him. Tears squeezed between their tight-pressed eyes.

'And you, hermit . . . Father,' Petru corrected himself. The man he'd thought of as just another lonely madman had been a priest once. Like the Abbess, he would be harder to kill for that reason.

The hermit did not move, his head still lowered, only his jaw and mouth revealed under the hood. He was smiling slightly, and then Petru remembered the madman not the priest and said, more sharply, 'Get up.' Annoyed, he turned, nodded at Bogdan who came forward. But as he did, the hermit rose, took a step beyond the confessional, stood there as still as he'd been sitting, head downcast, hands at his side.

It would be better to kill them where they'd killed the monks. Even if they were not going to use the sluice – for there must be no danger of these bodies ever being found – it was still best to keep the bloodstains in one area. Besides, up there near the dais was where they dined; and his wife, since her pregnancy, was easily nauseated. 'Come,' said Petru, calm again, 'to the feast.'

They moved away, and he followed.

Ion had begun to drag himself slowly. Bogdan stepped in, grabbing an arm, pulling. The second soldier took the other arm. The third walked beside Ilona, and Petru saw that the eager young fool already had his knife out, albeit hanging at his side. You didn't spook animals bound for slaughter, and that was doubly true for humans.

It was then that the hermit spoke. 'Wait,' he said.

His voice was low, the word softly spoken. Yet it carried, and everyone paused. At the door, Horvathy straightened. In the silence of the hall, the only noises came from outside, of men preparing horses for departure. And beyond it, the cry of a single bird.

'*Kree-ak, kree-ak.*'

The hermit turned to it slightly, then turned back as, on Petru's nod, the older guard left Ion and came towards him. The man did not have his commander's subtlety. 'Come on, you,' he barked, reaching and stepping in, then stepping back and looking down. 'What?' he asked, puzzled. And then he sat down suddenly, one hand wrapped round the knife that was inside him.

The hermit stepped around him. It had happened so fast that none of the guards were quite sure what they'd seen. It was Petru who reacted first. Drawing his sword, he shouted, 'Stop', took a step forward. But the hermit ducked low under the rising blade and closed with him, placing his left hand in Petru's armpit, reaching with his right to the sword-hand,

413

twisting it hard against its inclination. Petru grunted in shock, in sudden pain, dropping the sword. The hermit caught it as it fell, his grip on it reversed, the blade pointing back behind him.

The others began to move. The younger guard threw Ilona down, leapt for the wall, upon which hung a crossbow, a quarrel ever in its groove, a ward against sudden attack. He seized it, as Bogdan screamed, 'Let him go', drew his own sword, ran forward. But the hermit moved into Petru, driving his shoulder into the man's chest, pivoting as he did. The sword was still held in that reversed grip and it preceded the spinning bodies but not enough for Bogdan to see it properly, or do anything about it. His leather jerkin did nothing to resist the steel. He shrieked, dropped his own sword, staggered back, fell, clutching at the weapon the hermit had released.

Petru jerked, nearly freed himself from the grip. 'No,' he screamed, as the guard levelled the crossbow and snapped the trigger, just as the hermit stepped back, pulling Petru close.

The bolt passed through Petru's throat, taking his next command and, a few moments later, his life.

The hermit let the dying Spatar fall. He landed close to where Bogdan lay. The lieutenant's hands were wrapped around the grip of the sword whose blade projected a forearm's length from his back, as if he were deciding whether to pull it out or not. Then, before he could choose, he fell sideways and closed his eyes.

The hermit looked back. The guard who'd first come for him was still sitting up, but his eyes were also closed and he was no longer struggling. The younger guard dropped the crossbow, took a step back, realised there was no way out there, tried to come forward. But the hermit stepped towards him, bending to pick up the knife the youth had dropped when he'd reached for the crossbow. 'Help! For the love of God, help me!' the youth wailed at Horvathy. But the Count had not moved, could not. And those above were no doubt expecting such cries, and ignoring them. When he reached the far wall, as the hermit came closer, the guard realised that there was only one place left to go. With a last, despairing cry, he threw himself down the sluice.

The cry continued for a little as the man fell down the mountain; then it was suddenly cut off. The bird's cry came again, then that too ended sharply. And when it did, the four people left alive all looked at each other.

'Who . . . ?' whispered Ion, though he knew, even if he could not believe it.

Horvathy knew, too. Suddenly, clearly, without question. And it was he who breathed the name.

'Dracula.'

'Yes.' The reply came softly from within the hood.

'No,' said Horvathy, dropping the parchment rolls he held. He only had a knife in his belt. After what he'd just seen, it didn't seem enough. So he moved fast toward the dais, to the central chair, to the sword lying across it. He lifted it, turned . . .

. . . and Dracula was standing a sword's length away. 'That's mine,' he said softly.

Horvathy raised the sword before him, lifting the point till it was a hand's breadth from the other man's face. 'Don't . . .' he whispered.

'Don't take what's mine?' Dracula said.

As he spoke he stepped in, and Horvathy could not thrust, strike, cut. Could do nothing but look in the man's green, reddened eyes; watch him as he reached up, took the grip and pulled the weapon from the Hungarian's hands.

Dracula stepped back, lifted the sword high, squinted along its planes. 'He has done good work, the blacksmith of Curtea de Arges.' He smiled. 'And now I feel whole again.'

He looked back at Horvathy. And the Hungarian saw what he expected to see in that green stare – death. And seeing it, fear left him. He felt calm and he said, 'Do what must be done, Dracula. For you send me to join my wife.'

But Dracula shook his head. 'Your wife was a pious woman, I heard, Count Horvathy. No doubt she sits now at God's right hand. While you are bound somewhere else. To that special circle of hell reserved for traitors.'

Fear returned. Horvathy raised a hand. 'Brother Dragon . . .' he said.

'You called me that once before,' said Dracula.

The stroke came fast, from the high plane. It was halfway through his body before the Count fell to his knees, held up only by steel. His one eye remained open, though, when Dracula stooped to stare into it. 'And I am not your brother,' he whispered as he jerked out the sword.

Then he turned and looked back at the two other people alive in the room.

FIFTY-TWO

From the Dead

Ion's eyes were clear at last; yet he was unable to believe what they saw. He had only ever known one man who could kill the way he'd just seen these four men killed. That man was dead. Ion had seen his head impaled on a spike.

Then the answer came. Whoever . . . whatever . . . was laying the sword again across the arm rests, was walking towards him now, was that man's *varcolaci* – the undead, risen from his grave, come to feast on the flesh of men.

Yet the hand that now dropped upon his shoulder felt real enough, with its three fingers, its thumb, its stump. His own hand closed over it as he whispered, 'Vlad.'

'Yes,' Dracula replied, reaching down, lifting the frail prisoner, half-carrying him back to the confessional, lowering him into it.

'No!' Ilona was weeping as she came forward. 'No! It cannot be. Mother of God defend us all, for you are dead! Dead! I buried you.' She gave a last great cry, ran forward, reached up, threw back his hood . . . and gasped. For no living corpse, ripped from the shroud she'd sewed for him, looked back. The face was not rotten, worm-eaten. It was older, certainly, lined, and everything she had known to be black was white – hair, eyebrows, beard – but it was his face, beyond any doubt. And she knew, suddenly, certainly, that no night crawler stood before her but a man of flesh, the man she had always loved.

'I buried you,' she sobbed again.

Dracula looked down. 'You buried my son. And it was his

head that rotted upon the stake on the walls of Constantinople.'

'No!' said Ion, shaking his head. 'I saw them cut you down . . .'

'You saw a huge Turk slice off a head. But you never saw beneath the Turk's helmet . . . to Black Ilie, whom I'd sent away the night before, to dress as a Turk one last time, to do this last service for me.'

Ilona staggered forward, till she too could sink onto her confessional's seat. 'You killed your own son?'

Dracula shrugged. 'I did not. He died, as he wished to, in battle. For a cause. His father's cause.'

'But . . . why?' Ion shook his head. 'Why?'

'Because I decided to live – to see what a life I could control would be like. A cave for a kingdom, a hawk my only servant.' He nodded. 'And it was good. For a time.'

'For a time?'

'Yes. And then . . .' He frowned. 'And then last year I went to sell a fledgling at the autumn fair in Curtea de Arges, as I always did. A drunk stood up in a tavern and began to read a new pamphlet, more lies based on some truth of my life. Others in the tavern shouted him down – for this is my part of the country and its people have always loved the Draculesti. But I thought of those beyond, in places where they have never even heard of Wallachia, laughing in their palaces, their inns, their houses. And I realised that these . . . tales were not only damning my name, they were damning the Order I belonged to, blunting what had been the very spear-tip of Christendom. Instead of a crusader, I'd become a monster – and worse than any traitor.'

Ion shuddered. Yet Dracula didn't look at him but past him, to the widening pool of blood, the dead Hungarian at its centre. 'I wanted what Horvathy wanted, a Dragon resurgent. I wanted my sons, when they came of age, to ride proudly under its banner and with their father's name. But I did not know if what I wanted was possible. I was . . .

confused by the lies that had been told, could no longer see what I was, what I'd been. So I decided to ask the people who knew me best to confess. And those who stood to gain the most to judge.'

'Confess?' echoed Ion. 'There never was a confessor, was there?'

'Only once, in Targoviste, that night when . . .' Dracula looked at Ilona, then above her. 'What would be the purpose? No man could judge my actions and their reasons. Only God could.'

'So all this . . .' Ion clutched the side of the confessional. '. . . You arranged?'

'I had kept the seal of the Voivode of Wallachia, so I could draw up any documents I chose. I knew the secret ways of the dishonoured Dragons. And I had enough gold – for I have been training and selling goshawks now for five years.' He nodded. 'It is easy enough to arrange such things – when you understand both the hunger and the terror of men.'

Outside the hall, the sounds still came of preparations for departure. Dracula listened for a moment. 'I do not know if it will be enough. The Cardinal will take the testimony to Rome, along with his opinions. Perhaps the Pope will think it expedient to have this sinner redeemed, to have his name and his Order rise. Perhaps not. It is not something I can control. I have done all that I can.'

'But how will they explain this, my prince,' Ilona said, swallowing as she pointed to the bodies.

A half-smile came. 'A falling-out over spoils? Over a sword, maybe?' He pointed to the Dragon's Talon on the chair. 'Hungarian versus Wallachian, Roman versus Orthodox, as it ever was, while the Turk rejoices?' Dracula nodded. 'But we will be gone, and they will think us disposed of, like the scribes. For there are other ways out of this castle, out of this very room, that only I know.'

He went to the door, passing the Count's body, its lake of blood, drew back the bolt that Petru had shot. 'They will be coming soon,' he said. 'They will be wanting . . . this!' He stooped, picked up one of the rolls of parchment there. '"The Last Confession of Dracula". Do you think it will make a good pamphlet? Will the people of the world frighten their children to sleep with my true tale?' He smiled. 'Perhaps it is not bloody enough, eh?'

A cry came again, a hunting bird. Crossing, Dracula put the paper down upon a chair, reached within his jerkin, pulled out a gauntlet, pulled it onto his left, maimed hand. Then at the arrow slit, he leaned into the opening and gave a loud cry – 'Kree-ak! Kree-ak!' – as he thrust his hand through the gap.

They all heard what could have been an echo but realised was a response. Dracula suddenly bent, as if pulled outwards. Then he slid back. On his fist sat a goshawk.

As Dracula brought it back into the room, the bird blinked at the two people sat there, then craned its neck down towards the meat Dracula pulled from a waist-pouch beneath his habit. 'My beauty,' he whispered, then looked up because Ilona was rising.

'You called me that once. You could not call me that now.'

He watched her limp towards him. 'You will always be beautiful to me, Ilona.'

Ion was rising, too, slipping off the seat, dragging himself forward. 'And me, my prince? Am I still your servant? Or will I only now and forever be your traitor?'

'No, Ion. As I hope for forgiveness, so I must forgive.' He nodded. 'You did what you had to do.' He glanced at Ilona. 'For love and for hate. But you always were, and are, my only friend.'

Using the table edge to pull himself almost upright, Ion half-stood. This close, he realised his sight had indeed grown better for he could see, as if through a mist, the faces before him. Peering, he could even tell the colour of their eyes. Ilona's, that had bewitched him so long ago, still hazel. The goshawk's red. And Dracula's? That surprised him, for they were no longer just green but red also. 'What now?' he said.

Dracula raised his other hand. 'Listen,' he said. 'Do you hear them?'

They tipped their heads. Men shouted above. A horse snorted.

'Hear what, my prince?' Ilona asked.

'The bells on Mehmet's standard. He has raised his horse-tail *tug* before the walls of Constantinople. He is going to war.' He turned to Ion. 'Do you remember our game of *jereed*, Ion? The wager we made?'

Ion rubbed his eyes. 'No . . . wait, yes! Your foreskin against . . . a bird, wasn't it?'

'A falcon. And Mehmet never honoured the wager. So it is time to make him.' He leaned forward and his red eyes shone. 'Mehmet owes me a hawk.'

— EPILOGUE —

'His name was Death, and Hell followed with him.'
— REVELATIONS 6.8

EPILOGUE

Gebze, Anatolia, near Constantinople, four weeks later

For the longest time the sound was indistinguishable within
the low roar of a Turkish encampment settling for the night.
There were even other screams – of donkeys and horses, of
camels and men. Yet as the man whose trade was the sewing
of leather and hides walked slowly through the thickening
web of tent ropes, those other noises started to fall away.
Closer to the centre men were muttering to themselves, rarely
to each other, glancing over their shoulders, making warding
gestures as if to block the sound that grew ever louder as the
man approached – the bellowing of another man in agony.
Closer still and more men were facing inwards, standing
or squatting, most kneeling, some silent, others whispering
prayers.

No one paid him much attention, this squat *yaya*, with his
patched, mud-daubed tunic, his faded turban, straggling
beard and bare feet. He carried no weapon, just a small
satchel across his shoulder with many of the implements of
his trade stuck into the outside of it – bone needles of all
sizes, spools of camel hair thread, hide ties, a steel awl. If any
had studied him more closely they might have seen that his
bag dripped some liquid. But no one did.

It was easier than the last time he had tried to reach the
Sultan. He passed through the same order now as then.
Through the jumbled lines of *gazis* and *akinci* raiders, be-
tween the ever more splendid pavilions of the *belerbeys*,
around the small cones of hide in which the janissaries slept.
He noted some of their standards – the tower, the wheel, the

half-sun; even the familiar elephant of the 79th *orta*. When he saw the yellow oriflame of the left wing he knew that he was close. Though the silence of the *sipahi* warriors would have told him, too; that and the terrible screaming, so near now.

He was not the tallest of men and those he threaded between were the elite of the Turkish army and loomed over him. So he had to pass through these last before he could see what his ears had told him was there, a small, gentle sound beneath the louder, terrible one.

He stepped through the last ranks of warriors. And there they were – the bells that chimed upon the Sultan's *tug*, beneath the six horsetails. The standard stood before a pavilion identical to the one he had burned down twenty years before.

No one stopped him as he walked up to the twin-tiered gateway, passed through it, though warriors stood around with swords unsheathed and *solak* archers held arrows notched to strings. No one moved – for every man felt that if they did, even a little, then the balance of the world would change, and their Sultan, Most Exalted, Mehmet the Conqueror would yield to the devils that tore his guts apart, and die.

Thus, unchallenged, Dracula stooped, lifted an edge of canvas and stepped inside the Sultan's pavilion.

He entered a different world, for there was movement here, and noise, most of it coming from the divan that was at the centre of the vast tent and from the man thrashing upon it. Men in white robes and the purple sashes of physicians were attempting to force some liquid into the sick man's mouth. But the Sultan screamed, a mixture of prayer and obscenity, knocking the cup from their hands. Another was poured, lifted. Somehow some liquid slipped in, then a little more. Mehmet collapsed back, stilled somewhat, though his legs kept scything, as if he would run off the stained bed.

The screaming reduced to a low moan; the physicians stepped back, wiping sweat from their faces. A tall man, in the fine robes of a vizier – though even these were spotted yellow and brown, pulled one aside and whispered fiercely, 'What more, Hekim Yakub?'

The doctor shook his head. 'I do not know. I was called so late and I am not sure what my esteemed colleague, Hamid-uddin al Lari, has given him?'

'Esteemed arsehole,' the vizier hissed. 'I will pull the camel-fucker's guts through his teeth until he tells me – if I can find him. Is it poison, do you think?'

The doctor shrugged. 'Maybe.'

'How long?'

'I do not know.'

The vizier cursed under his breath. Then he looked up, at the faces of servants, slaves, soldiers, physicians, some twenty men who all stared back. 'No one is to leave this tent. Not a word of this must get out. If his son Bayezid hears of this before I can reach Prince Cem . . .' His gaze flew from man to man. Then, at last, it settled on Dracula, and his eyes went wide. 'Who, by the Devil . . . seize him!' he roared.

Vlad threw his bag aside before the four men fell on him, each grabbing a limb, hurling him to the ground. He did not resist them. There was little purpose . . . and it was not why he was there.

'Who are you? What are you doing here?' The vizier had rushed forward. Indeed, everyone in the tent was looking at him hard, as if he could provide some distraction from the sight and sound and stench of the man dying on the bed.

'I bring the Light of the World a most rare flower, Excellency,' Dracula said, his Turkish peasant-harsh. 'It is found in only one valley in the world. Across the Danube, in Wallachia.'

The vizier stared at him, mouth wide. All knew that Mehmet was a gardener, his trade against the day of disaster. But . . . now? Finally, he found words. 'What? You . . . you bring him . . . a flower?' He looked around and then screamed, 'He is either a liar, a madman or a spy. Cut him, one for each – eyes, balls and heart – and then throw his carcass to the dogs. Now!'

The soldiers jerked him upright. They began to move him to the tent entrance when the vizier remembered and bellowed after them. 'Fools! I said no one was to leave. Do it there! In the corner!'

Two held him upright. Two stepped back, drew daggers. And then a voice, weak from screaming, whispered from the bed, 'Wait!'

All, save the men who held Dracula, turned.

'Master!' The vizier went to the side of the divan, threw himself down. 'You have returned to us.'

'Bring him here,' Mehmet whispered.

'Who, master?'

'The one with the gift.'

The vizier shrugged in puzzlement, turned, beckoned. Dracula was dragged forward, one man still clutching him tightly on either side. He looked down . . .

He had last seen Mehmet that night twenty years before, in another tent, in another country. Both of them were young then and held swords. He knew what the years had wrought upon himself – but they had been even less kind to the Sultan. Years or illness or both. The red hair was gone, apart from a patch above each ear. The bronze skin was sallow now, green-tinged. And the *jereed* player's lithe body was now a soft, bloated mass that lay upon silk sheets stained with blood and excrement.

Yet his eyes were clear. He looked at the peasant before him and nodded. 'What have you brought me?'

'It is there, Lord of the Horizon. In my bag.'

'Bring it.'

Dracula was still held tight. Another guard fetched it.

'Open it,' Mehmet breathed, as a spasm shook him.

The guard did, then reached in carefully – all knew their Sultan's love of plants, and more than one guard had lost skin for carelessness – and pulled out a small canvas bag full of wet earth. In it sat a tiny flower, its mauve, spear-headed petals folded in upon itself.

'What is it?' Mehmet whispered.

'It is a crocus. It has just opened in the valley I spoke of, across the Danube. In the sun here it will open again and show you its yellow and crimson tongues. It is called, in the Latin, "*pallasii*".'

The vizier and the physician both looked sharply at the peasant mouthing Latin in their midst. Mehmet stared at the plant for a long moment then again at the man who had brought it. He turned to the side, retched, a thin stream of green bile trickling down. Then he looked up again. 'Leave us,' he croaked.

'Shall we still kill him before you, master?' The vizier raised a hand to gesture it done.

'Not him. All of you leave. Not him. All of . . . you!' Mehmet raised himself from the bed, his eyes ablaze, glaring at them, then sank back, his vast stomach convulsing.

'No one goes further than the gateway. No one,' hissed the vizier. One by one the men passed from the tent. The vizier, holding up the flap, gave one look back, shook his head, and was gone.

They were alone. Silence beyond the tent, silence within it, save for the rumblings coming from Mehmet's gut and his legs ceaselessly whispering across the sheets. The two men stared at each other. Then Mehmet broke the silence with a word.

'Dracula,' he said.

The prince started. He had not expected that, to be recognised. If Mehmet had changed then so had he. And he'd had no real plan, beside the crocus and Mehmet's love of plants. He had left it all to *kismet*: his own and Mehmet's, somehow the same. 'You know me?'

'I know who you were. I know you are dead. So I know you have come back from beyond. With a message for me.'

Dracula leaned down. 'No, Mehmet Celebi,' he said using

an old name, 'I am alive. I bring you no messages from any of the thousands you have killed.'

'And what of those you have killed, Dracula? You matched me, did you not, in your small way, in your small country. I saw your line of stakes.' A spasm took him again; he bent over, dry-puked, lay back.

'I will meet them soon enough, Mehmet.' He leaned closer, staring. 'But you will be meeting your victims before I meet mine.'

Something like a laugh came to Mehmet, transforming into a cough that wrenched him. But he recovered, looked up again. 'And do you think it will be anything other than Allah's blessing when my death comes?' He stared, shook his head. 'Alive, eh? I have no time to wonder. Only to ask . . . why are you here, Impaler?'

Dracula smiled. 'I came for the saker you owe me . . . Conqueror.'

'The . . . saker?'

'The wager of our game of *jereed*. My foreskin against your bird, Sayehzade. I won. You owe me a bird.'

'Sayehzade? Daughter of shadows. My beauty.' Mehmet's eyes rolled in his head, his voice came on a croak. Then he focused again, and suddenly shouted, 'Sayehzade's dead these twenty years.'

'Then I will take another.'

The two men looked at each other for a long moment. Then Mehmet waved to the side. 'Under the divan. A drawer. Open it.' Dracula did. 'There is a black token there, of onyx, my *tugra* engraved upon it?'

'Yes.'

'Only I and my chief falconer can use this token; we give it to someone who serves us to bring us a hawk. A hawk we tell them to choose. You may take it, choose any. Yet I tell you to ask for Hama.'

' "The bird who brings joy".' Dracula nodded, lifting the token. 'Will she?'

'She is young and fierce and still half-trained. But I think if you bend her to your will, she will kill for you as no bird has . . . since my Sayehzade. But it will take some bending. Do you have the skill?'

'Perhaps. If only Hamza *pasha* would return from beyond to help me train him. For he was the finest falconer that I ever knew.'

'Hamza!' The name came on another spasm. Mehmet clutched at his stomach, something roiling beneath his fingers. 'You killed him.'

'Yes. I loved him and I killed him. You loved my brother Radu and you killed him.'

'No! I didn't. I . . .' Suddenly, Mehmet doubled over, crying with pain. Then, mastering himself, he reached out, grabbed Dracula's hand, the three-fingered hand that held the token, pulled him closer, till their faces almost touched. The prince could smell the stink of the Sultan's guts, see the torment in the eyes. 'There is a price for the bird, Dragon's son. Though you will not think so, for you have waited your whole life to pay this one. Kill me,' he hissed. 'Kill me!'

Dracula stared into those eyes. He had stared into so many over the years, of those about to die. Atop a stake. Under a blade. He could usually tell how long a man had to live. And he could see that Mehmet had . . . just a little time yet.

'It is the other thing I came to do, Mehmet. To take your life, if I could. To die myself, happily, in that moment. And you are right, I have dreamed of doing that almost from the day we met. I nearly did take it, once before, the day I lost this.' He broke the Sultan's grip, lifted his maimed hand, stood straight. 'And yet, seeing you again . . .' He smiled. 'I think I will only take what you owe me.'

It was hard to make out what Mehmet was screaming when his doctors and servants and officers rushed in. It was all confused, an old dead enemy's name yelled out again and again. Hekim Yakub put that down to the opium. Still, he gave him some more, though he could see that it was starting

431

to have less and less effect. If he doubled the dose he could kill Mehmet. It would be a mercy. But you didn't kill a Sultan. Not if you hoped to live yourself.

It was a little while before the vizier remembered the peasant. But he was not hiding in the pavilion, and had not passed the guards at the rear. A closer search revealed a small slit in the canvas close to the ground on the western side. The vizier was going to order a search of the camp but then remembered that no one was to leave the Sultan's pavilion; no one who knew Mehmet was dying. They would have to wait till he did.

As for the rip, someone would be found to sew it up, eventually. There was no shortage of men who practised that trade, against the day of disaster.

Waiting for Dracula.

It seemed to Ion he had spent half his life doing that. Never expecting to see him again. Surprised when he did.

He did not expect to see him now. His prince had not asked him to come with him, on this last foray against the Turk. Ion had insisted. With his dungeon eyesight still poor, and his legs still weak, there was little he could do to ward his prince's back. But he could bear witness.

The shadows were reaching ever further down the valley, from the rock he sheltered beneath. Sunset was when he said he would return. 'If I am not here by then, all is decided. Mehmet lives, perhaps we both are dead. I surely will be,' he'd said. 'Tell Ilona . . .' He'd smiled. '. . . That I died a lion not an ass.'

Ion squinted down the valley. But he could see little. His sight was better closer to. The town of Gebze was a shadow to the left. The Turkish war camp was a far larger one to the right. He rubbed his eyes . . .

And then one of the horses snorted in warning. He picked up his bow. Any *akinci* scout who had found him would be a blur. But he wouldn't know that. 'Who's there? he called.

'It is I,' said Dracula, stepping into the lee of the rock.

Ion lowered his bow. 'You are back,' was all he could think to say.

'Yes,' said Dracula, squatting down.

'And Mehmet?'

'Mehmet lives.'

'Ah.' It had always been a mad dream. No one got close to a Sultan unless ordered before him, for punishment, for pleasure, to obey. He peered. This close he could see his prince's face. The green-red eyes were expressionless. Ion supposed that in the long walk back from the camp he had buried his disappointment.

Then he noticed the shadow on Dracula's arm.

'What's that? he exclaimed, though he could see.

'This,' came the reply, 'this is Hama.'

'Mehmet's falcon?'

'No. Mine.'

Ion leaned closer. Saw a dark-brown back, a breast slashed white and tan. The bird was hooded but sensed him, spreading her wings, darting her head, giving out her harsh shriek. 'A beauty,' he murmured.

'Yes. Strong. Fierce. But wilful, I am told.' Dracula raised a finger to the hood and the bird jabbed its beak at it, seizing flesh. 'I started to work her on the walk back up here. Hooded and re-hooded her. Turned her every way. Gave her a little meat.'

'Well, she is young, I can see.' Ion rose, groaning a little as he did. 'So. You have your *jereed* wager from Mehmet. Stolen?'

'Given freely.'

'Oh.' There was something to learn here. But Ion did not see why it could not be learned before a caravanserai's fire. The sun had dropped below the lip of the ridge and the cold was already finding his aches. 'Shall we go?' he said, taking a step towards the horses.

Dracula did not follow. 'Would you not like to see her fly

first?' He reached up, removed the bird's hood. The bird's head swivelled as she took everything in. The men. The horses. The darkening valley below.

Dracula stepped out from the deeper shadow beneath the rock, undoing the jesses that bound the bird to his three fingers as he did.

Ion followed. 'Vlad,' he said softly, 'she may not come back.'

'No,' replied Dracula, 'she may not.'

And then he flung out his arm.

THE END

AUTHOR'S NOTE

'Abuse not the dead, for they have gone on to what they
sent before them.'

        – from the HADITHA, or sayings of the Prophet

This was by far the hardest book I have written. That I am so
proud and pleased with the final destination cannot detract
from the toughness of the journey.

For a start, I was dealing with not one but two mythical
figures. There was the controversial – to say the least! –
fifteenth-century Wallachian warlord. And then there was
the vampire.

To deal with the blood-sucker first – Bram Stoker's
wonderful gothic chiller does indeed portray a mesmeric
vampire called Dracula. But it has been proven, by the brilliant Professor Elizabeth Miller, that Stoker knew very little
about the real fifteenth-century Wallachian. In his original
plans the villain was to be called 'Count Wampyr'. Then
Stoker discovered an English traveller's account of a trip
through the Carpathians taken in the 1820s. The traveller
briefly mentioned a notorious figure from an earlier century,
a man renowned for his barbarity. He also wrote that local
slang for the name 'Dracula' was 'Devil's son'. Perfect for
Stoker's vision of a good versus evil struggle. He used the
name, a region renowned for its gothic folklore, and little
else.

But I was not going to write about a vampire. I needed to
know about the real Dracula – and once again I encountered
a myth, tales of almost unbelievable depravity and horror
even for a region of the world well used to both. I had to do
an enormous amount of reading, talk to many people. I did
not want to 'abuse the dead'. Neither did I want to diminish

his sins in the manner of 'Yes, but after all, Hitler did like small children and German Shepherds.'

For the longest time, it didn't come. In despair I confessed to one of my advisers, Marin Cordero, whose detailed knowledge of the period humbles me, that I feared humanising him. 'You can't,' she responded. 'He's already human.'

'I am a man. Nothing human is alien to me,' said the Roman, Terence. Thus, Vlad's tale may not be 'alien', but it was still a very dark place to spend my time. Being still an actor in my heart, I always approach the characters I write as an actor would – through motivation. What events and relationships shaped their lives and affected their actions? What drove them? I sought for Vlad's motivations in the murky historical record, tried to piece together some plausible 'justification' for his actions. It was the hardest thing. And then I had an epiphany, about two-thirds into the writing of the first draft – written longhand for the first time ever in an attempt to viscerally connect imagination, heart and hand – I decided not to judge him. I decided to show what he did and stop worrying why he did it. Essentially, I let him be who he was, whatever that was, to set his actions against his recorded life and in the context of the brutal place and epoch in which he lived. I would let the reader decide.

The novel became easier to write after that decision, through each subsequent draft, as each puzzle-piece slotted into place. I didn't write the ending till the second draft. I changed it for the subsequent three. Not because I was dithering. I just kept discovering more and more. Surprises kept coming. Shocks.

I was also keen to stick to the historical record . . . so far as it is known! I've stated before that it is in the gap between so-called facts that the historical novelist lives. And there were huge gaps here. Partly because so little was written down, partly because so much that was was propaganda, told in the main by his enemies and conquerors. They had good reason to want to blacken his name. I am not saying that he did not commit horrendous acts against the Turks, the Saxons of Transylvania and his own people. But when he was eventually defeated it was these enemies who told his story.

Yet propaganda was not the only reason his dark fame spread. Vlad's defeat came at a time when new technology had just become available. The printing press with movable type had essentially been invented in the 1440s. As with that other great technological leap forward, the Internet, the new technology started producing what it was thought people wanted – Bibles, religious tracts, some manuals. But, as with the Internet in the 20th century, so with the presses in the 15th – what people really want is sex and violence. Dracula's tale supplied both, spectacularly, and his enemies flooded Europe with the viral videos of the day – pamphlets! And like all great political manipulators, Vlad's enemies took and 'spun' his tale for their own ends.

I, of course, have done the same. Yet I have tried to stick to the historical record so far as it is known. And all the following supposedly happened:

- his time as hostage, first as a privileged scholar at the *enderun kolej*, then in the hell of Tokat
- Radu's cutting of Mehmet
- the comet that heralded Vlad's return
- the impaling of the *boyars* at the Easter Day coup
- his brother Mircea's blinding and burial alive
- his cleaning-up of lawless Wallachia and the golden cup placed on the town well
- the nailing of the emissary's head to the table
- the night attack on Mehmet
- the slashing of a mistress
- the impalement of thousands before the gates of Targoviste
- the man impaled higher to smell the sweeter air
- his wife leaping from the battlements of Poenari Castle

- the granting of the sheepfolds to the men of Arefu for spiriting him away
- the forged letters of betrayal Vlad was supposed to have written
- the killing of the officer in Pest who 'invaded' his home, and calling it 'suicide'
- his supposed beheading in a final battle

To get to these 'truths' I have had to sift through many competing agendas. Of course, I have given the tales my own 'spin', my objective being to tell a good story, rather than vilification or propaganda.

I have lost count of the books I have read, the websites I have scoured. But I should mention, specially, four most useful books: Kurt Treptow's definitive *Vlad III – The Life and Times of the Historical Dracula*; M.J. Trow's witty and wide-ranging *Vlad the Impaler: In Search of the Real Dracula*; the obscure, brilliant, D.C. Phillott's *Observations on Eastern Falconry*; and, finally, a well-thumbed copy of Machiavelli's *The Prince*, which was written about fifty years after Vlad's death, but is filled with observations on 'realpolitik' and survival the Voivode would have well understood. I pasted quotes on the wall in front of my desk.

But inspiration does not only come from books. My research trip to Romania and Istanbul was vital in this respect. I stayed first in the house of the Tomescus, Gheorghe and Maria, in the village of Arefu, close to the site of Poenari, Dracula's real castle (forget Bran, it's Disney-Dracula, and he probably never even went there!). The village is a wonderful place, where people still live much as they have done for centuries – driving the unpaved hilly roads in bullock carts, eating what they raise and grow; which, in April, meant all pickled vegetables and every part of the pig, washed down with home-made *tuica*, a wicked, plum brandy. And the five hours I spent in almost sole possession of the half-ruined

Poenari Castle, 1400 steps up a mountain, gave me the essential setting and atmosphere for my novel.

I went to the gorgeous walled town of Sighisoara, Transylvania, where I drank a beer in the house where Vlad was born. The next day I had Vlad's Princely Court to myself in Targoviste so that I was able to sit where Vlad sat and channel the scene of the Easter Day coup. And I was determined to try to understand the religious impulses that drove these crusaders. In the village church of Arefu I stood and thought. And in a tiny parish church in Bucharest I listened to the beautiful chanted morning service as I studied the frescoed saints.

However, one of the greatest images came during a conversation with the time-generous, highly knowledgeable Nicolae Paduraru who has run Dracula-related tours since the 1960s. He told me how, just the previous week, the Romanian president had been impeached by parliament. The impeachment had to go to a plebiscite. Supporters were rallying for him in big demonstrations. And, instead of banners, they carried two portraits – his and Dracula's. For the former Voivode is still regarded as a benchmark of probity, justice and order. Romanians today long for a time when a gold cup could be placed at the town well and all could drink from it!

Istanbul, glorious Constantinople, is a stunning, sensuous place where you truly feel at the epicentre of the world. It informed all my writings about Vlad's Turkish enemy, especially Mehmet, and showed me a little about how his life among them must have shaped the young Wallachian. I was fortunate to have as my guide there my great friend Allan Eastman, film director, travel writer, acute observer of, and indulger in, life in all its colours.

I have already mentioned Professor Elizabeth Miller, foremost scholar on all things Dracula. And Marin Cordero, who so generously – and wittily! – shared her superior knowledge of all things Turk and Draculesti and was kind enough to review the manuscript for errors. But there were many others who also helped me greatly. My wife, Aletha, who had to put up with rather more obsession in this book than in any other; more dawn starts, more disturbed nights. To an extent I always take the characters I am living with to bed with me. Not so bad if that's Jack Absolute. Not great if it's Dracula! I also must thank Dr Howard McDiarmid and his son Charles McDiarmid who own and run the lovely Wickaninnish Inn, at Tofino, British Columbia, Canada. They lent me their family cabin near the inn to finish the first draft amidst some very distracting but ultimately inspiring beauty. Thanks also to the woman to whom this book is partly dedicated, Alma Lee, who not only arranged that retreat but has also given me much help and advice over the years and the considerable bonus of her friendship.

A tragedy happened just as I was finishing this novel – my superb agent, Kate Jones, died from cancer. The terrible suddenness was a huge shock for I lost not only my guide and mentor, so responsible for the direction of my career and of this novel in particular, but also a humorous, generous and lovely friend. Her influence is clear to me on every page and I miss her every day.

Many other people have helped. My Norwegian cousins, who took me to the 'Falcon Hut' in Oppland, Norway, and gave me an early idea. Rachel Leyshon, with me since my first novel, advised with her customary insight and wisdom. All at Orion, from management to marketing, sales, publicity and foreign rights have done a tremendous job. As has my Canadian publisher, Kim McArthur, who was her usual tornado of enthusiasm and skill.

Ultimately, though, this book would not be here without its editor, Jon Wood. Over a rather indulgent lunch two years ago it was Jon who actually came up with the idea of writing about the real Dracula – and then backed his hunch with generous support and penetrating advice. His editorial touch is always light and good-humoured and he admirably restrains my tendency toward the Hollywood epic. Unleash hell, indeed!

And as for Dracula himself? I make no judgement. I leave that up to those who heard his last confession . . . and, of course, to you, the reader.

C.C. Humphreys
Vancouver, Canada

BIBLIOGRAPHY

Dracula and Wallachia:
- Kurt Treptow: Vlad III – The Life and Times of the Historical Dracula.
- M.J. Trow: Vlad the Impaler: In Search of the Real Dracula.
- Elizabeth Miller: Dracula – Sense and Nonsense.
- Radu Florescu and Raymond McNally: Dracula, Prince of Many Faces.
- May Mackintosh: Rumania.
- Constantin Rezachevici: 'Vlad Tepes and his Use of Punishments' (Essay)
- The Borgo Post, various issues. (editor: Elizabeth Miller)
- Journal of Dracula Studies, various issues. (editor: Elizabeth Miller)

The Turks:
- Franz Babinger: Mehmet the Conqueror.
- Andrew Wheatcroft: The Ottomans.
- Jason Goodwin: Lords of the Horizons.
- Godfrey Goodwin: The Janissaries.
- David Nicolle: Constantinople 1453.
- John Freely: Inside the Seraglio.

Medieval Times:
- J. Huizinga: The Waning of the Middle Ages.
- Hans Talhoffer: Medieval Combat.
- Michael Walsh: Warriors of the Lord.
- George Riley Scott: A History of Torture.

Falconry:
- D.C. Phillott: Observations on Eastern Falconry.
- The Honourable Gerald Lascelles: The Art of Falconry.

Religion:
- The Holy Qur'an.
- The Orthodox Bible.

Psychology:
- Carl Goldberg: Speaking with the Devil.
- Steven Egger: The Need to Kill.

Inspirations:
- Niccolo Machiavelli: The Prince (trans. George Bull).
- Dante: The Divine Comedy (Trans. Henry Longfellow; Illustrated by Gustave Doré).
- Rumi Poems. (editor: Peter Washington).
- The Rubaiyat of Omar Khayyam (Trans. Edward Fitzgerald).
- Bram Stoker: Dracula.

GLOSSARY

Note on language:

Wallachians would have spoken a form of present-day Romanian, known as the 'limba Romana' or 'Roman tongue'. They would have written in Church Slavonic, the language of the Orthodox Faith, or in Latin.

'Osmanlica' was the language of the 'House of Osman', and spoken throughout the land. It was largely Turkish but with many borrowings from Arabic and Persian. For simplicity, I have rendered it without its many accents – cedillas, umlauts etc.

'Greek' means men of Constantinople. They were not referred to as 'Byzantines' at this time.

acemoglan – janissary recruit
agha – senior teacher
akincis – raiders
'bastard' sword – also known as 'a hand and a half'
bastinado – stick
Bektashi – branch of Dervish Moslems
belerbey – provincial governor
bey – lord
Bisierica Domnesca – cathedral in Targoviste
bolukbasi – captain of guard
boyar – Wallachian high nobleman
cakircibas – chief falconer
caravanserai – traveller's inn

cariye – female servant
cobza – stringed instrument
dar ul harb – Abode of War
dar ul Islam – Abode of Peace
dervish – mystical, Persian influenced, Moslem
destrier – large war horse
devsirme – levy of Christian youths
doina – Wallachian song/lament
donjon – central keep of castle
enderun kolej – Inner School
effendi – gentleman, master
enishte – uncle
eyass – fledgling hawk taken from nest
falchion – wide-bladed long dagger
Fatih – the Conqueror
Frank – Turkish term for most Europeans
gazi – holy warrior
gomlek – wool tunic
gozde – chosen girl
haditha – sayings of the Prophet
hafiz – one who can recite the Qur'an by heart
hamam – Turkish baths
harem – woman's quarters in house or palace
hospodar – governor of Wallachia. Warlord
imam – Muslim priest and teacher
janissary – elite soldier of Turkish army. Former Christian
    slave
jereed – javelin game on horseback
jupan – 'lord' – title of great boyars
kahya kadin – stewardess of the harem
Kaziklu Bey – Impaler Lord
kilic – sword
laladaslar – fellow students in the enderun kolej
languier – tree for snakes' tongues – poison detectors
logofat – Wallachian chancellor
mamluk – Egyptian military class

mescid – small mosque
Metropolitan – head of Orthodox Church, Wallachia
muezzin – calls the faithful to prayer
ney – Turkish flute
oriflame – war standard
orta – janissary company; school class
Osmanlica – language of Turks
otak – canvas pavilion
palanquin – covered carriage, often carried
pasha – highest ranking Turkish official
peyk – halberdier of the guard, with spleen removed
quillon – sword hand guard
Roma – gypsy
saray(i) – palace
Sfatul Domnesca – Voivode's council
shaffron – horse's head armour
shalvari – Turkish baggy trousers
sipahi – armoured cavalryman
solak – archer of the guard
spatar – cavalry commander/knight
taragot – trumpet
tellak – attendant in baths
Tepes – 'Impaler'
testudo – Roman 'tortoise' – a military tactic of interlocking
    shields
Thrace – Bulgarian Turkey
tilinca – flute
tug – horsetail war standard
tugra – sultan's symbol – brand or seal
varcolaci – the undead
vitesji – voivode's bodyguards
vizier – high official
voivode – warlord and ruler
vornic – senior councillor/magistrate
yaya – peasant recruits